DATE DUE

Cousin Susannah

Cousin Susannah

Hazel Hucker

St. Martin's Press ♏ New York

Library of Congress Cataloging-in-Publication Data

Hucker, Hazel.
Cousin Susannah / by Hazel Hucker.
p.   cm.
ISBN 0-312-13950-0
1. Man-woman relationships—England—Hampshire—
Fiction.   2. Married women—England—Hampshire—
Fiction.   I. Title.
PR6058.U27C68   1996
823'.914—dc20   95-43507   CIP

First published in Great Britain by Judy Piatkus
(Publishers) Ltd.

First U.S. Edition: February 1996
10   9   8   7   6   5   4   3   2   1

For Rupert, with love

The law locks up the man or woman
Who steals a goose from off the common,
But leaves the greater villain loose
Who steals the common from the goose.

Anon

Cousin Susannah

1

June 1794

Susannah never forgot the day she became a woman. It was preserved entire in her, vivid and clear, even when she was old, and from time to time some sight, sound or smell would recall those hours as if it were still only the dusk of that strange hot summer day. She would see again the river pouring past, scent the hay meadow, hear the sounds of the insects and the insistently calling cuckoo, and look again at the flattened grass where their bodies had lain, the crushed buttercups and cowslips spoiled on the earth and the blood-red splash of a newly opened poppy.

She had left the rectory immediately after breakfast that morning. Sent by the rector's wife to carry a jug of soup to a dying old woman, she had not hurried on her errand. The last of the early mist was just vanishing from the Hampshire valley, giving promise of a hot day to please the hay-makers; the air was fresh, the long walk an unexpected treat. Susannah dawdled, humming to herself, plucking sweetbriar leaves from the hedge to sniff as she picked her way down the rutted lane that led from the rectory to the village. The walk would take her the best part of an hour by the road, there and back, and she intended to enjoy it.

She was wearing a new gown, an attractive lilac print which suited her coppery-brown hair and soft colouring. It fitted snugly round her breasts, revealing their neat outline, hugged her neat waist and then curved sensuously down to her feet. Occasionally she switched her bottom as she walked and watched the pretty stuff swirl round her ankles. She appreciated the gown enormously. Mrs Bland, the rector's wife, had

1

bought the material from old Matthew Smith, who came to the village with his cart full of cottons, linens and muslins every eight to ten weeks. Usually Matthew's stuffs were drab, but this last time he had produced several pretty fabrics that Mrs Bland had been unable to resist, even for her maidservants. Susannah had obtained the most attractive length, for, after all, had she not a special place in the household?

The village street was disappointingly empty. An idle small boy kicking a stone and an elderly woman tottering into Duckett's shop offered no amusing possibilities. Normally, lads of her own age might be holding a horse for the farrier, or collecting items from the carpenter, and women going about their business would be happy to call a bit of gossip across the road. Disgruntled, Susannah quickened her step. All the available males must have been collared for the hay-making.

At the hump-backed bridge she paused. The river was gliding along in the oddly smooth fashion of such mornings, mist coming from its surface. She could see a trout lying inanimate in the shadow beyond the arch. If she walked along the river bank she would save herself several minutes and have time to sit in the sun and contemplate. Mrs Bland disliked her family or her servants using that path, because, she said: 'There are those who go down there to loiter and misbehave.' Susannah mused upon the alternatives. On the road now she would meet nothing but the odd farmwagon, creaking along in clouds of white dust, while she knew that the meadow by the river was being cut for hay. Her pretty gown should not go unseen. She turned to walk by the water, and by that decision changed her life.

The mowers were standing in a group at the edge of the meadow, put out by the lingering dew, unaware of its sparkling beauty, conscious only of potential dangers. Hay cut damp would be hard to dry efficiently, would probably ferment in the stack, and worse, would be in danger of spontaneous combustion. A high wind, a burning haystack, and a whole rickyard could go up with flaming straw flying off to be a danger to every thatched roof in the village. Only two years ago Mr Waterton's best barn had gone like that, over to Brambourne: a terrible conflagration. The men shook their heads and pulled their ears.

'Lord, what a waste o' time. Here we be, waiting to cut, and

2

that there grass as wet as a babe's bottom. Some'un tell the sun to come out proper, so's we can get going.'

That was her father's voice, raised in a plaintive bellow. Susannah stopped, kicked crossly at a dried cowpat and wondered whether to walk on. She had forgotten that he might be there, massive, noisy, flushed with cheerful exasperation, enjoying the first of the twelve or more pints of home-brewed that he would expect to pour down his gullet in the course of the day's labours. Would he notice that she was wandering down a forbidden path, or would he merely be aware that she was looking pretty and point this out to his companions with embarrassing persistence?

Before she could make up her mind, Dick Nutbeam, one of the rector's servants, saw her. 'Hey, look there, Tom. There's a sight to cheer your eyes! Miss Susannah, what d'ye think yer at, wandering down here?'

Caught, Susannah retaliated: 'Why, doing your boring errands for you, that's what. You stand in the hayfield guzzling beer, and I've to run about the parish carrying messages. Some folk know how to manage things so their work's done for them.' He wouldn't tell on her; he'd a warm eye for a woman, and besides, she knew too much about certain depredations in the rectory cellar.

'Mr Bland offered for me to help,' Dick retorted defensively, 'like he does every year ...'

He was interrupted by an explosive series of sneezes from Susannah's father. Thomas Trotter's nasal problems, particularly in the hay-making season, were heard from end to end of the village. 'Damn it!' he gasped when he could speak again. 'The prettiest girl in the village, and she my own daughter too, and I'm that afflicted I can't hardly speak to her nor see her.' He mopped at his swimming blue eyes with a large red handkerchief. ''Tisn't right that a man should have such a stupid ailment. I'll be in a regular state by tonight, that I know!' He peered at his daughter. 'Sukey, my gal, where're you off to, all dressed up like that?'

'Just taking soup to Mrs Oram, Father, helping her through her last hours. She can't eat proper food now, poor old soul. But I mustn't stay and gossip, Mrs Bland'll be needing me back in the schoolroom.' Susannah edged along the path as she

3

spoke, a pious look upon her face, intent on removing herself from his vicinity as quickly as she could.

'The very sight of you'll gladden Mrs Oram's eyes, I'll be bound. You're a good girl and that new gown suits you to the ground. Never say as your old father don't notice such things. I can see 'em all right, 'spite of this summer cold.'

'Yes, thank you, Father.' She smiled sweetly at him, glided several steps further on and cast her eyes swiftly over the group to see whether Luke Carter, the tall and silent Luke, was with them. She was pleased to receive the attention of several men in the form of grinning nods and waves, but she knew that to linger when both her father and Dick were there would be dangerous. Besides, Luke was not to be seen. Shame, he should have been here, sharpening his scythe on the whetstone, staring at her with hungry eyes, his shirt open to the waist to show the muscled and dark-haired chest that she liked.

She sighed, turned and hurried on. Even as she passed the end of the meadow she could hear her father, gripped by another sneezing bout, gulping and roaring for beer to ease his throat. Safely behind a belt of willows she slowed and gazed about her, sniffing the air. The course of the river was marked by a line of tall grasses, rich with wild flowers. Pale blue butterflies drifted, swallows wheeled and skimmed. Beyond lay other meadows and tangled copses, rising to the line of chalk downland guarding the valley. No one was about. She transferred the jug of soup to her other hand and sauntered along the bank, relishing the unexpected freedom from the schoolroom and her noisy charges.

Mrs Oram's cottage reeked of illness, of urine and decay. The shutters were closed and the dust-laden shaft of light from the doorway did little to dispel a gloom which Susannah feared hid all kinds of unpleasant matters. The old widow had fallen behind, as the village saying went, during the last weeks. Neighbours had brought food to her, too much one day, too little another. Her great-nephew, a sly youth called Arthur, had chopped wood for her occasionally, and had called in Jem Nutt, the local barber-surgeon, to dose her with his herbal remedies, but no one had stayed to give her the nursing she needed. So the cottage stank of Mrs Oram's sickness and inadequacy, and only in the last couple of days had Nutt, realising the mortal nature of her illness, notified the rector and brought in Martha Pither to see to her.

Martha, wife of the blacksmith and farrier, saw to the beginnings and the ends of most people in the village. A gossiping, downright woman, she was of an impressive amplitude, her stoutness confined within leather stays that gave her the solidity and strength of a rock: the villagers leaned on her. Clutching the latest of her babies tightly wound in its shawl she pounded from cottage to cottage, exhorting women in childbirth to 'Heave it away, then!'; brawling noisily with the menfolk; joking obscenely with the old wives and coping competently with the laying-out of the dead. Despite her bulk she could move quickly and dealt with a workload other women would have blenched at. Her own offspring started work at the age of six, and her dozen or so children worked in the forge or the fields if they were male, or, if female, helped in the cottage, ran errands for her and eventually entered service in one of the local big houses. Often she would have a second baby to suckle, helping mothers with an inadequate supply themselves. There was nothing inadequate about Martha.

She greeted Susannah with enthusiasm. She liked a healthy girl. 'Parson sent 'ee, then? Thought as much. Never forgets, do they, 'im and Mrs Bland? Not as their thought'll be appreciated this time. Poor old woman's past speaking now. She'll pass on tonight, I reckon, spoiling my sleep to sit up with 'er. They all do.' She beckoned the reluctant Susannah into the gloom. 'Sit on that stool a minute, m'dear. I'll just pour this into a pan so's you can return the jug. Tell 'em she relished it, would ye? Folks likes to have their good deeds give pleasure. An' I'll relish it, so 'tain't so much of a lie.' She beamed at the girl, poured the soup into a black encrusted pan that made Susannah shudder and passed the jug back. 'Wash this out in the river on yer way back, would ye? I'm nigh out of water now and just settin' down to have a sup of tea. Fancy a dish?'

Susannah refused and made rapidly for the door. Martha looked disappointed. 'Aren't 'ee going to say farewell to the old lady, then?'

Susannah suppressed a retch of horror. 'Oh no! No, thank you, I must get back to my work, Martha. We're heavy pressed today. I hope she'll go peaceful so's you get your sleep.' She ran

5

down the path, hearing Martha chuckling behind her as she went. 'No need to be frightened of it, m'dear, we all comes to it in the end. Tell parson she'll be needing his prayers.'

This time there was no hesitation about choosing the river path. The hay-makers would be expecting her to pass by, and in any case Martha had asked her to rinse the jug in the water.

The heat of the sun was warming the valley now, drawing into the still air the rich smells of cowdung, new-mown grass and dog-roses. Insects buzzed and hummed around her, intent on their varied tasks, seeking nectar or dung according to their natures; birds flew swiftly across her path or rustled importantly in the bushes; bees bumbled heavily about the spotted orchids and the yellow irises by the water's edge. It was a superb morning.

Susannah's steps slowed as she reached the most isolated part of her walk. Here there was marshy meadow on the opposite side of the river, pungent-smelling at times and alive with mosquitoes, but on her side, where the land swelled upward towards the beechwoods, there was a wide patch of grass and a small coppice, brilliantly green with new leaves. She stopped to stare about herself and experienced one of those moments of revelation that comes at times to the young. In comparison with the moribund old woman in the cottage she had just left she became aware with a vivid intensity of her own surging life-force: the colours about her were extra clear and brilliant, her body was full of zest and she had the feeling that she was on the verge of a breakthrough to some special level of consciousness, a feeling that had come to her once or twice before on hearing Fanny Bland playing the harp alone in the rectory drawing-room, hauntingly melancholy and sweet.

The little river beside her was clear as glass, surging along busily in the centre of the stream but allowing quieter patches to develop between the reed clumps by the banks. Sitting down on the bank, Susannah removed her shoes and stockings and dipped her toes into the water. The cold was biting at first, but exhilarating. A few feet away a grey wagtail flicked its tail, balancing itself on a damp log, ignoring her. She peered at the shallow, pebbled bottom, but could see no fish, only minnows. They swam in aimless intricate patterns, fleeing as her foot entered the water, but as the ripples vanished they returned to the same spot to resume their idling in the sunny water. A pleasing existence, she thought. A brown cow in the water meadow stared over the reeds at her, its white face freckled with flies.

She stood up in the water, holding her skirts high, then waded towards the centre of the stream, wanting to feel the water tugging at her legs. The cold was delicious. She took two more steps, the water swirled higher, and she knew that her lovely gown must be removed or show a tell-tale wet hem. Cautiously she glanced around, but only the cow returned her gaze and so the gown and her shift came off, to be thrown on to the grass.

A sudden movement by the trees gave her a terror that she was being spied upon, but then she saw a spaniel creeping through the long grass and recognised one of Mr Bland's six dogs, a young animal called Careless. The dog scuffled with something on the edge of the coppice, stopped, backed off for a moment, pranced high, then sprang. Susannah peered to discover what he was doing and saw the spaniel's head come up, a dead pheasant clasped in the soft mouth, one handsome wing extended across his chest. He began to trot homeward along the bank, his head held high so that the limp beautiful body should not trail in the dust. There was pride and pleasure expressed in his every movement; his eyes laughed at her as he passed.

'You bad boy, Careless,' she called softly. 'Your master won't thank you for that bird, he won't!'

She stepped into the pushing, surging current with care, for the gravel bottom hurt her feet. The water rose above her knees. She stooped to splash water up her arms and onto her face, then kicked a shower of water in the direction of the cow. 'Stop staring, stupid great thing!' The cow backed off, its head down. Her eyes glinting with mischief, she stepped forward to send another shower after it, her foot slid into a hole carved out by the deceptive current and her balance was gone. Arms flailing, she fell. Water fountained into the air. The shocked cow lumbered off, its udders swinging. Susannah did not see it: terrified, she was being swept down the centre of the stream, gasping and clutching at nothing.

Fifty yards away a man on horseback heard the splash and

7

glimpsed through the trees the agitated cow. His young horse side-stepped, blowing down its nostrils. He kicked it irritably, urging it forward to discover what had caused the commotion.

Susannah was unaware of his presence until, just as she had thought herself sure to die, a hand twisted itself in her hair and another grabbed her in the armpit and both plucked her with brutal force into a sitting position in shallow water. She gasped and spat, spouting water. A hand smote her between the shoulder blades and she coughed up more of the river.

'Devil take you!' said a deep voice from behind her. 'Why don't you have more sense? Learn to swim before you dive!'

She twisted round, still trying to heave air into her lungs. A large young man with heavy shoulders and an air of impatient authority was sitting on the bank above her: James Manning-ford, future owner of Abbotsbridge House. Of all men, he was the last she would have wished to see her in such a condition. After his cousin, Ambrose, he was easily the most important person in the community and quite the most personable male. She sat in the river in her shift and her drawers, all wet and slimy with weeds, and bowed her head between her hands. 'Oh, dear Lord!' she said. 'Dear Lord!'

He stood up, his boots squelching water, surveying her with intent dark blue eyes, half exasperated, half amused. 'Of course,' he said, 'you're the Blands' maidservant, aren't you? I thought I knew you.' He held out his hand. 'Come on, out you get. And don't worry, I shan't tell!'

She stumbled on to the grass, still shaking with fright, her face crimson. She grabbed her dress, holding it against herself in belated modesty. 'So stupid!' she muttered furiously. 'So embarrassing!'

He took charge. 'You'd best take off all that wet stuff and wring it out. Put on your dry clothes. D'you want my help?' She shook her head violently, shocked. 'I'll look away then. But you'll find it mighty difficult to pull that wet clothing off, it sticks so. And damn it, I must take off my boots and breeches and rid myself of as much water as I can. I'll never forgive you if my handsome new boots are ruined!'

'Oh, I am sorry, sir, truly. I do hope they aren't spoiled. And thank you for saving me.'

She stumbled away from him and crouched by the trees to

tug off her sodden underclothing, watching him from the corner of her eyes as she did so. He stood shaking the water from his boots, then removed his breeches. She averted her eyes and hurriedly flung on her shift and gown. Then she glanced furtively across to be certain his back was turned while she pulled on her stockings and fastened the garters.

As her skirt dropped down he swung round and came towards her to stand square-set against the brilliant sky, his massive head blocking out the sun. She blinked and shivered.

He laughed suddenly. 'What's your name, girl?'

'Susannah Trotter, sir.'

'Well, Susannah, it seems that each time I see you you're in trouble. Is that not so? Up to every kind of mischief. When I am at the rectory I hear Mrs Bland forever scolding you. And that vase of tulips, the last time I came – did they suspect that it was you who knocked it over in your game with the children and not that foolish greyhound as I told them?'

'No, sir. He's a naughty dog, that one. I was so grateful to you, you don't know! That vase would have been stopped out of my wages. You've been very kind to me.' She stopped, flushing. She could not look at him, his naked legs revealed. He was too close to her. Primitive feelings and fears fluttered inside her. She felt upset, weak, horribly conscious of the nakedness of her body beneath the upper clothes. He was not one of the village lads with whom she could have joked. With Luke Carter the situation would have been in her control. Not so with him.

He pulled a strand of weed from her hair, then took a handkerchief from a pocket to wipe her face in unexpectedly gentle fashion. 'What am I to do with you now? Or myself, come to that? I've no wish to ride through the village with or without wet breeches – and can you imagine if you return with sodden hair and clutching those wet undergarments what amazement you will cause, not to say gossip?'

'God rot all clacking tongues,' she muttered.

'Amen to that. We'd both better dry in the sun a little and then try to sidle through unobtrusively.'

'Yes, sir,' she said gratefully. She squeezed the water from their clothes and draped them over a willow branch. If only somehow she could avoid discovery of the morning's escapade she would be infinitely beholden to him. Mrs Bland could well

dismiss her for such behaviour, while as for her mother ...
Susannah shuddered to think of her fury. Highly respectable
Mrs Trotter was, as she tried to impress upon her daughter; a
one-time housekeeper at Abbotsbridge Park and a bettermost
person in the village, even if she had married somewhat beneath herself. Never would she have flaunted around in her
undergarments to disgrace herself before her betters.

James sat down on the rabbit-nibbled turf. He pulled off the
ribbon that held back his thick brown hair, ran his fingers
through it, then briskly retied the ribbon. Revealed by the
drawn-back hair were the strong features and clear complexion
of young manhood, faintly damp with perspiration. He indicated with a jerk of a strong chin that Susannah should sit
down beside him. Instinct told her to go; fear of the gossips
and, above all, the fascination of him, held her. She sat in
silence, one hand flicking nervously at the wet curls of her hair
to separate the strands. As the sun warmed her skin the goose
pimples vanished and she began to breathe more easily. Gradually she relaxed, leaned back on her elbows, raised her face to
the heat.

'I thought you were the Blands' nursery-maid,' James
remarked, 'yet here you are playing at nymphs by the river.
How do you explain that?'

'I had to run an errand,' Susannah said demurely. ''Tis a
long plod to Mrs Oram's cottage – I couldn't help getting hot.
The rector's man should've gone, but he's helping with the
hay-making in exchange for the mowers' help with our hay next
week.'

'So you escaped the nursery!'

She shook her head. 'The schoolroom. There's no young
ones left in the nursery now. I teach the little Blands their
letters, and more, too.'

'Do you indeed? What more?'

'Lucy and William study history now, and the use of the
globes.'

His eyebrows rose. A nursery-maid so literate was a rarity.
'Quite the little governess.'

'That's what Mrs Bland called me the other day – her little
governess.' Her voice was proud. She paused, then confided:
'That's what I'd like to become, a proper governess.'

'Would you indeed? Lucky children.' He turned to eye her with open appreciation. 'My sister never had so attractive a governess. Regular antidotes hers were, all of them, poor females. And talking of plain females, by God, when I first came to this village I thought the place must be under a curse. I never saw a girl that lay easy on the sight until I clapped eyes on you. What a relief that was!'

Susannah smiled, pleased. Not that it was so great a compliment, remembering his six female cousins at Abbotsbridge House. 'The Lord has laid a blight on 'em like the plagues of Egypt,' was the old churchwarden's view. 'The ugly sisters,' Thomas Trotter called them, more simply. And he reckoned his Sukey could beat them to a handsome husband any day. Only the youngest had any looks to speak of, and she was no rival at a mere thirteen. Poor Mr James, it must be lowering to live with that sad household.

He said condescendingly: 'But, you know, you'd need to have some French if you were to be a governess. It isn't so easy.'

Susannah sat up, ruffled. Clearly he regarded her hopes as mere dreams, her ambitions as pretensions that should be put down. She retorted: 'But I do have some French.'

'Truly?'

'*Mais oui, vraiment, je sais parler français.*'

He was taken aback, half-laughing. 'How the devil did you manage that?'

'Miss Fanny had a French tutor for nigh on a year, one of those who escaped from that murderous revolution of theirs. Mr Bland gave him a home and taught him English in return for his teaching the older children French. And when Miss Fanny had her lessons I had to be her chaperone. Well, you know what Frenchmen are like!' Her lips twitched at the remembrance of warm brown eyes and bony aristocratic hands that had to be forever slapped down. Fanny Bland had loathed him and was in no way put out when young Monsieur Decaen switched his attention to Susannah. Between bouts of protesting her virtue she had learned a surprising amount of French, both inside and outside the schoolroom.

'No, I do not know what Frenchmen are like! How should I? Tell me, would a Frenchman do this?' James picked up her

11

hand and kissed it lightly. 'Or would he do this?' An arm encircled her shoulders and pulled her forcefully and rather uncomfortably against him.

Her heart jumped. She twisted her head at the last moment so that it was only her cheek he kissed. 'He didn't ... No! You shouldn't ...'

'You mean the Frenchman didn't kiss you? Ridiculous fellow!'

He turned her head with his hand, his fingers pinching her chin. She tried to remove the hand, shaking her head. You could not be angry with the man who had just saved you from drowning.

'Susannah, you owe me a kiss. Am I to receive no real thanks for what I have done for you? I am hurt and disappointed that you value your life and my new top boots so lightly!'

He was acting reproach but his eyes were full of amusement. There could be no harm in a kiss of gratitude, she decided, flustered. Luke would never know. The other village girls would be tremendously impressed, if they but heard. The disjointed thoughts flashed through her mind as his mouth came down on hers. His kiss was totally different from Luke Carter's. It lasted a long time, while his hands found places that Luke's had never touched, arousing responses she had never known before. He smelt good, his face was as smooth as a boy's, his hands were gentle: there seemed nothing to be afraid of. She found herself returning his kisses, smiling inwardly at the compliments he was showering upon her between whiles.

'Your hair is deliciously soft,' he said, brushing the drying strands back from her face with his fingers. 'Your skin is as smooth as silk,' and a muscular hand caressed a breast. 'You smell of wild roses,' and his face was buried in her neck, but his hands were elsewhere. Susannah did not stop him.

She was just approaching seventeen, an age at which it is difficult to gather the strength of mind to reject either the insistent clamour of a healthy body or the bland but also insistent urging of a young gentleman from a class which she had always been taught to obey. The precepts of her absent mother had faded, and while she could not have brought herself to say: 'Yes!', the absence of any negative response led

12

him to further advances, of which her rapt sun-warmed acceptance informed him that he might attempt the ultimate act.

She did protest then, her head thrashing, panicking at the
last moment, but his body was a leaden weight holding her
down, her dress already pushed high, his hands clutching her
arms. His face was enormous, looming over her.

'No! Please ... No, stop it!'

'Lie still, you silly girl! We can't stop now. Lord, what a fuss!
Let me! Let me, will you!'

A cry clotted in her throat. She tried with hands and heaving
hips to throw him off, realised too late how her movements
were aiding him, and collapsed into limpness, biting her lips to
contain the whimpers of pain. Her world swirled into darkness
and him.

Afterwards they were both speechless. A cuckoo called
across the river, monotonously repeating its notes over and
over again. It was the only sound to break the silence in which
they sat. Heat shimmered on the distant downs. Susannah
could not understand why she was shaking when she was so
sickly hot. She felt bruised, stifled and robbed. James passed
his handkerchief across his forehead and round his neck for the
fifth time.

When at last he spoke it was almost with violence. 'Why the
devil did you not tell me you were a virgin?'

She shook her head, bewildered. 'I don't ... I didn't think ...'

'That it would make a difference? Of course it would.'

They stared at each other, dazed.

'I do have some principles,' he muttered. 'Oh God, what a
fool!'

She pushed the hair back from her face with a sticky hand.
Somewhere deep inside her there was an ache. She shifted her
position on the grass gingerly and clasped her arms round her
knees to stop them shaking. She wanted to cry, but she did not
dare: men had such strange reactions to tears. He was furious
and she could not tell why. He had had his way, after all. It did
not occur to her that it was himself with whom he was angry.

'The way you are,' he said accusingly, 'such a madcap and so
pretty and full of yourself - it never occurred to me that the
boys would have left you alone. Damn it, I thought you were

teasing me, leading me along like that. You were asking to be taken.'

'Well, no, sir. Not that.' The tears welled and one spilled down her cheek. He put his hand on her arm, a tentative conciliatory gesture. A bee, drunk from the flowers, overloaded with the yellow pollen on his legs, landed upon the flower-sprigged slope of her shoulder. She flinched. James released her arm, mistaking her movement.

'The bee,' she breathed, indicating with her chin. She was afraid of its sting, in no mood to cope.

'I don't see . . .' He followed her look. 'Ah!' He leaned over till his mouth was level with her shoulder and blew sharply. The bee's fat body was swept off, dropped, then achieved flight, buzzing heavily away.

'My poor girl. I'm sorry.' His voice was stiff, unpractised in apologies. He picked several blades of grass from her hair and her back. Contrition was in his gestures.

Her voice reproachful, she said: 'I hope I don't bear a bastard, sir.'

'Oh!' He let out pent-up breath in a gusty sigh. 'I hope not, too. But you are exceedingly unlikely to bear a child. Why, there are those who say it is impossible the first time. My sister Charlotte was three years wed before she had her first, and many others are the same. You must not think of it.'

'Mmm,' she said. ''Tis easy to say, not so easy to do!' Bearing a child alone, facing the fury of her mother who herself had endured the stain of bastardy, the ever-present threat of the poorhouse, sickness and pain – and he told her not to think of it!

She fell silent again. A butterfly flicked its coloured wings over her before alighting on a clover flower. She watched it with vacant eyes. He had not answered her in the way she craved. What did she want of him? Not words of love, that would be way beyond even her inchoate desires, beyond her sense of her own value. Appreciation perhaps; a renewal of the pretty compliments that had seduced her; reassurance that he would see that she came to no harm from their encounter. For she felt herself his now; he had possessed her. He failed her.

2

It was extraordinary, terrifying even, how time could have flown so. When Susannah realised how late it was she ran at full pelt back to the village, pausing only when she reached the hump-backed bridge, taking deep breaths in an effort to calm her heart and gain self-control. Not only the time but her dishevelled appearance worried her. Countryfolk were trained to be observant: they studied the weather hourly, they watched over their crops, they knew when a fox had prowled the poultry run. And they were aware of all their neighbours' doings. Perhaps they could even tell from her eyes, she thought, panicking. She slipped off a shoe, slid a tiny pebble into it, and replaced it. She would say she had fallen on the rough road and ricked her ankle. That should divert their attention.

She limped on past a straggling row of cottages and was immediately glad she had taken precautions, because, haling her from the doorstep of the last and most dilapidated cottage, was Betsey Pettifer, most sharp-tongued of all the village gossips.

Black Betsey and her father grumblingly farmed a few weed-ridden acres. They claimed to be of gipsy stock, and certainly they exhibited a typical cheerful bellicosity towards their neighbours, together with a hand-to-mouth existence which kept them out of the poorhouse only with the exasperated assistance of the neighbours from whom Betsey 'borrowed' food regularly as if it were her right. Betsey had two bastard sons: Arthur, a dark and wiry lad with a gift for poaching, who was reckoned to be about fourteen, and Harry, a sallow and smelly toddler.

15

Harry was squatting by his mother's feet now, his face intent, digging with his bare hands in the scuffed earth beside the house, mounding the soil and patting it.

'Hey, Sukey! Got a blister, 'ave yer? Where you bin?' Betsey called boisterously.

'I've been taking soup to your old aunt, Betsey,' Susannah called back repressively. 'She's in a bad way.'

Betsey snorted. 'Wastin' yer time there. Mean old maggot, she is. Wouldn't give you the pickings from 'er nose. Leave 'er look after 'erself.'

'She's past that now; she'll not last long. Your Arthur's been there. He's helped her.'

Betsey looked revolted. 'Soft in th'ead, that's what he is.'

Harry stood to water his mud pies copiously from his own natural source. His mother ignored him. 'Ere, they're looking fer you at the rectory, they are. That young curate from Brambourne, 'e comes riding past, all of a lather. "Have you seen the doctor, my good woman?" 'e calls, and then 'e says, "Have you seen Miss Trotter?"'

Susannah paused in her flight. 'What has happened?'

'I dunno. Didn' tell me. But main keen to find you, 'e was. Got a good leg on 'im that man 'as.' Her eyes squinted cunningly against the sun. 'Not the only thing good about 'im, I shouldn't wonder, hey? Got a fancy for ye, 'as 'e?'

'Nay,' Susannah retorted, 'for sure it's you he's after!'

Betsey's delighted cackle followed her as she limped on. It must be old Mr Humby, Brambourne's original curate, who was ill yet again. She hoped it was not one of the Bland children who was sick or hurt.

She was dangerously late in returning; Mrs Bland would be certain to ask questions as well as bestowing the inevitable scolding. As many as the rector's wife loved, them she rebuked and chastened, and as she prided herself on having largely raised Susannah to her present prettiness and intellectual attainments and was devoted to her, so the chastening never ceased. Normally it was as water running off a duck's back, but today Susannah felt she could not bear it. Her eyes prickled ominously at the very thought.

As she approached The Bull Inn she caught sight of the curate, Sedley Stacey, watching impatiently by the forge as

16

Martha Pither's husband, Josh, finished replacing a shoe on his chestnut mare. Susannah prayed fervently for the chance to pass unnoticed and reach the rectory before him. With luck she could scramble in through an open window and gain her room unseen: she could not face Mrs Bland as she was, whatever James Manningford's assurances as to her looks as she had darted off along the river bank. She slipped along the far side of the street, keeping an eye on the scene.

The Bull Inn and the smithy both stood back from the street, the ground before each flanking the lane that led up to the Winchester road and making together a sort of open square. Outside the smithy was an area of scuffed grass where a great horse-chestnut tree stood, its trunk encircled with a bench where the old men sat to drink their tankards of beer. Here was the clearing-house for the males' news-of-the-day as much as Duckett's shop was the centre for female tidings, and Josh listened tolerantly.

Suddenly, from beneath the bench of elderly drinkers, a lurcher erupted from his resting place beside his master's boots to bark at the hooves of the curate's mare. For a brief moment flared nostrils and an arched neck alone registered the animal's well-bred disgust, but as the lurcher's owner bellowed his commands for Dart's return, her eyeballs rolled and she began to cavort nervously around. The curate, attempting to mount her, was caught with one foot in the stirrup and forced to hop sideways as she danced away. He protested this indignity in vigorous and unclerical language, bringing a gleeful murmur of 'tuts' from his audience.

Josh, a large man with muscles that stood out like gnarled great tree roots, removed the lurcher by the scruff of the neck, booted him back to his owner, calmed the mare, and helped the curate to mount.

Susannah had scarcely covered ten more yards before there was a clatter of hooves beside her and a voice spoke her name. She looked up resignedly and found herself staring into the sun. It beat into her eyes with a blinding ache of light and momentarily dazzled her. She stumbled on a stone, winced as the pebble in her shoe dug into her foot, and recovered.

'Susannah!' Sedley Stacey said loudly. 'Where have you

17

been? I have been looking all over . . . But are you all right? Are you hurt?'

'No . . . Yes! My ankle was twisted. But it only hurts a little now. I shall be all right, sir. Please!' He was drawing attention to her.

'But you are limping,' he insisted, unexpectedly sympathetic. 'You must let me help you.' He slid from the mare and stood beside her, a sturdy young man of middle height, good-looking in a high-coloured, fleshy way. An arched nose and a heavy chin gave him something of the look of a senator of ancient Rome, a look enhanced by the self-confident carriage and thick sensual lips. 'You had better ride Coquette. Put down that jug and then I can help you up.'

Susannah thought quickly: it could be helpful to have him take charge of her and be there when she encountered Mrs Bland. 'You are very good,' she murmured.

She expected him to give her a polite leg-up, but no, his hands grasped her waist. 'Jump off your good foot!' he encouraged her, and she rose abruptly on to the mare's back, receiving as she did so the impression that Mr Stacey was enjoying himself. Riding sideways on a man's saddle was awkward; as she wriggled herself secure his hands lingered, holding her with a sticky intimacy. She took up the reins with a pointed briskness.

He put a hand over hers. 'Would you like me to lead her?'

'No, thank you. I can ride.'

He stepped back, bowing with ironic courtesy. 'I beg your pardon. I was forgetting what a competent young person you are.'

She blinked with surprise at such a compliment from someone who she thought had barely noticed her existence, but said, a smile flickering across her lips: 'Mr Stacey, you are all kindness and gallantry today!'

'A fellow creature in need of assistance,' he retorted. 'I am no Pharisee to ride by on the other side!'

As they moved off she lifted her eyes to look cautiously across the street to the smithy. Beneath the horse-chestnut tree a row of eyes was watching them unblinkingly, and from here and there in the shadows came the white flash of a grin. Susannah urged the mare on.

As they went up the lane she asked cautiously about the

trouble at the rectory, and the curate explained that Mr Humby had this morning been taken very ill. 'I do not think his life is in question, but of course I had to speak to Mrs Bland, the rector being out on parish duties, and then ride for the doctor.'

'Is he very bad?'

'He is shocking ill. But then he has been for some time. I cannot understand,' Mr Stacey added, 'why the Lord does not take Mr Humby to Himself. He will never be able to resume his duties and his life can only be a burden.'

And if he died, Susannah silently finished for him, you could become the curate of Mr Bland's second parish at Brambourne, not just the locum, and that would be to your considerable benefit. She shook her head. She had always been secretly sorry for Mr Humby and not only for his ill-health. He was a bumbling, absent-minded little man, but eternally willing. Despite his short-comings it was a pity that he had never managed to acquire his own parish: he would have worked in it with genuine and unstinting love. But Mr Humby had never had either money or connections to achieve what his abilities could not.

In this Sedley Stacey resembled him; he, too, was starting from nothing. But there the resemblance ended. Compared with the diffident Humby, Mr Stacey was a veritable Titan of complacent strength. He assumed that all about him would be as impressed by his intellectual and religious merits as he was himself - and, mesmerised by his self-assurance, they generally were. No one who knew him in the villages of Abbotsbridge and Brambourne harboured any doubts as to his ability to acquire a good parish and to rise in the Church hierarchy.

'Mrs Bland has been telling me of your accomplishments, Susannah,' the curate remarked. 'They really are quite extensive.'

'Mr Bland has always allowed me the run of his library,' Susannah said. 'And any books Miss Bland buys she lets me read too.'

'But your drawing and your embroidery! The oval fire screens in the parlour are delightful! I was complimenting Mrs Bland upon them, believing them to be Miss Fanny's work, when she told me it was you who had designed and worked them.'

'I enjoyed doing them.'

'I am favourably impressed,' Sedley Stacey pronounced. 'You are to be congratulated. Moreover, you are an example to the other servants.'

'I am?' Susannah was startled. She did not think that was what Mrs Bland would shortly be telling her.

'You have just been on a charitable errand. Do not misunderstand me, I admire you for it, but no smart London or Bath governess would condescend to run around the parish, risking infection to take soup to the sick.'

At the thought of being compared with a smart London governess, a reluctant laugh escaped Susannah. 'I don't mind helping,' she said. 'It is only when the Blands are busy and Dick not available.'

'It must be a tonic for the village folk to see you,' he said. 'I hope if I am ever ill I shall have so pretty an attendant.' His slightly protuberant eyes glistened up at her and she was startled to see in them the same hungry look with which Luke Carter often watched her.

As they entered the carriage-sweep of the rectory they became aware of a great bustle and noise. A horse was being put to the rector's curricle by the gardener; a maidservant by the front door was hissing instructions to an unseen person within; in the distance the rector's dogs were barking excitedly.

Mrs Bland came trotting out from behind the carriage, fanning herself rapidly, her plump face pink with agitation and heat. 'Where have you been? Where have you both been? No, do not attempt to tell me – I haven't the time to listen. But what are you doing on the horse, Susannah? It seems very odd. Really, there has been so much happening, such tracasseries here, you would not believe! And Mr Bland nowhere to be found. I must tell you ... But Mr Stacey, you should have returned half-an-hour ago, what did delay you?'

'The mare cast a shoe,' Sedley Stacey informed her, helping Susannah to dismount. 'I was forced to wait for Pither to shoe her, and then, luckily, just as I was leaving I saw Susannah ...'

'But why should she be riding and you walking? Is she injured in some way? Really! I was waiting for the doctor!'

'Susannah has sprained an ankle,' he replied, with a pained

and reproving look. 'She was looking white and shocked so I thought it best she should ride. The doctor will be here shortly, I assure you. Perhaps he could look at that ankle.'

'No, no. We must not delay him. A message has come to say that Mr Humby has worsened. An apoplexy, we believe. The doctor should not stop to look at Susannah's ankle – not unless it is broken – and even then ...'

Susannah interrupted hastily and with truth: 'There is really little wrong with my ankle – nothing that needs to be seen by him, that is. I'll put a cold cloth on it.'

'Yes ... I suppose. Then direct the doctor straight to Brambourne, Mr Stacey, as a matter of life and death. I am driving to the parsonage house myself to help, with all the necessaries I can think of. I place little reliance upon that housekeeper!' She swung round at the sound of trotting hooves. 'Oh, Mr Bland! At last!'

Her husband reined in his horse. From beneath a particoloured thatch of inadequately powdered sandy hair a pair of shrewd and lively eyes surveyed the scene. 'Don't curse me, pray. I was delayed by the landlord at The Bull. The fellow insisted on showing me the damage done by a fight in there last night - Barney Bidewell up to his tricks again. Hardly a chair left whole or a table unscarred. And Hayter himself with an eye like a plum. It must have been a rare to-do! And what's to do here?'

'My dear! Such a day! Poor Mr Humby!' His wife poured out her tale as the gardener assisted the portly rector to dismount.

'You seem to have it all well in hand. We shall go to Brambourne together in the curricle, as soon as maybe.'

'In one minute.' Mrs Bland snapped her fan shut and pointed it at Susannah's foot. 'Now, let me see that ankle, quickly. You had better go inside, child.' She shooed the protesting Susannah before her.

Mrs Bland was a kindly, short, full-bodied woman; a refined version of Martha Pither. Much of her time was spent on charitable works. Her round baby-blue eyes wide with amazement at the follies, not to mention goings-on, of her husband's parishioners, she strove nevertheless to scold them into propriety and prosperity. 'Would you believe it?' was her favourite exclamation, used with a cheerful lack of discrimination

21

equally upon the ribbons decorating her kitchen-maid's bonnet as upon the accident that left a labouring man crippled for life. To doctor a minor ailment was a delight.

She sat Susannah down in the hall and felt her ankle with pudgy probing fingers. 'No swelling that I can discover,' she announced, but added as she surveyed the limp form before her, 'though you do look pale, I must agree. You had better put a cold compress upon your ankle and set the children to something quiet.'

'Yes, Mrs Bland.'

'Fanny will be relieved to have you back. Since I was called away I have had to insist upon her supervising the schoolroom, and she was not best pleased, I can assure you! She had intended to try the new pieces the Manningford ladies so kindly brought her from Winchester upon her harp, and then to walk with Miss Waterton. She has been able to do neither. And Miss Waterton has already been kept waiting for fifteen minutes.'

Miss Waterton was the eldest of the squire of Brambourne's large family and not a person the Blands would wish to offend.

She and Fanny Bland were standing by the east-facing schoolroom window, Miss Waterton tapping her fingers on the sill. The boys and Lucy were all sitting with their heads bent over their books, unnaturally quiet.

'I have set them all to handwriting exercises,' Fanny said in a tired voice as Susannah entered. 'Miss Waterton has kindly contributed several excellent maxims and precepts.'

Fanny often reminded Susannah of Grecian figures she had seen in the schoolroom books. The droop of the head upon the long neck, the classic nose, the drapings of her high-waisted dresses and her shawls, all were reminiscent of those elegant ladies. And Fanny, bored and remote at a dinner party, was as stiff as any figure forever immobilised upon an urn. Today, however, Fanny was neither elegant nor remote. She was peevish. The schoolroom had windows to the south and east so that the morning sun poured in, delightful in winter but unbearably stuffy on a hot June day, and she had been trapped in it with her restless small brothers and her sister for most of the morning.

'You should have been back an hour since, Susannah,' she said, fanning herself with a book. 'I cannot conceive what you have been doing.'

22

Susannah shuddered with relief that she could not, and drew in a long sighing breath. 'Oh, Miss Bland, I twisted my ankle and that did delay me a little, but at Mrs Oram's ... well, you could not conceive how that was. Poor woman, left alone in her illness, not able to do anything for herself ... the place was in a shocking state – and the smell. Well, I could not describe to you how it smelt!' As she spoke she watched Fanny for her reactions; she knew her audience. 'Mrs Oram was terribly sick, dying sick. She had not proper control over ...'

The colour was draining away from Fanny's face. She put out her hand to interrupt Susannah. 'I do not wish to know the details. I simply do not wish to know! I only know that I have been inflicted with your schoolroom duties for hours, that I shall shortly have one of my headaches, and that Miss Waterton has had to be kept waiting.'

'One does expect some consideration,' Miss Waterton observed in agreement, not bothering to turn her head from contemplation of the view. Her lanky figure tensed and she leaned forward upon the windowsill. 'My dear Fanny, do but look! Is not that Mr Stacey riding off towards Brambourne? And the old doctor?'

Fanny glanced and nodded without interest. 'It would appear so. They say Mr Humby has had a seizure of some sort.'

Miss Waterton was not concerned for Mr Humby. 'Such a delightful man, Mr Stacey. Your papa must be relieved to have his assistance. So thoughtful, so considerate, always so truly gentleman-like. Quite a worthy addition to our society at Brambourne.' Her sallow face flushed; she touched her hair. 'I declare, his sermons have me spellbound.'

'Do they?'

'My brothers tease me. They tell me I have quite undergone a conversion since he arrived!'

'How gratifying for Mr Stacey. I must tell him.'

'Oh, pray do not! How embarrassing!' Miss Waterton said with flurried delight.

'I am sure he will relish your praise.' Fanny's expressionless gaze encountered Susannah's for a fleeting moment and one eyelid dropped and rose.

'Of course, should Mr Humby, er, depart from us, then Mr

Stacey would come in for the curacy?' Miss Waterton queried off-handedly.

'I have never heard Papa discuss the subject,' Fanny said. 'Shall we take our walk?'

'By all means,' Miss Waterton said graciously. Ignoring Susannah and the children, she gathered up reticule and parasol and preceded Fanny from the room.

There was a moment's silence; Susannah had just time to close the door before the four children erupted, leaping from their stools.

'Susannah! Why were you so long? Can we go outside? Please!'

'You have changed out of your pretty new gown, Susannah. You don't look so nice now!'

'What right has Miss Waterton to scold us and tell us what to do?' demanded Lucy, who at thirteen was deeply resentful of all instruction. 'It was rude to Mama to criticise us!'

'Look, Susannah! Look what Miss Waterton made us write!' William thrust a page beneath her nose across which it appeared a drunken spider had lurched with ink on all eight feet.

'You will have to write better than this when you go to Winchester,' Susannah warned him. 'Your brother Daniel says his dons flog him.'

'On, I can do it when I want,' William said impatiently. He seized the book back. 'But just listen to this! "Knowledge procures general esteem." "He who never makes mistakes never learns." "Misfortunes are a form of discipline." Does it not sicken you?' He saw her lips twitch. 'Of course it does!' he said triumphantly.

'You will let us go outside now, won't you?' the two smallest boys pleaded in chorus.

Susannah assessed the four hopeful faces. It really was intolerably stuffy; the children's cheeks were crimson. 'I think we should go and sit under the cedar tree, don't you?' she said. 'And I shall read you the story of Romulus and Remus and the founding of Rome.'

The suggestion met with unanimous agreement.

'But first you must tidy the schoolroom. Your mama would not be pleased to see this mess, would she?'

While the children tidied their books into the cupboard and washed the slates, Susannah walked to the south window and stared out. The rectory garden was sheltered by walls of rose-coloured bricks, against whose warmth apricots, peaches and figs ripened, and where roses flourished, but Susannah saw none of them. Her eyes blind to the present, she was staring into a bleak future in which angry faces spoke harsh words, while somewhere in the distance an unseen baby wailed.

Susannah had been born on a farm and brought up in a village. She had no illusions about the essential facts of conception and birth; no girl of her background could have. She had seen cows taken to the bull, seen a stallion mount a mare. She knew she would bear a child. It was not possible that so passionate and complete a mating as hers with James Manningford could prove unfruitful.

She could not think the worse of James for having seduced her. On the contrary, now that the first shock was over, she regarded his determination more in the way of a compliment. He had desired her, she had allowed the occasion to arise: he had taken her. That was how a proper man, a man of status, would behave. She had played with fire, she had been burned. But the flames were handsome. No, it was her own stupidity and vanity that were so exasperating.

Dear Lord! she thought. What should she do? She could encourage Luke Carter. She knew Luke cared more for her than any of the village girls who were avid for his attentions; she had seen it in his eyes time and again. But Luke, handsome and exciting as he was, was only a labourer. Her parents, yes, even her easy-going father, would be furious at her marrying so much beneath her. Her father was a farmer in a small way and the farmhouse was a respectable one; there was a Turkey carpet and a spinet in the parlour, not a piano-forte as her mother would have desired, but a spinet in good playing order. In the Carters' cottage there was an earth floor and little furniture – and she would loathe the life of a labourer's wife. Back-breaking toil from dawn to dusk, a baby every year, and the poorhouse at the end ... please God, not for her. She clutched the window curtains, biting her lip.

Perhaps she could lose the baby; she had heard such things were possible from muttered stories among the Blands' servants. Yet there were dangers in that, she was aware – and how could she discover the method?

A hand tugged at her gown. 'We're ready, Susannah.'

Swallowing hard, she let herself be led down into the garden.

3

James rode his horse slowly over the hump-backed bridge and into the village. From behind him came the cool plash of water and the grumbling rumble of the mill machinery. The miller, standing in the shade of his entrance, had raised a large white hand in salute and been ignored. James stared ahead of himself, holding in his young horse tightly, his mind elsewhere.

What the devil had possessed him this last hour? His heart lurched at the memory of Susannah's reproachful eyes, of her murmured, 'I hope I don't bear a bastard, sir.' Damn it, it was frustration, of course, and not just frustration of the physical kind: it was the whole stupid tenor of his life that had brought him to this pitch of aggravation. An outburst of some kind had been inevitable for weeks, months, even; that it had taken the form of the seduction of that enchanting, mischievous girl was the most ridiculous part of it. James was not one of those who took the same relish in breaking-in virgins as they did in breaking-in horses; he detested anything swaggering. A discreet young widow at a discreet distance was where his fancy had led him – but she had remarried two months ago.

A year past his father had been talking cheerfully of his marrying one of his six girl cousins. 'Must be one of 'em likely to suit and it would be the decent thing to do. Take a good look when you get to Abbotsbridge – no one's insisting but it would give 'em the feeling of keeping the estate in their family.'

James had looked and been shocked. His father, Peter Manningford, despite being heir to the estate, which was entailed in the male line, had not bothered to visit for many years. A barrister, he had a lively career and an interesting life in

27

London. His country cousin's place in Hampshire held no interest for him, and he had visited it only twice, in his early years at the Bar, when it had been convenient for him to break a journey there. In those days Ambrose had had a son, besides three or four daughters, and his wife seemed to be perpetually in pup. Even when smallpox had killed the heir it had not appeared likely to Peter Manningford that he would inherit; ever-pregnant Alice would be sure to produce another son. But Alice had not. Childbed fever, or possibly sheer disappointment, had carried her off after the birth of her sixth daughter. Peter, a lusty man himself, had anticipated that Cousin Ambrose would remarry, and had entertained few thoughts of inheriting, but as the years went by and Ambrose sat alone in his library reading Shakespeare, Peter realised that he might one day become encumbered with an estate of which he knew little and cared less. When Ambrose wrote to suggest a long visit to acquaint himself with Abbotsbridge, Peter shied from the idea in horror. To rusticate for months and see his practice go to ruin? Ridiculous! Eventually it was agreed that James, who showed no great aptitude for the law, and who frequently disappeared from the environs of Lincoln's Inn to hunt and shoot with his friends, should move to Abbotsbridge to acquire knowledge of what in the due process of time should inevitably be his own inheritance, and to assist his Cousin Ambrose in the administration of the estate. And it was then that Peter Manningford had made his remark to James about choosing one of his cousins as a wife.

James recollected this with a grimace of distaste. Marred by illness, by accidents or by upbringing, each of his cousins, once hopefully named for one of Shakespeare's heroines, was a tragedy in herself. He could not conceive of coupling himself with any of them.

Rosalind, the eldest, was twenty-five, an awkward, self-effacing woman. She struggled to run the house for her father, but the servants, while not ignoring her, rarely did exactly what she requested. Rosalind had recently taken to wearing a white cap. 'Not to show that she's at her last prayers,' said her sister Beatrice with tart humour, 'but that she's given up praying.' No man had ever looked twice at Rosalind. 'Or at any of us,' said Beatrice.

Katharine was next in age to Rosalind and should have been an attractive and vivacious girl, but the same vicious bout of smallpox that had carried off her brother when she was still small had eaten ugly holes into the soft skin of her cheeks and along with them had eaten away her self-confidence. Now she sat sewing in dim corners, her head bent low to hide the wreck of her face.

Beatrice was different; nothing could blunt her assurance, certainly not her lameness, the result of a riding accident ten years ago, when she was twelve. She ignored peering eyes and sympathy alike and strove to lead a normal life.

The Manningfords' heir had died while Alice was carrying Jessica, and the arrival of another girl, puny and sickly, was not welcomed. Unwatched by her nurse, Jessica fell one day into the fire and from then on faced life with a withered left arm and a puckered left cheek.

Two years after Jessica had come Julia. She was now fifteen years old; perhaps reflecting the household's resentment at yet another female she was a sullen girl, lashless, listless and anaemic, disliking everyone and disliked in return.

Only Silvia was relatively unmarred, but Silvia was still in the schoolroom and even she had bat-ears.

James rode at a walking pace through the village; he did not want to return to Abbotsbridge House, to the futility and the uselessness of his existence there. Ambrose, tired and cynical, allowed him to listen in at parish meetings, to attend his discussions with the overseers and the church wardens and the local magistrates; he rode with him around the estate and he had introduced him to his tenants, but that was as far as he would go in inducting James to the position that would one day be his.

The sun was beating down on James's head and neck and he wrenched angrily at his cravat, grown suddenly constricting. Ambrose was neither instructing him nor allowing him to take any real part in the administration of the estate. After nine months of semi-idleness he was bored and frustrated. He felt stupid in the eyes of the local landowners and magistrates and the tenants and all those other people who knew too well that his position in the village was only nominal. He felt denigrated to the level of some irresponsible pleasure-seeker, and this he hated. That this was how he had behaved when he lived in London, he acknowledged, but there he had been forced to a profession he disliked; here, where he was fascinated and longed to be involved, he was held at arm's length.

James liked Hampshire: the pale green line of the downs, the deep green shade of the beechwoods. He was at home in the narrow rutted lanes that led from village to village, lanes clotted with grey mud in winter, their hedges of hawthorn and dogroses white with dust in summer. He liked their peaceful homeliness as he had never liked the smart bustle of London. He enjoyed the relaxation of fly-fishing and hunting and coursing hares, but there was room in his life for far more than that. He knew from discussions with the local gentry and the younger farmers that agricultural methods were changing; new methods of breeding animals were being tried, experimental crops being sown. He had studied books upon these subjects. Ambrose was not impressed. 'Good old days, good old ways,' he said with a flat smile, quoting the villagers. But James wanted to become a part of these changes, to learn and understand enough to become an innovator himself, to immerse himself in the land and its ways as his cousin Ambrose, shut in his library, had never been.

The present situation should go on no longer, James decided. It was infuriating; worse, it was insulting. He would speak to his cousin today, now. He urged his horse to a trot, passing the rectory briskly and with averted head, looking beyond it to the avenue of great lime trees that led up to Abbotsbridge House.

As he turned into the avenue a jay flew up over the trees to arouse a mob of raucously cursing rooks. His horse took immediate exception to this, snorting and cavorting around in a joyous parody of fright, nearly unseating the master who had dared to let his attention wander. James cursed him for a damned fool and a lying monster, not worthy of being a gentleman's mount until he had learned some dignity, and was about to kick him into a gallop when he heard a chuckle. He wheeled round to see his cousin Beatrice emerging from the trees by the drive, riding her favourite horse, a remarkably ugly skewbald.

'My dear James, what an exhibition – and I thought you had been schooling him!'

'So did I!' he returned.

'To not much effect, evidently.'

'Are you offering to take on the task yourself?' he enquired on a somewhat acid note.

'Lord, no!' She had caught up with him and turned her mare to ride beside him. 'You know very well I could not. But I will offer any amount of good advice, if you wish it,' she added, her eyes bright with amusement.

'Thank you, no!' he returned. 'I detest advice, however good.'

She laughed and pushed the skewbald into an easy canter. James followed suit, riding slightly behind her, eyeing her seat on the animal appreciatively. The neighbours said that Beatrice was a strange and difficult girl, but he liked her best of all his second cousins, despite the astringent personality and the tart humour.

She was looking well today, wearing her favourite riding habit, a dark blue garment in a smartly military style with its gold braid and dashing scarlet sash. When she was seated her figure looked excellent, and her face well enough, with its alert grey-blue eyes and clear-cut features. The chin was a touch too determined for his liking, and the skin distinctly too tanned for beauty, but that was what came of riding at all seasons – and bareheaded in the sun, too! Her family disapproved, but Beatrice retorted, 'It lightens the house-mouse colour of my hair, and I like the sun on my skin. And what can it signify?' What indeed. For it was when she dismounted that her deformity became apparent, the shortness and lameness of one leg which gave a twist to her walk. 'A twist as if her backside were beckoning one,' said her sister Julia furiously. Beatrice's problem could have led to the same withdrawal from society as her two older sisters had made, but she behaved as if it were non-existent.

Down the wide grass ride and up the further slope to the handsome Palladian house they cantered, slowing as they neared the terrace, veering right to meet the drive and make their way to the stableyard beyond. As they turned to ride through the gatehouse arch the sun winked off the gilded

31

weather-cock on its lead cupola and James stared with affection at the elderly buildings. These were perhaps his favourite part of the estate, housing the horses he loved in an extravagant comfort typical of the Hampshire gentry.

In the courtyard a young woman was stepping backwards towards them as she ended what had evidently been a lively exchange with two lounging grooms. She shook a hand at them in a gesture of mingled admonishment and farewell, said, 'Told you he'd say yes!' and turned to leave. At the sight of the two Manningford cousins she grinned with embarrassment, dropped a curtsey and fled. The two grooms meanwhile approached James and Beatrice rapidly as if there could never have been any reason for their waiting in the yard but to take the horses.

'Harry,' Beatrice asked blandly as she was helped from the saddle, 'why were you both talking to Nancy Carter? Did she bring news of vast import?'

'No, miss. I mean, I can't say, Miss Beatrice. I believe she came to see Mr Manningford, partic'lar.'

'I see.' Beatrice shrugged and hobbled slowly towards the house.

'I, too, must see your papa,' James said, giving quick instructions to the grooms and then following her in.

Just inside the passage she stopped abruptly. 'James, if you wish for something from my father, or desire to persuade him to some course of action, do approach it discreetly, in a roundabout fashion. Papa detests people telling him what he should do. He considers it insulting. He likes to think that all ideas come from him – though I tell you frankly, he detests innovations.'

'I know it. But I am not practised in female schemings.'

'You charge in like a bull at a gate!' she retorted, and then laughed. 'And I am doing the same. Truly, James, I know you detest advice, but you would do well to follow this.' She glanced down at the skirt of her riding habit, brushing a wisp of hay off with a brown hand. 'I obtained this habit – way in excess of my allowance, you know – not by telling Papa that I had to have it, but by reporting to him that Miss Waterton had commented on my shabbiness and spoken of me as eccentric.'

'Feminine wiles!'

'Tact, my dear James. The tactful approach. Remember it!'

He found Ambrose Manningford in the library, a handsome, if faded, apartment, filled almost to bursting with well-thumbed books. He was seated in a tub-shaped leather chair, his long legs sprawling, staring morosely at the pile of papers and account books strewn across his mahogany desk. A young greyhound was sleeping at his feet.

He was in his late-fifties, a tall thin man, somewhat stooped now, his gaunt face seamed with downward lines from nose and mouth; a pessimist's face. Ambrose daily retreated to his library to indulge himself in points of pure scholarship, relishing knowledge for its own sake without regard to practical applications. History and literature absorbed him by the hour, the works of Shakespeare he read time and again as others would read the Bible. He did not seem annoyed by the interruption; James had the impression that he was relieved by it.

'Quarter days,' Ambrose grunted, indicating the dusty account books. 'Come round far too fast, and just when one least desires them.'

'A pity to have to be tormented by them,' James suggested.

Ambrose stared at him. 'Essential. But a damned bore. Filling out these ledgers, reckoning up the accounts, writing letters to all sorts of demanding persons – 'tis never-ending. And shut indoors on a hot day when I should be out and checking on the mowers – I take it they have started? Good!'

Normally he would not in the least mind being shut indoors: it showed the measure of his dislike for the work. Ambrose was a scholar, not an administrator. For the first time it occurred to James that his failure to instruct him in this part of the work might well spring from a natural reluctance to show him out-of-date records and ill-kept ledgers rather than from a lack of trust.

'You shame me, sir, that I have not insisted upon helping you long before this. I should have done.'

Ambrose uncoiled himself from his chair. 'Sit down, James. You'll take a glass of this Constantia wine? It is a favourite with me.'

'I should enjoy a glass. Thank you. But, Cousin, will you not school me in the keeping of these books?'

Ambrose handed him the wine. 'I would never have thought it in your line – but if you really wish it ...'

'I cannot be forever idle, sir. I would think it only right for me to take some of this work from your shoulders.'

'Then I shall endeavour to explain the system. We can start next quarter day – there is no hurry.'

If time was needed to straighten out the books then so be it. 'We are agreed. Next quarter day.' He had made a modicum of progress.

The young greyhound stirred, saw James, stretched extravagantly, yawned noisily, and then began to frolic, his head first on one side then on the other, inviting James to play. His claws made skittering noises on the polished oak floor. The two men ignored him.

Ambrose brought out: 'One thing I should tell you, James, before you discover it for yourself. The estate is not paying its way as it should do. Or as it used to do.'

James was not surprised. From his own judgment of the old-fashioned methods and the lackadaisical attitude of the men on the home farm he had already surmised that all was not well. And when Ambrose had introduced him to the tenants he had indicated that some were behindhand with their rents. It would be interesting to discover just how behindhand they were. 'Times are not easy in agriculture. You should not strive alone with your problems but confide in me, so that we can work together,' he said.

Ambrose was silent, sipping his wine, regarding his buckled shoes. The greyhound strayed off to snap at a bluebottle buzzing against a sunlit window. James waited, hoping for further revelations, but when his cousin spoke it was with a total change of subject.

'Spry, sit down! James, when you came in, did you see a young woman leaving the house? You may have passed her. Nancy Carter.'

'Yes, I saw a girl by the stables.'

'A sensible girl, sensible request. Her father is crippled with rheumatism – he was the old shepherd, you know. Can't earn a penny now. We thought he might end up in the poorhouse, but a subscription has been raised in the village to buy them a cow. I gave to it myself.' He paused to refill his glass, holding it up to the sunlight where it sparkled deeply. 'Nancy intends to become a dairywoman.'

'A good thought, but what ...?'

'She came to beg my permission to graze her cow on the common. She said she would be sure to pay the rent and keep her father from the parish, if only I would let her keep it there. For people like the school teacher and the Pither family there is no good clean source of milk and butter, you know, only Pettifer's daughter, Betsy, and she is detestably dirty.'

'So you agreed?' The waste of good farmland in the common was a matter James felt strongly upon: nearly six hundred acres, over-grazed at the village end, the rest of it neglected, a prey to encroaching brambles and thorn bushes. His lips tightened as he considered how to broach this subject. 'Most kindly of you, considering the poor state of the common.'

Ambrose drummed his fingers on his desk. 'Kindly? Perhaps. Kindly to myself. Consider the cost on the parish rates of keeping the family! If one can be the means of assisting such persons to support themselves and their families, how much better for all of us.'

'Possibly.' But cultivating those wasted acres could provide work for idlers who would otherwise spend their days gossiping round the forge or poaching. James opened his mouth to point this out, but Ambrose forestalled him. His cousin could be unexpectedly astute at times.

'If you are thinking we should enclose the common, James, let me tell you that I am opposed to it. I've no wish to have the village in an uproar of fights over land rights, nor to have bricks thrown through my windows, nor the ricks aflame! Doubtless you will have heard many arguments in favour from your young friends. But they do not convince me.'

'I am a relative newcomer to the debate,' James returned stiffly. 'I know that William and Squire Waterton at Brambourne speak strongly in favour, but I should be interested to hear your views.'

'Destroy a common and you destroy good folks' livelihoods. Every enclosure grant that I ever heard of threw more of the poor on to the parish than ever before, besides harming the small farmers,' Ambrose said tartly.

35

'How can that be? I thought that loss of common rights had to be compensated by an allotment of land.'

'That shows your ignorance of the matter. That applies only to the legal owners of right. The occupiers of common right cottages only have their right by virtue of their tenancy. If the common goes, their right is extinguished. And those who graze animals with my permission would suffer also – the Nancy Carters of this world and those who depend on them.'

'And are there many of those?'

'A fair number. Dame Harriman with her geese, cottagers with a cow or two or a pony. Aside from the small folk, those most concerned would be the landlord of The Bull with his carriage horses, and the Trotters.'

'The Trotters!'

'Yes, indeed. You must know Thomas Trotter, no one could fail to. He was elected churchwarden this year. A big noisy man.'

'I think I recollect him,' James said thoughtfully. 'A cheerful soul. If I am thinking of the right man, he gave me several thumbnail sketches of village personalities, possibly libellous, certainly witty.'

'That would be Thomas.'

'Not one of the tenant farmers, is he?'

'No, no. He has land of his own.'

'A smock-frock farmer?'

Ambrose shook his head. 'He is of yeoman descent. He has sixty acres or thereabouts.'

'Good Lord!' James was silent for a moment, stunned. Then he asked cautiously, 'It is his daughter who is nursery-maid to the Blands?'

'More than nursery-maid nowadays. One could almost call her the governess, I suppose – if one could imagine that lively creature as a governess! A strange business, that. Susannah was virtually raised with the Bland children, particularly Fanny, half servant, half friend.'

'Really?' James took out his handkerchief to mop his forehead. It was intolerably hot in the library and the buzzing of the bluebottle was sawing through his head. 'But if her father is a farmer, why was she not educated at home?'

'There were incessant money troubles. I know no details,

36

naturally, but Thomas is far too interested in his neighbours' doings ever to do well with his own. He would have sold up, I believe, if it had not been for his wife's hard work and careful management. She is of better stock than he is.' Ambrose smiled wryly. 'I am afraid Mrs Trotter found it impossible, for all her strivings, to make a silk purse out of a sow's ear.'

'Nor even a pigskin one?' James responded.

'Nay, there's good fibre in her, true enough, but he's a rustic boar, content in his wallowings.' Ambrose took out his enamelled snuffbox.

'The girl takes after her mother, then.'

Ambrose took a pinch of snuff, delicately, carefully inhaling. He snapped the snuffbox lid down. 'No, she takes after her grandfather. He was a man of great character – mostly bad character!' with a twist of his lips. 'She is in sort a cousin of ours – not yours, of ours – distant, but a cousin, nevertheless.'

James could sit still no longer. He began to pace up and down the library floor. Spry rose to trot after him expectantly. 'How could she possibly be a relation of yours? She is a servant.'

'An old family scandal, my dear James, an old family scandal. Her grandfather was Sir John Ovington, the baronet, a cousin of my mother's.' Ambrose was clearly enjoying making his revelations, his light eyes amused as he watched James's reactions. 'He was young then, and damned good-looking, a man to turn any woman's head, I daresay. He certainly turned the governess's head. Miss Lacey, her name was, my sisters' governess. She was a charming girl.'

James picked up the *Hampshire Chronicle* to kill the bluebottle with a vicious slap across the window pane. The greyhound flinched.

Ambrose was rambling on: 'Sir John had come to us to escape the duns. Gambling was his problem; he'd lost a packet at the tables, on the horses, cock-fighting – anything you like. He'd had to ride out of London fast to lose his creditors or he would never have been travelling in one of the worst winters for years. I remember well his arrival in a screaming blizzard.' His shoulders shook gently. 'I must have been about eight or nine years old then. I was mightily taken with him. Thought him devilish dashing, y'know. That blizzard continued all night and most of the next day, so there he was, snowed in and stuck. For it froze hard, you must know, and did not let up for, oh, five or six weeks. But at least the duns could not pursue him! Instead he pursued Miss Lacey. Wasn't much else for the poor fellow to do in that weather, was there?'

James shrugged. 'So the inevitable happened.'

'Mama was most put about. When the thaw came John naturally travelled on, and two or three months later it became apparent that Miss Lacey was in a condition no governess should be in. She had to go, of course.'

'Of course,' James echoed faintly.

'She went off to Andover, or some such place. Her family disowned her. John could have been willing to marry her – who knows? But the poor fellow'd died in a hunting accident near Exeter. My parents sent her a little money from time to time. They felt partly responsible – and knowing Cousin John they certainly should have taken more care! Emily Trotter is Miss Lacey's daughter. When Emily was about twelve years old her mother was found to be sick of a tumour. She knew her days were numbered for she brought Emily to us. She asked only that we should provide the girl with a suitable position in the household. Mama felt that she must, and indeed, it answered well. Emily was such a quiet stolid little thing, always reliable. Eventually she became our housekeeper and only left when she married Thomas Trotter.' He took another pinch of snuff. 'So there we have it. A little scandal to lighten your morning, James.'

'Indeed,' James muttered.

'And,' Ambrose added, suddenly brisk, 'if you were thinking, like Cousin John, of pursuing the governess, don't! I'll admit she's the prettiest girl for miles about, but she's not for you. She's too near us to be treated as any village wench, but too far from us to marry. You understand me.'

'I understand, sir.' James wanted to kick something.

'Not that you've much chance,' Ambrose was continuing, grinning, 'with Kitty Bland playing the dragon to the beauty. She keeps a constant watch.'

One part of James wanted to terminate the conversation immediately and leave the room, another had a horrid fascination for the subject. 'What is the relationship with the Blands?' he heard his voice asking.

'Friendship, no more. No skeletons there! Mrs Trotter and Mrs Bland were married in the same year. Kitty Bland was young and naive, drowning in parish problems: Emily Trotter came to the rescue – she was born capable. When the Trotters could in no way afford their daughter the education she deserved then Mrs Bland was glad to repay an old debt. I daresay she would have helped her for nothing, being a foolish good-natured soul, but Emily Trotter's pride would reject anything smacking of charity. Susannah did the work of the nursery-maid and learned her books at the same time. And I'm told her accomplishments could stand comparison with Fanny's – even though she does not play the harp!'

James was silent.

'Matters will change vastly for the Trotters when Master Jack inherits the land,' Ambrose added. 'It is young Jack who runs the cattle on the centre of the common. His own venture, and one likely to pay, too. There 'ud be sheer fury to counter from that quarter if you enclosed.'

James raised his eyebrows but said nothing. Ambrose could not apparently visualise the benefit of ploughing up all the great common, despite the enormous rises in the price of corn recently. James calculated that if the war with France were to continue, and the new navy that the French were so desperately building came to blockade the Channel, none of the corn imports that England depended upon could reach her shores. The opportunity was there for the taking; the profits could be enormous. Ambrose should be buying land as well as enclosing the common.

How to persuade him of it? that was the problem. James needed more than William Waterton's enthusiasm or his own intuition as to the length of the war. He needed facts and figures. He must obtain them.

'You know, sir,' he said slowly, 'if I am truly to assist you here I feel I need to learn more. My father has solved legal problems for Mr Coke of Holkham upon a couple of occasions – they are friendly acquainted. I shall seek an introduction. I am told Mr Coke is vastly knowledgeable in farming methods, both the old and the new, and most helpful to young farmers. He holds festivals of agriculture, sheep-shearings and so forth, every year. I think I might show filial affection by visiting my father shortly, and then journey to Holkham. Should you object if I left you for a month or so? I should be back for the harvest.'

'You must do as you wish,' Ambrose said indifferently.

4

Susannah celebrated her seventeenth birthday by fainting in the big hall at Abbotsbridge House.

When she came round she was lying on a sofa, feeling hot and very sick. Four of the Manningford sisters were standing staring at her. She drew a shaky breath and held it, terrified lest she vomit over their feet. A face loomed nearer, a face she had never seen before without a veil. She focussed on the smallpox scars as they blurred and cleared again – they were not so shocking as gossip said – and slowly the sickness ebbed and her head cleared. She breathed carefully and tried to sit up.

'Miss Trotter,' Miss Katharine's soft voice insisted, 'Miss Trotter, you must not rise yet.' A hand pressed her down, and a fan wafted the cool air of the hall over her.

Miss Katharine's face was replaced by Miss Manningford's, long and bony, nervously smiling, clearly worried.

'Miss Trotter, are you unwell? Have you the fever?'

'No, no! The heat,' Susannah reassured her. 'It was only this thundery heat.'

She moved her eyes. Miss Manningford and Katharine were looking concerned, while the younger Jessica and Julia were regarding her as if she were one of the more repulsive exhibits at a fair. In the background two maidservants peered. She levered herself to a sitting position.

'You have been most kind and I thank you, but I must go directly. It is my afternoon off and Mama expects me.'

'Then it was good of you to bring my sister's tapestry wools first,' Miss Manningford said earnestly, 'and on such a hot day, too.'

Not goodness, but a violent illogical need to see James Manningford, or, if he were not returned from his journeying, somehow to discover when he would come. Susannah did not know what, if anything, she expected from him, only she knew that she had to share her terrifying secret with James: she had to confront him with the problem he had created. But he was not here.

When her monthly curse-of-Eve had failed to arrive she had slipped to the privy so often to discover whether the miracle she prayed for had not occurred that Mrs Bland had made embarrassing queries as to the state of her bowels and the summer flux. She had no one to turn to, only the sweating terror of the nights alone that turned her thoughts to James.

She stood up, needing to get away from Miss Manningford and Katharine's kindly fuss, from Jessica and Julia's cool stares, from the maids' inquisitive eyes. 'Thank you. I shall do very well now.'

Miss Katharine insisted that she be lent Julia's old pony to save her the walk in the heat, and a manservant accompanied her to the farmhouse gate. Susannah was touched by their thoughtfulness.

Her mother's rare smile told her approval, but she spoke drily: 'A strong girl like you should think nothing of the walk, but it does show in what light the Manningfords regard us, that they should take such trouble to repay your little kindness. I am pleased, Susannah. We do well to stand high in their estimation.'

Mrs Trotter was a woman of dignity, high-bridged of nose, calm of manner, reticent of speech, a woman of a different mould from her gregarious neighbours. She led the way into the buttery, where she poured them both a cooling glass of lemonade and then drew a tankard of beer from the cask. 'Your brother is in the barn. He will be glad of this. Take it across to him, will you, please, while I fetch the present I have for you.'

Susannah picked her way across the cobbled yard. A quartet of hens clucked and pecked in the shade of the open shed, while their accompanying cock surveyed his harem from the rim of a cart-wheel. Two sows, hugely near their time, lay somnolent on the steaming midden. The barn, long and low, old and dilapidated, formed the bottom side of the yard, its thatch, like some monstrous uncut fringe, dipping down on both sides till it almost touched the ground. Her brother was perched precariously on its summit, a pile of straw beside him. 'A very happy birthday to you!' he called.

'Goodness, Jack, are you safe?'

'Of course I am. Is that beer? Then I shall descend.'

He wriggled crabwise across the lumpy thatch to a ladder, which Susannah ran to hold as he descended. He gave her a casual hug, seized the tankard and drained it in great gulps. 'That will strengthen my arm.'

'What is the problem?'

'Neglect, in a word. That roof has been leaking for weeks, months even. Father keeps insisting: "'Twill be done, son 'twill be done!" But nothing happens.'

'I know.'

'And the harvest will soon be upon us – how can we store the corn in a sieve? Besides, while I do not wish to speak in a carping and unfilial manner of our beloved progenitor, Father 'ud make a rare botched job of it.' He cocked a knowing eyebrow at his sister, who grimaced back.

Jack was twenty-one and already did double the work of his father, his lithe muscularity making light of loads that Thomas never would have attempted. Jack had a driving ambition to develop the farm and double its acreage. The way his father muddled through chafed his keen and critical mind, and only his naturally calm temperament restrained him from the outbursts of wrath that would have been natural to his sister.

'How are your cattle?'

'Progressing excellently on the middle part of the common, up by the old dewpond. I have hired a good boy to watch them and I should turn a handsome profit.'

'I will pray so,' Susannah said with affection. 'And what will you do with your profit?'

'Buy more land, if I can. The price of wheat is going ridiculously high with this war, and that will turn me an even better profit.'

'I believe you are right.'

'I know I am right. I shall become a rich man and give you a handsome dowry, Sukey! Which reminds me – I feel I should warn you that our mother has fixed upon a highly suitable husband for you. She is charmed by her own perspicacity!'

'Dear Lord,' Susannah exclaimed crossly. 'I wish she would not plot and contrive so. But who is it?'

Jack looked slantwise at her down the aquiline nose he had inherited from his mother, his eyebrows tilted ironically. 'I leave it to you to discover!' He flexed the muscles of his arms and looked up. Beyond the barn the sky was piled with great dark clouds, motionless and menacing, though above them the sun still shone. 'I must get back to my thatching or all my efforts will be in vain, for unless I mistake me, there is a storm brewing. I thought this heat too good to last. The weather this year seems generally determined to be unkind.' He scrambled back up the ladder.

Mrs Trotter's present was a length of cream silk for a gown, an expensive gift that had her daughter catching her breath with delight. 'Seventeen! A delightful age, Susannah, but we must now seriously consider your future. You cannot forever stay a nursery-maid, nor, indeed, a governess.'

'No,' she agreed warily.

Mrs Trotter gently touched the folds of silk as they lay in her daughter's arms, then she turned away. 'I have no immediate changes in mind, but we must begin to make plans. We will talk together, you and I. Fold that stuff up and put it on the walnut table in the parlour and then bring me the sewing box and the pile of socks you will find beside it. We shall work under the pear-tree in the garden.' It would never occur to her that anyone might sit and chat without useful occupation.

Susannah did as she was bid, following her mother along the garden path to the wooden seat. The air in the garden was still, the birds were silent. She had loved her mother's garden since she was a small child; it was to her the epitome of a safe haven, walled and quiet and tucked away. The garden, like the farm-house, dated back to Stuart times, with neat geometrical beds divided by mellow brick walks edged with lavender and box. This formal structure time and Mrs Trotter had softened with exuberant clusters of plants that spilled over on to its paths, leaving thymes and pinks peering up from the cracks between the bricks, old roses hanging their untidy heads and the scent of honeysuckle rich on the air. Today the stillness and the silence were oppressive, the scent sickly.

Susannah picked up a sock and examined the hole in its heel with absent eyes. She threaded a needle with wool. What was her mother saying?

'. . . we shall make the silk up into a suitable gown for evening wear. I have fashion plates being sent from Winchester 'specially. I feel we should hold a small party after the harvest – we could invite Timothy Goddard, Daniel Bland, perhaps the curate, Mr Stacey. We could hold one at Christmas, too.'

'Yes.' The needle had pricked her finger; she sucked the welling spot of blood. Christmas was beyond contemplation.

Her mother pushed a darning mushroom into a sock. 'But I do not wish to learn of any more village flirtations, Susannah. Luke Carter is mighty handsome, and a good man besides. But to marry – no!'

'There has never been any talk of that.'

'Good.' Mrs Trotter turned her penetrating eyes on Susannah. 'But there is always talk in Abbotsbridge. Most of it is just puff and smoke – but where there is smoke there is always some fire, even if only a spark.' With unusual humour she added: 'And there are too many young sparks languishing after you, my girl! Discourage 'em. Village sparks will do your reputation no good. Remember, I look to you to marry well!'

Susannah kept her eyes lowered. Perspiration trickled between her breasts. She longed to snap at her mother, but did not dare. She loved and feared her mother in almost equal measure. Mrs Trotter ruled her family, not in the fashion of the village matron with a swift cuff or a smack, but with a code of behaviour that brooked no exceptions, and kept Susannah's conscience ever pricking.

As a young woman, secret pride had sustained Emily Lacey: pride in her breeding, the daughter of a baronet and a governess who had come of gentlefolk; pride that she had risen above the stain of bastardy and achieved a respectable place in the village community; and, as time passed, pride that she had acquired a husband and a family of her own. Thomas Trotter had been the means to the desired end: she did not love him, but she was loyal. Her devotion centred itself in her children; her lovely daughter should achieve all that she had not.

45

Emily snipped off her wool and pulled another sock from the pile. 'They tell me that Mr Stacey has moved into the rectory now,' she remarked, her voice amused. 'Those foolish kindly Blands – they are forever put upon! How is Mr Humby progressing?'

'But poorly. Mr Stacey says he is paralysed still on his right side and can move neither arm nor leg. He is confined to his bed, mumbling and dribbling.'

'How lowering it must have been for Mr Stacey, living at the parsonage house with that sad man, perpetually ill and now speechless.'

'That was why Mrs Bland took pity on him – that and the housekeeper's complaints of all that she had to do for Mr Humby, and the terrible pains it was giving her in her back, her shoulders and her bunions. Mrs Bland said she could not bear to see Mr Stacey withering away there, living on boiled pig's cheek and cold turnips, with no one who cared for his comfort!'

'Mrs Bland tells me he is a good, hard-working young man, who should do well in the Church. Do you like him?'

'He is well enough.' Perceiving the drift of her mother's remarks, Susannah added swiftly: 'It is said that he is taking an interest in Miss Waterton and that she will have a fortune of nigh on ten thousand pounds!'

'Miss Waterton?' The darning needle flashed in the sunlight as Emily gestured her contempt. 'She is no great catch for all her money. A plain girl with no charm at all. She has a wasp's buzz of a voice – and a stinging tongue to go with it. You could cut her out any day.'

Susannah winced. To discuss her matrimonial prospects at this juncture would be unbearable, but once started on the rival merits of a farmer, a hopeful curate or even a younger son of the gentry, her mother was like a river in spate. She must fend her off nonchalantly.

'Mama! What charms do I have that could compete with ten thousand pounds?'

Her mother pursed her lips and nodded, as was her habit when intent upon a subject. 'You have plenty of charms, and accomplishments too, and I am not the only one to say so. Yes, and any young man would vastly prefer a pretty and complaisant wife to a long-nosed humourless old dowd!'

46

'When you put it like that, how can he possibly consider anyone but me?' Susannah said, giving her mother a humorous look.

'You keep that in mind!' Mrs Trotter admonished her, but she smiled reluctantly back at her daughter and let the subject drop.

Susannah settled back to her darning with a sigh of relief, but resolved nevertheless to leave the farmhouse as soon as the present sock was mended. The approaching storm was excuse enough.

She walked back through the village struggling to think. 'You look pale,' her mother had said in bidding her goodbye. How could she help but be pale? she had responded quickly. This heat made everyone pallid. The sky beyond the church tower was inky, dramatically dark, throwing the silhouettes of trees and tower into lighter relief. In contrast the village street was a white world of dust, shrouding hedges, chickens, pigs and children alike in pale layers of pulverised chalk. Her feet were dry and weary with the stuff.

Only the horse-chestnut reared itself tall and darkly green outside the smithy. From beneath it voices came and went in waves of sound. There was a rumble of argument interrupted by a burst of laughter. An elderly man stumped across the patch of scuffed grass to stand by the roadside, legs planted apart, haranguing the group under the tree, hurling abuse at them with the gestures of one who wishes he were hurling stones. 'Shame on ye! Minds full o' muck as a midden!'

Two small-holders who had come to collect items from the forge were standing to one side listening, slapping their approval on their thighs at every telling point. They were men different in temperament but similar in views, both forces to be reckoned with in the village. Sam Truckle, an aggressive weather-beaten man plagued with an intractable cough, had called for his plough-coulter. He was the father of six grown and half-grown children, one of whom, Berry, was apprenticed to Josh. His friend and neighbour Peter Page, a gnomish man with a mobile jovial face, player of the trumpet with the church players, was waiting for Josh to produce his new gate hinges, and gleeful at the unexpected entertainment.

47

'Slut, is it? Our Charity's no slut!' the old man snarled. 'Time and times I've said 'tis all lies and now I'm going to make ye swaller them words!'

'That's right, Master Jurd,' Page grinned encouragingly, 'you push them down their throats!'

'Scan'lous tongue eternally clacking,' Jurd threw at the ancients, thrusting his hands into the pockets of a large new pair of leather breeches to hitch them up. 'Like a gaggle of ole women you be!'

The lurcher beneath the bench glimpsed a cat sauntering on the far side of the street and dashed after it, hurtling between old man Jurd's legs and upsetting him into a pile of fresh horse droppings. The ancients on the bench roared their delight, while Peter Page clutched helplessly at Sam Truckle.

Jurd rose, spitting fury as he twisted his head to view the damage. 'My new britches! Ruined as like as not ... an' all I paid for 'em! Why d'ye keep an animal like that? Useless misbegotten crittur!'

Stung, its owner retaliated: 'No more misbegotten than the babe that's swelling the belly o' your grand-daughter Charity!'

'You did oughter 'ave charity about sech things,' a woman onlooker smirked.

'Ah,' capped Page, 'a lot of men 'ave 'ad Charity, seemingly!' and thumped Truckle in the ribs. The old men roared again.

'You'll see,' old man Jurd shouted. 'You'll see – Bidewell'll wed her.'

'Going to make 'im, are yer?' the crowd enquired.

'Squire'll make 'im, when I tells 'im!'

'Yer durst not go to Squire,' an old man taunted. 'I'll wager a shillun ye dursn't.'

Picking up her skirts, Susannah hastened past, catching her breath in her throat, dust spirting from every step she made. With each day that passed she had become more worried that the worst had happened: her faint today had made her certain. Dear Lord! was that how it would be for her family in two or three months' time – all the village laughing and nudging and making obscene jokes? Susannah Trotter to be dragged up to the squire's house by her angry father to lay a charge before him as magistrate as to the father of her child?

That was for rustics, to keep mother and child from becoming an expense to the parish. That was not for her. She must not allow herself to consider anything so dreadful: her parents would never take such an action. Or would they? Suppose her mother insisted she should be thrown out? Her father would object to that. If she named James Manningford as the father no one would believe her. Naturally old Mr Manningford would believe Charity if she named Barney Bidewell; it would be to the benefit of all those who paid the parish rates to believe her. But James Manningford? The gentry would protect their own. Certainly there would be no question of a forced marriage. If Susannah had not been so miserable she could have laughed at the idea.

Damp was springing in the roots of her hair and a queasiness was rising in her throat. Barney was protesting that he was not the father of Charity's baby, but, of course, he could prove nothing... *He could prove nothing!* Her footsteps slowed as her brain wrestled with the implications of this thought. Before her was Duckett's shop, its door wide open to let out the heat. The curate, Sedley Stacey, had emerged from its dark interior and now stood blinking in the sulphureous light, two beribbonned parcels dangling awkwardly from his fingers.

An idea hit Susannah, the most shocking ever to come to her mind. She stopped dead and put out her hand to support herself against the window shutter of the shop, turning her face aside as though Mr Stacey might read the thought written upon it. Push it away, it could not be. God would condemn her wickedness. But it would save her, whispered her mind ... and it would save her baby. No one should point the finger at her child. God would understand that. Her mother rarely mentioned her childhood before she came to Abbotsbridge, but Susannah did not need to know all the details to understand that there had been terrible times. The marks were on Emily Trotter still, in all her thoughts and ways. It was wrong that the innocent should suffer.

Sedley Stacey glanced round and saw her. His face visibly brightened. 'Ah, Susannah! Are you returning to the rectory?'

Beyond her in the dark cavern of the shop two women were gossiping. They were safe, snug and smug, each married to her man. Susannah's mind raced, considering, examining, determining; the idea that had come to her crystallised – and was

49

rejected. No, to seduce a man in order to name him as the father of her child was a bad thought, an evil beckoning Will-o'-the Wisp whose temptations she must ignore, however alluring.

She took a deep breath and smiled at the curate, a smile extra brilliant from the rush of shame at her guilty thoughts. 'Yes, indeed. Mr Stacey. Do not tell me – you have been on an errand for Mrs Bland!'

His nostrils flared with annoyance. 'For Miss Fanny, in fact.' He held up the two packages disdainfully. 'Muslins, newly arrived, and velvets for next winter. Little did I think when I entered the Church that a curate could become an errand boy.'

'Such a shame! Mr Stacey, you are too good.' Her voice was warm and clear and full of sympathy. In the shop the two women craned their heads to look. She stretched out her hand. 'Let me carry them, please.'

He relinquished the parcels. 'I trust you will not find them a burden? They are not heavy, but I did hear you had been unwell.'

'Unwell? Me?' she said innocently, her brain in a turmoil. 'What nonsense! You can see I am in fine fettle.'

'That was not what I heard from Miss Manningford but five minutes ago. She told me you had fainted in their hall.'

'Oh, what a hum! A moment's dizziness when I came in out of the sun was all.'

He looked at her; she gave him a glance tinged with mischief and a tiny shake of the head before turning to walk up the lane.

An expression of pleased understanding spread over his face. 'I understand. You would not care for Mrs Bland to fuss.'

'She has so much to bother her,' Susannah said demurely. The last thing she wanted was Mrs Bland asking probing questions.

'You do not have the fever? I know it is about in Brambourne. Indeed, tomorrow I am burying an old woman dead from it at the poorhouse. You do appear a touched heated.'

'No, no. No fever! And I am brave now.'

The walk past the church to the rectory was steep. Sedley seemed to be finding it an effort, for he walked at a stroll, while Susannah chatted about the Blands and daringly teased him about his prospects.

'When poor Mr Humby departs this world for a far better

50

one, then you will have a proper curacy and a handsome house. We shall all be mighty proud to know you then.'

Sedley looked down his arched nose, resentment heavy on his face. 'I have no promise for when that time comes. There is a cousin ... I do not know the details, but I believe him to be at Cambridge. The place is being kept warm for him, and after him for Master Daniel Bland.'

Susannah twisted up her mouth and shook her head. 'Daniel will never become a clergyman. He dreams of the army, of a dragoon's uniform. I know this, for we are of an age and he has told me in confidence. Though it is an open secret! Anyway, he is still at Winchester College. And as for the cousin – pooh! He will not be wanting to settle upon a curacy here for years yet, and in the very nature of things he can have no definite expectations. No, we shall see you established at Brambourne very soon.'

Sedley Stacey was silent, shortening his stride still further, his head down. Above the church tower swifts were circling in mad exuberant flight, screaming as they went, sorties flying low across the meadows, up over the elms and so round and back again. Sedley glanced up at them and said in a fretful tone: 'Such a noise those birds make. It quite pierces my head. And the weather is so heavy. I wish the rain would come.'

'You are tired?'

'I have the headache. I have been threatened with one all afternoon. Your cheerful conversation quite made me forget it, but walking up this slope has caused my head to throb most unpleasantly.' There was a greasy sheen of sweat on his skin and his normally high-coloured cheeks were pallid.

There was a low rumble of thunder and the first great drops of rain pocked the dust.

'I think it is you who have the fever,' said Susannah.

5

Sedley was sure he had never felt so ill in his life. He ached
everywhere: his head, his neck, his back, his legs. He turned and
twitched in his bed, unable to rest whatever his position.
'Sleep!' Mrs Bland entreated him from the doorway and he
dutifully tried, only to fall prey to nightmares that endlessly
tormented him. Fiends were hammering him into a coffin and
the nails were piercing his head; a lancet was cutting his veins
and the blood was draining hotly from his body; iron bands
were crushing his temples. A door opened and dogs leapt
towards him; panting slavering animals with lolling red
tongues protruding between sharp and shining teeth.

'Pray do not worry about the funeral,' one of them barked at
him.

The funeral ... Funeral? Was he dying?

'The service, services,' he managed to mumble.

The animal metamorphosed into the rotund figure of the
rector, looming above him. 'The Sunday service is attended to,'
he said. Spaniel-brown eyes blinked at him, the surge and
stench of dogs retreated and Sedley dropped back into a half-
world of clashing hammers and clamouring bells.

On the third day he struggled back to reality. Birds were
singing behind the curtains and his head was no longer trying to
burst its bounds. He had a memory of Dick, the rector's man,
clumsily ministering to his most intimate needs, and other
memories, of cool hands touching his forehead and holding
cold drinks to his lips, and of a soft voice that had calmed his
troubled sleep. Strange that Susannah should have nursed him;
he must tell her of his gratitude. While it was only natural that a

52

young unmarried woman should have an admiration for a handsome clergyman, her devotion was special and should be rewarded.

He became aware that something unusual had happened to the house. Normally it was full of sounds. What had become of the noisy dogs, of the piping trebles of the children, of the servants' feet clumping on the polished floors?

Dick enlightened him when he appeared to attend to him. 'Mr and Mrs Bland have both taken the fever, and two of the maidservants, too. Young Lizzie, she's gone with the little ones down to Mrs Trotter's to help feed the ducks an' chickens, an' watch the butter-making. Very helpful, Mrs Trotter's bin. And Squire Waterton came in his carriage with Miss Waterton to take Miss Fanny to stay at Brambourne Manor.'

'And those dratted dogs?'

'Them? Susannah made me lock them up in the far stables. She couldn't be holding with them underfoot. Can't say as I miss them any!'

'No!' Sedley agreed. He struggled to raise himself to a sitting position and fell limp against the pillows. 'I'm as weak as a kitten,' he complained.

'Likely you are, sir,' Dick nodded, thrusting a clammy flannel at Sedley's face and dabbing inexpertly. 'Dr Huskett bled you proper.'

Sedley submitted to the flannel. 'Did he?' From a jumble of recollections he plucked a picture of Susannah averting her face from a blood-spattered tin bowl, a handkerchief pressed to her lips. 'Good Lord,' he added faintly.

For the rest of that day and the next Sedley lay quietly recovering his strength, Dick nursing him and Susannah appearing from time to time with herbal infusions, bowls of strengthening broth and delicious little messes that he understood she had prepared with her own hands, Cook still being confined to her bed. On the first evening he made her his speech of gratitude, telling her how vastly impressed he was by her ardour in her care. 'My own mother would not have done as much. Your position here hardly required it – and it took courage, too.'

It was dreary alone in his bedroom and she was an attractive, indeed desirable, young woman; Sedley contrived excuses to

53

hold her talking whenever she appeared, Susannah perched on a chair's edge ready to leap up and escape should someone approach, for to be found closeted alone with a man abed would be shocking, compromising to her virtue and his position. Their low-voiced conversations wove a web of conspiracy about them; for a man naturally conventional it was an exciting novelty.

The second evening, encouraged by her interest, he spoke of himself and his ambitions. Susannah knew of his anxiety to obtain a good curacy; she must also be aware of the difficulties for one who had no patronage in the Church, no friends in high places who could speak for him to the Dean and Chapter. His father, also a clergyman, was long since dead and his mother was a widow living a retired life in Bath and plagued by ill-health. Sedley was glad to be living now in Abbotsbridge and helping to serve the churches of two parishes; this was widening his social contacts; one never knew who might not be of help. Besides, Sedley confided, his aim was to stay in Hampshire. He wanted a rural parish; his long term aim was to own land, a gentleman's seat, and to combine as squire the running of an estate with the work of a parson. He knew there were many who successfully combined the two. 'A squarson!' Susannah said, laughing admiringly. He smiled back. She truly was a most understanding girl.

Sedley was surprised at how pleasant it was to talk to Susannah: to think of women in terms of friendship had not occurred to him before. In Bath, his social contacts had been few and dull. His mother had not considered that Sedley might need a circle of friends: he had only too much contact with those noisy ruffians at school; a poor invalid widow could not entertain such as those. Oxford had widened his horizons; Oxford had produced his dolly Molly, as his friends referred to her. Molly had not been a friend, precisely; Molly had been for other things. They had never talked, or not what he would call talking; the merest exchanges of words. She was the niece of his college servant. Molly. He recalled her with complacency: a plump brunette with lively dark eyes. To her, serving Sedley's body had been of no more import than serving him a meal: his needs were fulfilled and she was well paid. She made no bones of the fact that Sedley's money and that of four other undergraduates was being saved – after her uncle's slice – for when her sailor came home from the sea.

There had been more than two years of Molly. But since then there had been only frustration. Really, Sedley told himself, life could be most difficult for a man in Holy Orders. He had reconciled his dolly with his religion by telling himself that no man could counsel others where he himself was ignorant, but now he envied William Waterton when he slapped the milkmaids' buttocks and chased them under the haycocks, but dared not emulate him. His need for a parish of his own was urgent; his need for respectability paramount. He must not allow himself to dwell upon a nursemaid's breasts, of which he'd caught such exciting glimpses as Susannah bent to plump his pillows, nor the richness of her russet hair, nor ... nor anything else about her.

The following day Sedley felt his strength returning. He sat in a chair by the window that afternoon, thankful to be out of bed, but he could not concentrate upon the volume of the Revd James Fordyce's sermons on his lap. He had never felt so restless. He tried to distract himself with plans for his future, but something major had affected his attitudes. All seemed grey and lifeless. In pursuit of his ambitions he had been paying attentions to Miss Waterton, a plain but genteel lady, William's oldest sister, at twenty-six only two years older than himself. Although he was but a penniless curate, the lady had been graciously pleased to accept his attentions. Her eyes, her smiles, were all for him. Now, perhaps through some natural perversity, he was not sure that he wished to proceed. Her handsome fortune seemed the merest dross. Sedley stood up and retrieved the book of sermons from where he had flung it on the floor. This was folly, doubtless some effect of his illness. He must concentrate on regaining full health, mental and physical.

He read for perhaps three minutes and then the sound of childish voices from the lawn below interrupted him. Susannah was playing ball with the children; they were running up the garden and back again, jumping, throwing, calling, laughing, the dogs barking among their feet. He rose to lean on the windowsill. The scent of crushed grass and roses came to his nostrils. Across the lawn Susannah was standing still now, encouraging the boys to throw further, harder. A puff of wind blew the muslin of her gown against her body, outlining her nipples, the curve of her belly, her thighs, teasing the tendrils of her hair. All sorts of wicked thoughts crowded into Sedley's mind and his body reacted shockingly. He groaned.

That evening he could not sleep. He flung off his bedclothes in a sweat, he gathered them untidily up again in a shiver, he thumped and turned his pillows: all was to no avail, sleep eluded him. His thoughts kept racing wildly over the wind's impudence with Susannah's body, and the way her hair had shone and floated. Hair had a special allure for Sedley. He had lit his candle to read the sermons – they should prove soporific enough – when the vision of a glass of brandy came to him. The very thing. The rector would not object, surely, not for medicinal purposes. He got up, pushed his feet into his slippers and padded off to find the decanter.

The door to her room creaked. No matter how slowly he moved it the sound persisted, monstrous in the night's silence. A dog barked. As the door opened the curtains fluttered and the bright disc of the moon shone through the window. Susannah sat upright in her bed.

'What? Who? Does someone need me? Please!'

He was in the room and the damned door closed behind him at last. 'Ssh!' he hissed. 'It is I, Sedley.'

'But Mr Stacey ...!'

Her white nightrail shimmered over her breasts in the dark, moonlit, beckoning. He stumbled across the room, put a knee on the high bed, captured her hands, held them close against his chest in a melodramatic gesture.

'I have been dreaming of you,' he breathed. 'Yes, dreaming. I have feelings for you that are ardent, too ardent to be suppressed. Dear girl, you must allow me to give them the fullest expression ...'

He swung the second knee up and heaved himself on to the bed. She leaned away into the pillow, wrenched her hands from his and pushed hard at his chest, almost unbalancing him. 'No, no,' he said, 'you must let me, you have to!' And in recovering himself he lurched forward with sufficient impetus to throw his left leg across the bed and straddle her.

56

'Mr Stacey,' she said, her hands still pushing at his weight, 'you must stop. You must go away. You've been drinking. You'll regret this in the morning.'

He was deaf to her words, his face lunging forward towards hers, his body's weight forcing the inadequate hands away.

'Never, never,' he mumbled meaninglessly, 'never regret such beauty and such charm. Such hair, lovely hair, so, so ...'

His voice trailed off as he shifted his weight to one elbow, clutched a lock of her hair and drew it across his mouth.

Her body wriggled beneath his, long limbs tossing in an effort to throw him off. Her struggles were intolerably provocative; he had never been more sexually aroused. 'You must,' he moaned. 'You must allow me! You know you wish it, too. You know you do!'

She was not crying out, not screaming. Women made these protests only for form's sake where a handsome virile man such as he was concerned; he knew that for sure.

'No, Sedley, you can't ...'

But his mouth fixed on hers, smothering her words, his tongue pushing between her teeth. He would show her that his ardour was not to be denied, stop this petty pretence of distress. Bottom briefly in the air, he tugged away the last restraining bedcovers, scrabbled to raise her nightgown. His greedy mouth moved downward to an uncovered breast, licking and biting at the nipple.

'No,' she breathed again. 'No!'

'Yes,' he panted, his hand pushing roughly between her clenched thighs. 'You must! Please!'

For a moment he raised his head to look into her face, illuminated by a thin shaft of moonlight. Their eyes met. A strange look passed across her face, her eyes fell and were veiled, her hands stopped fighting his. He had known it, he had known his will and his ardour would overcome her. Didn't she adore him? Sedley wasted no time in pushing himself between her legs.

Afterwards his memories of the act were confused. He had a dim fancy that she had muttered: 'You will be gentle, won't you?' then only too swiftly had come the jolting return to earth after the ecstasy of his climax, the sight of her tear-wet face on the pillow, the cold shock of the thought that she must have been a virgin, and, as he crept from the bed, clear in the light of the moon, the sight of two dark spots of blood on the sheet.

6

When James rose to follow Ambrose into his library on the
evening of his return from Holkham, his cousin Beatrice
caught his eye and gave him a faint shake of her head. James
raised his eyebrows.

'Papa,' she explained, 'has just received a box of new books
from London. It would be useless to expect him to concentrate
upon anything else for at least five days.'

James considered her. 'I suppose you are of the opinion that
I should be better occupied playing piquet with you!' he said
sarcastically.

'Oh, thank you, James. How kind of you! But I should prefer
backgammon myself. I have the pieces to hand on the sofa
table.'

He shook his head. 'An old man's game. But I suppose I
should be grateful you do not choose chess.'

She chuckled. 'Both are games of strategy. A useful study for
a man.'

'Ah, I understand now. More good advice!'

Beatrice limped to the table and seated herself. She began to
push the men into place on the board, her face amused. 'How
gratifying it is to find someone in this household so swift to
follow my mind!'

James sat down opposite her. 'But I fail to comprehend why
you interest yourself so much in my affairs.'

She made no reply to this, but picked up the dice and threw
them. 'A five and a six. Beat that! It is good to have you back,
James. Was your journey to Norfolk worthwhile? Did you find
Mr Coke helpful?'

'Exceedingly helpful.'

Mr Coke had been kindness itself. Dressed in a shooting jacket and long boots, with a broad-brimmed hat clapped on to his head, he had spent three days conducting his guest around his great Norfolk estate, showing him new farmsteads built on farms carved from reclaimed common and marshland, explaining how he had introduced covenants into all the leases on his estate to insist upon certain modes of cultivation, and discussing the new methods of farming with all the enthusiasm of a man half his age. His soil was sandy, while Hampshire was chalky, but both were light soils so that the problems and their solutions were similar.

'Mr Coke is an advocate of enclosure, is he?'

James threw the dice in his turn. 'Double two! Since Mr Coke inherited he has spent a great deal of money on enclosing and consolidating his lands and then on improvements.'

'And to what result?'

'He has already trebled his revenues.'

'Truly? That is amazing! Tell me how – in simple terms, please.'

James moved a piece and then sat back. 'When Parliament agrees an act of enclosure then every farmer receives all his land together in one compact holding, instead of scattered in strips throughout the three great open fields of the village, as we have it at present. Added to that he is given an additional acreage to represent his rights in the old common. That is allocated in proportion to his total ownership of land.'

'In other words, the more land a man owns, the more acres he can grab from the common. Yes, I know all this.'

'My apologies. At the time enclosure takes place, when all the village land is redistributed, then the old leases naturally must be rewritten. Land in a compact easily worked farmholding is worth at least double what it was previously in a straggle of small parcels.'

'Goodness,' Beatrice said slowly, 'Papa could increase his income dramatically ... and rid himself of incompetent tenants into the bargain.'

'He could. And there is more to it than that. Each farmer, tenant or owner, can then decide for himself what crops to grow on his land. He can put money into improving his soil. He can experiment. He is no longer tied to what the village meeting decides.'

James had seen acres of golden ripe wheat where, said Mr Coke, until his improvements no wheat could be grown; he had been impressed by Mr Coke's experimental breed of pigs and by the superb flocks of Southdown sheep, and he had admired the great new barn at Holkham – 'The largest in England!' said Mr Coke – waiting to receive all the bounty from the fields. James was no dreamer, but in Norfolk he had seen a vision of what could be achieved at Abbotsbridge. In his room he had a sheaf of notes, neatly annotated. The antiquated inefficiency and disorder of the Abbotsbridge farming traditions were a challenge. He was not afraid of hard work or responsibility, or of dislike. Not even Ambrose's indifference repelled him. He would convince him: his success would be the greater.

'And now you have to persuade Papa.' Beatrice contemplated the backgammon board gloomily before making her move. 'But James, there would be a shocking amount of work to do in organising this enclosure. Papa would loathe it!'

'The work would be mine – that is, if he would allow me to do it. I'd enjoy it. The benefits would be his.'

'What could anyone offer more?' Her grey-blue eyes met his and he saw a look of mischief come into them. 'And he will need those benefits. My goodness, James, he will need them! The roof here is in need of major renewals, and there is dry rot in the attics and damp in the pantries.'

'You do not surprise me. Many of the cottages and the farm-buildings are in poor repair.'

'Yes, indeed. And there are other matters to be planned for.' She leaned forward and a confident little smile hovered about her lips. 'My three young sisters will need to make their come-out, a matter I believe Papa has overlooked. Katharine and I were hardly suitable for a grand launch into society and Rosalind never cared much for such fripperies, but if the others are to have a ball each in their honour and to be suitably attired for their débuts, Papa will be at some expense!'

Rosalind and Katharine looked up from the sewing they were doing for the poor basket.

'But I have never heard Papa mention such a thing,' Rosalind protested, her naturally worried look deepening.

'No!' Beatrice said blandly. 'Papa is so vague. It is high time it was brought to his notice. I am surprised at you, Rosalind, that you have not done so.' She moved a piece triumphantly across the board. 'There!'

'Now you have blockaded me.' James shook his head reproachfully. 'Cousin Beatrice, you understand strategy all too well. I think I had better resign the game to you. Or should I say, games?'

'Coward!'

'Really, Beatrice!' Rosalind remonstrated. She let her sewing drop into her lap. 'But tell me, do you truly consider that Papa should give a ball for Jessica? Her poor face ... that arm ... how could he?'

'Very easily. Long sleeves, cleverly sewn, will disguise her arm, and surely some new style might be devised for her hair that would mask the worst of her cheek? Her figure is pretty enough.'

'But not her temper,' James remarked.

Beatrice regarded him from beneath her brows. 'If Jessica had some hope for her life, something of which to dream, I believe her temper would improve overnight. James, you ask why I take an interest in your affairs? I can only say, this is the affair of us all. We three, Rosalind, Katharine and I, will never leave Abbotsbridge. We're beyond hope. But Julia and Jessica and little Silvia could find themselves husbands if they but had a fortune each to recommend them. Perhaps this enclosure business may succeed there; our present portions are very small. And I devoutly pray it may succeed for your sake as well as ours. I can imagine little worse for a man than to be encumbered with six spinster cousins!'

Katharine's soft voice came from her corner, observing in amused tones that even Miss Waterton had her curate.

'There you are, indeed!' Beatrice said.

Rosalind leaned forward. 'Well, no, I have heard different,' she said, anxious at all costs to preserve accuracy. 'I hear in the village that Mr Stacey has frequently been seen talking to Susannah Trotter, that he has even invited her to ride his horse. It is she whom he admires.'

Beatrice made a gesture of resignation and then began to laugh.

'I applaud Mr Stacey's taste!' James said.

Mr Stacey would not have agreed. Mr Stacey's admiration for Susannah Trotter had suffered a sudden eclipse. No longer did the rectory servants come across him and Susannah laughing and chatting in quiet corners, no longer did the villagers glimpse them together as they had done over the past few weeks: Mr Stacey avoided her as if she were suffering from some contagious disease.

To his mind that would not have been far from the reality. The infection that Susannah carried could spread throughout his life, contaminating and withering all that was good in it: his position of trust with the Blands, the respect of the communities of the two villages, his hopes of preferment within the Church. Nothing would be saved.

A baby! He could not, would not, believe it. It was too soon for her to know, surely ... She had come to tell him in the garden late one evening, slim and seductive as ever, and he had been charmed to see her there. It made him feel ill now to think how his senses had yearned towards her – such folly, such delusion, such wickedness – but then he had been tempted by a Delilah, a lovely wanton whom no normal man could have withstood, and never a man whose natural instincts had been thwarted as long as his had. The Church demanded too much of a man, he thought bitterly – but the Church would never forgive his transgressions. He prayed nightly for God's understanding, prayed nightly that Susannah might be mistaken: 'Take away this cup from me!' he pleaded.

Marriage! That was what Susannah was demanding now. But marriage was out of the question. He could not afford to marry. Yet equally, as she had pointed out, he could not afford not to marry. 'I do not believe there is a baby,' he had said. 'You are hysterical.' He turned and walked away.

Yet every evening she found an opportunity to whisper: 'That which should've occurred has still not happened.' 'Matters have not changed.' He did not wish to know of such sordid matters; it was grossly indelicate that she should mention her body's malfunction to him. He ignored her.

Thus a week passed. Sedley Stacey went through the motions of his daily work automatically. He preached a sermon upon the Beatitudes to the villagers of Brambourne: 'Blessed are they which do hunger and thirst after righteousness: for they shall be filled', receiving Miss Waterton's fulsome praise unsmilingly; he discussed various problems with his clerk and with the churchwardens, offending them with his terseness; he christened a baby that squalled and squirmed the entire time that he held it. At the rectory Susannah instructed the children in English history and in French, and rebuked William for slovenly work. She also found the opportunity to tell Dick of Mr Stacey's worryingly ardent pursuit of her and to let drop a hint concerning certain watered down bottles of brandy.

At the end of the week, on the Saturday morning, Susannah came to find Sedley in the dining parlour, where he was drinking fresh coffee.

'Mrs Bland wishes to speak to you urgently,' she said.

He saw that her face was tear-stained. 'You have not told her of your ridiculous ideas?' he demanded, appalled.

'I had to,' she said, putting a handkerchief to her drenched lashes. 'I was so sick this morning that I could not attend to the children. She pressed me and pressed me as to why I was ill.'

He could have hit her.

She looked at him sideways. 'I told Mrs Bland of our great feelings for each other. I said that our love had run away with us. I pleaded for her understanding.'

He could have strangled her.

'I could deny that I ever touched you.'

'You could, but I know you would not. You're too good for that. Besides,' she added, in a voice that was almost pitying, 'Dick knows that's not so.'

He took an unwary gulp of coffee and scalded his throat and tongue. He choked, speechless for several seconds. 'Dick? How the devil does Dick know? Is this some plot you have hatched?'

'You came to my room,' she reminded him, 'on several occasions. The floor creaks, the door creaks, even the bed creaks. Dick was asking questions, so I had to swear him to secrecy – but he will tell the Blands if I ask him to.'

Sedley crashed his cup into its saucer and coffee splashed across the tablecloth in a widening brown stain. 'This is unbelievable, quite unbelievable. It is blackmail!'

He strode out of the room, feeling more than ready to take a stand with Mrs Bland or anyone else who might be wishful to compel him into a marriage so clearly unsuitable in terms of his position in life, his financial situation, or, indeed, any other basis that might be adduced. But he reckoned without that redoubtable lady.

Mrs Bland burst into a torrent of speech before ever he had a chance to take breath. 'Mr Stacey,' she said, the moment the parlour door was shut, 'Mr Stacey, I feel more disappointed in you than I have ever felt in any man in whom Mr Bland and I have placed our trust. We have always thought highly of you – of your devotion to your duties, and of the desire you expressed to be of service in the villages. We have believed you to hold to all the moral principles of a Christian and a gentleman. Now Susannah has come to me, full of sorrow and contrition, to tell a terrible tale. A tale that implicates you as a seducer, and in our house, too, under our very roof! My belief in you has been swept away. Mr Stacey, what have you to say?'

'Mrs Bland,' he said, struggling to keep afloat on this flood of eloquence, 'I beg of you to listen to me. It is not as you have been led to believe.'

'It is a dreadful blow to me,' she said. 'And after all we have done for her and for you! It is incomprehensible to me that those for whom we have cared the most should treat us so uncaringly. Well, there is only one thing to be done, you must be married – and soon!'

He flung back his head haughtily. 'I cannot marry a servant ...'

'Susannah is our governess,' she cut in snobbishly, 'and the daughter of very respectable parents.'

'... or one who has shown herself to be wanton!'

'Mr Stacey! I do not know under what circumstances you and Susannah came to commit these shocking acts, but I am certain that she was a virgin until you came to this house. For myself, I always despised Adam in the Garden of Eden when he blamed the woman for man's first sin. Even conceding that Susannah was your willing partner, was it not your duty, rather than succumbing to her naive passion for you, to have shown her the error she was in? It seems you have totally forgot your role as a clergyman – your duty to teach and counsel those in

65

doubt or led astray, your duty by your own example to set a standard of decency and morality.'

'These are matters for Mr Bland, madam, not for you.'

'You are correct, Mr Stacey, and as a clergyman, as your rector, he must and shall speak to you. But I speak to you as Susannah's employer and as her friend!'

A wind was rising; spatters of raindrops hit the window. Sedley glared at his tormentor, seething with impotent rage. Whatever he said she twisted about to put him in the wrong. 'How can I be certain Susannah is ...' He could not say the word. 'How can anyone? She could be mistaken.'

'Nevertheless, it is your duty to marry her. You have sullied her.'

'I cannot afford to marry!' he burst out.

'Ssh! The servants! You should have thought of that earlier, Mr Stacey, before you took such thoughtless, nay, such wicked, advantage of her.'

The sound of the front door being opened and shut and hasty voices in the hall made them both pause. The door opened and the rector appeared, his kindly face working with emotion. He spoke gruffly.

'I have just received a message that Mr Humby has had a heart stroke. Dr Huskett believes he cannot survive. Mr Stacey, if you will come with me, we will both ride to Brambourne to ease his parting.'

Mrs Bland pressed her hands to her flushed cheeks. 'My dear, there are certain matters here that I have to confide to you – but they must wait. Is there anything you require to take with you?'

'No, no. I believe we have only to prepare Mr Humby for his end. When all is over, we shall return.'

Mr Humby took his time in dying; shy in life, he seemed shy now of meeting his maker. The compelled marriage of Barnabas Bidewell to Charity Jurd had been organised for late that morning. While Mr Bland sat with his old friend Humby, Sedley Stacey rode back to Abbotsbridge to tie the knot ordered by Ambrose Manningford, Esquire, Justice of the Peace.

Abbotsbridge and Brambourne villages lay less than two

miles apart: Abbotsbridge was the older and larger; Brambourne was expanding and bumptious. The villagers were invariably competitive and frequently antagonistic. 'Them wild 'uns over the hill,' the inhabitants of Abbotsbridge would sourly murmur of their rivals. 'That smug lot down by the river,' Brambourne's villagers retaliated.

Both churches were ancient; both gave the rector endless headaches over their repairs. The church of St Swithun at Abbotsbridge had walls built with flints that Saxon and Norman children probably were forced to remove from the chalky fields much as the present children laboured to do. Gargoyles vomited the rain from the roofs through their agonised mouths, while in the winter gulls stalked the leads, frightening the local pigeons from their bespattered haunts. Rarely in its hundreds of years of history could the churchyard have been desecrated by such language as Barney Bidewell used that day in early-September, shocking the villagers of Abbotsbridge and causing the residents of Brambourne to smirk knowingly behind their hands.

Sickened, yet held there by a morbid fascination, Susannah watched the scene from behind a landing window in the rectory.

The wind was blowing the rain in gusts across the tombstones, drenching the cheap finery in which Charity had hoped to carry off the occasion. As she ran for the shelter of the church porch her dress was driven against her figure, distorting it grotesquely, blown rats-tails of hair smearing themselves across her cheeks.

Barney Bidewell trudged up the path behind her, flanked by Josh Pither as village constable and Susannah's father, Thomas, as churchwarden. Behind them came the overseer, clutching the licence, followed at a distance by Charity's family, determined to see justice done. Barney's head was down, his shoulders hunched. He had just been released after two days locked up on a warrant granted by Mr Manningford. In all his erratic life such a thing had never happened to him before; he was deeply shocked. Worse still, he was stone-cold sober. Barney was not used to being brought to account for his misdeeds; the largest and most truculent of the young men of both villages, he had gone his own way. Now a slip of a girl and her aged grandparent had combined together with the Squire to bring him to this: his reputation would be ruined.

Beneath a thick old yew a group of Brambourne women stood sheltering from the rain, gleefully observing his discomfiture. One of them shouted something Susannah could not catch.

Barney turned, snarling abuse. 'An' 'oo wants ter know what Brambourne women thinks?' he added. 'Bastards the lot of ye, ugly as sin an' cursed by the devil, born o' poxy whores wi' knock knees an' cross eyes! Everybody knows yer nuthin' but a lot o' gaping holes!'

The men around him closed up to hustle him along the path, their ideas of propriety outraged by this behaviour.

'Scummy ole hags!' Barney growled.

Mr Stacey appeared abruptly in the church porch, Charity disappeared from view, and Barney quietened. Mr Stacey snapped out an order and the procession shuffled into the church with Charity's family bringing up the rear, her grandfather's bow-legs the last that Susannah could see of them.

She remained by the window, shuddering, gazing down at the empty porch, wondering what effect this ceremony would have upon Sedley Stacey. Would he connect it with his own situation?

At times the enormity of what she was doing hit Susannah like a blow; it was not for nothing that she had been brought up in a religious household. But her conscience was soon wrestled down. Her baby: it was all for her baby. Besides, had James Manningford not already impregnated her, Sedley Stacey could equally have done so. His readiness to take advantage of her was a greater sin than Mr James's, for he was a man of the cloth. He deserved no pity, for he had shown no compunction with her.

'Dear Lord,' she prayed silently, 'let Mr Humby die. Let him pass over easily, but let him die. He were better dead and in Thy care, anyway.' His death would be the lever she needed for success. That, and, she thought, her mother. She must fling herself upon her mother's mercy and involve her in the struggle. Remembering her mother's strict principles and the all-pervasive rules, her mouth went dry with fright; that would be the worst part of all.

Sighing, she left the window and returned to her young charges, who were painting with water-colours in the schoolroom. Thank God, today was her half-day: there was a great deal to be done.

James Manningford was engrossed in discussion with his friend William Waterton of Brambourne as they rode along the village street on Monday morning. Three hours spent hacking their hunters round the fields, meadows and common of Abbotsbridge, scrutinising their condition and debating their potential, had left both men stimulated and entirely in accord. The harvest was not going to be good, that was clear. William remarked that it was the same all over Hampshire, probably throughout England. There would be shortages and high prices this winter: please God, it would not be a harsh one. 'Though,' he added, 'if it were, the inevitable distress amongst the poor would soon bring home to your cousin the inadequacies of the present farming system in Abbotsbridge.'

'It might,' James agreed. 'But I've no wish to kick my heels for a year while the obvious is made grievously evident to him.'

'You wish to begin the enclosure process this year? Good Lord, James, you've left it a trifle late, have you not? Are you any nearer to persuading Mr Manningford?'

James gazed between his horse's ears. 'Let us say, he's asking questions.'

'Pertinent questions?'

James nodded. 'Pertinent questions.' Ambrose had recently enquired in an offhand manner about such matters as the cost of enclosure, the time the process would take, and the procedure for obtaining the necessary parliamentary sanction. James had given the information in a similarly offhand manner, and waited.

'You have the patience of Job!' William said, with a big laugh that set James's hunter stepping sideways away from the noise. Everything was big about William Waterton: his solid head, his hands with the thick curls of hair on the backs, his muscular shoulders, his slightly crooked teeth. He was fair and blue-eyed in a way that suggested Saxon forebears, his looks bearing out a family claim to have lived in the area since before Domesday. Perhaps it was a long-inherited interest that gave him his own concern with the development of farming. 'Do you think you will succeed in convincing Mr Manningford, James?'

'It is not I who have to convince him, he has to convince himself.'

'Very subtle!' William observed in the tone of one scornful of such deep doings. 'Well, should you wish my father or me to speak to him on the subject, we'd be only too glad to oblige. It was my grandfather, you know, who dealt with enclosure in Brambourne, and we've never ceased to be grateful to the old boy. You know how much more productive our lands are than yours.'

James did. 'If you'd care to speak to him along those lines, I'd be most grateful – but whatever you do, do not allow yourselves to be drawn into argument with him; it could be disastrous.'

'Stubborn old coot, wouldn't you say?'

'Oh, I would never be so uncivil! Let us merely say, cautious in the extreme, and with a great loathing of being pushed!'

William's great laugh rang out again. 'Put it as you wish, I don't envy you your task.'

Three geese waddled rapidly along the street towards them, necks outstretched, hissing like a trio of kettles as they pursued a fleeing small boy. Reined in, the two horses stood stockstill, their knees and ears twitching with outrage. A slim female form darted across the road, picked up the small boy, dumped him out of harm's way at the side and then ran at the geese to disperse them in an undignified rout. 'That is what you should have done,' the girl observed to the little lad. 'You'll never grow to be a man if you cannot say boo to a goose!'

'That's the way!' William Waterton said. He urged his horse forward, ready to give the girl a friendly buffet on the nearest suitable part of her anatomy, but was stopped by something in her erect stance and her quiet unsmiling face.

'Thank you, Miss Trotter,' said James. 'Most helpful.'

'Mr Manningford,' Susannah said, 'I should be grateful for a word with you, if I may?'

'Yes,' James said. 'What is it?'

'Privately, if you please.'

James looked doubtful and faintly annoyed. He hesitated.

William said in his boisterous way, 'No need to worry about

me, my dear fellow, I must be off. An interesting morning. Goodbye, Miss Trotter!' He leered happily down at Susannah, the confident lustful look of a man who was sexually attractive and knew it. He kicked his black stallion and it sprang off up the hill, its haunches gleaming.

'Yes?' said James, as the hoofbeats dwindled.

'I have to tell you ...' For a moment she seemed at a loss for words, standing rigid and silent, her mouth slightly open, until abruptly they came. 'I am to have a child,' she said. 'I always knew it would be so.' At his blank look she enunciated softly but very clearly, 'I am carrying your baby!'

'A baby!' He was thunderstruck; it was not a contingency to which he had given a thought. 'Are you certain?' Susannah nodded. He could not talk to her from on horseback, they might be overheard by some villager. He dismounted.

His arrival on her level appeared to unlock her tongue. Words poured from her. At first James could not take in what she was saying; the words were rushing through his head, turbulent and muddled, distorted by his guilt. He struggled to listen and gradually his brain made sense of the confusion. Susannah had always known what would happen; at first she had been desperate, but now there was a gleam of hope. There was a man, the young curate from Brambourne, living at the rectory with the Blands, who had said he would marry her, if, and only if, he became the curate now that Mr Humby was dead. There were many and frightful complexities: there was a cousin whom Mr Bland did not wish to disoblige; there was Mr Bland's anger with Mr Stacey and Susannah; there was the inadequacy of the stipend Mr Humby had received. She did not see how she was to succeed in her plan unless she had James's help, and, through him, Mr Manningford's.

James seized upon the one incontrovertible fact he could find in all this confusion. 'But the living of Brambourne is not in Mr Manningford's gift – it is a Winchester College living, I believe – certainly he will have no influence there.'

Susannah gave him a patient look. 'No,' she agreed, 'but in Abbotsbridge he does have. Mr Bland will not ignore any representations from him. And your own words in Mr Stacey's favour would be well received also, as Mr Bland's future patron.'

71

He searched for more facts. 'Does Stacey know the child is not his?'

Her eyes were on the ground. 'No.'

'I see.' So she had been sleeping with the young parson. His horse shifted impatiently, sidling his rump round, not understanding the reason for the delay. James tightened his grip. 'Stand still, damn you!' He felt oppressed and driven by the irritating complexities of his life, the endless need to manoeuvre Ambrose. 'I will see what can be done.'

'It must be soon – it is urgent!' she urged him. Her chin came up, she said: 'It is all I have asked of you. It is really very little. And it is for *your son*.'

Her eyes sought his and held them for a long moment. He saw unspoken messages in their depths; undeclared hurts, accusations of outrageous behaviour. He had a sudden perception of her position, understood why the words of anger and disgust had not been spoken: as much her pride as shyness or embarrassment.

'It is not so simple. I cannot tell Mr Manningford what to do.' He knew he was behaving badly, that there were many things he should have said to her and somehow could not. He was taut with self-fury, so taut that any words he attempted would sound false and condescending.

'You must speak to him today,' she insisted.

'I will do what I can. I have said so.'

He called to a youth across the street to give him a leg-up on to his horse, mounted and rode on, his lips compressed. Devil take it, the girl could have no idea of his difficulties with Ambrose. Any further interference with his cousin's way of running his village and there would be no hope for his own enclosure plans. But Susannah had a simplistic view of the situation; she saw the problems in black and white, wrong and right. And he was wrong, he saw that: he had wronged her. He gave a wry smile. He would involve Beatrice, she was her father's favourite, she would be able light-heartedly to prompt Cousin Ambrose to urge the rector to act in Mr Stacey's favour. Good God, what a tangled web ... And all because there was a baby coming and it was his – his child. He relaxed in the saddle and felt the tight muscles in his shoulders unknot themselves. It

72

was an extraordinary thought: that bright attractive girl and his child.

Yes, he would somehow manage what Susannah asked, though subtlety would be necessary. He could speak to Mr Bland directly. And there might be other ways in which he could help her, help them both. He could ensure that they had some place, some recognition in local society. His lips twitched. Damn it, he would see that no one snubbed her. It would be amusing to make her positively fashionable, her and that prosy parson she had seized upon to father the child.

7

Mr Bland called Mr Stacey to speak to him in his bookroom shortly before noon three days later. Susannah heard from the schoolroom above where she was wiping the children's slates over with a damp cloth. For once she was alone: the children had been taken out visiting in the carriage with their mother. She piled the slates together to put them in the cupboard but her hands were shaking so much that she dropped them and one shattered. Cursing under her breath she kicked the pieces aside and tiptoed to the top of the stairs to listen. There was a steady murmur of voices from the rector's bookroom, but she could hear nothing. Dear Lord, how aggravating it was to be shut out. The voices rose in furious disputation, and she gripped the newel post with both hands. The voices dropped again and she gasped her relief, her knees like melting candle-wax. Men were such fools with their bluster and their noise.

After Mr Humby's death she had spoken at length to Sedley. Their talk had been acrimonious at first, but later it had become surprisingly thoughtful. Susannah had been able to show him where his own best fortunes lay; how to build out of the ruins of his plans. Pathetically, as a last protest against the inevitable, he had said: 'How can I tell my poor mother that I am to marry a nursery-maid, a servant?' 'You will tell her no such lies,' Susannah had retorted. 'You will be marrying a governess of genteel breeding, the grand-daughter of a baronet!' After his initial disbelief, Sedley had brightened noticeably. Clearly, breeding was important to his mind. 'There has never been any question of the Manningfords not admitting the relationship,' Susannah assured him. 'Mr Manningford has always favoured my mother with kindness, and my brother Jack has been allowed to run his cattle on the common far beyond any entitlement that our land gives us.'

Sedley had commented upon the wretched poverty that a portionless wife would have to endure upon his stipend. 'You could ask Mr Bland to increase it,' Susannah observed. 'Forty pounds is shocking little. It is bad enough for an elderly bachelor, but for a man with a wife and child it cannot be contemplated!' Sedley considered it highly unlikely that Mr Bland would look favourably upon such a proposal; indeed, he would count himself damned fortunate to obtain the curacy. Susannah ventured to disagree. There were, she murmured diffidently, certain arguments which might sway the rector that possibly Mr Stacey had not considered.

Susannah crept down the stairs to the bookroom door but no more than a murmur reached her ears. Tantalising, but dear God, better that than shouting. She had memories of too many raised voices in the last week: Sedley Stacey, damning her impudence; her brother Jack, threatening to mill the fellow down; her father, swearing that he would publicly duck her seducer in the smithy horse-trough.

Her mother had been far more frightening in her low-voiced rage, white with shock, calling both her and Mr Stacey terrible names, names she had never thought her mother could know. Mrs Trotter's anger, though shattering while it lasted, had been short-lived. She was too concerned for the future to waste time railing over the past: she had taken the situation in hand and her tactics were subtle. Thomas was instructed to talk to the rector after the Sunday morning service: dismay coupled with sympathy for the rector's predicament was the right note to strike, Mrs Trotter settled it – 'And none of your gossiping!' For herself, she would speak to Kitty Bland, more in sorrow than in anger, on a note of confidence that the Blands would see the situation resolved aright.

Susannah could stand it no longer. Crouching at the keyhole would not do, it was too easy of detection; she had a better idea. She slipped out into the garden, sidling round to the bookroom window. No one seemed to be about, and, as she had guessed, the bottom sash was pushed up to let in the soft air; better still, there was the big bay tree just to the left of the window to conceal her. Careless of the twigs and cobwebs that brushed her clothes, she squeezed between the bay tree and the wall, creeping forward till she could hear the voices.

Sedley Stacey was speaking, very quietly, saying that on a smaller stipend than fifty pounds per annum he could not afford to support a wife and child. So it was settled that he was to be curate of Brambourne parish! Susannah leaned against the wall in weak relief. 'In sober earnest, Mr Bland,' Sedley's voice continued, 'I feel I have been punished for any misdoing and so has Susannah, by losing your regard and good opinion. Now we must build a new life together. I do not see how we could attempt that on a lesser sum. And at that we should be devilish poor.'

'In offering you the curacy,' Mr Bland's voice came flatly, 'I have exceeded what my conscience told me was right. You were fortunate that Mr Manningford spoke on your behalf; were it not for that and for my wife's long friendship with Mrs Trotter, I doubt if I should have done so. And as I have already said, I have been most grieved at your behaviour and at your apparent wish to shed the blame upon your partner.'

'I have already expressed my contrition,' Sedley said stiffly. 'And you know that I am grateful for what you have done.'

Somewhere Fanny was playing her harp, ripples of notes ascending, delicate and clear, a startling contrast with the gruff voices in the bookroom. Susannah pushed back a tumbled lock of hair and inched forward.

Mr Bland was informing Sedley of his embarrassment at having to let down a young cousin, and of his own financial problems. 'As you know, I now have the expense of setting my son Daniel up in his chosen regiment, of purchasing his cornetcy, and making him a suitable allowance. Another shock for my wife and me. Daniel was at home for only two weeks this summer before he went off to stay with his friends, and he confessed this change in his career designs only the day before he left. As my wife says, we have been most sadly treated by those whom we cared for most.'

Sedley mumbled something and there was a short silence.

'You must appreciate that the income from Brambourne, although small, for it is not a rich living, is most important to us at this juncture,' Mr Bland said. He would offer forty-five pounds, a gesture of great generosity.

Sedley refused to budge. He was not prepared to be that poor. He would rather, if regretfully, leave Hampshire and start again elsewhere. He hinted, delicately, that Mr Manningford would be deeply shocked to have his cousin Susannah produce a bastard. Both villages would be upset: Susannah would be a living reproach to the Blands. Naturally, Sedley would rather do his duty by Susannah. She was a lovely and accomplished young woman, a credit to them both. But she should not be turned into a drudge. Did they not feel they owed it to Susannah to be more generous?

Sedley achieved his fifty pounds, the marriage to take place by licence next Wednesday. Time, they did agree, was of the essence.

James Manningford was spending a busy week: time, for him, was also of the essence. Should his cousin finally agree to his enclosure plans he must be ready to commence work immediately. He spent a day in Winchester closeted in a stuffy room with an attorney. On the succeeding days he sent for his curricle early, and, dressed with his usual casual elegance, drove behind his greys to make calls on various neighbouring landowners and farmers. He was, he told them, just passing, and felt it a pleasure to pay his respects. In each case he managed, after the preliminary courtesies were over with the wives and families, to have a word alone with the master of the house.

On the Thursday afternoon he was greeted by Beatrice when he drove into the stable yard. She was just dismounting from her skewbald, flushed with exercise, her eyes bright with amusement.

'Well, James! An unusual encounter! But then you have been having a busy week. Dares one ask what you have been busy about?'

'One dares. Today, I have been visiting Mr Knight and his family.'

'Good Lord!' For a moment she looked puzzled, then her face cleared. 'Ah, I see. Good groundwork, James. I could not picture you as enraptured by the little Knightses! But I fancy Adam Knight will require several visits before he is convinced of the glories of enclosure. And have you also paid your courtesies to the Goddards, the Fulbroads and the Trotters?'

'To the first two, yes. I imagine the third would be a waste of time.' He handed the reins to a groom and leapt lightly down from the curricle.

'You are probably right. But courtesies are courtesies and should be observed in full. Do not, I beg of you, ignore the Trotters. To have your enemy's respect is the first step in disarming him.'

'I might try to go this week,' he said. He felt a strong reluctance to meeting Susannah's family, yet he appreciated Beatrice's argument.

The amusement was back in her face. 'You will find them in high fettle and bursting with news.'

'How is that?'

'Their daughter Susannah is to marry Mr Stacey, and he, as you recommended, is confirmed as Brambourne's curate. They cannot help but be delighted. He is quite a prize for the family.'

The breath was short in his chest. 'Who told you that?'

'I encountered Mrs Bland by the rectory. Apparently it was only arranged this morning. They are to have the ceremony next week, she told me. I daresay we shall have an invitation. I wonder why the hurry?'

'I know not.'

A servant came scurrying from the house, calling to him. 'Mr James, sir! Mr Manningford asked me to tell you on your return that he'd like to see you in the library. He is anxious to speak to you before dinner.'

'I shall be with him directly.'

'Perhaps he has made up his mind,' Beatrice murmured mischievously.

James snorted. 'Pray for a miracle!'

He found Ambrose pacing the library floor, as agitated and annoyed as he had ever known him. His brow was furrowed and snuff was spilt down the normally immaculate folds of his cravat.

'Have you heard the news about that fellow Bidewell?' Ambrose shot at him.

James closed the door. 'The man who was compelled to marry his slut? What of him? Has he murdered her?'

78

'Good God, no! But this is no joke. The fellow has built a cottage on the edge of the common! And there is worse – I have not seen it yet, but according to my information he is busily enclosing a couple of acres for his own use.'

'Damned impertinence,' James said.

'He has been a thorn in my side since he was a boy. He is a drunken bully and a trouble-maker. This is a deliberate gesture of defiance, a retaliation for my having exerted my authority.'

James raised his eyebrows. 'Then I presume you will order it to be pulled down?'

'Can't be done,' Ambrose said, red with anger. 'Damn his eyes!'

'Why not, sir? If you can force the man to marry, surely you can remove his hut?'

'Not so simple – I wish it were. This is a tangle of ancient rights and traditions. If a cottage is built overnight and smoke is coming from the chimney by morning, then a right is established.'

'And he achieved it? That is incredible!' James perched himself on the arm of a chair. 'I wonder that the work could be done in so short a time. Even with help it must have been a struggle to have the chimney's foundations laid and its brick courses finished overnight by lantern-light, quite apart from the walls and windows and some sort of roof.'

Ambrose grunted his disgust. 'He has built on the far side of the common, by the woods. There was, I gather, considerable enthusiasm from both families and from his neighbours to have him so well removed from them. He had help a-plenty. There is nothing I can do to be rid of him.'

There was a moment's silence. Then James gave a brief laugh. 'There is, you know, Cousin. Enclosure! With less than twenty years upon the land a squatter has no claim, no claim at all!'

The two men contemplated each other.

'I could, couldn't I?' Ambrose pushed the papers about on his desk with bony nervous fingers.

James walked over to where the greyhound, Spry, was lying in a patch of pale sunlight. He began to rub the animal's narrow head, murmuring to him, hiding the excitement in his face from Ambrose. A minute later he heard his voice addressing him.

79

'Over these past weeks I have been giving serious thought to this matter,' Ambrose said. 'It is not a change to be undertaken lightly. I have sought information, I have consulted Mr Waterton upon his experience, Mr Bland and I have explored the possibilities on several occasions. In view of the shortages of corn likely from the war with France, I think that we should increase the acreage under the plough. It is our public duty, our duty to our country in troubled times. In short, James, I feel we should enclose. I take it that you are in agreement?'

8

On their wedding day Mr Stacey's bride was greatly admired; he could not fault her. She looked lovely, the wedding dress hastily sewn from her mother's birthday present length of cream silk setting off her creamy complexion and ruddy brown hair to perfection, its newly fashionable high waistline conveniently hiding her thickening middle, and its point d'Alençon lace – an inheritance from her maternal grandmother – showered with compliments by the ladies. Susannah's manner was correct, calm, almost demure, as she received the guests with him, speaking pleasantly and without confusion to them all. Except Mr James Manningford; she was abrupt with him, surprisingly brusque. But Mr Manningford appeared not to notice anything amiss; he smiled and bowed and kissed her hand in most handsome fashion. In general her demeanour was much as it had been over the past week, subdued if not downcast; clearly she was awed by the honour Sedley was doing her in making her his wife.

And at times he thought he had not done so badly himself. He had been astonished, almost taken aback, by the warmth of the congratulations showered upon him by the local gentry. Persons whose judgment and approbation he prized had praised his discernment in choosing Susannah. Mr James Manningford had conveyed the Manningford family's congratulations and invited him to shoot partridge with him, 'As soon as you have time for other matters!' Mr William Waterton had clapped him on the back and called him, 'A devilish lucky fellow, by George! You'll be the envy of us all. Far better than that long-nosed sister of mine!' It helped to make the disaster bearable. But it was still difficult to thrust the consideration of ten thousand pounds from his mind.

The rector lent the newly married couple his carriage to take them to Brambourne vicarage. As Sedley handed his bride into the carriage and Mrs Trotter turned from checking that her daughter's boxes were safely secured, he saw mother and daughter exchange a swift smile. Mrs Trotter's bosom was expanding with the relief of having her erring daughter safely married and with the triumph of a wedding-breakfast attended by the notables of both parishes. Sedley felt he could allow her triumph; she behaved towards him with a most proper consideration and respect and had consulted him upon all matters of importance regarding the occasion. And the refreshments had been excellent; everyone had commented upon them; nothing stinted, everything done in the best manner. Undercurrents there may have been, the Blands clearly feeling the reproach of Susannah's downfall while in their care, and Miss Waterton and her mother conspicuous by their failure to attend (and Sedley was still gravely embarrassed by the way he had been forced to act there), but such matters had been more than compensated for by William Waterton's readiness to act as his groomsman, and by both Mr Manningfords, together with Miss Manningford and Miss Beatrice, gracing the ceremony. It quite made his own chest swell.

Jack Trotter pushed him out of the way – most rudely, Sedley thought – to give his sister a farewell kiss and then Thomas Trotter had to fuss over her, too, but at last he could climb in, the steps were swung up and the door closed. The assembled guests called their good wishes and a couple of handkerchiefs fluttered. As the horses moved off a group of farm servants and villagers uttered a ragged cheer. They should not have been there; the ceremony was intended to be private and quiet, but their presence did, he supposed, give a pleasing demonstration of his own popularity.

'Goodness,' Susannah said, leaning back in her seat beside him, 'I can hardly believe it is all over! Such as rush as it has been. To say that I am fagged would be inadequate – I am exhausted!'

'That is hardly surprising,' he said. 'We have had so much to do in so short a time. But I must admit it has been well done.'

He hoped she was not too tired. He did not wish his bride to long only for sleep on their wedding night. It would be the first time that he could fully explore and enjoy that tempting body of hers without the need for subterfuge and creeping in the dark, without the fear of discovery. His fingers slid up her smooth arm, grasping and kneading the flesh beneath the falls of lace. If he had to be married, by God, he would make the best of it; she would soon learn how to please him.

The carriage lurched violently as it reached the top of the narrow rutted lane. Sedley roused himself from his alluring reverie to comment: 'This hill is a disgrace; it is positively dangerous. One would think the parish could put some repairs in hand to level out the ruts.'

'They do from time to time,' Susannah said, easing her arm away. 'Stones and gravel are put down, but each time it rains the water cascades down and removes all their mendings.'

Sedley peered. 'The men should be ordered to dig a channel on either side to divert the water. Then they could mend to some effect.'

'D'you know, I believe you are right,' Susannah said. 'How sensible. I wonder no one has thought of that.'

He grunted. They were driving into Brambourne now, past a little farmhouse with pear trees before it, past a row of old thatched cottages leaning companionably towards one another, past the solid square worth of the White Hart Inn with its chaises and its carts on its forecourt, and on towards the squat-towered church and its parsonage.

Their new home was built on simple dignified lines; a flint and brick rectangle dating back to the days of Queen Anne, with its garret windows projecting from the warm brown tiles of the roof and a sturdy porch swathed in late honeysuckle. Unfortunately, as Sedley knew, its attractions from a distance bore little relation to the reality nearto: on Saturday morning a party consisting of the Blands and the Trotters and himself had inspected the whole place, exclaiming over the dust and disorder of the rooms, where grey velvet cobwebs bracketed the angles of the walls and ceiling plaster threatened to descend upon their heads, and lifting eyebrows and tutting at the grease and mouse droppings in the kitchen. 'The housekeeper, Mrs

Dismore – Mrs Dismal, I should rather call her – was past her work, poor soul,' Mrs Bland had sighed.

Upon receiving his cogent representations as to the unreasonableness of expecting a young and penurious curate to bear the costs of the previous incumbent's neglect, Mr Bland had agreed to deal with the dilapidations to the house, but the grounds, unhappily, remained Sedley's responsibility. Had it been Miss Waterton sitting beside him now as his bride, expense would have been no problem. Indeed, had he so desired, he could have commanded the best of the new landscape improvers to effect a transformation. As it was, he foresaw an unpleasant degree of back-breaking work. The garden was overgrown and desolate; withering stalks of nettles rearing themselves above couch grass and ivy, old man's beard trailing from skeletal rose bushes, and the muddy paths glistening with snails' slime. As for the little orchard and the two vicarage meadows, where they were not choked with brambles they were deep in docks and nettles.

As the carriage slowed to turn into the short and muddy driveway of the vicarage a little woman darted out to stop it, a covered basket clutched to her bosom, brown eyes intent in a wrinkled brown face: Prudence Paine, self-appointed nurse and midwife, Brambourne's version of Martha Pither.

'Mr Stacey, sir, Mrs Stacey, my best wishes for all your 'appiness, an' I thought you could make very good use of 'er!' She thrust the basket at Susannah with a satisfied nod.

'But what ...?' Susannah jumped as the canvas cover heaved. An anguished mewing assailed their ears. 'Dear's my soul, a cat!'

'Half-grown! An' she comes of good mousing stock. Just what you do need from all I hears. Mrs Dismore's my cousin – not that I'd boast of it. An' don't you feed 'er once she's settled in. She's to find for 'erself.'

'Oh, yes! Er, thank you.' Susannah took the lurching basket on her lap.

'You'll call on me when you need me for any nursing an' that, won't you?' Prudence called as the carriage creaked on again.

'Oh dear,' Susannah said. 'There is great rivalry between her and Martha Pither. If I need help in illness or ... or in anything

84

else, I cannot imagine calling on anyone but Martha. How unfortunate.'

'I cannot believe they would squabble over us,' Sedley said.

'Can you not?' said his wife. 'I can.'

They ate their supper in the dining-parlour, cleaner now than when they had last seen it, its shabbiness less apparent in the candle-light. Mrs Bland had sent servants from the rectory to scour it from the attics to the cellar and Miss Manningford had released the Pithers' oldest daughter, Becky, an Abbotsbridge House parlourmaid, to work at the vicarage, on production by Martha of a sturdy younger sister to take her place. Becky waited on them, her plump, good-natured face earnest with her endeavours to please. Maid-of-all-work she might be, but housekeeper at the vicarage was what she meant to earn and be recognised as, so a new cap sat precariously on her fluffy dark hair and a new apron encircled her ample waist, and all was done according to the standards she had learnt at Abbots-bridge House.

Sedley was in amorous mood. Each time that Becky left the room his hot hands groped for Susannah, feeling her neck, her breasts, her thighs, interfering with her eating. She was tired and she was hungry; she did not wish to be handled while she was having her supper, it made her feel nauseated. It was a relief when the kitten appeared from the kitchen, prancing in as Becky came to remove the plates that had held the veal collops, distracting Sedley. She was a silvery tabby with darker markings like raised eye-brows bestowing a look of hauteur to her pointed face. She sniffed suspiciously at every corner, flinched at shadows thrown by the flickering candles and scampered upon the chairs, finally leaping on to the table, whence she was removed by a scandalised Becky and dumped on the floor. She stalked away on stiff legs, a picture of affronted dignity.

'Proper little ladyship, 'ent she?' said Becky.

The kitten discovered a mousehole in the skirting board and thrust down an exploratory paw.

'An' a sharp little soul. Knows 'er job, you can see.'

'As you do, Becky,' Susannah said. 'The veal was delicious.'

'Aw, thank you, ma'am!' Becky blushed with pleasure. 'I'm glad it suited ye.' She collected the plates and trotted out, returning with a dish of almonds and raisins and a dish of greengages.

The kitten was examining Sedley's buckled shoes.

'Should I take 'er now, surr?'

The kitten leapt on Sedley's knees, sniffed, hesitated, then curled herself nose to tail.

'She likes you,' Susannah commented.

Sedley touched her gingerly; he looked pleased. 'Leave her here,' he decided. 'Cats are sensible creatures. I've no objection.'

'Very good, surr.' Becky's firm tread dwindled away down the passage.

Susannah took a gulp of wine and a deep breath to fortify herself. Somehow she must keep Sedley in this mellow mood; somehow she must set the pattern for their married life. She fussed over him, pushing the dish of almonds and raisins close so that he could reach it without disturbing the kitten, and refilling his glass. The wine was one of half-a-dozen bottles sent over by Squire Waterton, and she was glad of it.

There was a silence. Susannah remembered the horrid silence in the church before he had brought out the words, 'I do!' and pushed the memory away. She looked around; no rooms in her parents' house could match this or the drawing room for size or proportion. Whatever Sedley might mutter about pokiness or dilapidations, to her the challenge of transforming the vicarage was appealing. The floorboards might be splintered and creak beneath their shoes, the half-panelling of the walls be in shocking condition, but she knew, as Sedley did not, what a good carpenter and a few layers of beeswax polish could do. She sipped her wine, her mind busily deciding upon pattern of wallpaper, colour of curtains and hue of carpet. And furniture ... her mind jerked at the thought: to dream was delightful, but how would they afford even the most basic items?

'Sedley,' she asked cautiously, 'what are we to do about furnishings? When old Mr Humby's sister has come over from Whitchurch to collect what is hers, we shall be left with almost nothing.'

He finished his wine and filled the glass again. 'We shall ride to Winchester and purchase what is necessary.'

'But the cost, Sedley! Do you have any money set aside? I –

my father has been splendidly generous, he has given me twenty-five pounds.' It had seemed an enormous sum to her a few hours ago, but now, when she contemplated furniture, clothes and the coming baby, it was nothing.

'There is no need for that to be touched,' Sedley told her. 'I have more than sufficient.'

'For all we shall need? Truly? But what do you estimate the cost will be?'

'I do not know exactly, but my expenses have been so small since I came to Hampshire that I have not had to touch my own little income.'

'Your own income!' Susannah was stunned. 'But you never ... I knew nothing of this! So how much can we afford?'

'I have a sum comfortably in excess of one hundred pounds put by.'

Susannah gasped and did a swift mental calculation. 'But that means you must have a capital sum of about two thousand pounds!'

Sedley looked put out by her understanding of financial matters. 'Something in that region,' he admitted.

'But that is magnificent!' She jumped to her feet in her excitement. 'We shall be quite rich!'

'Hardly that,' he snapped. 'We must still watch every penny. I shall have no carriage, no manservant, no hunters.' His lack of hunters galled the most. When he thought of William Waterton's splendid horses, especially his black stallion, Lucifer, he ground his teeth with jealousy.

'I know,' Susannah said hastily. 'I know. But compared with what I'd thought it's handsome. More than three times as much! And there you were, bargaining with Mr Bland as if you'd not a shilling in the world.'

'That has no bearing on the matter, none at all. It is a matter of principle. The labourer is worthy of his hire. My private affairs are no concern of the rector's – whatever he may think.' Inflections of rancour sounded in his voice.

Susannah broke into laughter. 'You are absolutely right! Of course he must pay you properly for the work you perform. Oh, how splendid!'

The sound of her mirth was so infectious that Sedley began first to smile and then to join in her laughter. He put an arm round her waist to pull her upon his knee, forgetful of the kitten, which, finding itself suddenly endangered, shot from his lap spitting and cursing. Startled, Sedley swore back at it, while his wife, still shaking with laughter, sank onto his lap. He took a hard grasp upon her, biting and kissing her neck and then moving his wet mouth round to hers, licking and biting and sucking in a sudden ecstasy of desire. His fingers hooked themselves into the neckline of her gown in a struggle to reach the breasts concealed beneath.

'No,' Susannah said, jerking her mouth from his and pushing his hands away to save the precious silk. 'No, don't do that. Please!'

'What d'you mean – no?' he snarled.

'I will undo it – see?' With fresh trimmings her wedding dress must serve as an evening gown. She added quickly, 'But should we not go upstairs? Becky – Becky may come in. I should not like her to see . . .'

'Yes,' he said. 'Hurry then!'

The bedroom was cold and dark and musty, its heavy furniture looming at them in the fluttering light of the one candle Sedley had grabbed. It seemed to dampen his passion momentarily. He stood staring only, breathing heavily, as Susannah undressed to nakedness. But when she took the pins from her abundant hair to let it tumble he snatched the hairbrush from her hand and brushed till her scalp smarted and gooseflesh rose painfully on her breasts in the wake of the bristles, his pleasure evident.

At last he tugged her on to the bed, his eyes hot on her body; she saw no affection in his look, only desire and a tincture of resentment. A moment's delay to peel off his clothes and then the four-poster creaked as he clutched her. Gritting her teeth as hard and greedy fingers pushed between her thighs, she vowed to make the night memorable for him; she owed it to him in gratitude that he'd married her. His weight bore down on her; she moved her body to his, striving to meet his rhythms.

'Lie still!' his voice commanded. 'I wish a wife, not a wanton!'

Her body went rigid with shock.

'Yes,' he said. 'Like that!' His fingers gripped her till they

bruised,while his body continued to take its thrusting pleasure.
'You understand me – a wife!'
'Yes, Sedley,' she managed, wincing and hating. 'I understand.'

He went to sleep afterwards, a stertorous sleep of satisfaction. Susannah lay awake, staring into the blackness of the curtained bed. She was sore in body and sore at heart. Downstairs she could hear floorboards creaking as Becky finished her work; there was a soft padding sound as she mounted the stairs to her garret bed, and the click of a latch. Then there was silence. Outside an owl hooted, to be echoed by another hoot, far distant. Occasional snufflings revealed the presence of the mare, Coquette, in her stable.

A strange noise came; a rustling, no, a scratching noise. A mouse, perhaps? A rat? She parted the bed-curtains and peered mistrustfully. The scratching came again and this time she smiled with relief. She slid from the bed and tiptoed to open the door. The little cat trotted in, her tail high, heading straight for the bed and the warmth created by Susannah's body. 'Little ladyship!' Susannah breathed. She wriggled back under the bedclothes and the kitten curled beside her, vibrating with purrs. Companionably they slept.

9

Twelve men took their seats round the big table in the dining-room of the White Hart Inn at Brambourne at noon on Friday, September the twelfth. It was a dull, drizzling day and they crowded in cursing the weather and shaking the droplets from their coats.

This was a meeting of the principal landowners of Abbots-bridge to discuss with their squire a matter of vital importance: whether or not to hazard their gold in the expensive business of enclosing the open fields, commons and wastes of that place. When the discussion was over they would dine. Ambrose had objected to this: 'Suppose there are rancorous arguments?' 'All the more reason to heal any breach over the wine,' James had replied.

He watched with cynically assessing eyes as the men seated themselves. Mr Fulbroad, silk merchant from Winchester, whose acres, acquired twelve years ago, were second only to the Manningfords', elbowed his way to the chair next to Ambrose – profit was his sole concern. Old Mr Munday, glaring, hobbled on rheumatic joints to the next seat; more subtle than Ful-broad, he lit a long pipe and directed its fumes at his neigh-bour's nose. Munday's impatience with the present farming system was well known. Next came Mr Bland, who, with his extensive glebe and as impropriator of tithes, had a strong interest in the proposals. At the bottom of the table Thomas Trotter had the support of his son Jack; Trotter would be certain to oppose the scheme, as would Stent, another small farmer. Mr Goddard, on the other hand, had sufficient acres to make enclosure attractive. Last to take his seat was Mr Knight, the slender, highly-strung and uncommitted owner of one hundred and sixty acres. Upon his vote, as James judged it, the success or failure of the meeting would depend.

Two outsiders were present, Mr Fewtrell, an attorney from Winchester, and Mr William Waterton, whose natural inquisitiveness had led him to offer to take the minutes of the meeting.

Mr Fulbroad was favouring those seated near him with his views upon the war with France and the effect it would have on agriculture in Hampshire. 'The position of our troops in the Low Countries gives me no hope for a speedy end to the campaign. The Austrians are treacherous allies and the Dutch are but weak; if the Duke of York does not act immediately we shall have those murdering Frenchmen not only romping all over Flanders, but breaking through even to Amsterdam. I tell you, gentlemen, we are bound to increase our forces there. The pressure for supplies is already great and sure to increase.'

'True enough,' said Mr Goddard, polishing gold spectacles upon the lace of his cuff. 'Why, one can hardly journey upon the Winchester road without falling foul of one great wagon train after another.'

'Aye,' Mr Fulbroad replied. 'I hear that crops and pigs for the navy are being raised as far inland as Basingstoke.'

Ambrose Manningford rose to start the meeting. 'Gentlemen! Gentlemen. Now, we are all aware of the purpose of this meeting, so I propose merely to outline ...'

He was interrupted by Mr Fulbroad. 'Might I enquire why that young man there is present?' He pointed a hairy forefinger at Jack. 'He is not a landowner to my knowledge, Mr Manningford.'

Jack stood, tall, erect and not at all abashed by the company he was in. 'I am glad you have given me the opportunity to explain my presence here, Mr Fulbroad,' he said gravely. 'I represent the interests of Mrs Sarah Pern, widow, owner of thirty-nine acres, and Mr Page, Mr Pettifer and Mr Truckle, small-holders.'

Mr Fulbroad leaned forward, his heavy stomach pressing against the table. 'Were those persons invited to this meeting, Mr Manningford?'

Ambrose shook his head.

'No,' said Jack. 'They were not. And it puzzles me as to why not? They are landowners, same as you are, even if small, and therefore have a concern in this. More important, they have a vote.'

Mr Fulbroad snorted. 'On their acres, much good may it do them.'

'I believe the consent of four-fifths is necessary,' Jack said quietly. 'If the small proprietors vote against enclosure – and they will – then you will not have a majority decision, nor anything near it.'

Mr Fewtrell, the attorney, started to speak but Ambrose Manningford's voice cut through his words. 'Mr Trotter, I believe you are under a misapprehension. We are dealing here in terms of property, not of people. It is a man's property interest that counts and we calculate its value in acres. The acres held by the small proprietors in total barely reach one hundred, not even a thirtieth part of the whole.'

Silence. A gust of wind threw rain against the window.

'You mean that you vote in acres?' Jack looked sick. His eyes searched the company, desperate for denial.

James moved restlessly as the eyes found his: they were Susannah's eyes again, large and accusatory, their smoky-grey depths sending the same messages of shock and injury. He should have visited the Trotters, he knew he should. This moment could have been avoided. But he had not wanted to spoil the family's pleasure in Susannah's wedding, or so he had told himself, and afterwards, with time so short – well, he had never gone. And the devil of it was, he liked the boy, he had his sister's intelligence and her mettle. His voice placatory, he said: 'That is why the small-holders were not invited to this meeting. It is among these gentlemen that the decision will be made.'

'That is monstrous,' Jack said.

'It is the customary method,' Mr Manningford said.

'But this means that the smaller owners have no say whatso-ever. And in a matter which affects their entire livelihood, their whole lives!'

'You could hardly expect that a man with four or five acres should have as much say as one with four or five hundred!' Mr Fulbroad retorted. He lifted a pinch of snuff to a hairy nostril and sniffed his scorn.

'And what about those with common rights?' Jack flung at them. 'Are you saying that they will not be heard?'

'Why should they be?' Mr Fulbroad asked. 'They have no stake in the land!'

Mr Manningford intervened, the lines on his gaunt face deepening with distaste for this scene. 'You are moving ahead of yourself, Mr Trotter. We have not yet taken the decision to enclose. You are interrupting the process of that decision. Pray be seated.'

Jack remained standing. 'Mr Fulbroad has objected to my presence here. Do you other gentlemen wish me to withdraw?'

Mr Bland, benign and smiling, told the company, 'I've no objection to Mr Trotter.'

'Nor I, indeed,' said Mr Goddard, frowning over his spectacles.

'Well, I have,' said Mr Fulbroad. 'Dammit, if he can come claiming to represent God knows who, then before we know where we are we'll have every commoner who thinks he might lose a pig by it clamouring to have his say.' Hector Fulbroad had red hair and a red face and the two shades of red fought an endless battle for dominance; now, in his anger, his face deepened to plum and won. 'I want him out, sir!'

It was at this point that Mr James Manningford amazed those present, including himself, by rising to his feet and saying, 'Then by the same token I must withdraw. While I may be Mr Manningford's heir, I own no land in Abbotsbridge.'

Jaws dropped. Mr Munday spluttered over his pipe. William Waterton muttered, 'Bravo!'

'You, sir? You? Rubbish!' Hector Fulbroad said. 'Not the same thing at all. Never heard such nonsense.'

Mr Fewtrell spoke sharply, his face taut above the starched white bands of his profession. 'I see no reason why either gentleman should go. It is perfectly proper for Mr Trotter to hold a watching brief for certain small proprietors if they have so instructed him, and equally proper for the heir to the Lord of the Manor to be present. Indeed, one would expect it.'

'Then let us continue,' Ambrose said firmly, drawing the attention of the meeting. 'When you are both seated ... Thank you, gentlemen.' In his quiet aristocratic voice he outlined the gains to be anticipated by enclosure, but qualified any

93

enthusiasm he might have shown by adding that vehement opposition could well arise among the villagers.

'We know how to deal with trouble-makers!' Mr Fulbroad interjected.

Ambrose ignored him. 'And it will be a lengthy and expensive business for us all,' he concluded, 'let us make no mistake. It will mean the re-drawing of the map of our village – even our roads will not be safe. But our reward will come in greatly increased land values and in the knowledge that we shall be increasing the nation's production of food at a time of vital necessity.'

A moment's pause, then Mr Knight addressed himself to Mr Manningford, his reedy voice nervous but determined. 'Sir, you spoke of the loss to the villagers with common rights. Like young Mr Trotter, I am, ah, concerned for them. They barely make ends meet as 'tis. Without their free pasture, are we not going to force them on to the parish, into the poorhouse?'

'I doubt it,' Ambrose replied. 'Several hundred acres will be fresh brought into cultivation, giving work to many, but in addition, visualise the employment that will arise from enclosure itself . . .' He spread his hands.

James took up his theme and warmed to it. 'The new farms will have to be fenced and hedged and ditched – tasks of months. And those hedges and ditches will have to be maintained – regular winter work. New buildings will be needed; new roads will have to be laid out. No man should find himself idle.'

The cool young voice of Jack Trotter broke in. 'It is not only idleness that concerns the men – it is the loss of their independence. That is what they fear.'

'How d'ye mean, their independence?' old Munday asked.

'Without common rights, and without the right to cut fuel in the woods, the men will be forced to sell their pieces of land – they will become mere day-labourers, living on a pittance and tied to their masters. Their lives will no longer be their own.'

'And a damned good thing too!' Mr Fulbroad proclaimed. 'None of 'em are steady or trusty that I've met. Ask 'em to do a day's work for you and they tell you they've to fetch the cow from the pound or take the pigs to market.'

94

'With no hope of betterment they might as well be slaves,' Jack said shortly. 'Is that what you'd wish?'

Mr Fulbroad's neck swelled and his plum colour intensified. 'You are impertinent, young man!'

'Gentlemen,' Mr Bland intervened, 'it is unfortunate but true that someone must suffer in all human progress. Consider the upheaval that the wheel must have brought – the brawny human carriers must have suffered loss from the advent of the cart. But we would not now do without it!' Heads nodded relieved agreement. 'But we must be certain that the benefits of enclosure will outweigh the drawbacks. I am convinced they will. We are ourselves slaves to an outmoded and antiquated system, with no hope of betterment.' Having picked up Jack's words and tossed them back at him, the rector continued to speak, as assured as if he were in his own pulpit, observing that it was impossible as things were to try new crops because the manor court persistently voted out all change; hence nearly a third of the land was wasted lying fallow each year, while diseases attacked the animals on the common and spread like wildfire. But all this would be changed. Under his wise vision a new village was created: snug farms lined the valley, their fields rich with bountiful crops and healthy animals, tended by men whose work would always be in demand. His voice deepened with conviction. It would be a benefit and a blessing to all.

James reached for a wine bottle and poured himself a glass. Then he switched his gaze to the man who held the casting vote.

Mr Knight was an earnest church-goer; Mr Knight was listening to the rector's sermon with unblinking attention. He had told James that he was most anxious to do what was right; he must ask advice, take counsel. James did not know which exasperated him more, Mr Knight's mincing speech and his lace handkerchief, or his inability to take decisions. William Waterton had once remarked in his robust way, 'Knight'll never move upon anything. Hah! It has ever amazed me that he managed to sire one child, let alone five!' Perhaps the rector's persuasions would succeed where James's had not.

In the discussion that followed no more tendencious matters arose – facts were what the men wanted. Munday enquired how long the whole damned business would take. Mr Manningford replied, to the attorney's nods, that if Parliament heard and granted a petition presented this autumn, then the Bill for Enclosure could, with proper management, obtain the Royal Assent by the spring. The commissioners appointed would then have to start their work of receiving and determining claims, measuring the land and finally mapping out the new farms. Given that not too many people had lost their deeds or started arguments over boundaries, he would estimate – and it was only an estimate, mark you – a total of three years.

'Three years of turmoil!' Mr Knight said, looking dismayed.

Stent, silent until now, spoke up to ask whether a small portion of land could be set aside for the use and benefit of the poor. 'For they stand to suffer badly, sirs!'

'It would be possible,' Mr Manningford said non-committally.

They moved to a vote. The large owners voted without hesitation.

'For, of course!' said Mr Fulbroad, glaring at the Trotters.

'I vote for enclosure,' said Mr Bland.

Munday took his pipe from his mouth. 'I am for it.'

Jack nudged his father to start a counter-attack. 'I vote agin it!' Thomas growled. ''Twill do me great personal harm, and I don't see how 'twill do the village aught but harm.'

'That is my view, sirs. I am against!' said Stent.

Jack followed him swiftly: 'Mrs Pern, Mr Page, Mr Truckle and Mr Pettifer vote against.'

Hector Fulbroad's lips thinned. He looked as if he would snarl an interruption but a shake of the squire's head stopped him.

'Mr Goddard?'

'For!'

All faces turned to Mr Knight, who flushed deeply and passed his lace handkerchief across his damp forehead.

'Well, sir?' challenged Mr Fulbroad. 'Are ye for us or agin us?'

Mr Knight's adam's apple bobbed. 'I vote for enclosure,' he jerked out.

There was an outburst of exclamations. Mr Fulbroad banged the table triumphantly, half-drowning Ambrose Manningford's quiet conclusion: 'I, too, vote for enclosure. Then it is agreed, gentlemen, we enclose.'

In the noisy conversation that followed no one seemed to notice Jack Trotter shove back his chair and walk out of the meeting. Only James saw him go and felt some of the fire of exultant achievement die within himself. He had an abrupt vision of the blow that the loss of the common would be to Jack's ambitions, and realised with shock that the boy had not once spoken of this: his concern had been for the lesser members of the village, the unlettered and inarticulate poor who had no outlet for their distress and anger. James knew he could not have been so objective in such a situation and the realisation annoyed him.

More wine bottles were brought in and circulated, toasts were drunk to enclosure and the meeting settled down again on Ambrose's request, to consider the weighty matter of the commutation of the rector's tithes, and whether the Church stood to gain or lose by having land in lieu of tithe. James found it impossible to concentrate.

10

The notice was pinned to the church door early on Sunday morning, while the dew glistened thickly on the grass. While not expecting the classical reaction of, 'Kill the messenger!', the bearer of these particular tidings wished to keep his skin whole and his bones unbroken, thus his business in the church porch was seen only by an illiterate lad driving a pig down the lane. Yet through that strange alchemy which spreads village news, by the time the bell-ringers had commenced their call to morning service there were few in Abbotsbridge who had not heard of it, and the churchyard was packed with an angry jostling crowd. Men and women milled over the mounds that marked the burial places of their ancestors, folk who had toiled and farmed and lived with the aid of the common and who would have been as horror-struck as themselves by the great change that menaced the village. 'How are we to manage without the common?' 'What about my grazing rights?' 'We'll stop this, no matter 'ow!' The voices came in a cadence of despair, asking unanswerable questions, uttering meaningless threats, rising in an anguished and mutinous chorus of protest.

By the church porch stood Josh Pither, as constable, and Thomas Trotter as churchwarden, flanked by the verger and the overseer, their faces impassive but their eyes intent, ready to prevent any attempt to tear down the notice.

Near them Jack Trotter stood, his face pale with emotion. As if by unspoken agreement the small farmers and the small-holders moved towards him; they needed Jack to articulate their grievances. Young as he was, he had argued with the landowners on their own level at the White Hart Inn; he'd fight for their rights now. And Jack looked at them all with his steady grey eyes and nodded as he listened.

From the lych-gate the big bass voice of John Hayter, landlord of The Bull, rose above the noise of his neighbours' and silenced them momentarily.

'We'll not permit it,' he bawled. 'That common has belonged to this village since time immemorial. It can't be taken away from us just because Mr Manningford and a handful of grasping landowners covet it. That's not English justice, never 'as been, never will be!'

The crowd vociferated its approval.

'We'll fight it!' Hayter proclaimed. He paused to find a resounding phrase and brought out: 'We've got prescriptive and inalienable rights that no man shall take away from us!'

'Aye,' shouted Dame Harriman, whose flock of geese was entirely dependent upon the grass of the common. ''Tis Magna Carta and that. We knows. An' I'd liefer die 'n let 'em trample upon me!'

Barney Bidewell pounded in through the gate, his great chest heaving from his long run over the common and up the village street, his jaw jutting. He thrust his way to the centre of the crowd. ''Ere, what's all this? Enclosure? Plough up our common? I'll not 'ave it!'

Hayter, whose inn furniture had suffered many times in Barney's drinking bouts, vented some of his own rage in spite at Barney. ''Tis what'll happen unless we band together to stop it, yes, and they'll tear down all the squatters' houses, too. Your habitation's doomed, Bidewell!'

'Tear down my 'ouse what I builded wi' my own 'ands? Let 'em try, that's what I say, just let 'em try. I'd tear down their 'ouses and barns – aye, an' see 'em burn, too!'

'Set their ricks afire!' a high-pitched voice called. Was it Black Betsey's? She was there, her lank black locks wild about her head, her dark eyes snapping with the excitement of the occasion. 'They oughter be made to suffer fer this! Where does they think I've to put me dairy cows?'

'That trio o' walking skellingtons? I'd bury 'em if I was you!' That was Thomas Trotter. The crowd relieved its tension with an explosive guffaw.

Betsey rounded on him, shrill with vituperation. 'Ye're a fine

99

hypocrite, ye are! Oo's side're you on? Churchwarden! Ye're givin' yer help to the gentry, 'ent ye! So's they can rob us of what's rightly ourn. Ye should take shame to yerself!'

The sounds of a carriage in the lane caught the villagers' attention; they turned and surged forward. A low growl came from them, the menacing rumble of an approaching storm. The carriage rounded the bend into sight – it was Mr Fulbroad, the first of the landowners to appear and the most disliked, riding in his spanking new barouche with his two oldest daughters. The storm broke. A hail of abuse and gravel fell about their ears, followed by a large flintstone that shot through the air to crack the paintwork of the door with a bang. The horses reared and kicked while the two red-headed girls screamed their terror, clutching the sides of the carriage. 'Drive on, ye fool!' Mr Fulbroad bellowed, his voice cracking with strain. The coachman laid his whip on the horses' backs and they dashed off in the direction of Brambourne, the barouche swaying violently as it went.

The crowd jeered and chanted and stamped its approval of this rout.

'An' we'll do the same wi' Squire when 'e comes!' Barney yelled jubilantly, tugging another large stone from the church wall.

'No, we'll not,' said Josh Pither, turning on him. 'Not with stones, we'll not! Put it down, Barney!'

'Make me!' he snarled, chipped teeth showing in his dark face, his great fist high, poised to smash the stone in Josh's face.

But Jack had edged his way behind Barney and now chopped his hand down on the man's biceps. The stone fell as Barney yelped with pain and swung round. Jack ducked nimbly to avoid a sledgehammer blow from the left fist; Josh seized the arm on its descent and used its own momentum to force it up behind Barney's back. A viciously mouthed threat was sharply cut off as Josh jerked the arm. 'Quiet!' Sweat broke out on Barney's face and he stood still.

A second carriage rumbled along the lane. In it sat the squire with Mr James and Miss Beatrice Manningford.

As the carriage slowed James caught his breath in shock. While he had expected some protests he had never visualised a crowd of this size, a wide barrier of faces between the three of

100

them and the church. The horses stopped and the faces moved forward. In the rising mutter of voices he heard the anger that Ambrose had feared and that he had discounted. Beatrice said something in a low voice and James felt a spurt of anger with her that she had insisted upon coming and with himself that he had not bodily prevented her – and in an open carriage, too. He saw that her face was curiously calm and composed, as if she knew that the villagers would not touch her. And then he knew with a flash of intuition just why she had come with them, and his self-anger deepened, black and heavy.

He stood up and caught Beatrice's hand to help her out. The hand tugged at his for attention and he realised that she was speaking again. 'Wait!' she said. 'Wait!' And he saw that Ambrose too was not moving but was staring at something or someone among the mass of faces.

From out of the hubbub came a voice, not loud, but in its steady assurance dominating the crowd so that the sounds of their hostility ebbed and the angry flushes faded from their faces. He searched for its source and saw it was Jack Trotter, urging the villagers to refrain from noisy or violent demonstrations, explaining that if Mr Manningford and his friends presented a petition to Parliament for enclosure, those who were against it could equally present a counter petition – and they were many. He himself would be prepared to organise it. And Parliament must hear their case.

By the church wall James saw a girl who had been crying take a deep shuddering breath and smear away her tears, her eyes now fixed upon Jack. Her face was familiar, yet somehow connected with a distaste – and then he remembered who she was: Nancy Carter, the old shepherd's daughter who had obtained Ambrose's permission to keep a cow on the common . . . on that hot day in June . . . that day when he and Susannah . . . He thrust the memory away to listen again to Susannah's brother. And gradually as he sat there in the carriage, chafing at his own inaction, the realisation came that he could never have calmed the villagers as Jack was doing, that he would not have known what to say, nor how to express it in their words. And with that realisation came a profound feeling of humility. He was, he saw, a stranger to them all.

When Jack ceased speaking James rose and assisted first

Ambrose and then Beatrice from the carriage. And the crowd pressed back and slowly parted to let them through. As he drew level with Jack he wanted to nod an acknowledgment to him, but an instinct born of his new humility told him it would be wrong, even dangerous. He lowered his eyes and walked through the silence to the church door where the rector stood, white-faced, waiting to receive them. As they passed into the church a rising murmuration began again behind them.

The sun was like a great silver coin suspended in the autumn mist as Sedley and Susannah drove out of Brambourne early one morning soon after their marriage. Spiders' webs were festooned on the bushes, stitched along each thread with silver beads of water; dew was sparkling on the shaggy grass; the air was cold but exhilarating. Susannah pulled the hood of her cloak close about her head and filled her lungs with relish.

Plough teams were out on a flank of the downs ahead of them, painting brown stripes across the creamy stubble. Rooks and starlings were swooping from the mist and landing behind the ploughs to peck at the newly turned-up food. And as the horses plodded forward so the birds swirled behind them, greedy and exuberant. Then the gulls came to join them, out of nowhere, sleek and aggressive, wheeling down in effortless spirals to strut on the brown folded waves of earth with the same lordly self-confidence they displayed on their own element. Susannah watched them in fascination as the curricle drove up the narrow lane towards the Winchester road.

That big field must belong to Squire Waterton. She looked about herself. All this land was his; the smooth neat fields, the well-trimmed hedges. It was very different from the land around Abbotsbridge: the three great sprawling open fields with their untidy strips and baulks. But within a few short years Abbotsbridge farms would look like this – unless, by some miracle, the enclosure plans could be stopped. One by one the plough teams reached the headland and turned; slowly the brown stripes widened. Ploughing on this scale was impossible in Abbotsbridge. The treacherous thought sneaked into her mind that this was a better way to farm. She shivered and wished the sun would gain some strength.

Jack and her father would be out ploughing too. She visualised Jack walking a straight furrow, the muscles on his arms standing out as the ploughshare sliced through the earth, his face taut as the automatic performance of the physical task left his mind free to grapple with the strategy needed to persuade the villagers to present a petition against the Bill of Enclosure. Jack had already determined that this was the proper way to oppose the landowners, but to convince the men of it was a Herculean task. To folk such as the Pettifers and Barney Bidewell and Peter Page, inarticulate and illiterate, noise and violence were their primary means of expression, not pieces of paper. Attorneys-at-law and Members of Parliament were part of a mysterious and distant system whose officials lived lives of strange splendour and spoke a different language. They were men to be feared and loathed and avoided, never people who could assist in any battle of theirs.

Jack spoke of calling a meeting at the farmhouse, but Susannah was convinced this would be dangerous. There were too many hotheads about spoiling for a fight; bring them together and their pent-up fury would find a vent in broken heads and broken windows. And as their leader, Jack would be a clear target for the magistrates' revenge. No, better that he should persuade men like John Hayter and Josh Pither to help: The Bull Inn and the smithy were the natural meeting places of the village; if those two men declared to their customers their conviction that Jack's plan was the right one to defeat the landowners, then the villagers would soon be equally convinced.

She would speak to him about it. Jack was over-young for the role that he had taken upon himself, and with a youngster's headstrong idealism. His lithe and lively masculinity and his warmth of personality had always evoked an answering warmth in her; now she wanted to protect him. Like their mother, like herself, he was part neither of the village, nor of the gentry: this was an unequal and rancorous struggle that could go badly wrong; if it did, neither side would have the least compunction in turning on him.

The curricle turned from the rutted lane on to the smooth surface of the turnpike road. It was the rector's vehicle. When Mrs Bland had discovered that Sedley had planned for them both to go on horseback to Winchester, she had been horrified. 'Ride? In Susannah's condition? Do you wish to have her totally knocked up, you foolish man?' Glaring, Sedley had retorted that they would be staying overnight, not riding both ways in one day, since Mr James Manningford had told him there was a play worth seeing at the theatre – a delectable comedy by Mr Goldsmith – and had kindly suggested it as a treat for his bride. 'He did, did he?' had said Susannah, her eyebrows raised. 'How remarkably thoughtful of him.' 'Dear me, no!' Mrs Bland concluded, ignoring them both; she knew that Mr Bland had no immediate engagements that he could not reach on horseback; she would inform him that the Staceys were to borrow his curricle.

Susannah was grateful; the first days of her marriage had been tiring. Unexpectedly echoing her thoughts, her husband spoke: 'How pleasant it is to be away from the vicarage,' he remarked, 'free from all the bustle of settling in and the endless stream of callers.'

'It is wonderful to be out,' she agreed. 'This is a rare treat.'

'I think when we return, Susannah, that you might contrive to reduce the number of visitors.'

Sedley had been greatly put out: her father, her mother and Jack had all invaded the vicarage to denounce the iniquities and greed of the Manningfords and the other landowners, and to plan how to stop them; Fanny had appeared with the children to tell them of the excitements; Mr Bland had been closeted with Sedley for nigh on an hour; and even, most embarrassingly, Miss Manningford had called, proffering a basket of trout with Mr James's compliments and insisting how wonderful dear Mrs Stacey's brother Jack had been in calming the crowd: 'Cousin James tells me that but for him we should have had our carriage stoned like the poor Fulbroads!' And finally Mrs Bland had come to pour out her indignation with Fanny, who, she said, with that dreadful fracas going on, had wandered off to play her harp and left the children to hang out of the landing window, seeing violence and hearing coarse language to which no well-bred person should be exposed.

Mr Bland had requested that Sedley should take the next Sunday service at St Swithun's at Abbotsbridge, while Mr Bland took the Brambourne service: the enclosure notice would be on the church door for the second of its three statutory Sundays, red rag to the village bulls, and the rector thought it best that a neutral person should be there. 'A good thought for him, but hardly enticing for me!' said Sedley. As he had fulminated to Susannah the previous evening, this was their honeymoon period, supposed to be a period of peace in which they could become intimately acquainted – and what had it become? Something akin to an unending village meeting.

'I can hardly request Mr and Mrs Bland not to call on us,' Susannah protested.

'No, no!' he said testily. 'You know very well I was not alluding to them. The rector and his wife must always be welcome. No, it is to your family that I was referring. While you must behave as a daughter should to them, I see no reason why they should be forever on our doorstep.'

'My mother is being exceedingly kind,' Susannah said reproachfully. 'She says she will help me remake some old silk damask she's got put away in a trunk into a new evening gown. How can I turn her away?'

'Your mother is a sensible woman. Naturally you cannot turn her away. Really, Susannah, you are being wilfully obtuse. Since you force me to put it into plain language, I object to your father and your brother turning my vicarage into a political forum.'

'But they would never do that,' Susannah said, the hurt note deepening in her voice. 'They came only to tell us of the blow that has fallen upon them. Why, you cannot be happy yourself to know that your wife's family is to have its income reduced so unexpectedly, its hopes of increasing its land-holding dashed to the ground.'

'There is that, I can see,' Sedley admitted, taken aback.

'If Jack's plans had been allowed to come to fruition then he could have doubled our acreage. We'd have become land-owners of standing.'

'A boy's dream!' Sedley retorted, making a comeback. He settled his three-cornered beaver hat firmly on his head and shouted at the driver of a wagonload of squealing pigs to pull over so that he could coax his snorting, sidling horses past. This achieved, he added, 'In my position, Susannah, one cannot be too careful.'

'How do you mean?'

'It would be intolerable for either of us to be involved with the leader of a mob of malcontents.'

'My brother? Jack? How can you speak of him so? You know he is opposed to violence.'

'So I believe. But that is not as others see it.'

'But who?'

'Mr Fulbroad, for one. I met him yesterday. There have been threats overheard of rick burnings and destructions. He spoke of a nest of Jacobins in Abbotsbridge.'

'A nest of Jacobins? Oh!' For a moment Susannah clenched her teeth with fury, then the ludicrous aspect of the accusation caught her sense of humour and she burst into laughter. 'Oh, that is really pitching it too high. No one who knows Jack could ever take any notice of such nonsense.'

'I trust you are right. But you must acknowledge that it is singularly unfortunate for me to be associated with one against whom a charge of Jacobinism could be laid.'

Sedley was an intelligent man, yet his views were smeared by other men's prejudices. Susannah bit back a tempestuous reply to that effect and they fell silent. The road was busier now, with wagonload upon wagonload of produce heading for the coast, and Sedley concentrated on his horses.

Susannah studied her new husband's face obliquely. They could be at the start of fifty years of marriage ... that thought was not alluring; she pushed it away. For her, as for him, the indisputable fact was that their marriage was infinitely to be preferred to the scandalous, the unthinkable alternative. She must take life day by day. And her life now was filling with exciting matters – fine new clothes, a house of her own, a life as a somebody in the community. She was infinitely, guiltily grateful to Sedley, however grudging his capitulation. She meant to make him an excellent wife, seeing to all his creature comforts and working without stint to help him in the parish. No one should fault her. She could contrive on little money; she had seen her mother perform miracles on next to nothing all her life; she, too, could manage poultry and pigs and conjure tasty meals from odds and ends and create a charming room from pieces of velvet and vases of flowers.

But Sedley's values were different from those of other men she knew well – Mr Bland, her father, or Jack. Money and position, she suspected, called to him above loyalty, duty and service. He would not be won over by simple goodness. Besides, his moods veered with such startling rapidity. He could not bear to feel himself under attack or denigrated; the slightest criticism and he would lash out, his tongue vicious with spite; yet while he felt himself to be admired and respected he could be pleasant, even generous. Marriage to Sedley, she concluded, would not be easy.

And marriage had made vast changes in her life. She missed the lively atmosphere at the Blands': the children's comical comments; the servants' gossip; even the surging, panting, scrabbling dogs whose noise and smells permeated everywhere. She saw now that Mrs Bland had behaved like a second mother to her, with her scoldings and her unexpected kindnesses. In running the vicarage Susannah coped with an unconscious ear for the observations she would expect from that lady.

And Fanny. The fascination of Fanny, her brilliance on the harp, her tart tongue, the morbid pre-occupied moods that would overtake her for days, even weeks, and then the sudden bursts of sardonic humour and the childlike fits of giggling that turned her into a different, an enchanting person: it was strange not to see her every day. It was Fanny who had coerced Mr Bland into being generous over the kitchen refurbishments at the vicarage. 'But Papa,' she had said – and in front of everyone, too – 'if it is a question of money, then I shall willingly forego my new ballgown. I know what an expense outfitting Daniel is proving!' Whereupon her father had hastily declared that there was no problem, no problem at all, that all the dilapidations would be made good, and the latest Robinson's patent range installed. Susannah was touched that Fanny insisted upon their continuing friendship; she would have disliked not to share with her the books that Fanny bought, especially the novels; she always enjoyed her vigorous critiques of their spineless heroines – 'I should never permit a man to treat me so! Why do females have all to be so foolish?' And Fanny had been her bridesmaid, though wondering aloud as she helped to dress Susannah how any sensible female could actually wish to marry. She would buy some music for Fanny in Winchester; perhaps she could find some pieces new published that would please her.

She would buy Sedley a present, too. For whatever motives she had tied herself indissolubly to him and there was no going back. And at the thought of today's expedition and the play to come, her naturally ebullient spirits rose. There were compensations. She tucked her hand into the crook of his arm and gave it a squeeze. Sedley lowered his arched nose a degree and his features relaxed. 'We are making good time,' he remarked.

They entered Winchester through the Westgate, after waiting behind a broad-wheeled cart that had barely room to pass through.

'One would think the corporation would have this old gateway pulled down,' Sedley grumbled. 'It only impedes the traffic.'

'They removed the Northgate and the Eastgate some years back for the same reason,' Susannah said. 'It is a pity to lose these memories of the past, but they are crumbling fast.' She gazed about herself, mentally saluting familiar landmarks, the handsome clock that projected from the Guildhall to their right; the old Buttercross, its steps, as always, crowded with market women; the steep slope of St Giles' Hill rising above the River Itchen at the High Street's end. A damp, low-lying city, Winchester, its great Norman cathedral built on a marsh; brooks bubbling along its lower streets; the cellars of its houses flooded with water each winter: no wonder that its inhabitants groaned of their rheumatics. Yet despite these disadvantages it was a bustling place: the county town of Hampshire, a market town, and, above all now, a military town, its mediaeval streets thronged with redcoats. Susannah found it exhilarating.

The George was a large coaching inn with a driveway leading from the High Street into an inner courtyard. As Sedley drove in, an ostler leapt to hold the horses and two footmen each presented an arm to help Susannah alight. Startled, she managed to descend with a fair assumption of nonchalance. She noticed Sedley giving her a reflective look, but thought no more of it, until, after their bags had been deposited in their room and they were seated in the parlour drinking coffee, he informed her that she must order herself a modish pelisse.

She opened her eyes wide at this extravagance. 'But my cloak is nearly new.' She looked down at it. It was a crimson cloak, of a colour so intense that the hood cast a glow upon her face. Its purchase had cost Mrs Bland all of thirteen shillings and Susannah was proud of it.

'It will do well enough about the vicarage garden or for walking in dirty weather about Brambourne,' Sedley stated, 'but it is not suitable to my wife on other occasions. Every other servant girl and country woman wears a red cloak. Besides, you cannot wear such a thing to Abbotsbridge House and we are invited to dine there next week.'

'Next week! But how will there be time?' And how could she face James Manningford through a whole evening?

'You will tell the dressmaker to hasten the work.'

'Yes, Sedley.' His generosity might arise from social reasons, but it was not unwelcome. 'How very kind you are. Thank you!' And she and her mother would work till the candle-light hurt their eyes to have the blue silk damask from the garret trunk transformed in time.

'Then that is decided,' he said. He swallowed the last of his coffee and stood. 'Excellent coffee, but we must hurry to make our purchases.'

They bought two wing chairs of a style Sedley particularly favoured; a handsome mahogany card-table and a tripod table with carved ball-and-claw feet; two Turkey carpets in rich colours – 'Stained-glass window colours!' Susannah said; and two big rectangular gilt mirrors which she vowed would double the size of any room they were put in, through their reflections. 'And increase the light,' Sedley approved, 'especially if we put sconces near.'

They both liked a grandfather clock with a silvered dial made by Joseph Fifield here in Winchester because of its sweet chimes, but when it came to choosing between dining tables nothing could be found to suit Susannah. One was an ugly colour, others of a style quite wrong for the room; finally, irritated, Sedley agreed to leave it for another day. 'You have made the right decision,' Susannah assured him.

The hours passed. In mid-afternoon Sedley left Susannah at the dressmaker's while he paid a courtesy call upon a canon living in the cathedral close, to whom he had once been introduced by Mr Bland. 'One should never neglect any contact which might prove of influence,' he said.

Any embarrassment Susannah might have felt at her first

visit to so modish an establishment as the dressmaker's was swiftly dispelled by the chic proprietress, a refugee from France with a strong accent and an equally strong sense of style. Mme de Courcy admired madame's figure, understood the need for haste, rolled her eyes in sympathy at a hint that madame's girth might be expected to increase and designed a pelisse that would not only allow for such an eventuality, but disguise it.

So efficient was she that Susannah had time to visit the bookshop next door before she and Sedley met at The George to dine and prepare for the theatre.

The bookseller was an elderly man wearing gold-rimmed spectacles. He blinked thoughtfully at her description of Sedley's interests and produced *The British Sportsman OR Nobleman, Gentleman and Farmer's Dictionary of Recreation and Amusement* by Wm Augustus Osbaldiston, Esq. The contents included the secrets of choosing and training good horses, instructions for shooting flying and finding game of every species, and hints for breeding greyhounds, pointers and other dogs. 'A regular country gentleman's compendium' the bookseller proclaimed it, 'invaluable to all sportsmen.' She bought it. Sedley yearned to be thought a thorough sportsman.

The theatre had a resplendent interior brilliantly lit by what seemed to be thousands of candles. The ceiling was painted to resemble a blue sky with a scattering of clouds and in the four corners were paintings of the comic and tragic muses, Thalis and Melpomene, of Apollo as the representative of opera, and of Pero as the representative of pantomime. Sedley had seen it on a previous visit and was pleased to explain it to Susannah. The absurd charms of the paintings intrigued her. 'That poor painter – lying on a scaffold at such a height and painting upside-down – 'tis amazingly skilful!'

Susannah had never been to the theatre before, although she understood acting through the games of charades the Blands played and the one-act pieces they sometimes produced for their own amusement. This was different. *She Stoops To Conquer* had a sharpness of wit beyond anything she had ever encountered and the actors playing the Hardcastles and Tony Lumpkin had her rapt attention. She could not remember ever having enjoyed herself so much; she was weak with laughter. If this was the theatre, it was all that she had heard it made out to be and more.

The following morning was spent in selecting curtain materials and linen, china and glasses. When she and Sedley mounted into the curricle and drove off it was in the comfortable knowledge of time and money well spent. With reproachful hints at over-pricing coupled with a suggestion of future patronage should the price be right, Susannah had secured substantial reductions in the price of the linen, and the addition of some extra items of china – 'As a token of our wish to be of service.'

She leaned back in her seat. It had been good to walk streets where no one knew her, to be away from the tight little world of the villages where every inhabitant seemed to be scrutinising and judging her. These two days had been a complete break; a means of distancing herself from the guilts and tensions and fears of the past weeks and the perplexities of the future. And at the theatre she had been transported for an evening into a different life, a life radiant with nonsense, illuminated by mischief. It had restored her old sense of fun; she was refreshed and alert.

Into her mind, uninvited, came a vision of James Manningford, big, confident, sensual, powerful, staring sombrely from the saddle of his horse. It was his suggestion that had led Sedley to take her to the theatre, to spend this time away from home. Mr Manningford, she thought scornfully; easy for him to toss out that suggestion for her amusement, it cost him nothing. The very thought of him roused her antagonism; this was the man who had seduced her so light-heartedly and caused her such agony of mind; this was the man who was behind the enclosure of Abbotsbridge Common and who had shattered the peace of the village. Unthinking, uncaring, arrogant, he represented everything she detested and despised most in the gentry. And yet . . . she could not stop a creeping warmth about her heart at the knowledge that he had thought of her.

'I wish,' she said wistfully, 'that we could have stayed another day. It has been delightful.'

'I have my sermon to prepare,' Sedley reminded her, 'and it is an important one.'

Susannah was immediately wary; she had thoughts for this

sermon; the attitudes and actions of many people in Abbots-bridge could depend on it. She enquired cautiously, 'Have you decided on which text you will preach?'

11

The Staceys were late in arriving at the Manningfords' dinner party and they came separately. Susannah was the first to appear.

When the butler flung open the drawing-room doors and announced her name the gentlemen rose to their feet, but it was as though they had risen to stare rather than to receive her; a sudden silence had fallen on the company. James saw her chin lift and her back straighten, and heard the susurration of silk against her long slender thighs as she walked alone into the room. Then Ambrose threaded his way through his guests to take her hand and welcome her. 'Mrs Stacey. How delightful. But is your husband not with you?' And following him, Rosalind, all elbows and awkward movements, greeted her with fussing earnestness.

Susannah made her explanations, ignoring the curious eyes, her voice calm and clear. James had forgotten what an attractive voice she had; a boyish soprano, and with those moments of huskiness that a boy's voice acquires just before it breaks. Mr Stacey would be with them shortly, she said, and he had requested her to convey his apologies for the untoward delay. It transpired that Prudence Paine from Brambourne had stopped the Staceys just as they were turning into the lime avenue that led to Abbotsbridge House, and urgently requested of Mr Stacey that he should christen a new-born baby. 'A dying baby!' Susannah said. Naturally, her husband had not hesitated. Somehow James received the impression that it was she who had not hesitated to urge Mr Stacey to his duty.

'Ah, the Bidewell baby,' Mr Bland replied. 'Yes, indeed. Prudence came to me earlier with the same request. She was

113

vastly distressed. "The babe is main weak an' pickéd an' like to go back!" she urged me. Methody or not, the woman has a good heart. Over the common I rode, only to be turned back by Bidewell himself, who threatened me and all Abbotsbridge landowners with violence should we come nigh his cottage again – for we are plotting to destroy it.'

'True enough,' Ambrose murmured.

'However,' Mr Bland concluded, smiling at Susannah, 'despite Barney's declared resolution not to allow any prating preacher near his child, Prudence and that poor girl Charity between them must have prevailed upon him to allow Mr Stacey to christen it. I doubt that Mr Stacey will feel any desire to linger and we can expect to see him shortly, his duty done.'

'Mr Stacey is most punctilious in doing his duty,' Miss Waterton commented sharply, her eyes on Susannah.

'Barney also refused to have Martha Pither attend Charity,' Mrs Bland put in rapidly and inconsequentially. 'Prudence was quite smug about it, I'm sorry to say. He told her he'd have none of those interfering Pithers about his cottage. I fear we shall see more trouble from that young man.'

The room was thronged with guests; Ambrose ushered Susannah slowly through them. Mr Waterton, large and genial like his son, bowed and greeted her in friendly fashion before continuing his conversation with Rosalind Manningford, but his wife managed only a cursory nod before she turned away. Mrs Waterton always reminded James of a moulting sparrow hawk, with her beaky nose and her hard bright eyes and the shawls that slipped untidily from her hunched shoulders. Yet though, like her eldest daughter, she was no beauty, her face had all the character that her daughter's lacked. Mrs Waterton delved into every concern of the poor in Brambourne and regulated their behaviour with a firm hand: 'As good as any magistrate!' her husband boasted. The villagers grumbled, but respected her: 'A ring on every finger and a finger in every pie!' was their comment on her.

William Waterton made up for the coldness of his mother and sister in the warmth of his salute, kissing Susannah's hand with an enthusiastic smack that had those ladies drawing in sharp breaths. Even Elliot Fulbroad, Hector Fulbroad's

114

twenty-one-year-old son and heir, gave her a look of startled appreciation from his bulbous eyes as he made his bow.

The challenge of her first formal dinner party had brought out the best in Susannah, James thought; the russet hair cleverly curled and tied, the flowing lines of the blue silk gown against the lithe young body, the eyes wide and dark. The contrast between the scantily-clad girl he had met by the river in June and the young wife in all her new dignity of silk and lace was staggering. He heard Mrs Bland murmur that the tout-ensemble was quite charming and saw Susannah's quick smile of gratitude. So she was not so self-assured as she appeared.

On a sofa by the fire his cousin Beatrice and Fanny were talking, or rather Beatrice was briskly expounding and Fanny looking languidly amused. As Susannah approached they both looked up; Beatrice indicated the sofa in invitation and Susannah seated herself on its edge.

James had a sudden thought that here was the real test: not the Watertons, not Ambrose, nor any of the others, but Beatrice. If she could hold her own with Beatrice, she could hold her own with any of them; Beatrice was the arbiter for his taste.

'Well,' she was commenting to Susannah, 'you have been among us for many years, now you are with us. An interesting transformation.'

'I find it so,' Susannah said calmly.

'And enjoyable, I trust?'

'I trust so, too.'

A brief pause; their eyes met and he saw a glimmer of amused comprehension pass between them. Beatrice said: 'We must make it so.'

Fanny's attention was held by the cameo at Susannah's neck. 'I have not seen it before, have I? It is unusual in design. Onyx, too. Is it a present from Mr Stacey?'

'No,' Susannah said, turning to accept a glass of wine from a manservant. 'No, it was given to me by my mother. It was my grandmama's.'

'Then it must be quite old,' Beatrice said. 'Would that be the grandmama who was governess to my aunts? The one who left so abruptly?'

Susannah considered her sharply. She nodded. 'Yes, it would.'

'Papa was speaking of her only the other day. He admired her, you know. He says you resemble her strongly.'

'Does he?' Susannah looked at once fascinated and embarrassed. No doubt her delectable but immoral grandmother was a forbidden topic at home. Only Beatrice would have the hardihood to raise it openly.

'Yes, indeed. A lady of charm and character, he told me. Tell me, do you think that she was badly treated?'

'Badly treated? By whom?'

'By the society of her day.'

'Who am I to judge?' Susannah fenced.

'You? As good a judge as any, I should have thought.'

Was Beatrice implying what he thought she was implying? James wondered. She was treading on thin ice whether or no.

Susannah's chin went up. She said: 'Since you ask me, then yes, I think she was. And she would be treated no differently now.'

'Do you believe that society should ignore illicit relationships and their results? That they should be condoned?'

'No, for it would undermine morals, family life, inheritance – the basis of society. But what disgusts me is the hypocrisy of the condemnation, then and now.'

'Pray continue,' Beatrice said. 'You fascinate me.'

Susannah twisted her glass between fine-skinned fingers, drawing flecks of light from the wine. 'We are told that the woman is the weaker vessel, that she needs protection, that she must leave the handling of all her affairs to men. St Paul said: "The head of the woman is the man." Yet suddenly, in this one matter, the belief is turned upside-down – the woman is expected to be the stronger vessel, and to control the man, and that even when he may be far higher in society than her, or in authority over her.'

'And when she fails the man is called a devil of a fellow, and the woman is disgraced! You are right, it is hypocrisy. Dear me!'

Fanny interrupted: 'And we are in danger of becoming far too serious for the occasion. My sentiments agree with yours entirely, but let us talk of less provocative matters, Beatrice, please! Mrs Stacey is new to this company.'

'Mrs Stacey seems capable of holding her own in any company,' Beatrice said with a grin. 'But I suppose we must be duly insipid. Shall we return to the cameo as a suitable topic? I must say, it is delightful!'

James turned away; a stab of something hitherto unknown had passed through him as they spoke, leaving him shaken, a state not normal to him. He found the gentlemen still discussing Barney Bidewell. Mr Waterton wanted to know if he could be the fellow who was taking his pheasants; the depredations this year were shocking.

Ambrose doubted it. 'Barney is too large and loud ever to make a poacher. ''Tis more likely that young Arthur has moved on to new ground.' He fished out his snuffbox and took a pinch of snuff.

'Arthur? Arthur who?'

'Pettifer. A sly rogue. Son of Black Betsey, a gipsy slut. He rarely works, yet they never come on the parish for assistance. I fear our butcher knows more than it would pay him to tell.'

Mr Waterton snorted his disgust, his weather-beaten face ruddier than usual beneath his powdered wig. 'If that's who 'tis, then I'd thank you to keep your poachers to yourselves, dammit!'

His wife said: 'The fellow's depriving my menfolk of their shooting. If I had ought to do with it, I'd have poachers flogged through the village at the cart's tail, before ever they were sent to the quarter sessions. That would stop 'em in their tracks.'

Her husband agreed, but added: 'Trouble is, this fellow leaves no tracks. Not to speak of. He's as little substance as a shade in the night. How are the keepers to catch him? I've a mind to set man-traps, though I don't care for the infernal machines in general.'

From the corner of his eye James saw Susannah's head jerk up and round. 'But man-traps can maim a man for life,' he said. 'Or kill him.'

'If a man goes after game he knows what he can expect,' Squire Waterton said hardily, taking a gulp of his wine.

Elliot Fulbroad concurred. 'My father would agree with you, sir, 'tis shocking the amount of game that is taken. The rogues think they can do as they wish. Property is no longer sacred – not now they're affected with this revolutionary rub-

117

bish from across the channel. Action must be swift and strong to succeed.' His thick neck reddened with his indignation.

The doors opened and the butler announced Mr Stacey. As Ambrose and Rosalind rose to welcome him, James saw Rosalind glance at the clock and murmur something to her father. He suspected they would go in to dinner almost immediately and he was right. Ambrose spoke briefly to Mr Stacey, assuring him that he had behaved with propriety in having attended to his duty before his pleasure, and, no, that he had not caused the company any untoward inconvenience in keeping their dinner waiting, paused to congratulate him upon a most thoughtful and cogently argued sermon last Sunday upon the theme of reconciliation: 'Blessed are the peace-makers, indeed, Mr Stacey!' and then made his way to Susannah to suggest that they should lead the party to the dining-parlour.

James puckered his forehead to stop himself from laughing aloud. Of course, a bride came first in any company, be the others whom they might.

Susannah walked beside Ambrose with her eyes lowered, concentrating whole-heartedly upon his conversation, her face showing no awareness of the reactions of her fellow guests. It was clear that it stuck in several throats that she should take precedence. They could not overlook her having compounded her original misjudgment of birth with having been the Bland children's nursery-maid, and, worse, with having a brother who was leading the village opposition to their enclosure plans. There were dilated nostrils and averted faces. He saw Mrs Waterton peering at him with impatience and his desire to laugh vanished; the horrid truth dawned that since Ambrose accompanied Susannah, he was doomed to take the hawk-faced old bully in to dinner himself.

'Come, Mr Manningford,' she said, curling her bejewelled talons round his arm, 'this will not do – you are wool-gathering.'

Mrs Waterton conducted to her chair, there was a delay while the rest of the party strolled in, lively now, talking and exclaiming, tapping fans on arms and calling over shoulders. James seized the opportunity to speak to Susannah.

'I trust you are happy in your marriage, Mrs Stacey?'

She turned her head to examine him with grey eyes that were

118

intent and searching, but challenging, too. He returned her gaze until its intensity forced him to look away, dazzled.

'Naturally I am happy.' Her voice came with cool sarcasm. 'How could I be otherwise? Do I not have the husband of my choice?'

It seemed as though there was some demon of perversity within him that forced him to say or do the wrong thing every time he saw her. He cursed his own ineptitude.

He said: 'I apologise. That was ill-put. I wished ... I wished only to express my concern and my ... my desire to assist you ...'

Stammering like a schoolboy now, made stupid by her composure. Words would not convey what he felt – indeed, he was not certain what he did feel, only that the mixture of guilt and liking was intolerable inside himself and must somehow be given an outlet in words. Yet he could not say what he wished to say, not here, not now, not among this crowd of gossiping, gaping neighbours.

He said stiffly: 'If you should have any problems, any problems at all, you must let me help you. I shall put myself entirely at your service. You have only to let me know.'

Along the dining table the great silver candelabra were full of candles and their light seemed to flicker in her eyes as she considered him. 'That is kind of you, Mr Manningford. Thank you.'

The indifferent note in her voice was tactful in the circumstances, yet he felt rebuffed. He had to reach her. He said: 'That was a clever sermon of your husband's last Sunday. It had subtlety I had not expected. Was it you?'

'Me?'

'Yes, you, Mrs Stacey. Your work.'

'My husband would never allow me to write his sermons, Mr Manningford.'

'Don't prevaricate! Writing is not the same as influencing. And I detected a strong influence at work. The address was not in his normal style.'

'No?'

'No. It was gentle, thoughtful. And it showed understanding. Well?'

119

'I did give my husband some advice,' Susannah admitted, and a half-smile parted her lips a little.

'You are a clever woman,' James said.

Dinner at Abbotsbridge House was an occasion to be celebrated in style and without haste; it lasted for almost three hours. Ambrose was an austere man and abstemious for his age and time, but he knew how to entertain his guests. The long mahogany table was handsome with silver and cut-glass and great bowls piled high with autumn fruits. The meal commenced with pea soup, cod and oyster sauce, a roasted cock-turkey, boiled rump of beef, ham and mutton steaks, followed by a second course of roast duck, cheesecakes, damson pies, tarts and raspberry puffs. There were oranges, pears and apples, almonds and raisins, brandy cherries and filberts for dessert; the whole washed down with wines, port and sherries, porter and strong beer.

With Mrs Waterton concentrating greedily upon her food on one side of him and Mrs Bland chirruping to her far neighbour on the other, James was free to survey the table.

It was a mercy that the senior Fulbroads had been unable to come: Fulbroad would have choked with spleen at being asked to greet Jack Trotter's sister on a footing of equality, but if his son reported that members of the gentry found her acceptable, Fulbroad would be forced to rethink. His own presence was not so warmly demanded that he could afford to take a stand against Susannah's.

Young Fulbroad, stocky and stiff in his high-collared mulberry coat, was sandwiched between Fanny Bland and Miss Waterton. For a while he struggled to engage Fanny's attention, favouring her with his views on the situation of the allied armies in the Low Countries, explaining with comprehensive gestures of his knife around two strategically placed forks and a pepper pot, how, were he in the Duke of York's shoes, he would sweep the monstrous French into the Sambre – or, alternatively, drown them in the Scheldt. Fanny paid him no attention beyond the occasional 'Oh, yes?', but picked at her food, staring dreamily ahead of herself. James liked to look at her, but from a distance; her pale elegance did not draw him as Susannah's warm russet looks did; Fanny had more the abstract attraction of a work of art, an object to be admired but

120

not touched. Her hair was very fair, drawn up at the sides and then allowed to fall in delicate ringlets that reached to a point just below the nape of her long neck; her skin had the cool translucent beauty of porcelain and its fragility, too. James preferred something more robust.

Elliot Fulbroad seemed to be arriving at a similar conclusion. His brilliant campaign to reduce the French army to a mere rabble having been received with a total absence of applause, he turned from Fanny to his neighbour on his left-hand side, and was awarded a very different reception. Miss Waterton hung upon his every word, receiving his ponderous sallies with shrieks of delight. She was resplendent tonight in a gown of mauve satin loaded with lace and spangles; diamond drops sparkled from her ears; the expanse of bony chest revealed by her décolletage was decorated with a diamond-studded pendant hanging from an elaborate silver chain and her arms tinkled with bracelets. James suspected that the shrieks and the flashing diamonds were designed to attract Sedley Stacey's attention and remind him of all he had forfeited by marrying Susannah. Several times her eyes flicked sharply right towards him.

William Waterton was drinking heavily. The company was not to his taste. There were four females in his vicinity, but as one was his long-nosed sister, and one Mrs Bland, that narrowed the field of his interest to Beatrice, whose physical deformity and astringent tongue alike made him nervous, and Fanny, who responded to his rumbustious overtures with no more interest than she had shown in the military manoeuvres of Elliot Fulbroad, finally yawning without concealment. He tried hallooing up the table to Susannah, but she was listening attentively to Ambrose on literature and pretended not to have heard him. William beckoned to a servant, and, dismissing the claret, as 'Thin, washy stuff, not to be contemplated by gentlemen of style!' settled for downing glass after glass of port and informing the table in general of the merits of his black stallion, Lucifer, describing its exploits, swearing there was not another to match it in the length of the county. James noticed Sedley looking sour and grinding his meat between his teeth with vicious thoroughness. 'A horse in a thousand – nay, in a hundred thousand. A bit of blood there – something slap, dammit! I'd match him against anybody's, any day!' William boasted.

Ambrose, distracted from a discussion of Miss Burney's *Evalina*, murmured contemplatively: 'He doth nothing but talk of his horse.'

A look of mischief crossed Susannah's face. She returned softly: 'God made him, and therefore let him pass for a man.'

Ambrose, startled, said: 'You naughty minx!' and broke into a low grating chuckle that lasted for some time. The idea that Shakespeare might be quoted back to him for amusement as well as edification was evidently a new one.

'What's this?' Mrs Waterton demanded, rearing her turbanned head from her plate. 'Have I missed a joke? I enjoy a joke.'

'Mrs Stacey was enlightening me with Mr Shakespeare's words,' Ambrose replied, still smiling.

'Ah, was she? Mr Shakespeare, I protest. 'Tis a dull subject for a dinner table.'

'An excellent subject, if you've the knowledge to discuss it.'

'Too dry for me.' Mrs Waterton dismissed the bard, spearing herself another piece of roast turkey.

Ambrose returned to Susannah. 'So you believe there should be more to a man than prowess with horses?'

'I prefer a man of many parts.'

'I am told you have many talents yourself, Mrs Stacey,' Ambrose said reflectively. 'Tell me, have you read much of Shakespeare's works?'

'Only those that I read with the Blands.'

'And which are those?'

'We would read aloud of a winter's evening: *As You Like It*, *Twelfth Night*, *The Merchant of Venice*, of course – '

A loud crash interrupted her. The curtains of the centre window blew in, a heavy object thumped to the floor and slid across it; glass tinkled. Miss Waterton screamed; the men gasped and leapt to their feet; William Waterton's chair crashed to the floor behind him.

'Oh! Whatever was that?' Rosalind uttered, a hand to her mouth.

'A brick, I believe,' James said, striding round the table to the window.

122

'Be careful!' Ambrose whipped out.

'Are we under attack?' Beatrice enquired.

'God knows!' James said. He twitched back an inch or two of the curtain to the side of the long window and looked out. A three-quarter moon was riding above the trees, but it was partially obscured by mist and his eyes were still dazzled by the myriad candle-lights of the dining-parlour; he could see nothing but blackness beyond him. But that was reassuring: no blazing torches menaced the house. Everything seemed still. 'Nothing to be seen,' he reported.

Behind him Ambrose was ordering the menservants to run to the next room to look; should they perceive no immediate danger, no angry crowd, they were to collect reinforcements as they went and hurry into the garden and into the park and search. If there were any men lurking then they could perhaps be apprehended. 'Now go – and fast!'

James bent to retrieve the brick that had caused the damage. A piece of paper was wrapped round it, a note pierced and torn by the glass it had smashed through. James read it aloud.

' "Wee will not suffer you to Inclose. You shall not take what is rightly ours not Land nor Beastes nor Monny. We are all minded to this and Bound by it. If you do not concede our Will then we shall have our way and God have Mercy upon you." '

Beneath was a crudely drawn dagger and the words 'Beware the fatel Blade'. James did not mention this.

'Good Lord!' Ambrose said. 'An unpleasant missive.'

The other men crowded round James at the window, peering and exclaiming, voices clashing as each made his own assertions as to which man or men had made this cowardly attack. 'That man Bidewell again – ' 'A group of village bullies – ' 'The Bull's landlord is bitter enough – ' 'And so is Truckle – ' 'Transportation's the answer to such threats – '

Only William was not with them; he had decided that young Mrs Stacey needed reassurance and was happily breathing port fumes down her neck as he patted her shoulder.

Rosalind was dithering by the table. 'Perhaps I should go to the kitchens,' she said with obvious reluctance. 'The maids may be upset.'

'You sit down, my dear,' Mrs Bland advised her. 'Your

cook'll deal with any hysterics soon enough. That's if she's any sense herself. There is nothing we ladies can do but keep calm.'

'I agree,' Beatrice said. She was peeling a pear, the skin sliding neatly between her fingers. 'The more you fuss over them, Rosalind, the more they'll believe there is something to be fussed over. Fanny! For heaven's sakes, are you all right?'

Fanny had turned so white she was almost green, but a part of James's mind noted that she looked repelled rather than afraid.

William's hand was stroking the nape of Susannah's neck. 'No need to worry over the ruffians, m'dear,' he said. 'I'm here to protect you.'

Susannah twisted her head to look up at him. 'With you beside me, Mr Waterton,' she replied, 'I shall not worry over anything further.'

Beatrice's eyes blinked her appreciation of the double-entendre.

'William!' Mrs Waterton squawked. 'Stop mauling Mrs Stacey – she's no need of your attentions. Make yourself useful and pour Fanny a brandy, do.'

William scowled and went for the decanter, only to be fore-stalled by Sedley who grabbed it from beneath his hand, poured a glass for Fanny and then moved ostentatiously to comfort his wife.

One of the servants reappeared and spoke rapidly to Ambrose from the doorway. Ambrose listened and nodded and turned back to the company.

'It would appear we have nothing immediate to worry us. Two of the maids were in the stillroom when they heard the crash and they report hearing running feet. Both are adamant that it was only one pair of feet. No one has been seen outside. I imagine the man, whoever he was, has long since gone. I think we can safely return to our meal.' He ordered the broken glass and the brick removed and sat down.

Elliot Fulbroad said: 'The rogue who has done this must be caught and severely punished.'

Ambrose gave him a look of faint hauteur. 'I doubt that he will be caught,' he said repressively. 'But should he be, then we shall know what to do with him.'

Elliot was sensitive neither to overtones nor to implications.

124

'I'd have that man Bidewell arrested, sir. He stoned our carriage – a brick would not come amiss to him. If his child has died 'tis likely he would be in just that sort of temper.'

Mr Bland leaned forward, looking annoyed, but Susannah's cool voice spoke first.

'It could not possibly be Barney.'

'And why could it not?'

'He can neither read nor write.'

'Precisely so,' Mr Bland nodded.

Elliot looked disconcerted, but not for long. 'There are plenty of men in the village who could have written that note for him. There is a regular little nest of Jacobins preaching sedition and stirring up opposition to enclosure.'

Susannah said in a humble voice: 'Mr Fulbroad, I am but a woman and perhaps do not fully understand the words you use. Pray, what do you mean when you speak of Jacobins?'

'Why, revolutionaries, Mrs Stacey. Men who have caught the infection of those murdering Frenchies. Folk who plot to destroy the way we are governed, to pull us all down.' He gave her a supercilious look. 'Envious persons of the lower sort who think they are as good as their betters because they have a smattering of education.'

'Revolutionaries seek to change our lives utterly, do they not? Violently to overthrow all the old ways?'

'Yes, I think you could say that.'

The whole table was silent now, listening.

'So those who oppose all change could hardly be called Jacobins?'

'No –' Too late, he saw where her questions were leading him and stopped abruptly.

'Then, Mr Fulbroad,' Susannah concluded triumphantly, 'how can you possibly accuse those who oppose enclosure of Jacobism and sedition? They do not urge anyone to violent change. They wish only to preserve rights that have been theirs for many hundreds of years. Is that not so?'

'Ho!' William Waterton let out a great roar of delight, banging the table with his big hand till the wineglasses jumped and tinkled. 'She has you there, Fulbroad! She has you there!'

She has us all, James thought exultantly. She has shown us all up for the blustering bigots we are; idle fools mouthing catchwords and pompous phrases without a thought to their true meaning. As pretty a piece of cross-examination as ever I heard, by God.

Fulbroad was crimson. He spluttered something, but nobody heard; they were all too busy exclaiming and chuckling and arguing. James glanced along the table. Ambrose's lips were twitching, Beatrice was applauding; even Fanny was smiling as she sipped the last of her brandy.

'Your wife has as sparkling a wit as ever I heard, Sedley, damme if she hasn't,' William exclaimed, mopping a dribble of port from his chin. Sedley inclined his head, but he did not look pleased.

At most dinner parties James welcomed the withdrawal of the ladies from the gathering; he enjoyed the more relaxed atmosphere that prevailed in their absence, the male discussions of politics or gaming or the breeding of livestock, the passing of the port without the disapproving eyes, the occasional bawdy stories, but tonight the conversation seemed flat, the spice was missing. When the time came to join the ladies for coffee and tea in the drawing-room, he led the way.

The ladies were deep in discussion of Jessica's first ball, to be held in a few weeks' time, and gave no sign of having heard the approaching men. Miss Waterton was addressing Susannah.

'Of course, this must all seem very strange and new to you, Mrs Stacey,' she said in a voice of honeyed vinegar. 'All of us had to make our come-out, but you never did, did you?'

Beatrice interposed: 'My dear Augusta, no such thing. I had no coming-out celebrations, nor, come to that, did Rosalind or Katharine.'

'Oh! Well, no, naturally ...' Miss Waterton stuttered with embarrassment. James could read her thoughts upon her face. Beatrice could never have – not with that indecent limp! Or her sisters – Katharine so pock-marked and Rosalind with dyspeptic red nose and her awkwardness. 'But that was different. So difficult for you ...'

Beatrice continued gently but implacably, 'My cousin Susannah came out upon her marriage.'

'Yes, well, I suppose ... one could say ...' Miss Waterton was writhing, but recovered sufficiently to make her protest. 'Your cousin, did you say, Beatrice? I do not understand you!'

'My cousin. You must know that we are related – through Susannah's grandfather, Sir John Overton.'

Miss Waterton, shocked but determined, her mother's beady eye upon her, said: 'But I thought, I believed – Beatrice, you are speaking of an illicit relationship. You cannot wish to claim – no, no, it is unthinkable.'

'Whatever the birth,' Beatrice said, 'it is the breeding that counts, is it not? Breeding and accomplishments. I have heard you say so myself. And my cousin has both.'

'My sentiments entirely,' said James.

12

Sedley found himself a prey to conflicting emotions in the weeks that followed the Manningfords' dinner party. He had anticipated that the first big social occasion of their married life would be a testing time for Susannah, but while he had not feared that she would let him down, it had been disconcerting to find her the success of the evening.

He was considering this as he went to the stable to saddle his mare, Coquette, one morning in late-October. The day was bright, with thin streaks of cloud flung across a blue sky; the still air held a fresh, damp, sweet smell of fallen fruit and rotting leaves and cool earth. The mare snorted a welcome, her breath steaming out towards him. He slapped her neck absently as he opened the bottom half-door of her stable.

Susannah had made Elliot Fulbroad, a guest of the Manningfords, look foolish upon a matter that was dear to their hearts and they had applauded her. Sedley found this unaccountable. Indeed, he had feared that somehow the episode might rebound upon them, but it had not been so. The Manningfords having made clear their approbation, all those people of any importance who had not previously waited upon his bride had now made good this deficiency – with the exception of the Fulbroads – and invitations to dinner parties and evening parties had been showered upon them. Sedley shook his head and reflected upon the hollowness of social success.

Coquette was skittish this morning, jerking and sidling about as he struggled to saddle and bridle her. Perhaps he was communicating his own unease. He barked at her to stand still.

In one instance Susannah's popularity was particularly vexatious: William Waterton did not bother to conceal his interest. 'A lively filly,' he called her, and flirted outrageously. Sedley felt that his familiarity demeaned her; he thought Susannah should be far more repressive in her manner. Indeed, he warned her, he should not wonder if the younger men were not placing wagers upon the outcome of William's advances. But Susannah was unconcerned. She had actually laughed, saying that Mr Waterton was the same with every pretty woman and that it was a shame for him there was such a dearth of them in Abbotsbridge and Brambourne.

Sedley frequently found it hard to persuade Susannah to his own way of thought. Not that she ever argued, she was as adept at side-stepping contentious issues as anyone he had ever met, no, she simply went steadily on in her own way. At times he longed for a quarrel, a vehement dispute in which he would demonstrate her total wrong-headedness and reduce her to tears, thus marking himself as master in their marriage. He pictured himself as mopping her tears afterwards; he was not, he thought, an unkindly man. But the opportunity never arose.

Her family now: he had spoken to her before about their too-frequent visits, yet still they continued, and twice Mr James Manningford had called to find Jack at the vicarage. Such encounters unnerved Sedley, but not Susannah. A disagreement upon principle should not make men enemies, she said, such meetings were just what was needful to make them understand each other better. And somehow she contrived to have the two men sitting together in apparent amity discussing the merits of Mr Tull's seed-drill, or the four-course, as opposed to the three-course, crop rotation, while he, their host, followed their discourse with difficulty.

Despite this, her attitude to James was not conciliatory. She said she did not care for him; at various times she had spoken of him as high-nosed and condescending, as a hard man who cared little for the poor and as shockingly opinionated. Sedley could not agree; he considered James a friend, and a generous one. He pointed out the numerous small gifts that came from the Manningford household and the courteous visits. Susannah shrugged and her manner towards James continued cool, even when he brought her with his own hands a Dutch vase to hold the autumn flowers and berries with which she liked to decorate their rooms.

Sedley tugged irritably at Coquette's girth. It was extraordinary how infuriating women could be – and how often they could contrive to put one in the wrong, even when one was not. Just take this business of made-up dishes. He had always despised hashes and ragouts and piquant sauces as frenchified, an excuse for masking left-over food. But when he protested she opened reproachful eyes and said: 'Well, had I known, I would not have served it. But it was a special recipe Mama had from the cook at Abbotsbridge House. And if we can save money in small ways, Sedley, perhaps you could afford to have a curricle, if not a barouche.'

He had to admit she was clever with the house-keeping. For a third of the sum his mother spoke of expending they lived twice as well. Of course, it was a different matter living in the country from living in a town. Already Susannah had set herself up with a cow and poultry and her parents had provided a side of bacon for the freshly white-washed kitchen and three young pigs to root about in the orchard. Susannah had christened the pigs Alpha, Beta and Gamma. Becky said that Gammon was a suitable name, to be sure, but what alphabets had to do with pigs she couldn't tell. Becky looked after the stock well, forbidding her mistress to carry the heavy buckets. Sedley found the vicarage economy fascinating. Nothing was wasted; all their left-overs – peelings and stalks and whey from the cheese-making – went to feed pigs or poultry, while they were blessed with fresh eggs, milk, cream, butter and cheese. And Susannah was never idle; when she walked in the village her eyes scanned the fields and hedgerows for the promise of sustenance: mushrooms and hazel-nuts, crab-apples and blackberries. 'Food free from God,' she would say. There was food free from other sources, too. Bath and Oxford could never vie with the generosity of the countryside. Hardly a day passed without its gift to his doorstep: a hand-plaited basket full of duck eggs from a grateful parishioner, a hare from Mr Bland after a morning's coursing, damsons from a neighbour. Sedley's breeches were beginning to be tight about his middle.

He was intending to have a word with his clerk this morning; the singing in the church was intolerably bad; only the clerk and two other men and they the worst he had ever heard. He swung himself up into the saddle and was urging the mare forward when the half-grown cat, Ladyship, shot under her nose in hot pursuit of a rat. Coquette promptly seized the excuse to buck-jump and jiggle her way round the house to the road, causing her master to swear breathlessly as he struggled to restrain her. The mare calmed, he became aware of William Waterton and James Manningford riding towards him, both with a look of barely suppressed amusement on their faces. Red-faced, he acknowledged their greetings with a curt nod.

'On your way to do good?' William enquired. 'What fellows you churchmen are! But first, you could do us some good if you would!'

Sedley raised his eyebrows.

'We were unfortunate enough to run into that appalling man Fulbroad in Abbotsbridge,' James said.

'He invited us to shoot his coverts with him tomorrow morning,' William continued. 'Neither of us can stand the man, so ...'

'So we told him how delighted we should be to accept had we not already engaged to go shooting with you,' James ended with a grin. 'And there'll be the devil in it if you cannot oblige us! Can you come?'

Soothed and flattered at being preferred to the powerful Mr Fulbroad, Sedley expressed himself delighted. This when all was said, was why he had desired a country parish.

The men gathered up their reins and prepared to ride on.

'I trust your wife is well,' James flung over his shoulder. 'Do we see you both at the Goddards' tomorrow?'

'Yes, indeed,' Sedley replied. 'But you may see Mrs Stacey before then. She will be at Abbotsbridge House later this morning. Your cousin Miss Katharine invited her to discuss her tapestry work, I understand.' There was a note of complacency in his voice. He was gratified that there should be friendship between the Manningford ladies and his wife.

As the two men rode off Sedley glanced towards the vicarage. As he thought, his wife was sitting sewing on the window-seat of the dining-parlour. Her head was bent; she gave no sign of having noticed the conversation in the lane. Quite correct, he approved, he would have disliked to have her

131

call from the window, or, worse, come running out as ladies like Mrs Bland would do. Susannah would be putting the finishing touches to the new covers for the dining chairs. A most satisfactory saving there.

His wife had been more than a match for old Miss Humby, a stout body with a hairy wart on her chin and a dominating manner. It had been clear from the start that the cart she had hired would not accommodate all the furniture left by her dead brother. 'I am loath to relinquish relics that hold memories of the poor dear man,' had said Miss Humby, patting her nose with her handkerchief, 'but I feel sure you would like to offer me something for the better pieces. It would be to your advantage, after all, Mrs Stacey.' Susannah smiled, but declined. Her generous husband was buying all they needed in Winchester; she would burn anything Miss Humby could not take. Sedley thought of intervening at this stage, but a twitch of Susannah's eyebrows stopped him. After consideration, Miss Humby abandoned the dining-table and chairs as past praying for, together with an oak bedstead, a Queen Anne walnut lowboy on cabriole legs ('So out-dated – do pray give it to one of the cottagers!'), and a brass mantel clock with an eight-day movement. She also instructed Susannah to dispose of Mr Humby's clothes to the deserving poor.

After she had gone Susannah danced a jig of triumph round the dining-table. 'You have taken leave of your senses!' Sedley protested. 'Look at those scratches and white rings! And all the chairs are rickety.'

She stopped, breathless. 'You wait and see ... they all will be ... transformed.'

Two days later Jack appeared with a spotty youth he introduced as a joiner; when they left the table glowed a burnished red mahogany and the square taper legs of the chairs sat firm on the floor. 'Astonishing!' Sedley admitted, but pointed out that the stuff on the seats was still tattered and shabby. 'When I have time I shall embroider handsome new ones,' Susannah assured him, adding briskly, 'but first they must have temporary covers – and I can obtain the material at no cost at all! My mother has some snuff-coloured brocade in her garret chest, hideous in its present form as a hooped gown, but just the thing for the chair-seats. She will be delighted to have a use for it.'

Sedley allowed Coquette to break into a trot and then a canter. If Susannah was transforming the vicarage, so must he enlighten and transform the church and the parish. Mr Humby's regime had been shockingly lax. The matter of the music was not the only matter to be raised with his clerk, Kimber, but since it ranked high with the Waterton ladies it would be best to sooth their wounded susceptibilities before embarking on more contentious matters. In the meantime there were all the mundane problems that one had to contend with in any mediaeval and previously ill-run church: doors that squealed on their hinges, leaks from the roof, frayed altar-cloths, an overgrown churchyard, a cracked bell that rang flat and a belfry colonised by noisy and dirty bats. When all this was put right and the parish reverberating with his praises, then he would venture into matters of doctrine.

Susannah put the final stitches to the last of her brocade seat covers, stood, stretched and went to smarten herself for Abbotsbridge House. Beatrice Manningford thought it a good scheme for Susannah to discuss the designs for the final covers with Katharine; comparing ideas could be an inspiration to them both. Beatrice called upon Susannah regularly, watching the progress of the refurbishment of the vicarage with interest, admiring her eye to colour and to style, remarking that she had no such talents, which, in any case, would be wasted, since it was hardly likely she would ever be in a position to renovate a house of her own. Susannah enjoyed her company despite the perverse delight Beatrice seemed to take in provoking her over the matters of enclosures. Although she disclaimed any wish to improve her mind, Beatrice read widely, including, she admitted, several of James's books on agriculture. 'When one has nothing else to hand,' she said, 'anything is grist to the mill. I am become quite an expert upon the better breeding of cattle and the cultivation of turnips and clover and the artificial grasses! Cousin James should lend his books to your brother Jack. He would understand then why enclosed farming is necessary.'

Susannah put on her new pelisse, and brushed her hair with

care. The nursemaid might have been elevated to the curate's wife, but she was still far from the Manningfords' eminence; Susannah was determined not to give them or their servants anything to despise in her.

She was surprised how different the drawing-room at Abbotsbridge House looked in the morning light from when she had first seen it. A servant ushered her in and Katharine rose from where she was sitting with her back to a far window and came forward to greet her, but Susannah found it difficult to concentrate upon the soft platitudes coming from beneath the half-veil as to the weather and her husband's health. In candlelight the room had been sumptuous with rich fabrics, sparkling with handsome ornaments and portraits. Now she saw that the rose-red silk hangings on the walls were faded in streaks, the gilded frames of the ancestral portraits were dingy and that the central medallion on the carpet was showing signs of wear. It disconcerted her; a family as reputedly wealthy as the Manningfords should have all about it perfect: she could not conceive how they could have allowed such decay to occur without rectifying it.

Katharine requested the servant to bring refreshments and invited Susannah to sit beside her, taking up an embroidery frame from her chair and showing her the work. 'Not an exciting piece this, and quite coarse. It is to cover a carriage stool for Beatrice.'

The strongly oriental cone and medallion design was being carried out in tent stitch, in deep reds and blues. Susannah thought it handsome and said so. What she could see of Katharine's face looked pleased but embarrassed. 'And I greatly admire the chair seats in your dining parlour, that formal scroll and flower border enclosing a different exotic bird on each chair is the most skilful design I ever saw. I'd be grateful to have your help with my work.'

'Oh, I make no claim to genius with design,' Katharine said in a flurry of self-disparagement, 'and I am sure you have your own ideas. It is just ... my sister thought we'd both be glad to find someone to share our interest.' The mouth beneath the veil smiled diffidently.

It occurred to Susannah that Katharine was nervous. It was unexpected in someone of her birth, but then she had always hidden herself away; she could never have been used to sharing her concerns and ideas with friends. 'She was right for my part, Miss Katharine,' she said, adding lightly, 'Mr Stacey is less than enthralled by stitchery, and while Miss Beatrice said she liked to see good work, she confessed she loathed sewing herself.'

The smile widened. 'My sister occupies herself in other ways, as you will know. But, Cousin Susannah, I am sure Beatrice has told you to call her Cousin. Please do the same with me.'

'I should like to,' Susannah murmured. Then, almost without her willing them, the words sprang out: 'But please take off the veil, Cousin. I hate to talk to someone whose eyes I can't see. 'Tisn't natural.'

The veil shuddered. 'I never inflict my disfigurement . . .'

Susannah said gently: 'It's no infliction to me. Remember, I have seen your face before.'

'You have? But when?'

'In the summer, when I fainted in your hall. I felt such a fool that day! But you were kind to me and I was very grateful. You were not veiled then and I remember as I came round seeing your face and thinking that it was nothing near so bad as folks made out.'

'Oh! Oh, truly?' Doubtfully, 'Well, I do not know . . .'

'I do. I think the veil is more disfiguring. And there is no one else here. Please!'

Reluctantly, slowly, a hand went up to pull off the veil; Katharine averted her face. The skin of her jawline was drawn taut; the tendons on her neck stood out: Susannah could feel the anguish of her embarrassment as though it were tangible, and it caused a responding stab of anger in her that Katharine should have to suffer and to hide for such a wanton cruelty of nature.

'Your pockmarks are nasty,' she said slowly, 'but most of them could be hidden.'

'How?' Katharine asked vehemently. 'Do you think I have not agonised over them endlessly? I could wear my hair as long and shaggy as a tramp and still they would show, and still I should not be fit to go about. When I was a child the villagers stared and the children shouted. Never again!' She began to stitch angrily at her tapestry.

A servant came in with refreshments, and with her limped Beatrice, flushed from riding in the fresh morning air, hungry and cheerful. She helped herself to a slice of cake and stood eating it without a plate, the crumbs scattering on the carpet.

'I have ridden over the downs,' she told them, 'and I have a devilish appetite. And how have you progressed? Have you brilliant designs ready for Susannah to work upon?'

'Heaven help us, not yet!' Katharine protested.

'I have been distracting my cousin with talk of disguising her pockmarks,' Susannah added.

Beatrice's eyebrows shot up. 'Have you, indeed? I noticed the veil was off. How would you disguise them, then? What special ideas do you have that the rest of us have missed?'

Aware of antagonism in them both, Susannah forced herself to speak. 'I have two main thoughts. The first would be to change the hairstyle so that the temples were concealed, the second to design a cap to hide the forehead: those are the worst areas, the rest are nothing. Old-fashioned patches would mask the pits on the right cheek and the eyebrow, and that shallow mark on the left cheek is no worse than many ladies have.'

'As simple as that! The magic wand indeed!' Beatrice's voice was lightly satirical. 'But how does a cap conceal the forehead? It would have to resemble a nun's wimple to do that.'

'Not as I would have it. It would have to be carefully designed, of course, but I envisage it in the finest muslin with a ... with a frill, as it were, of delicate lace to fall round it, just long enough to conceal the pocks.' She added, rather desperately, 'It could look most romantic and unusual. If I had a cap with me, and some fine lace, I could show you.'

A short silence. Beatrice asked: 'And the hair?'

'Parted in the middle and drawn back on either side but softly.' Her fingers gestured over her own face. 'No fringe, no curls, but pinned up at the back under the cap. The temples would be covered.'

The sisters looked at each other.

'Like a Quaker woman,' Katharine said. 'Do you know, I rather like that.'

Beatrice pushed the last of her cake into her mouth and dusted off her fingers. She went to the door. 'I shall ask Rosalind for one of her caps. And I shall find some lace.'

When James came into the room twenty minutes later Katharine was studying her reflection in the big gilded looking glass over the fireplace, with Beatrice and Susannah on either side anxiously awaiting her verdict. All three turned as the door opened.

James greeted Susannah, then hesitated, stared, and stared again at Katharine. 'Good God!' he said. 'What a transformation. I would not have believed it.'

The colour rose in Katharine's cheeks. 'Do you like it? It was Cousin Susannah's idea. I own, I had my misgivings, but I do think it is an improvement. Is it too outlandish?'

'Certainly not. I confess I hardly knew you, but that was the unexpected change. You should keep it that way.'

This male appreciation of her new mode clearly pleased Katharine, who turned back to the mirror for a further lingering scrutiny.

James stayed talking to them for several minutes, refusing Beatrice's offer of cake with the observation that he could not understand the female prediliction for such sweet stuff, but pouring himself a glass of wine and eating a couple of figs. Beatrice wanted to know why he was about the house at such an unusual time of day.

'What's that? Oh,' James said, 'I remembered I had to look out some papers, some stuff for William Waterton. He is interested in the notes I made when I stayed with Mr Coke at Holkham, those on his farm leases containing covenants requiring certain methods of cultivation to be used.'

'I remember you telling me,' Beatrice said. 'A sensible idea.'

Susannah looked from one to the other, her eyebrows raised. James turned to her, asking how she proposed returning to Brambourne.

'On foot,' she replied brusquely. 'How else?'

'On horseback,' James said. 'Our ways lie together; you could ride with me. I daresay Beatrice would lend you a horse and my groom could return it. No need for you to trudge.'

Beatrice nodded. 'Harry will know which to saddle.'

'I will leave you ladies to talk while I collect my notes, and we shall leave in, let us say, half an hour,' James decided. 'Unless you would rather not ride with me, Cousin?'

'I will ride,' Susannah replied, her voice cool.

It was not Beatrice's precious skewbald that she rode, but a young bay with a sensitive mouth. They had cantered in silence down the avenue between the autumnal limes, dropped to a walk and turned into the Brambourne lane before James spoke.

'You are very quiet, Cousin Susannah.'

'I was thinking, Mr Manningford.'

'I have asked you before to call me Cousin,' he said.

'We are not cousins, Mr Manningford. Your branch of the family is not related to my family in any way.'

'It is related by marriage,' he retorted. 'That is sufficient to my mind. What were you considering so quietly?'

'I was considering how it might feel to be a future tenant at Abbotsbridge, having my freedom to farm constrained by my lease.'

James glanced drily across at her. 'The present system has its constraints, has it not? No one is free to experiment as he wishes in the open fields, be he tenant or owner. Every man is tied to the level of the worst and most backward-thinking farmer. The covenants I wish to introduce combine, for example, the old idea of forbidding the sale of manure off the farm, with more positive instructions, such as following a sensible modern course of crop rotation and not taking more than two crops of corn successively.'

'My father and brother would farm in such ways anyway,' Susannah said scornfully. 'Why must you treat men as fools?'

'Because, dear Cousin, some of them are. The Truckles and the Pettifers and the Smallwoods of this world put nothing into their land and they wear it out. With the country at war with France we shall need all the food we can grow. Nothing will ever persuade me that it is right to encourage foolish farmers to continue in their folly, above all, never on Manningford land.'

She frowned. There was truth in what he said. But he showed no comprehension of the difference between stupidity and misfortune; he lumped the lesser folk of the village together as if they were all alike – and, indeed, his plans would reduce them all to the lowest level. 'How,' she asked abruptly, 'did you come to the decision it was right to enclose?'

There was silence for several seconds. Susannah's horse tossed his head, fretting at the tense pull on the reins. James contemplated her. 'You tell me,' he said, 'how you come to the decision to kill a pig.'

'Well, really,' she said angrily. 'That is hardly ...'

'No,' he interrupted swiftly. 'Do not misunderstand me, I am interested in the steps of making that decision, what stages you would go through.'

'Well,' she said reluctantly. 'I should consider whether the pig could produce more flesh yet, against the need for the meat now.'

'Yes,' he said. 'Pray continue.'

'If it was ready to be killed off and we were almost out of bacon, well, then the job would have to be done.'

'And then?'

'Then the butcher would be called in.' Her head was haloed by the rich colours of the beech hanger to their left, where the turning leaves gleamed gold and copper and bronze. Against their brilliance her eyes had a smoky darkness.

'Yes,' he said. 'Yes, that is how it went. I considered that the land under today's system could produce no more food, but we have a need for that food now – another year of war and our village larder will be almost empty. The old system is ready to be killed off.'

'And you are the butcher!' she flared at him.

'If you like. Your butcher does a necessary job. He takes on the unpleasant task of killing the pig so that you shall enjoy the meat.'

'But these are people you are dealing with, not pigs, Mr Manningford!'

He raised his eyebrows. 'The Pages? Black Betsey Pettifer? Oh, come now,' he teased, 'I have frequently heard their hovels compared with pigsties – and to the pigs' credit!'

For a moment he thought he saw an answering glint of amusement in her eyes, but then her lips compressed themselves and she turned so vehemently upon him that her horse jerked his head in fear.

'That is you entirely,' she said. 'Arrogant, condescending and selfish. Scorning everyone, caring nothing! You despise these people for their poverty where a better man would sympathise. You think you can take what you want and leave them to suffer – well, you'll soon learn 'tisn't so easy, my brother 'ull show you that! He's going to fight you over the common and go on fighting.' Caught up in her tension, the horse half-reared and almost threw her. As she struggled to control it, she added furiously: 'And I'll tell you this, too, a pig would show more understanding of poor folks' predicament than you do, for all your fine education and your knowledge of the law.'

His hand flew out and she thought he would strike her, but instead he snatched up her reins to calm the upset horse. For a moment they jostled for control, their animals wheeling, his body looming over hers. When he jerked his horse back again they sat staring at each other, breathing fast. A faint wind stirred the fallen leaves and sent them scuttling round the hooves of the stamping, shuffling horses.

When he spoke his voice was very quiet. 'I would not take such words from anyone but you. And I do not acknowledge any truth in them, though you may have cause to think it from my actions in the past.'

'Yes,' she said. 'I do.'

He continued as though she had not spoken, ignoring the matter of the common, going straight to the heart of her anger. 'I have not asked your forgiveness for what I did to you, because it was unforgivable. I acknowledge that. But all that I can do to make your life with Mr Stacey more tolerable I have done, and shall continue to do.'

'Invitations to dinner and to evening parties!' Susannah interjected with scorn. 'Oh yes, I am aware of your contrivings!'

'I don't believe Mr Stacey despises such parties,' he said. 'He now moves widely in our local society and his contacts may well succeed in obtaining him the preferment in the church that he courts.'

'And then you could be rid of us both, rid of the embarrassment of my presence. What a sensible manoeuvre!'

'Do stop lashing out at me,' James said tiredly. 'You cannot lash me more than I have been lashing myself these past weeks. And an excess of spleen cannot be good for the baby. Cousin Susannah, I do not wish to be rid of you. It is not you I dislike, it is myself.'

A dozen matters that she wished to throw at him had jostled on the end of her tongue and now, in an instant, had vanished.

Unexpectedly disarmed, she found herself speechless. They sat motionless, silent, one flushed with emotion, one pale, until an outburst of coughing from a middle-aged man walking down the lane recalled them to their surroundings, and they set their horses into motion.

The man approaching them came with a bow-legged trampling gait, tugging a lurcher on a piece of rope behind him. He was a man in his forties, with the weather-beaten face and slightly hunched shoulders of one who lived his life in the open. He was wearing an olive-green smock frock over corduroy breeches and ribbed worsted stockings. As he drew level with them he hawked and spat fluently, directing his spittle at the hooves of James's horse. The horse stepped sideways, its haughty lift of the head mirroring that of its master. The man stared at Susannah, jerked his head to her and tramped on.

'So Truckle will not truckle to me!' James remarked.

'Are you surprised?' Susannah returned. 'You are planning to ruin his life.'

'I am? I think perhaps you had better tell me about Master Truckle. No, wait! First, tell me if he can write.'

'I believe he can.'

'And he certainly looks capable of hurling a brick.'

'I would think so.'

'But you would not commit yourself?'

'I would not know.'

'No? No, I think you would not. Pray forgive my interruption and tell me about him.'

Susannah paused, collecting her thoughts. 'You will already know,' she said, 'that he has about fifteen acres. And you have commented that he puts little into them. But he did once. And he does his best now. It was a series of misfortunes that did for him. And you are the last and worst of them, you will probably finish him.'

'I see,' James said evenly. 'Continue.'

'There was an outbreak of sheep rot a few years ago, not long before the war started. He'd put his savings into sheep, ran a score or so with the others under the old shepherd, and the rot took them all. He wasn't the only one to suffer, but he lost the most, and I suppose he had borrowed to buy some of them, because I remember my father speaking of his debts and I know he had to sell a couple of acres. Then he broke his arm the next spring which for a man working virtually alone is a terrible disaster. I know how bad it can be because my father broke an arm when I was young and that meant hiring someone to do his work. Dear Lord, that was a bad year we had. It was then that I went to be nursery-maid at the Blands. But Sam Truckle could not afford to hire anyone. His wife and his sons did what they could, but they went downhill badly and they've never been able to pull back since. His arm isn't as sound as it might be, either. If you take away the common from folk like him, it is the end. His pony, his two cows, his wife's geese – they all depend on the common.'

'Even with the common it is a struggle for men like him,' James said slowly. 'I wonder they keep it up for year after year.'

'A struggle?' she repeated. 'I do not think you could possibly understand: no one could unless he had lived it. You have only been here a year, you have seen nothing yet.'

'Then why do men do it rather than seek employment?'

'Because they know nothing else. And because it is their land, their one great possession, and while they work it they are beholden to no one, and because there is always the hope that *this year* the harvest is good, *this year* the animals will do well, perhaps *this year* they will be able to expand. And the land has its own attraction, its own beauty, daybreak and twilight, spring and autumn.' She looked across at him. 'You know this, you must do, else why have you chosen to come here?'

James nodded. 'It is true. But then I have come on different terms.'

'Very different.' She gave him a look that was almost pitying, and then she was speaking swiftly, her body leaning towards him, drawing him a word picture of that life that he did not know. She told him of the battle to turn the land from an adversary into a friend, a personal, deep and endless battle, for to the countryman the land was not only the acres he worked, but an array of elemental matters that sometimes would work with him and at other times fight him: it was windswept downs and marshy valleys; it was fields of green blades rippling in the spring breezes and smashed acres of oats lying in the mud of a storm; it was the crying of new-born animals and the lowing of the dying. Susannah was determined that through her words

142

James should feel something of the sweat of carrying swill and heaving muck; the backache and chill of cleaning turnips in the winter fields. It was slow work, she said, trudging work, for a reward that was never immediate. In spring the land was mild and lovely, vibrating with bird-song and the bleat of lambs; at harvest-time it granted men its bounty of corn and fruits. But at all times it demanded service, and a love that was often close to hate.

Although they were walking the horses slowly, they were at the gate of the vicarage before the words stopped. James slid from his horse to help her dismount; her body was heavier now and she landed awkwardly. From the way he looked at her she thought he was aware of her thickened waist, and the thought constrained her. At the house a curtain twitched; Sedley had seen them and would be hastening out to offer James wine and biscuits. Quickly, formally, she thanked him for accompanying her.

'It is I who should thank you, Cousin Susannah,' he said, equally formal. 'It was an instructive ride. You make your case well.' He swung himself back up on to his horse, the groom appeared to lead the bay Susannah had ridden, and they were gone.

Sedley appeared at her shoulder, scolding her for not bringing Mr James in.

'He was expected at the Watertons',' she said absently. 'He would not have stayed.'

'I do not know what he will have thought,' Sedley said.

'No,' she murmured. 'Nor do I know what he thought.'

13

Two days later Fanny came to visit Susannah. She had just carried a message from her mother to the Watertons, and she was in a fretful mood. Susannah was not in the best of moods herself, for she was feeling unwell and the fact that it was her own fault merely increased her discomfort. At the Goddards' the previous evening she had hoped for an opportunity to continue her discussion with James, only to find that her bridal eminence as usual placed her next to her host at dinner, while later, to her disgust, when the gentlemen at last joined the ladies, he had not so much as glanced towards her, but took his coffee into a corner with Mr Bland and Mr Knight and stayed there. In consequence, Susannah had drunk too much wine at dinner and too much coffee afterwards and was now suffering from headache, nausea and bad temper.

Becky brought in refreshments, but Fanny declined to take anything. 'Ugh, no, thank you. I have already addled my insides sufficiently at the Watertons'. I do wish they would not be so avid in pressing one.'

'Are you suffering too this morning?' Susannah asked sympathetically. 'No, no thank you, Becky, take them away, do.'

Becky removed herself and her tray with a reproachful glance and could be heard in the passage muttering to Ladyship about certain ladies who overdid themselves. ''Tis a crying shame, puss, 'tis indeed!'

'Becky!' Susannah called and the muttering stopped. Susannah and Fanny giggled faintly.

'At least she cares about your health,' Fanny said.

Susannah looked at her discontented face. She knew Fanny.

144

'What is it?' she asked. 'There is something more than indigestion bothering you.'

'Mama. What else? She kept me up until the small hours, scolding. Apparently I was unforgivably rude to Timothy Goddard, ignoring him at dinner. I was entirely unaware of it, I assure you, but she says I interrupted him right in the middle of some story about a poacher to speak to Miss Manningford about having her pianoforte tuned. Did you notice it?'

'To be truthful, yes. He did look hurt, poor man.'

'Oh dear! Did he? And I didn't believe Mama. No wonder she was cross. And I quite like Timothy. At least he doesn't prose on endlessly about the political situation to impress me or leer and strive for opportunities to touch me like William Waterton!'

'Does he?' said Susannah. 'And I thought it was only me he favoured, being so recent arrived.'

'He does it to you, too? How horrid men can be. And Mama thinks I should admire them and flirt with them, and strive to persuade one to marry me!'

'But you must get married soon,' Susannah protested, half-laughing. 'What else could you do?'

'That,' Fanny said, 'is the root cause of my disagreement with Papa and Mama. Susannah, I have seen an advertisment in the *Morning Post* offering special tuition on the harp – from a famous musician in London. Only think how wonderful that would be! I could stay with my Aunt Anne while I studied, and then I could give concerts. Only very select concerts, I assure you, in private.'

'And they disapprove?'

'They are not averse to my having a season in London – I might contract a suitable marriage there – but they say such specialised music teaching is unnecessary, and to give concerts unthinkable for a lady of quality.' Fanny had rejected the offer of a season out-of-hand; the marriage mart was not to her taste: 'Being ogled like a maid at a fair? No, I thank you!' Frustrated in her dearest wishes, she was more than ever at loggerheads with her parents.

'Your father and mother wish only the best for you,' Susannah murmured. 'They care greatly.'

'For the person they would like me to be,' Fanny retorted,

'and not for me as I am, otherwise they would not have expected me to replace you in playing nursemaid to my brothers and sister. I her Mama complaining that I am heartless, that I have no care for them, but it is not true. I am fond of them, but I am not fond of listening to William endlessly reciting off his Latin verbs or correcting Humphrey's spelling. Nor can I be any help in the parish or the house, I simply have not the gift. But I do have a gift for music, and if I do not concentrate upon it now and develop it I shall be nothing but second-rate all my life.'

'Untrue. You are beyond that now.'

Fanny rushed on as if she had not spoken. 'Oh, I could escape through marriage, but to what? To more cares of household and to having a baby every year and to listening to the tiresome conversation of my husband and his friends? Men's interests are so narrow. When James Manningford first arrived from London I thought he might be different. It was fascinating to hear him speak of concerts and theatres and books and he plays well, but now ...'

'What do you mean, he plays well?' Susannah interrupted.

'He is no mean performer upon the pianoforte. Did you not know? Yes, indeed, and his voice is not to be despised either. But he has now become as excruciating as the rest of our local turnips, and talks of nothing but crop yields per acre or Ransome ploughshares. I declare, it makes one quite despair.'

Susannah nodded absently, gazing into the little darting flames of the fire that Becky had kindled, mulling over this latest piece of information about James. It was unexpected, out of character with her image of him: it made her uncomfortable, as though somehow, ridiculously, she had misjudged him. She wished she could hear him play.

She became aware that Fanny, who had fallen moodily silent, was speaking again. She looked up. Fanny was leaning forward, her voice low. 'Susannah, you are married and ... I am not stupid ... I know you are in a certain condition ... pray forgive me for discussing it but there is no one else I can talk to ...' It came in a rush: 'Susannah, it's so dreadful – how can you bear it?'

'Bear what? Having the baby, do you mean? The birth?'

'All of it.'

'Oh, it's not so bad. I'm not frightened. I know that some women have problems, but I don't expect them for myself.'

Fanny shuddered. 'It horrifies me. It always has. I remember when my mother had the boys. Each time ... first the sickness, then her body, so gross and distorted ... and then, when her time came, I would hear her moaning – I would cover my ears from the sounds, but still I would hear them. And once I saw one of the maids rushing from the room with the towels all bloodied. I nearly fainted. I was sure she would die. It was terrible. It still is terrible.'

'You mustn't think like that,' Susannah said urgently. 'It's only nature working, after all, and I can't believe God intended it to be dangerous or frightful. I remember when Sedley and I drove to Winchester, watching the crowds of people in the High Street and thinking that every one of them had been born of some woman – and there were so many that clearly it could not be so very bad!' She chuckled. 'It was amazingly reassuring! Think of it in that way.'

Fanny shook her head, her eyes turned away from Susannah, her embarrassment clearly at odds with her need to unburden herself. 'It is not only that,' she said, so low that Susannah could bearly hear her. 'It is another matter ... I do not wish to be married.' She swallowed. 'The thought of ... that ... disgusts me.'

Susannah drew in her breath. She was not the person to help Fanny there; her own experience was not such as to make her wax lyrical. The sexual union between her and Sedley had not noticeably improved since their wedding night; at times she wondered if his refusal to allow her to participate was not a subtle punishment for her seduction of him. She did not know his views for he refused to discuss such matters; they were forbidden territory. Yet despite her disappointment, she was certain there was more to a man and woman's relationship than she had known. She remembered the warm sensations James Manningford had aroused, and she recollected how, in the novels Fanny lent her, the heroines went through unimaginable vissicitudes to fly to the arms of their lovers: surely not for the performance Sedley inflicted upon her in the stuffy confines of their curtained bed, every night except Sundays.

147

She looked at Fanny's averted face. 'If you love someone,' she attempted, 'it is surely different.'

Fanny shook her head, her fingers busily pleating and unpleating the folds of her gown. 'I have thought about it and thought about it – about marriage, that is, and I see nothing in it for me. Not in any aspect. And I have tried to make my parents understand, but all they do is shake their heads and look mysterious, and say that I am young yet and innocent; these things will be revealed in God's own time. Susannah, what am I to do? I cannot forever go on as I am.'

'I know. But surely there must be some way out.' Susannah eased her body into a more comfortable position on the sofa, picked up the curtain she had been hemming when Fanny arrived and threaded her needle; she could think better when her hands were busy. Fanny's revelations had not taken her by surprise: her distaste for most men ... that constant preoccupation with music ... her brilliant playing of the harp. Concerts, she had said ... Susannah's mind ranged ... and twitched into action. 'Wait, I have a thought.'

'It is more than I have. What, pray?'

'Concerts, you said – and your parents were shocked. Yet you are asked to play at evening parties here ... and others play ... Miss Waterton, who constantly tells us she is doatingly fond of music, Miss Manningford. And James Manningford. Why should we not get up private concerts here?'

'A musical club?' Fanny asked doubtfully.

'Exactly.'

'Do you think it would answer?'

'You can but try. And then your Papa and Mama would understand the harmless nature of concerts given to a select party. It would take time to establish it, but by then, why, you would be old enough to be your own mistress!'

'Goodness, yes! How clever you are! Ah, but, Susannah, who would do the organising? Mama leaves me so little time to myself.'

'We'll manage somehow,' Susannah urged her. 'No, I have it – Miss Waterton! Put the problem to her – not the whole of it I don't mean, but the arrangements – she will leap at the chance; she loves to organise!'

Fanny giggled, her eyes alight with excitement. 'So she does.

And perhaps her efforts will distract her from the botanical walks she urges upon me, and that Mama will not let me evade. I see it all.'

'And there is more. If you have to practise for a concert, Mrs Bland will realise that you need more time to yourself. One of the servants will have to keep an eye on the boys while they are playing – young Lizzie, for example.'

'Indeed!' Fanny jumped to her feet, seized her reticule and prepared to leave. 'Do you know, I have to go for a walk with Miss Waterton tomorrow and I was dreading it! Now I can put your idea to her and it will actually be a pleasure. And I will tell you someone who might play with us – Katharine Manningford. Yes, I have seen the great changes you have made; her poor face will never be perfect, but at least she can face her friends now. And she plays the flute – did you know?'

'Do not rush her,' Susannah said firmly, putting down her sewing. 'To show her face to her friends is one thing; to face the world again is another. She has been many years in seclusion, don't forget.'

'Oh, I know,' Fanny said happily. 'I shall not push her, only coax. And it will take some time before we are ready, naturally. But it will be such fun to plan. For once in my life, Susannah, I shall have something good on my mind.'

As Fanny walked away from the vicarage, Susannah had an urgent thought. She called softly after her: 'Do not let Miss Waterton know it was my idea, will you? That could be fatal.'

Fanny returned her a sidelong glance of mischief. 'Do not worry, it had already occurred to me – only I was not so impolite as to mention it! And I shall not tell her that you have a Voice either, not yet.'

October gave way to November and Susannah's father and Jack came to the vicarage armed with bill-hooks, scythes and a saw, to help Sedley clear the second vicarage meadow; they had dealt with the other two weeks previously. The day dawned fine, if damp, and Susannah planned to enjoy herself; she would relish a day in the open, even if she were not permitted to do more than tend the bonfire.

Starlings were chattering among the chimney pots as she walked down the path to the meadow and she thought how pleasant it was to hear them; homely, almost human. But the eerie squawks of half-a-dozen seagulls circling and squabbling above the meadow were far from homely; she had seen too many of them this autumn and it made her uneasy. She had noticed the rich crops of berries in the hedges and the way the rosehips hung in profusion; now she made a mental note that the winter would be a bad one.

The three men were hard at work. Thomas was hacking at the brambles amid loud curses for the thorns that clutched at his clothing, Sedley was tugging ivy from the hedge, while Jack had taken himself off to the far boundary to saw up the branches that had fallen from the old elm trees there. Near the gate an overladen bonfire was emitting pungent gusts of smoke. Susannah smiled, seized a fork, removed the tangled skeins of ivy that were choking it and with expert hands thrust dry twigs into its heart until first little tongues of fire ran among them and then the whole pile burst into flames, sending sparks sailing up into the raw air.

Mid-morning, Becky brought a jug of ale and tankards out on a tray and the men gathered round her, wiping their brows with their cuffs and easing their shoulders and backs, discussing the progress of their work. Thomas strolled over to speak to his daughter, a moustache of foam on his upper lip.

'Sukey, my gal, you may look well, you may feel well, but you shouldn't oughter be doing this. No. An' pulling branches about is no work for a lady, neither.'

'They're only small ones and nobody can see,' she protested, casting more sticks into the fire. 'If I get tired or cold I'll go in, I promise. I'd die of boredom if I had to sit with my feet up all day.'

'Ah,' her father said meaningfully. 'But if you're too restless the babe 'ull come early, an' then you'll not be able to say it come early – if you take my meaning. 'Twill be too early!' He mopped his mouth and then his forehead with his red handkerchief, scowling affectionately at her.

'I'll take care,' she said. 'I'll save your good name.'

'No light matter,' he told her, putting his handkerchief in his breeches pocket and pulling on battered gloves. 'Your mother worries.' He trudged back to the brambles.

'Look' Jack said, joining Susannah. 'Your little cat has come to discover what you are about. Curiosity incarnate, cats.'

Ladyship was stalking along the hedge, lifting her feet high to avoid the lank grass, darting glances about her. Sensing their attention she sprang up a sycamore sapling and scrambled out along a branch, crouching and lashing her tail. Susannah stood on tiptoe to twiddle a twig for her.

'You are all right, are you?' Jack enquired softly. 'The parson treats you well?'

'I have no complaints,' she said, her back turned to him.

'That is no reply.'

The cat pounced and caught the twig. The narrow branch swayed dangerously; Susannah jerked the twig away to tap it behind her, coaxing Ladyship back to safety. 'He buys me clothes, he spends money generously on the house, we are well entertained by our neighbours – what more can a woman want?'

'There are other things, especially for a woman like my sister.'

The cat leapt for the trunk, clung precariously, her claws rasping, then slithered down backwards. Susannah turned to face Jack. 'You have no need to worry – I am content.' She continued rapidly as he seemed about to question more: 'But what about you? You are the one with the problems. Mama tells me of meetings in the village, of discussions with attorneys, of endless arguments. What is happening?'

He shrugged. 'Endless arguments – in a nutshell. Mr Manningford is having the petition for enclosure prepared. It will be presented to parliament in December, to the best of my knowledge. We are having our petition against enclosure prepared likewise. But there are still many who disagree with this method of fighting it – violently disagree.'

'Sam Truckle?'

'Among others.'

'Did he throw that brick?'

'No, I believe he did not throw it.'

Something in the tone of Jack's voice caught her attention. 'Oh, of course, how stupid I am. Sam wrote the letter, Berry Truckle threw the brick! Does Josh Pither know?'

'No. Or Berry would be out of the forge in an instant. Josh, thank the Lord, wholly backs my petition, and bellows his wrath against any who threaten violence. I only wish John Hayter would do likewise at The Bull.'

'How do you reckon your chances of success?'

'With the House of Commons landowners to a man? Not good! Oh, if it is well prepared and well fought we must have some chance. We would not be doing it otherwise. But there are those who would prefer to burn barns.'

'At least the hopes for the petition are stopping them for the moment. And maybe the lapse of time will cool their tempers.'

'That is my prayer.'

Susannah bent to pick up more trails of ivy and flung them on the fire. In the heat they spluttered and twisted; flames licked through them. ' "Yet man is born unto trouble, as the sparks fly upward," ' she quoted softly. 'Tell them from one who was there, that the brick broke the Manningfords' window, but it did not dent their resolve.'

'I will.' He grimaced, his eyes tired. 'And you in turn can tell me something, Sukey. What is Mr James Manningford up to now?'

'I have no idea. Why?'

'He has been visiting people in the village, Mr Stent, Mrs Pern, even Sam Truckle and the Pettifers, and asking questions. He wants to know in detail about the animals they keep on the common and their importance to each household, but also whether they have any surplus from their produce to send to market.'

'I know nothing of this,' Susannah said, her face thoughtful.

'And he has asked about their families and how they live and even how healthy they are. Some found this offensive; Sam said he swore at him to tend to his own business. Does it all not seem strange to you?'

'Strange in him,' she said slowly, stirring the edge of the fire with her foot. 'But anything I discover, you know I will tell you.'

By mid-afternoon the meadow looked like a meadow again rather than a wasteland, though the grass was lank and muddy where it had been trampled upon and the dead stems of thistles and nettles and docks poked up through it in stark clumps. 'Pigs!' Thomas advised Sedley when they stopped for a drink of

152

tea. 'Loose your pigs in here for a short while. They'll nose up the nettle roots and eat 'em, love 'em, they do! They'll drop a useful mite o' dung, too.'

Susannah stood with the men gazing into the distance. The sun was disappearing behind a scattering of clouds, lighting them rosily as it went; against its glow the freshly denuded branches of the trees stood in skeletal beauty. Rooks were starting to fly homeward across the fields, straggling in twos and threes. A flock of long-tailed tits appeared in a wild cherry halfway down the hedge, exploring it, somersaulting about the bare twigs. Something disturbed them and they flew off, their white tail feathers flashing. Then a blackbird startled up its warning call: 'Pink, pink, pink!' repeating the one note endlessly.

Jack said: 'There's someone behind the hedge!' He called, 'Who is it? Come here, will you.'

A silence; nothing moved. Then abruptly, seeming almost to emerge from the ground beside them, a gipsy-looking boy appeared. The men stepped back, startled.

'Arthur!' Susannah said. 'Hullo.'

The boy looked at them warily, only his dark eyes moving. He wore a filthy shirt under a torn leather waistcoat laced together with string, and breeches that hung in folds over his bony thighs. He looked about fourteen, possibly fifteen. 'I wor doin' no 'arm,' he told them. 'Jus' lookin'. No 'arm in that.'

A wayward breeze stirred the bonfire; sticks crackled, sparks rose. Arthur's eyes slid sideways towards it. 'I'll 'elp ye with that,' he offered to Susannah. 'You bin goin' slowish an' light ent goin' to last long.'

Susannah looked at him. He stared back, pushing matted black curls from his forehead with his wrist. 'That would be kind,' she said. 'Thank you.'

'Really, Susannah!' Sedley protested. 'If this youth is the person I take him to be, then I hardly think you should encourage him.'

'I am a little tired,' she acknowledged, 'and who are we to refuse an honest offer of help?'

'Well, I hope you know what you are doing,' he said, and stalked back across the meadow to where he was raking up the debris.

Thomas and Jack shrugged, picked up their tools and followed him.

Arthur moved quickly, silently, stoking the fire and stirring it to new life. From time to time he stood back to survey it, lifting his head to watch the smoke sailing in a long plume towards the dying sun.

'You like bonfires?' Susannah asked.

'Them's clean,' he offered after a moment's deliberation. 'Smell good, too.'

'They do, don't they,' she agreed. She took a deep breath and snuffed the scents of the evening appreciatively; woodsmoke, crushed grass and the cool, clear smell of the earth. Beside her Arthur flung wood into the heart of the fire, turned to collect a heap of old man's beard to add to it, held out his hands for a moment to the heat. He must have been cold creeping up the hedge, Susannah thought; his rags were hardly adequate covering for November's chills. She looked at his gipsy's head against the sky and thought that the life of Black Betsey's son could never be easy: no one would trust him, employment would be nigh impossible to come by. It was known to their neighbours that the pair of them squabbled constantly, for they cursed each other with uncaring vehemence and an unrivalled line in obscenities. Yet Arthur could not be wholly bad, as the gentry made out; it was Betsey he poached for, he had cared – in his own rough way – for his dying aunt, and he was said to have some feeling for his little brother, Harry.

'Arthur,' Susannah said, pouring him a mug of ale and thrusting it into a grimy hand, 'would you set some rabbit snares for me?'

He drank the ale, his eyes watchful over the mug.

' 'Tis the kitchen garden where I've seen them,' she explained hastily. She grinned. 'Nothing illegal. And any you catch we'll share – first to you, second to me, and so on.'

He put down the mug, wiped his lips on his hand. 'Could do,' he nodded.

She gathered a handful of twigs and stood beside him to throw them on the fire. 'I heard a nasty tale the other evening,' she said softly. 'It could go hard on anyone who goes poaching in Squire Waterton's preserves – he's talking of using mantraps.'

He glowered. 'Them's evil.'

'Yes,' she said. 'Poaching may be wrong, but maiming a man's worse.'

Arthur thrust a hand through his hair and went back to work with a vigour that was almost frenzied, running up and down the field to collect the last of the rubbish; poking the bonfire till its flames lit up the dusk like a beacon.

As the men turned to leave the meadow, Susannah approached Sedley, carrying a large garment that she had run back to the house to collect. 'Arthur can have Mr Humby's old coat,' she told him. 'Miss Humby said to give it away.'

'Give it to that ne'er-do-well?' Sedley protested. 'Miss Humby meant it for the deserving poor!'

'He deserves it,' Susannah said flatly. 'He has no coat.' She turned and thrust it into Arthur's arms. 'You have worked well,' she said, 'and I am grateful. And I hope you can make good use of this.'

The boy clutched the coat, holding it against his thin chest. He looked at her, then at Sedley, who was muttering that he had intended to give it to his clerk's eldest boy, and then he bolted.

'You see!' Sedley said. 'He did not even have the grace to say thank you.'

'He would not know how,' Susannah said. 'He has no one to teach him manners.'

With the improvements to the vicarage largely completed, Susannah and Sedley gave their first dinner party, inviting Mr and Mrs Bland and Fanny together with the Goddards and their son Timothy. This would give Fanny the opportunity to lavish attention on Timothy, Susannah remarked with amusement, not only requiting him for her previous snub but also delighting her parents. Sedley would have preferred to invite the Manningfords and the Watertons. Susannah disuaded him: people might think them pretentious to have invited the great folk of both villages; besides, to have James Manningford's satirical eye upon her, not to mention Mrs Waterton and her daughter judging them upon every matter of little moment –

'Dear's my soul, no!' said Susannah. 'My knees would knock with nervousness – and imagine should Becky spill gravy down

Miss Waterton's latest gown! 'Twill be Becky's first dinner party, too.' Sedley was not concerned over pretentiousness, but her last point carried weight.

When the ladies withdrew after the meal, Mrs Bland took Susannah into a corner for what she called a comfortable coze. She was full of news and worries, but first she had to enquire in embarrassing detail about the progress of Susannah's condition. 'And no swellings of the ankles? No low backache? I am relieved to hear it. You have been doing far too much – do not deny it, I know it – the changes you have wrought here speak for themselves. Not that you have not done well, this room is quite charming and the dining parlour, too – most elegant! I don't hesitate to say that you are a credit to your upbringing. But Mr Stacey will not want to be calling in the doctor to a sick wife, will he? Oh, and Lord bless me, I nearly forgot to tell you, Dr Huskett is to retire, his gout is so very bad now, poor man.'

'When does he go?'

'Not until the spring, I believe, and he has promised to find us a successor. I'd as lief have someone young and with modern ideas; one cannot deny that Dr Huskett is a stick-in-the-mud.' With a glance at Fanny, sipping coffee and dutifully persevering with the delicate and dull Mrs Goddard, Mrs Bland dropped her voice. 'I will not hide it from you, Susannah, I am concerned for my husband. The good doctor may say he sees no cause for worry, but I do not like the look of him.'

'What is worrying you?'

'There is a mixture of symptoms that point to ... to something nasty, that's where my suspicion lies. He is always so tired nowadays, and he never was used to be. He has headaches. And he is breathless from nothing. Why, I saw him walking up the rise to the rectory t'other day and he'd had to stop to rest. He said 'twas naught but I'll swear he was in some pain – and his lips were a horrid sort of mauve.'

'Oh dear,' Susannah said. She knew now where Mrs Bland's suspicions were heading, and she had an uncomfortable feeling she was right.

'Yes!' said Mrs Bland, with a kind of macabre triumph. 'Precisely! And I cannot say I am surprised at it, not with the troubled year we have endured. Mr Humby's death was most upsetting, and then there was the worry over you and Mr

Stacey, and worst of all that business over enclosures – my poor husband took it dreadfully to heart the way the villagers turned upon him, and who can blame him? Then Fanny has been so difficult and unhappy. What am I to do with her? I don't wish to seek for another governess: at the ages the children are now we should be able to manage between us, but Fanny is hopeless. She thinks of nothing but music, music, music.'

'And you know you are truly proud of her,' Susannah said quickly, uneasy at being confidante to them both. 'Such skilful playing is quite out of the ordinary, everybody says so. She has the touch of a great musician.'

'But I don't wish for a daughter of mine to be a great musician,' Mrs Bland wailed. 'I never expected such oddity. I expected a daughter who would enjoy balls and assemblies and marry to the credit of her family and give me grandchildren. As I did for my mama and as you are doing, Susannah. No,' she corrected herself hurriedly, 'not exactly as you have done, but ... well, you do understand what I mean, don't you? I am at my wits' end with Fanny!'

Susannah said with diffidence: 'Perhaps if she's happy with her plans for a concert then she will be more cheerful over her teaching duties.'

Mrs Bland gave her a straight look. 'If you believe that, Susannah, you must be more of an optimist than I am. But I shall try it, yes, I have said I shall try it.'

The appearance of Becky with fresh coffee was a welcome interruption. Fanny, Susannah thought, was a nightingale caught up in a flock of starlings; something remote, uncommon and exquisite; it was absurd to expect her to find contentment in the commonplace bustle of the rectory. How the chubby, chattering Kitty Bland could have produced such a daughter was incomprehensible. But it was also a tragedy. Her mind met this unexpected thought, jerked with shock, and was forced to abandon it unexamined as Mrs Bland started again upon her family's saga of problems.

'And Daniel, too. A grave disappointment there!'

'But he is happy now with his cornetcy?'

'In the Fifteenth Light Dragoons,' Mrs Bland told her. 'As his uncle was. He's busy purchasing his accoutrements and arranging for the transport of his charger. He will be paying us a visit shortly and then he will be off to the Low Countries. That does not make us happy, I can assure you! Mr Fulbroad tells us terrible tales of the campaign there. There has been an undisciplined retreat into Holland, he says, and all the men are suffering from fevers and agues. And one cannot help thinking, suppose those dreadful Frenchmen, those Jacobins, should capture Daniel? He could be guillotined!'

'I do not believe that prisoners-of-war are ever guillotined,' Susannah said reassuringly. 'They put them in a camp.'

'If only I could believe so,' Mrs Bland sighed. The sound of the dining parlour door opening and cheerful voices in the passage told them that the gentlemen were relinquishing their port to rejoin the ladies. Mrs Bland leaned closer towards Susannah. 'Quickly, tell me, has Mr Stacey heard again from his mama?'

'Yes,' Susannah admitted reluctantly. 'A letter came two days ago.'

'And is she to visit you shortly?'

'No, she is unwell.' The heart spasms that had afflicted Mrs Stacey at the abruptly presented news that her son had married an unknown and portionless girl had not yet abated, the shaky lines of writing had informed them; Mrs Stacey could only thank God for the dear friends in Bath who comforted her in this crisis and the excellent apothecary who attended her.

'Then when does she plan to come?'

'Possibly in the spring. Sedley tells me she has a horror of winter travel.'

'Well! A horror of winter travel, indeed! Heavens,' Mrs Bland hissed as Sedley appeared, 'if a son of mine were in such a situation I should be on the road in a trice, come snow or hail or floods. I should not rest until I had met my daughter-in-law!' And she rose from her chair and took herself off to talk to the be-spectacled Mr Goddard.

Susannah went as a good hostess should to deal with the gentlemen's coffee and tea and found herself being told by Timothy Goddard how highly he thought of Fanny's notion of a musical club. 'The very thing for her!' Timothy was in his early-twenties, not long down from Oxford, compact in build, ingenuous, with the trusting and candid eyes of a young animal. The eyes slid now to where Fanny was sitting with his mother, rested for a brief moment and then swung guiltily back to his hostess. 'And an inspiration to us all to keep up our music,' he added. 'I'm sure it must prove so,' Susannah agreed and he beamed at her and told her how much he had enjoyed his dinner. He asked if Mrs Stacey played an instrument and chuckled when she said that her performances on the spinet or the pianoforte were for her own amusement, never the public's, and assured her he was the same. But she could sing? She admitted she could, a little; he said he would look forward to hearing her. Susannah wondered why so pleasant a man had so little appeal and concluded that he was too pleasant; there was no edge to him, no challenge. Recently she had seen a stag standing on a knoll in a woodland clearing, his antlered head raised, a wild and handsome animal defying all comers, his does behind him. He'd had that male arrogance, that air of natural self-confidence that men like James Manningford and William Waterton radiated: Timothy was too tame.

Mr Bland coming then to have his cup replenished, Timothy sidled away and managed to manoeuvre himself a chair next to Fanny. Susannah scrutinised the rector covertly: his bluff good-natured gossip about the Brambourne village characters was as it always was, but his eyes were tired, and there was an underlying greyness to his skin that she had never seen before. And brown blotches were developing on his hands: grave spots, Martha Pither called them.

14

Winter came swiftly, frosts pinching, dank mists rising from the
ditches and the river; the polished floorboards were cold to
Susannah's feet in the mornings; the cow lowed her complaints
at being permanently in her stall. Susannah kept busy, using
work as an outlet and a distraction from pangs of conscience at
how she had used Sedley, from unbidden worries over whether
her baby might, as her father had said, come earlier than early.
She cooked, she baked, she sewed, she arranged dried autumn
leaves and berries in great vases for the church, she agreed with
Mrs Waterton which of Brambourne's sick and needy she
should visit. She adjusted herself to her new rôle without
conscious effort, suiting herself to its changed rhythms as an
actress would dispose herself to the rhythms of a new performance. By the time dusk fell her body was lulled with the tiredness which fell on her more heavily now, her mind drugged with
the day's achievements. Then came the evenings, the long
candle-lit hours of silence and Sedley's recounting of his day's
accomplishments and silence again, he staring into the fire, she
endlessly stitching. And then to bed and the dull submission to
Sedley once more.

She had no complaint against Sedley, no complaint against
Fate: she still strove to deepen the relationship with him, but
was fast coming to the conclusion that it was impossible; it was
not in him to respond. Only their social life was proving an
unexpected bond. Sedley encouraged her developing friendships with Beatrice and Katharine Manningford and was prepared to spend money on entertainment if it was carefully laid
out to forward his preferment schemes. The plans for Fanny's

concerts were excellent, in his view; his wife's participation would bring them both to the notice of a wider circle of acquaintance. The times when they dined out together were pools of light in the dull landscape of their marriage. But with winter these dwindled; the nights were long and dark, the lanes treacherous with mud; only the Manningfords' ball shone as a great event.

The Manningfords had planned for full moonlight and they got it; the great arc of the heavens was cloudless and the mud was frozen hard. Susannah had the unaccustomed luxury of a fire in the bedroom and the help both of her mother and Becky in preparing herself.

She had not wanted to be among the early arrivals and to her relief, by the time the Blands had themselves arrived and then sent their carriage for the Staceys, the ballroom was rapidly filling. She and Sedley entered unobtrusively behind the Fulbroads, who surged in on a wave of gushing exclamations to the squire and Miss Manningford: 'So delightful ... such delicious greenery!' 'Hothouse plants, I vow and declare!' 'A dazzling gatherin', Mr Manningford!' Nothing could have exceeded the dazzling nature of their own attire, father and son in suits of cut velvet silk with opulently embroidered waistcoats, and mother and daughter robed in the most expensive gowns, loaded with lace and trimmings and sparkling jewellery. Susannah had not met Miss Fulbroad before, for the eldest of the three Fulbroad girls had only just returned from a long stay in Bath, but she did not care for the haughty tilt of the heavy-chinned head as Ambrose Manningford introduced them, still less for the words she caught, muttered to her nodding father as their group moved away, of Miss Fulbroad's surprise at Mr Manningford's asking her to meet such a person.

Inside the ballroom Susannah took a deep breath and blinked at the brilliance of the lighting; what seemed like hundreds of candles shone in the Venetian chandeliers, their flames reflected back from the magnificent polished clusters of glass in a thousand points of light. As at the start of the Manningfords' dinner party, her heart was thumping; she was more used to social occasions now, but at least there she had known everyone by sight, tonight there were many strangers, powerful-looking men with freshly powdered hair talking to

161

patrician ladies wearing modish creations that made her own efforts, so elegant in the vicarage bedroom looking glass, seem the pathetic contrivances of a nobody. She looked for the Blands, whose party they were to join, but could not spy them through the surrounding knots of chattering guests. People she knew began to pass and greet her and Sedley; fans waved and snuffboxes snapped; she curtseyed this way and that, a touch awkward from the tight bandage round one ankle. The Goddards arrived and introduced a friend of Timothy's, John Forbes, a wealthy banker's son; like Timothy, he was dark and earnest and his eyes were shy. The Watertons nodded as they passed, an odd glint of humour in Mrs Waterton's hooded eyes; in their rear strolled William, over-large and clumsy in fine velvet and lace. At the sight of Susannah, he veered away from his parents and sister to demand that she partner him in the first of the country dances.

Susannah apologised that she could not: 'So stupid of me, but I have sprained an ankle – nothing of any moment, but I dare not dance upon it.'

'The devil you have! How'd ye do that?'

He jerked his chin at a footman and she took a glass of wine from a tray, her eyes sliding sideways at William as she sipped. She was beginning to feel better. 'I slipped on the stairs as I came down tonight.'

'Then tell that girl of yours not to use so much polish. Dangerous things, stairs, eh, Stacey?'

Sedley helped himself to wine. 'You were saying...? Oh, the fall, yes, a pity.' But Sedley showed little regret over the accident that prevented his wife from dancing with William. He turned away to catch the eye of an acquaintance.

'And I was planning to show all these folks how the country dances should be tackled,' William mourned. 'Of recent, they've become as staid and dull as a minuet. But you're a sweet goer! Together we'd give 'em a grand show!'

She shook her head, smiling. 'Not tonight.'

He made a disgusted sound. Lowering his voice, he said: 'But we can still sit one out together, hey?'

He was interrupted by the appearance of Mr and Mrs Bland, together with Fanny and a sandy-haired young man of about

162

eighteen, thickset and self-conscious in the dashing uniform of an officer of dragoons.

'Mrs Bland, Fanny – Daniel!' Susannah turned from William to clasp the hands of the rector's son, who, when home from school, had treated her with all the casual friendliness and teasing of a brother. 'What a glorious surprise! But why did no one tell me Daniel was to come so soon? You did not know? If that is not typical!'

'Nonsense! You'll have me acting a shabby part next. Truth is,' Daniel said, his eyes flicking to the stern face of his father, 'I got my military gear together faster than I thought possible, discovered a fellow I know about to head for these parts and persuaded him to take me up in his carriage.'

'And we were not complaining at his early appearance, were we, my dear?' Mrs Bland said, her eyes, too, turning to the silent rector.

As Daniel began to ply Susannah with questions about her new married status – 'Your stunning transition to parson's wife!' – and how she relished the rôle, William stirred restively, tried unsuccessfully to regain her attention, shrugged his shoulders and detached Sedley from the little group to bear him off to the card room, where, he said: 'The entertainment 'ull be better and polite conversation ain't required.'

The orchestra was tuning up; Timothy Goddard appeared, lean, palely adoring, blinking with self-consciousness, to claim Fanny as his partner; a ripple of movement passed through the assembled guests; the chaperons and the elderly sought seats by the great log fire at the far end; Jessica Manningford appeared with Elliot Fulbroad to lead off the first dance.

Daniel said: 'You don't want to dance, do you?'

Susannah laughed. 'Clearly you do not. Remember your Latin – a negative question requiring a negative answer? And mine is no, my ankle has a slight sprain, so I cannot.'

'Then you should be sitting, not standing.'

'I have been standing like a patient heron, on one leg, longing for some kindly person to help me to a chair by the fire.'

He studied the chaperons. 'By those old toughs? You are joking!'

'Never in my life,' she murmured demurely.

He led her to a nearby couch. 'Still the same irrepressible

Sukey! When I first saw you tonight I thought you utterly changed, so poised and serious – and Mama was saying you had taken on maturity overnight – but I suspect 'tis surface only!'

As the guests prepared to take the floor Susannah watched Jessica curiously. Beatrice and Katharine had asked her to advise Jessica on concealment of the puckered cheek, since she had been so successful with Katharine's problems, but, oddly, Jessica's problem, though the lesser at first sight, had proved the more intractable. Perhaps this was partly the girl's character. She was resentful of the need for help, scornful of Susannah's credentials to give it, angry that her sisters should have invited her without permission; her eyes had been clear and hard as pebbles in a stream as she stared at the mirrored comparison of her own looks with Susannah's in her bedroom. Susannah had played with her hair, making suggestions, receiving no encouragement. In the end, exasperated by the girl's rudeness, the mantle of her mother had descended upon Susannah and she had been blunt. 'There is no way you can hide the cheek, the damage is too great. What must be done is to distract attention from it.' Against all logic this approach had worked. In the glass Jessica's face had looked back at her, startled, the mouth slightly open. The lines of irritability vanished as though a hand had pass over them, smoothing them away. Jessica had blinked, once. 'How?' she had asked.

The music started. Elliot bowed, Jessica curtseyed; the dance began. At first the couple were alone on the floor, performing together for the acclamation of the watching guests. Susannah noticed that Elliot appeared more self-conscious than Jessica. He made a couple of forced remarks to the girl; his laugh was overloud. In comparison Jessica was calm, her back very straight, her steps exact. The new arrangement of her hair had been well done; the mass of ringlets twined with seed pearls suited her, softening the long, rather bony face, while the rich fabric but simple lines of the ball-gown displayed an excellent figure. Beyond them stood Hector Fulbroad, the centre of a group of guests, gesticulating, full of comments, his thick neck swelling with complacency.

Other couples began taking the floor; Rosalind Manningford's gloved hand was on James's arm, a lieutenant from the navy was partnering Miss Fulbroad, Timothy's friend John Forbes had been captured by Miss Waterton. She was surprised to see how many of the older folks were ready to dance; she had thought this pastime the interest solely of the young, but clearly she was wrong; even old Mr Waterton and Mrs Bland were there, their stout bodies performing the movements of the dance with quite as much enthusiasm as their young. Susannah longed to be with them. She shut her eyes, blotting out the sight of the mass enjoyment, the enticing rhythms, angry with her swollen belly for preventing her. And from now on she knew she should keep to the house, make excuses to avoid any entertainments, hide the growing evidence of her pre-marital sins from the gloating disapproval of her neighbours. Depression pounded behind her eyelids, its beat that of the feet on the ballroom floor. But it was no use lamenting: the very problem that prevented her from joining the dance was the indirect cause of her being there at all. And if she could somehow pass the terrifying obstacle of the over-early birth of her child without the revelation of her secrets, then there would be other occasions like this when she could enjoy herself wholeheartedly, no gnawing worries to eat away at her confidence and her pleasure. The depression lifted slightly; she opened her eyes to see Daniel looking at her doubtfully.

'Have you a headache?' he asked. 'Is the heat too much for you?'

'No, no,' she said hastily. 'Only a momentary soreness of the eyes.' And she began to ply him with questions on his future life, about how the army was provisioned as it crouched on the bank of the River Waal, about what clothing he would need to keep him warm there in the Low Countries, and about his horses. Horses Daniel could talk about all evening and possibly would have done, had she not interrupted his description of the magnificent steed he had recently acquired (through great cunning and sagacity at a most reasonable price), to enquire why he had stayed away from home so long.

'There was much needing to be settled about my cornetcy and my equipment,' he said, eyeing her defensively. 'And, as I was telling you, my horse, Caesar, had to be bargained for . . . and there's no need to raise your eyebrows at me, Susannah. You know why, too. There'd have been such a rumpus. I

165

cannot abide being jawed by Papa. He makes a fellow feel such a cur.'

'He was desperately hurt by you.'

'And by you, too,' Daniel retorted.

Susannah winced and acknowledged a palpable hit. 'I know.'

'He does not understand,' Daniel said. 'He is still asking me why I should want to go off and kill other men. As if slitting Frenchmens' throats were one's sole aim. I try to make him see that 'tisn't like that. 'Tis more a matter of controlling a murderous rabble that's hell bent on rampaging across the continent and killing thousands there. As it already has in France. Do you know how many they say are being guillotined in Paris alone every month? More than two thousand. And at Nantes some beast had several hundred children killed – massacred. Papa deplores it from the pulpit – and over the dinner table. What good does that do, safely here in England? I want to be one of those actively helping to stop this terror.'

'You must tell Mr Fulbroad, you will have him on your shoulders.'

'God forbid! Why? Oh, of course, over this enclosure business. Yes, I have heard of the part your brother Jack is playing from Papa, and Fulbroad's stupid views about a Jacobin threat to the village, and James Manningford's new plans also. Mr James called upon my father yesterday about some parochial matter or other and stayed to drink a bottle of wine with us. He is a good fellow, you know. He may only have been in Abbotsbridge for a short time, but he is full of modern ideas and plans for expanding our crop-growing and I am all for them.'

'Indeed?'

'Lord, yes. And Mr James knows what he is talking about in politics, too – you'll hear no croaking from him, he is all for continuing the war. Why, if the French rascals do succeed in over-running Holland then they will have control of all that coastline of the continent that faces us – our life-line, Sukey, in famine years.'

She was irritated to hear James's words in Daniel's voice and even more irritated to know they were true. She stared half-blindly down at the twisting fingers in her lap. Dear Lord, how low it all made her feel.

'But you won't want to hear about politics,' Daniel was saying. 'Let me find us both another glass of wine.'

As he returned so William Waterton appeared at her other elbow, announcing that Daniel need not stay, Mrs Stacey would be well looked after should he wish to join the lively game of faro just being set up in the card room. Daniel hesitated, grinned, and vanished.

'Well,' William said with satisfaction, 'told you we'd sit one out together, didn't I? What d'ye say, we move to the conservatory? You'll not have seen it yet, I'll be bound. I can show you one or two things there.'

She looked at him from under her lashes. 'I did not know you were interested in botany, Mr Waterton.'

'The deuce I am! But other matters take my interest, Mrs Stacey. There are certain ... blossoms, one might say, blossoms of a ripe loveliness, fit to be picked by a man who knows how to handle 'em!' William's eyes were not so much exploring her figure as sucking it in.

'You shock me, Mr Waterton. You cannot mean you would pick a flower belonging to another!' Her voice mocked him. 'And you a magistrate's son, too! Suppose you were found out?'

'Never have been yet!' He let out a great chortle. 'And Parson Stacey's too busy fleecing Fulbroad of his guineas at whist to come snooping and sermonising!'

She shook her head. 'My ankle would never take me there and back.'

He sighed noisily but took the setback in good part, sitting himself down to entertain her with some highly salacious anecdotes about his fellow guests. According to him the powdered gentlemen and their patrician ladies had the morals of alley cats. The baronet talking to old Mr Manningford was well known to be have fathered the heir to the short fellow partnering Mrs Knight. The lady in the primrose muslin was said to have dropped an unwanted infant down a well not a year before she married. And had she heard about Elliot Fulbroad, invited to a lady's boudoir in Winchester and then heard the husband outside? 'Grabs his breeches and flings up the window sash, sees a bush below in the dark he hopes 'ull cushion his fall and launches himself into a holly! Pricked himself, by God!' William shouted with laughter and slapped his thighs. His sister, stalking past, cast him a rancorous look. Three minutes later Sedley appeared, staring down his arched nose at them, a Roman senator outraged.

'Ah, Stacey,' William said easily. 'Cleaned Fulbroad out yet – or have you lost your winning streak?'

'I have played cards enough for tonight. But your friends are looking for you to play basset, Waterton.' His full lips were tight, his tone a breath away from offensiveness.

William shrugged. 'Then you amuse your wife, Parson Stacey, and I'll give her my thanks for a delicious interlude and take myself to the card room.' He bowed to Susannah and sauntered away.

Sedley stood tense, glaring, almost threatening, his head thrust forward towards Susannah. 'You are making a show of yourself, yes, a show of yourself, flirting with Mr Waterton.'

'On the contrary,' Susannah said in a cool voice, one hand playing with her fan, ' 'tis you are making a show of yourself by scolding me in public for the entertainment of the malicious. Pray do not look round, half the room is watching. If you sit down and smile they will turn away in disappointment.'

He half turned, then sat abruptly.

She smiled then, and put her hand on his arm. 'You have no cause for concern, Sedley, I assure you, but I am glad that you care sufficiently to rush to my protection.'

He was taken aback. 'You should have sent him about his business,' he said more moderately.

'I know, I do see that. But I was desperately wondering *how* when you arrived. Your squire's son ...? Without giving offence ...? Perhaps I should ask the other ladies how they manage it.'

'That is what you should do. You, of all people, must take care.'

The evening wore on. Mrs Bland became overheated in the dance, requiring dabs of lavender water on her forehead and revival with a cool glass of champagne; Sedley danced a minuet with Miss Waterton and a gavotte with Miss Fulbroad, then went to converse with Mrs Waterton; Beatrice came to sit with Susannah for several minutes, making amusing and astringent comments on the dancing, telling her she was a fool to have lamed herself.

'I am,' Susannah agreed wryly. 'But one learns much by watching. And I can hardly lament my luck to you, who never dance.'

'But I never have, so I have nothing to lament. I resemble those ladies who never ride, but who love to watch the hunt – and there is hunting going on tonight!' To Susannah's raised eyebrows she added: 'My vixen of a sister, Jessica, and Elliot Fulbroad for a start. But he is riding for a fall with Papa. One would think he might consider his ...'

She was interrupted by Rosalind with a request that she rescue timid Mrs Knight, trapped in a corner by the senior Mr Fulbroad, and eyeing him with the startled fixity of a baby rabbit mesmerised by a stoat. Hector Fulbroad, a widower, habitually stood alarmingly close to the ladies as he made them his florid compliments. Beatrice rose with a grimace to make her way along the room, her halting walk seeming particularly awkward tonight against the lively figures of the dancers in the gavotte.

The music ended: having made their bows and curtseys the ladies and gentlemen drifted from the floor. Susannah watched them, and suddenly, out of the crowds of turbanned heads and curls and feathers and wigs, she saw James Manningford standing fifteen feet away, staring at her. He was wearing a coat and breeches of deepest blue, his waistcoat cream silk embroidered in deeper cream; their simplicity emphasized the breadth of his shoulders and the height of him. Against the background of the gaudy dress of the babbling guests, nothing could have made him stand out more. She clenched her hands on the new shawl that she had so carefully arranged about herself; resentment boiled up in her as abruptly as it had done in the lane to Brambourne, resentment that she must sit in dullness while he danced, that his belly was flat and taut while hers grew daily more distorted. She turned blindly away, her hand searching for her wineglass and then he was there, standing over her, detaching the glass from her fingers.

'Cousin Susannah. Cousin, your glass is empty. This will not do.'

Some man ... John Forbes, the banker's son ... asked her

where Fanny was; Mr Bland passed them, throwing out a comment about the healthy nature of the dancing exercise; a group of gentlemen surged after him, arguing a minor variation to a country dance; she felt dizzy from the constantly varying scene. James leaned to take her hand.

'I can't dance,' she snapped. 'My ankle ...'

'I know,' he said. 'Your husband told me. You have twisted it or sprained it or some such thing. No, I thought you might care to keep Katharine company for a while. She sits alone on these occasions and as you can't dance it would make a change from watching others enjoy themselves. Take my arm.'

It was almost an irritation that he should prove so thoughtful. She rose to her feet, muttering: 'I don't need your help.'

'Take my arm!' he repeated. His tone was quiet, but it was a command: Susannah found herself obeying. As she limped from the ballroom he asked her what exact damage she had inflicted on her ankle. 'Just before your first ball, too. What a ridiculous time to choose!'

'There's nothing whatsoever wrong with my ankle,' she informed him in a low and steely voice.

'Nothing wrong? But why ...?'

'Do you truly imagine that in my condition I can dance? Even in a dignified dance like the minuet I couldn't turn about on the floor without everyone noticing my ballooning shape and gossiping behind their hands and their fans? So ... I have put a pebble in my shoe and a bandage on my ankle and no one raises an eyebrow at my sitting quietly.'

'And you have their sympathy, too!' James began to laugh. 'I never met a female so resourceful as you. Are you never at a loss for some ingenious scheme?'

She could feel his mirth vibrating in the muscles of the arm she was holding. She said: 'My situation has compelled me to be resourceful, as you must admit.'

She felt his arm stiffen and still itself. He said: 'Yes. I know.' And there was something of understanding in his voice. Then he added: 'And I'm about to use similar tactics myself. Perhaps I'm learning from you.'

'Similar tactics? How do you mean?

'In a moment.'

He pushed open a door and she found herself being ushered

170

into the snuff-scented dimness of Ambrose Manningford's library. There was a small branched candelabra on the great mahogany desk, but as the light from its candles fell only on the dark leather-bound spines of books in bay upon bay of shelves, little of it was reflected back; it stood in a lonely amber pool. The curtains at the two great windows had not been pulled and the thin light of the moon and the stars filtered through the glass to fall in two more pale pools before them. On the desk an uncorked bottle of wine and two glasses stood on a silver tray, flickers of candlelight glinting in their depths. James picked up the bottle and poured. She saw that the lace at his wrists was exceptionally fine, his hands immaculately manicured. A vision of her father and brother's muscular hands was suddenly in her eyes, their skins chapped, the fingernails and their cuticles broken and rough; they had no time to tend them; they would never resemble James's. She thought, I do not belong here, why should I be here with folk who understand so little of how life is shaped for others? But then, in unexpected contradiction, as James pushed the cool smoothness of the wineglass into her fingers, she felt that the knotty blistered hands of her father were alien hands also, that his uncouthness was an affront. She was halfway between two lives, not properly a part of either, isolated. She shivered.

'Are you cold?' he asked. 'I shall not keep you long.'

'Not too cold,' she said. 'A goose stepped over my grave, is all. But Cousin Katharine – she isn't here. I thought you said ...?'

'She's trying to persuade Beatrice to retire to her bed. Beatrice has not rested all day; she's been endlessly busy. She will not say, she never will say, but I believe she is in some pain with her back.'

'You are beyond me, Mr Manningford. We spoke together not many minutes since. She seemed cheerful then, her usual self.'

'Yes, she would. But I suspect, and others do too, that the way she hobbles puts a strain upon her back. She goes suddenly white and will hardly speak. She detests giving way to any weakness, but there are times when she must lie still.'

Susannah shook her head. 'I didn't know. How horrid for her. Do we wait for Cousin Katharine here?'

171

'No, I'll have you taken up to her room. But first we must talk. Sit down, please.'

She could not imagine what he had to discuss with her that could not be discussed elsewhere. The half-lit, high-ceilinged room with its smell of old books and snuff made her uneasy, and so did he, so big and assured and dominant and yet underneath, she was beginning to realise, as full of unease as her. She could sense it in the way he looked at her and then looked away, in his handling of his glass, twisting it in his hands till the wine spilled over and dripped unheeded onto the floor. She sat, stiff-backed, waiting.

He took a chair opposite her and by the desk, as if they were both awaiting an interview with the invisible Ambrose. From the ballroom came the thin sounds of the violins playing a country dance, the faint thuds of feet accentuating its beat.

James opened his mouth. 'I'm to be the baby's godfather,' he brought out.

Shocked and unprepared, she blurted back: 'That's impossible. You're his father.'

'Who is to know that?'

'God will know.'

'I think that God might understand my motives.'

'The world would think badly if ever it knew.'

'Damn the world.'

'And I should know.'

A pause. Then: 'Would it worry you overmuch?'

'Yes. Yes, it would. It would be wrong.'

'But it would help the child. Mr Stacey has accepted my offer with gratitude.'

'You have offered this to him? Before speaking to me?'

'I spoke to him not ten minutes ago. I told you I was learning your tactics.'

Silence. A silence seething with emotions while she struggled to find words to express her fury. 'My answer is no, and no again. How could you even suggest such a thing? It – it is indecent!'

He shook his head. 'Stop and think, Cousin. Your genius for achieving the maximum with minimum resources should show you the advantages in this. Unless I stand in some formal relationship to the child I cannot help him. As his godfather I

172

can give him gifts ... a watch, a pony ... More importantly, I can contribute to his education, insist that it is of the best. I believe it is right that I should shoulder this burden.'

She looked across at him dryly. 'Suppose the baby is a girl?'

He exhaled a breath of laughter. 'But you've assured me many times that the child is male. Your son – that's what you said to me. Whichever it is the care will be mine.' He stood to refill their glasses and as he handed hers back he asked, 'Have you always been so argumentative?'

'Oh no,' she said swiftly. 'I was ever easy-tempered.'

'Don't tell me – I know! Circumstances have changed you.'

' 'Tis you have said it,' she returned, but could not prevent her lips from twitching.

He did not sit down again, but wandered with his glass behind the desk to the big window there, to stand in its pool of moonlight, staring out. The cold light fell on his face from above, showing it strangely bleached of colour, all the strong planes and hollows exaggerated. He looked concerned, his lips tight, his shoulders hunched. His eyes were staring without seeing. Gradually, as she watched, wondering whether she should not be leaving the room, fearful lest their absence together should be noticed, she saw him relax and gaze at the landscape. He turned and said softly: 'Come here!' and when, doubtfully, she stood beside him, said: 'It's beautiful, is it not?'

The land was white: all the grass, all the branches of the trees, all the twigs, were stiff with hoarfrost, sparkling and bristling with it. Above them rode the full moon and thrown like dust across the black sky were thousands upon thousands of stars. There was a quality of silence in the beauty of the still land and the endless glinting sky that was eerie, almost frightening.

'I have seen nothing like it before. It is unreal, a different world.'

'Incredible,' he agreed, his voice low and quiet. He turned from the white vision outside to contemplate her. 'Cousin Susannah, we must go. But first, will you drink with me?'

'To what do we drink?'

'To our child.'

She drew in a sharp breath, hesitating. 'To our child.'

Formally, deliberately, following the custom, they drank together until the glasses were empty. And as they did so, his

173

body beside hers, their eyes locked, Susannah felt changes taking place inside herself. Blood was beginning to flow warmly through her. It was as if she had cramped a limb and now it had been eased; the relief was both exquisite pleasure and pain. The pleasure deepened suddenly, surged through her, became demanding, aching for him to close the tiny moonlit gap between them, to hold her against him, his mouth on hers. She wrenched her eyes from his and thrust her wineglass onto the desk, shocked by the shameless behaviour of her body. Fear struck her that somehow he might discern the sensations that rocked her; she could not bear to betray a thing so intimate, so embarrassing, not to him, dear God, not to him. She must go now, at once.

Her voice sounded high and unnatural in her ears as she asked him to find a servant to show her to Cousin Katharine's bedroom, and to let Sedley know where she was and why. 'I don't wish him to be worried and perhaps think I have been taken unwell.' She was reluctant to go and talk to Katharine, though in other circumstances she would have been pleased. Her need now was to go home and huddle up in bed, her back to the stertorous Sedley, one hand twined in the warm fur of her little cat, and unravel her thoughts. Her mind was reeling from a complexity of emotions that had her baffled by their contradictions.

15

A petition of Ambrose Manningford, Esquire, Lord of the Manor of Abbotsbridge in the county of Hampshire, and owner of several estates within the said manor and parish of Abbots- bridge; of the Reverend Edward Bland, Clerk, Rector of the said parish; of Hector Fulbroad, Gentleman, and of several other persons, whose names are thereunto subscribed, being also owners of estates, copyhold messuages, cottages and other pro- perties within the said parish; was presented to the House and read, setting forth, that, within the said manor and parish, is a common or waste, called Abbotsbridge Common, and also open fields and meadows, the holdings being at present intermixed and dispersed, that the land in its present state is incapable of Im- provement, and that it would be of great Benefit to the several persons interested in the same common and fields if they were divided and enclosed into specific allotments, and all rights of common and average thereon, or upon any other commonable lands in the said parish, were extinguished ...

James pushed the papers across the desk irritably and breathed on his fingers. Leave to present the bill had been given four days earlier, on the twenty-second of January, and he should have been enjoying this phase of the work, but he was so damnably cold that his brain refused to concentrate. Besides, he was uneasy. The enclosure process, which had seemed so straightforward and right when first decided upon, he now saw as beset with unforeseen considerations and conflicting demands that it would be impossible to reconcile. Ambrose was no help to him; he had retired to bed with a head cold three days ago and only snuffled damply when James went to discuss

175

certain changes from the original plans, mumbling: 'I told you, I leave the matter entirely to you.'

The fire burning in the library grate could have been a red paper imitation for all the heat he could feel; James went to stand with his back to it, thawing his nether limbs. Frost had held all England in an iron grip for many weeks, with the snow that had given her a white Christmas remaining on the ground; the old men huddled round the forge said they never remembered a winter to compare with this one. The window panes at Abbotsbridge House were etched inside with icy traceries, only those rooms with constantly tended fires could melt the frost ferns and flowers by noon; milk and cream in the larders froze overnight; even new-baked bread, left on a kitchen table, was found rock hard in the morning. Katharine had taken to feeding the wild birds daily, and it was an amazing sight to see them swirling round her, the ungainly pigeons fluttering on her head and shoulders, and blackbirds and robins and chaffinches so tame with hunger that they would feed together from her hands.

The *Hampshire Chronicle* was full of gruesome stories of people who had frozen to death by the roadside, or perished in rivers by skating on ice insufficient to bear their weight. The floats of ice on the Thames were of tremendous size, the *Chronicle* said; several lighters were dashed about by them and a lighter laden with precious coal sunk. Far more worrying than this to Mr Bland had been the accounts from Holland of the fighting around the River Waal, and the frantic efforts being made to keep it from freezing over by breaking the ice. A discharged soldier with half a hand missing was found dead behind a haystack just outside Brambourne; he had been making his way back to his parish. 'That could have been my son Daniel,' the rector said hoarsely.

Now events had moved beyond this. Winter had taken the side of the French, freezing the Waal and the Maas solid enough to bear the weight of men and cannon. The ragged revolutionary forces had pushed across at General Pichegru's command, forcing back the outnumbered British and Hanoverians over the frozen wastes of Gelderland in a retreat that became a nightmare of frostbite and hunger. A third of the allied forces died, the corpses of six thousand men together

176

with their dead horses and abandoned waggons strewn across the whitened countryside. The Prince of Orange fled with his treasure and his wife in a fishing boat to Harwich. On January 20th the first day of Dutch freedom was proclaimed in Amsterdam, the French general assuring the populace that fraternity was the sole order of the day. The stolid sensible Dutch rejoiced vigorously with their conquerors in the towns while quietly assisting the British wounded in the countryside to escape. The British Admiralty had hoped that the Dutch fleet at least might be saved, but the Zuider Zee froze for the first time in a hundred years, allowing a dashing body of French cavalry and artillery to gallop across its surface and capture all but a few of the battleships ice-bound in the Texel.

All James' and William Waterton's gloomy prognostications for the winter had been borne out: the harvest poor, the weather harsh, the French triumphant. The price of corn had already leapt to unbelievable heights and was bound to go still higher. The fact that he had been correct in foreseeing the disaster potential did not please James, however. In a village like Abbotsbridge it was impossible to ignore its effects. He knew that in Southampton charity sermons had been preached in all the churches at the beginning of January and generous donations given for the purpose of lowering the price of bread to the poor, and a similar successful meeting had been held in Winchester's Guildhall recently. Yet his Cousin Ambrose had done nothing beyond sending a few sacks of logs to old retainers. James suspected that it was Mr Bland who was normally the generator of any benevolent schemes but his mind seemed to have frozen round the plight of his son; he looked old and grey-faced and his eyes constantly hunted the papers for any news that might indicate Daniel's survival.

James stared from the window, slapping his arms round his body to revive his circulation. The gardens, the park and the fields beyond were all white, reminding him of the night he had stood at this very window with Susannah Stacey, but this morning there was none of the glitter that had fascinated them then; the view had the bleached pallor of old bones. He turned to the desk and picked up his papers, but worries gnawed at him; his once total confidence in his own judgment had been eroded. Sometimes he felt as if he was being forced through some process of change almost as turbulent and entire as the enclosure process was bringing to Abbotsbridge. And it was Susannah's fault, hers and that brother of hers, Jack Trotter. He tapped the papers on the desk, struggling to judge conflicting needs one against another. The villagers had been suspicious of his questions and reticent to the point of surliness: 'If I lack understanding, then help me to it!' James had snapped, then cursed himself for impatience. Was there a genuine case for retaining part of the common? He had consulted several of the landowners and large farmers, but there had been no consensus of opinion, indeed, opposition in some quarters had been decided; James had put the matter aside for reflection. Now the conclusion came clearly – a new clause must be inserted into the enclosure bill – a small common must be retained for the villagers' use. He must call a meeting of the landowners, defeat opposition by a vote. He would talk to Mr Bland first, distraction from his fears over Daniel would be no bad thing for the man, and, James decided, feeling better by the second, he would discuss combining his visits to those who had signed the enclosure petition with collecting donations to provide corn or whatever for those in need.

He was cantering his horse down through the lime avenue when he became aware of a young woman in a crimson cloak making her way along the lane beyond, but it was not until a gust of the cold east wind caught the cloak and blew it against her body that he realised who she was. Like a yacht with her sail bellying to the wind, he thought, admiring the rich curve of her figure, checking his horse so that they would arrive together at the avenue's end.

'Cousin Susannah!'

'Mr Manningford.' A brief smile, a lowering of the eyes.

The bay danced impatiently at being stopped. James wanted to tell her how lovely she looked, flushed and vivid against the white background, but it was inevitable that any such remark would be misinterpreted. Instead, he asked where she was bound and why she was not indoors on so unpleasant a morning. She skirted a treacherous patch of rutted ice. She was going to the Blands, she said, hoping for news of Daniel and then to Duckett's shop on her husband's behalf. The lane was narrowed by snow wind-piled in dramatic and grotesque shapes against its hedges, its centre slippery where snow had half-melted and frozen again; she was battling sturdily on but God knew what would happen if she should fall: Stacey was stupid to allow her out alone. James would have put her on his horse but Samson was over-lively this morning and not saddled for a woman. He dismounted.

'I, too, am going to the Blands. I will walk with you.' If she lost her footing he could catch her. He was about to tell her of his mission when they were hailed by a scurrying little woman who was made almost circular by the numerous shawls knotted round her. 'Prudence Paine,' Susannah muttered. 'From Brambourne.' Prudence slithered towards them, brown eyes alert with sensation.

'Mr Manningford, you oughter know that the Bidewells' baby 'as gone to a better world at long last. The Lord's name be praised! Called in I was an hour ago to lay 'im out. So if Barney goes an' gets drunk this evening you'd best look out, for he's as stuffed with evil thoughts as a pudden is wi' currants. An' if I don't find Mr Stacey at home when I gets to the vicarage, p'raps you'd be good enough to let him know there's another buryin' to be done, Mrs Stacey.'

'I shall,' Susannah promised.

'An' you mind what I say, Mr Manningford, excuse me. I don't want to find you the third, do I? Not that there aren't plenty could go, this tar'ble weather. I'd not be surprised to find it three times three yet. God's will be done.' She nodded her head portentously and scuttled off.

James stared after her. 'What does she mean, "the third"?'

'She's methody,' Susannah began.

'I did suspect that,' he interjected drily.

'She has her own views on matters of life and death. She reckons death is ... well, almost catching, one could say.'

'Truly?'

'Oh yes. She says, where one goes, three goes. A trinity of souls for the Trinity that's above. A soldier died, a baby died – so who'll be the third?'

'Good Lord!'

Susannah continued, explaining with a mock-solemn face how Prudence believed that every baby delivered alive was a possible force for good – a future preacher, teacher, physician;

that she had a mystical view of the unplumbed depths of their minds, that they understood more than the cleverest ancient, for they came straight from God. 'She could be delivering a new Christ. Martha Pither is scornful, naturally. "I dunno about delivering no Christ-child," she said to me once, "but I do know a few young devils as 'ave bin through my 'ands!"'

They stopped before the rectory and burst into laughter. It was the first spontaneous laughter he had heard from Susannah and he thought what an uncommonly pretty sound she made, piquant but not mocking.

'How divertingly you tell it! Your accent is exact. I like Martha Pither,' James said.

'Of course,' Susannah said, still smiling. They turned to enter the rectory carriage sweep and impulsively she put out a hand to delay him. The smile had faded. 'Mr Manningford, do you know that Mr Fulbroad put pressure on certain men to sign your petition? There is talk at the smithy of veiled threats of rick burning and crop damage as well as bribery.'

'I had heard,' James said grimly.

'It was a wicked and dishonest thing to do. And when your bill comes before the House of Commons they will retract their consent. That will make you and your friends look exceedingly stupid.'

He looked at her.

'And more,' she said, her indignation mounting as she spoke. 'He is using the same threats to make those with smaller parcels of land sell to him. The more acres he owns, the more he will obtain in proportion when the common goes. Then he'll be richer and harder than ever, employing the men when 'tis fine, letting them starve when 'tis bad. If you know what he's doing, why do you not stop him?'

'No one could stop him from buying land. It's up to the men whether they sell or not. But I know nothing of any threats to force them. Acquit me of this at least.'

She stamped snow from her shoes in an impatient gesture. Sarcastically she said: 'Yes. Oh, yes, I acquit you of making threats.'

'How very good of you! How can I defeat Fulbroad's plots when I know nothing of them? I am not possessed of second sight.' For the first time he was retaliating to her taunts with anger, his blue eyes hard.

She took a step back, then said: 'You *should* know, Mr Manningford. If you cared more about village matters you would. As you would know that there are families here which are sick from the cold, families which have no fuel and no one fit to gather it, folk who are nigh starving. But what do you care? – you in your selfish preoccupation with taking away what little they have!'

His voice was as frigid as the air. 'I care sufficiently to have come here to discuss with Mr Bland the setting up of a fund to deal with this situation. I intend to draw up with him a list of potential contributors and to visit them all by the end of tomorrow.'

A pause. She cast him a baleful glance. 'Oh. Well, you must admit that you have given me reason in the past to doubt your concern.'

'I do admit it.'

'I am glad to know that something is to be done.' She gave him a straight look. 'And *I* will admit you were right when you said the village larder would soon be empty. And,' she said gloomily, 'you were right about the effect of the war.'

'Believe me, that gives me no pleasure.' He felt the anger drain from him to be replaced by respect for her directness. 'If we are to be so honest with one other, then I will say that you have opened my eyes to many matters also.' He looked for a moment longer at her troubled young face and saw the tenseness leave it. He was tempted to tell her of that other reason for his visit to Mr Bland but stopped himself. If he were to be unsuccessful in his pleas to the landowners then Susannah would think him a mere braggart.

His horse was restless. He led him into the carriage sweep, saying over his shoulder: 'You should persuade your family to invest in any land that has to be sold.'

'To profit by others' misfortune? They would never do that!'

'Better them than certain others. You know there are men who are bound to sell and there is already pressure on them. Your brother could make sure they were not cheated by offering them a good price.'

'I doubt he could afford it.'

'The price of corn will go higher still. Land values will be leaping. A mortgage would be easily obtained, soon paid off.'

The Blands were delighted to see both James and Susannah, told them that they had no news of Daniel, but they prayed no news was good news; fussed them into the morning room to warm by the fire and insisted they must at once take hot possets. Maids were sent scurrying, the dogs barked and jumped up unrebuked, the children came tumbling downstairs to talk to Susannah, even Fanny demanded that James confer with her over which of two Haydn piano sonatas he should play at the concert; it was the normal Bland bedlam. Their cordiality, which once he would have found excessive, now warmed and heartened him. It was only after several minutes that he could draw the rector to one side and ask for an hour of his time.

'Of course. In my bookroom,' Mr Bland said, and they were walking from the room when a shout came from Humphrey, kneeling on the windowseat.

'There's a man riding up to the house. A man in uniform.'

The silence that fell on the room was total; even the dogs were still. A maid went to the front door, but Mrs Bland could not bear to wait and stumbled from the room after her. The man had dismounted now and James caught a glimpse of his face: it was white with cold and fatigue ... and something else. Instinctively he put his hand on the rector's shoulder.

The house trembled to Mrs Bland's cry. For a brief moment the morning room was full of statues and then they came to anguished life, sobbing and groping towards each other. He heard Mr Bland say: 'He's dead. My son Daniel is dead.' And then pity and anger gusted over James. He remembered the proud foolish boy at the ball, glorying in his new uniform, defying his father's censure and his concern. And now he was one of those thousands of bodies lying on the ice of a foreign land, a useless sacrifice to an ill-planned, ill-fought war in whose action he had barely had time to join. He saw the face of Mr Bland and the anger goaded him into activity. He seized a chair and made him sit down. He found the manservant, Dick, and told him to deal with the rider's horse and then to fetch the brandy, no, to fetch brandy and glasses at once. He told the maid to stop snivelling and find her mistress's vinaigrette. Then he turned and took in rapidly what was happening in the room:

182

Mrs Bland collapsed on the sofa, her gown rucked up, her mouth agape in a rictus of distress, her daughter Lucy crouched beside her, clutching her hands; Susannah bending over the two smallest boys, her grey eyes infinitely calm. He saw a greyhound push its long muzzle under the rector's hand and as his eyes moved on, Fanny, her face the colour of putty, swaying ... As he crossed the room he saw Susannah look up and move with great speed so that they caught Fanny between them. She seemed extraordinarily heavy for so slight a girl.

'We'll put her on the sofa,' Susannah said.

'No!' James said vehemently. 'You will not carry her. How can you be so foolish? William, come here!'

With the boy's help Fanny was laid down, her head in her mother's lap. He heard the heavy indrawing of Mrs Bland's breath as she struggled for control, and he saw Susannah take a handkerchief to wipe the tears from the quivering face, her hand using gentle but firm strokes that seemed to impart some of her own calmness to the woman. Mrs Bland pulled herself more upright, then took the vinaigrette from the maid's hand to wave it under Fanny's nose. Susannah pulled James aside.

'Mr Manningford, please ride to Brambourne and fetch my husband.'

She was shivering, keeping that air of calm only by force of her determination, but she was not flinching from the pain and grief in the room, and her colour was reasonable. He was not sure what Sedley Stacey would contribute, but he nodded and instructed Dick to bring his horse round to the door.

He was back in little more than fifteen minutes, having left Stacey to saddle his mare and follow him. As he prepared to dismount the front door flew open and Susannah appeared.

'Don't dismount,' she called. 'You must ride to fetch Dr Huskett. Mr Bland has had a seizure.'

The seizure, whatever it was, was worrying. Mr Bland, like his daughter Fanny, had lost consciousness, but he had not come round easily and when he did, lay limp on the bed to which Dick helped him, mumbling his grief at having parted from his son on poor terms and without giving him his blessing. 'My heart was hardened, and now he is gone. I shall never forgive myself ... never forgive myself.' He complained of dizziness and nausea to Dr Huskett, but showed no signs of having had an apoplexy, which was what his wife audibly feared. The doctor, bending bristling white eyebrows upon him, expressed the opinion that shock coupled with an excess of the sanguinaceous humour had caused his symptoms, and bled him. This seemed to give some relief. James would not allow Susannah to hold the bowl for the operation, and since no one else in the household appeared steady enough to cope, he held it himself.

In the meantime Sedley had arrived, and saw, he said to James, no reason for Susannah or him to stay: he would minister to the Blands now. James nodded and ordered Fanny's pony to be saddled for Susannah; he would ride with her. Mrs Bland was assisted back to the morning room to sit with her children while Sedley made consoling remarks and read to them from the Bible. As she pulled her cloak about her, Susannah heard verses from St Paul's First Epistle to the Thessalonians: 'For if we believe that Jesus died and rose again, even so them also which sleep in Jesus will God bring with him . . .' and as she walked out into the bitter cold the words followed her '. . . Then we which are alive and remain shall be caught up together with them in the clouds, to meet the Lord in the air: and so shall we ever be with the Lord. Wherefore comfort one another with these words.'

'Your husband will do better with them now than either of us could,' James remarked, assisting her into the saddle.

'Yes,' she said. 'He is not so troubled.' She gave him a puzzled look. 'But you are angry. Why are you angry?'

'The waste,' he said briefly, swinging himself onto his horse. 'Unforgivable.'

'But I thought you were in favour of the war?'

'I was. I am. But not of running several campaigns together, each worse supplied and more forgotten than the next.' One hand made a furious gesture. 'Any task that is undertaken must be tackled whole-heartedly, with detailed planning from its conception to its end, then, and only then, is its success assured.'

Yes, that was how he would think; it was how he worked. He looked very large and determined there on the big horse, and for the first time his size and his self-assurance seemed to her right and male and protective, not an insult.

In a different tone he said: 'I'm sorry, Cousin Susannah. This bears hard on you. Someone you've known all your life.'

The sympathy in his voice caused her throat to close up convulsively and the backs of her eyes to smart with tears. She shook her head. He looked at her and then they rode in silence. At the entrance to the lime avenue she protested that there was no need for him to accompany her further and he retorted that there was every need, and it was not until they had slithered and struggled up the rise beyond in the teeth of the freezing wind that they spoke again.

It would be stupid to hope, James said, that Mr Bland would shortly be in any fit state of mind or body to help over the raising of funds to aid the poor. But the need was immediate. To whom could he turn for advice? He had been racking his brains. His cousin Ambrose was sick abed; Mr Stacey would now have the burden of running both churches; Rosalind was struggling to cope with Abbotsbridge House with servants who dripped with colds or moaned that they were crippled with chilblains; only Susannah could guide him. She had lived many years with the Blands and she was the curate's wife: who else would have her knowledge? He would not, he added firmly, expect her to be risking her health in going into houses where there might be dangerous fevers; advice on the hows and wheres of the matter was what he desperately needed.

Susannah could think of nothing she would be better pleased to do. When they reached the vicarage she would order hot soup to warm them both and then they could set to work. James said he would not dream of troubling her today in her grief and fatigue; he would return tomorrow. Susannah argued that he would be condemning her to sit and cry alone; she had liefer by far be occupied. James gave in with pleasing meekness.

While he unsaddled the horses and stabled them, Susannah entered the kitchen through the back door to speak to Becky, and narrowly avoided tripping over a dead pheasant lying on the step. With a glance behind herself she grabbed it and shut the door. 'Becky!' she called.

Becky emerged from the pantry. 'Oh, you're back, ma'am. Dear, oh dear, so cold you do look, an' your poor eyes all red from the wind. I warned you goin' out was madness, didden I?

Let me take your cloak then, and you warm yourself by the study fire and I'll heat some milk.'

'Hot soup, please. Mr James Manningford is with me. Becky, Mr Daniel Bland is dead. The news has just come.'

Her shoulder was patted comfortingly. 'An' you feared it, too. Them poor Blands. 'Ere, what's this you've got?'

'It was on the doorstep.'

'Well!' said Becky, her eyes thoughtful. 'Handsome, he is. An' nuthin' to say 'oo he come from? That makes three rabbits and two pheasants now, dunnit? Someone admires us, so to say.'

Their eyes met. 'I cannot refuse a present that comes from nowhere.'

''Twould be a wicked waste to throw un out,' Becky agreed.

'Hang it in the pantry, quickly,' Susannah said. 'Mr Manningford must not ...'

James blew in on a blast of arctic air. 'Damned if I walk round the house in this snow,' he said, stamping lumps of ice onto the kitchen floor. 'And what must Mr Manningford not do, Cousin?'

'Be kept waiting for his soup,' Susannah replied promptly.

Becky's ample rear disappeared into the pantry.

'A pheasant?' James commented, his eyebrows raised.

'We have gifts from grateful parishioners at all levels,' Susannah told him, allowing a note of smugness to creep into her voice.

They worked together in the study, he big and bulky, seeming to take up half the fire as he leaned over it, his hand shielding his eyes from the heat; she seated on the other side of the hearth, her little writing slope on her lap, quill-pen and paper to hand. She analysed three elements to be considered: which people in the village should be approached for donations and how much each should contribute; how the fund raised could best be utilised, and who should benefit. The third was the simplest: as Susannah commented to James between sips of scalding beef broth, the overseer of the poor would know where the urgent need lay, while those who needed help because of sickness could be easily discovered from Martha Pither and Jem Nutt, the barber-surgeon. James had determined a basis for the contributions, he said: he would call on all in the village who owned more than twenty acres, together with the doctor and the better-off tradesmen. Susannah shook her head vigorously: did he wish to cause offence? Those who could barely afford sixpence would be huffed not to be approached. James sighed into his soup. Susannah told him severely that the exercise would be good for him and his horses, to which he retorted that if he died of pneumonia he would hold her responsible. And what if Sam Truckle told him to go to hell? Then he must allow Sam that pleasure. A devil of mischief lurking in his eyes, James then suggested that he should prepare, on the very best paper, a list of the wealthiest members of the community and note with a flourish what each donated. The mean would be shamed into generosity – no man would want a nought against his name. Susannah relished his scheme, and together they drew up the list, fitting a figure to each name which James noted on a separate aide-memoire. They parted in pleasant amity, agreeing to ask Mr Goddard to join them, and to meet next day to decide how to allocate the fund.

It was while Becky was making up the parlour fire ready for their discussion next day that Susannah heard of the excitements of the previous night, and how only Josh's intervention had saved the Manningfords' barns from being set alight. 'Barney Bidewell, 'twas,' said Becky, making a wigwam of kindling. 'Foolish folks bought him tankard 'pon tankard of beer to drown 'is sorrows, 'spite how everybody knows what drink does to Barney. Haranguing 'em all he was in the ale house, and them him and 'is cronies moves on to The Bull an' starts shouting there 'bout the wickedness of laws that do permit the rich to steal our common, an' pull down the habitations of the poor, an' force men off their own precious bit of land. An' then Sam Truckle an' Dick Pettifer joins in, saying they're right and how the corn factors and the millers are all sittin' there waxing fat on high prices while babes do wither away, an' my father's tucked in a corner keeping mum because he reckons mebbe if they can spew their ill humours out of theirselves – begging your pardon, ma'am – then it'll all die down an' none the worse. Only it doesn't. Next thing he knows they're all for lighting brands at the fire an' marching to burn the squire's barns.' She paused to take breath, sitting back on her heels.

'Go on,' Susannah urged her. 'Dear's my soul, how'd they get stopped?'

' 'Twas my father,' Becky said, flushed with pride. 'Leaps for the door, he does, an' puts his back to it. And then he tells them. Tells them that they've every right to be angry, but how they won't do their wives and their children ought but harm by gettin' 'emselves put in gaol fur arson. Who's to feed 'em then? An' he tells Berry Truckle who's shouting with 'is father, that his apprenticeship at the forge is over if he don't help stop this. An' then he tells that fool John Hayter a thing or two 'bout 'citing men to mischief. Long an' short of it is, Barney shouts 'tis burning whether or no, an' there's a fight starts an' stools and tankards gets thrown. So John Hayter loses his temper and him and Berry takes a leg each an' my father takes Barney's shoulders an' they're throwing him out. But he's cursing so shocking they upends him in Father's cooling trough.' She swept up the hearth thoughtfully. Then she giggled. 'They broke the ice on the trough with 'is head. Even so, Father said, you could hear 'im fair sizzling as 'e went in!'

Over that week and throughout February Susannah and James worked together; the baby was not mentioned, enclosures were not mentioned: it was a period of unprecedented peace between them. They settled with Mr Goddard that bread, meat and fuel were the items most needed by those in distress, and that it was better given in kind than in coin. Money, Mr Goddard observed, peering with benevolent cynicism through his gold-rimmed spectacles, would likely vanish in drink before wives and children could benefit. The total raised was fifty-nine pounds, ten shillings and sixpence, which Susannah and Mr Goddard assured James was very great, far more than in any previous year of dearth. Mr Fulbroad had actually been coerced into giving ten guineas.

With the distribution of essentials to those in need, the rumblings of discontent seemed to die down in Abbotsbridge. Appalling conditions and near-starvation in several cottages were revealed by the search for recipients for the charity. Mrs Waterton excused Susannah from parish visiting in Brambourne: 'I shall have to manage without you for a while,' she said. 'A pity my daughter considers herself unavailable.' 'Dear Fanny's concert!' Miss Waterton said reproachfully. 'I must hold myself ready for rehearsals to start again.' So Susannah plodded regularly over the snow to Abbotsbridge where James saw her emerging from a tumble-down cottage hardly bigger than a cow hovel one morning, and hailed her.

'You look dispirited, Cousin. A bad case of distress? Of sickness?'

She gave him a challenging look. 'See for yourself.'

He ducked his head to enter and stared in silent wonder: a floor of beaten earth, a crippled man inert on a chair cobbled from discarded bits of wood, a sick woman struggling for breath on a palliasse on the floor, three children with tumid bellies and stick-like limbs crouching before a smouldering turf fire. Five pairs of eyes surveying him with numb indifference. A stench of smoke and sickness.

Behind him Susannah said: 'Nat Jurd and his family. It was a choice between separation in the poor house or this. They chose to be together.'

James said: 'I had no conception of such a level of misery. How has this come about?'

'In his good times Nat spins flax to earn a shilling or two, and his wife goes weeding for Widow Pern, but in this weather neither has work. Today I brought soup and a blanket and woollens from the poor box and they have been given a little bread, but neither meat nor fuel has come.'

'I shall see to it,' James said grimly. His fingers searched a pocket for a coin and pressed it into the man's fingers. He reeled back outside and stood taking in great lungfuls of the clean cold air. 'Dear God, Cousin Susannah, what can I say?'

'Nothing to be said,' she responded wrily. 'Plenty to be done.'

'I will see to it,' he said again. 'But there is one thing I must say – and that is that you will cease these visits. God knows what disgusting diseases you could pick up ... may well have picked up already. No, no argument! If necessary I shall visit every cottage in the village myself, to reassure you as to its every member's welfare.'

The sharp frosts continued on the days following, the temperature staying below freezing point all day long in any room without a fire. From the cottages by the river came reports of moorhens and wagtails invading the rooms for warmth.

189

Though Susannah would never have admitted it, she was grateful simply to sit by the fire stitching baby-clothes; her body was clumsy now and the paths and lanes were treacherous. She was not dull: James came from time to time to tell her how the charity fund was being used, Beatrice rode over to take tea, members of her family visited her.

Her mother, her brother Jack, and Sedley were all with Susannah one morning when James was seen dismounting at the vicarage gate. A groom was given orders to keep his horse walking and James came in briskly, saying that he was in haste, but that he had certain news to impart to them and was pleased to have discovered them together. Sedley and Mrs Trotter were anxious to press warming refreshments on him but he refused.

'As I am sure you, Mr Trotter, will already know, the Enclosure Bill has its first reading next week. Your petition against the Bill will, I assume, now have been presented.'

'Two days ago,' Jack said.

'Yes. You are opposing in total the enclosing of Abbotsbridge Common and that is your right. However, there is a matter which you may now wish to tell those supporting your petition – or alternatively reveal at a later date, whichever you think fit. The landowners of this parish have considered carefully the loss which certain villagers will suffer in the event of the Enclosure Bill being passed by both Houses. They are agreed that there should be an allotment of land for a cow common.'

'I had heard that it was being discussed,' Jack said quietly. 'Thank you for informing me. It will be something to be grateful for – should it be necessary to be grateful.'

'A cow common?' Susannah questioned, pushing herself to her feet. 'Of how many acres?'

Sedley intervened sharply: 'There is no need for you to question Mr James, Susannah. This is not a matter for you.'

'That is perfectly all right,' James said. He turned to Susannah. 'It would be thirty-five acres.'

'Thirty-five acres?' Susannah ground out with contempt. 'From all those hundreds available? Lucullus dines with Lucullus at the Manningfords' table – and they can scarce spare a crumb for the poor! Thirty-five acres! Such condescension!'

'Susannah!' Mrs Trotter gasped. 'You must not speak like that ...'

'How dare you! How dare you speak to Mr Manningford with such insolence!' Sedley hissed. 'Apologise at once!'

Susannah stood silent, eyebrows raised at James. Contempt had coated her anger with an external semblance of calm. A leaden quietness fell on the room. From the lane outside came the steady clop of the horses being led up and down. James turned on his heel and walked from the house.

Sedley and Mrs Trotter spoke together in a rush of shock and indignation. 'How could you? What possessed you to speak in such a way?' Mrs Trotter gasped. 'Your behaviour was insolent to an unbelievable degree,' came from between Sedley's gritted teeth. 'You are mad, wicked, evil! How could I have brought myself to marry such a stupid slut? Never would I ...'

Jack's quiet voice cut through their noise to pierce Susannah's consciousness. 'You are wrong, Susannah. Totally wrong! Mr James wanted double that amount of land, but Mr Fulbroad and Mr Munday opposed him furiously. He fought and fought for what he did get. And remember, he is no landowner himself: he was at a hopeless disadvantage.'

'He fought ...?' A hand flew to her mouth and away. 'Dear Lord, what have I done?'

'Ruined us, I imagine,' Sedley snapped.

Susannah was not listening. In the lane James had just mounted. She turned, wrenching at the doors as she ran, heavily, clumsily, out of the house and over the snow towards the now moving horses.

'Wait!' she called urgently. 'Mr Manningford, wait, please!'

The groom looked over his shoulder and said something to James. A snapped reply. The horses were kicked to a trot.

'Cousin James! Please!' she screamed.

His back stiffened. His horse slowed; his head did not turn. 'Ride on ahead,' he ordered the groom.

'I'm sorry. I'm sorry. I was wrong!'

'Always you believe the worst of me,' James said. 'Always I must be wrong, always I am to be despised.'

'No!' she said wretchedly, tears beginning to run down her face. 'You are not. I know that now. My brother told me what

191

you had tried to do. It was I who was wrong ... again ... in jumping to false conclusions.'

He turned his head to look down at her.

'I don't know why ... I am being very stupid, I think. I can only apologise ...' She searched hopelessly for a handkerchief and found one being pushed into her hand.

'Take mine,' he said. 'It is clean.'

She mopped and sniffed and blew. 'Please forgive me.'

It seemed an age before he spoke. 'When you have forgiven me so much, how could I not forgive you?'

'Oh!'

'But peace between us now, please.' He pulled off a tan leather glove and leaned down. 'Give me your hand.'

She held her hand up to his. 'Thank you.'

'Promise me you will always ask me first about any matter that has you concerned.'

'I promise.'

He kissed her hand. 'Now go indoors, at once. Your hand is icy.'

It was sometime before Susannah's mother and brother left the vicarage. Mr Manningford's reaction to her apology had to be discussed in detail and then Mrs Trotter and Jack wanted to explore with her the effect a cow common might have in the aftermath of enclosure, but at last they went.

Sedley stood by the window: when they were out of sight he walked across the room to Susannah. 'Stand up!' he ordered her. Then he gave her two stinging slaps on the cheek with the flat of his hand. 'You miserable bitch!' he said. 'You could have ruined my career today with your rudeness. And you nearly wrecked a most beneficial friendship. You are not fit to appear in company. And if you are ever rude to any gentleman again, then I shall forbid you to go into company. I mean it.'

16

Susannah's baby was born into a wet and weeping world, but Susannah did not consider this an unfortunate omen, rather as a felicitous occurrence that kept the elderly and inept Doctor Huskett from her bedside till all was over. It was also lucky for a different reason.

Hampshire is in general a warm and well-drained county; the Rivers Itchen and Test do not overflow their banks in the wayward fashion of the Trent or the Severn and the fields are seldom waterlogged. In March of 1795, however, the great thaw and the subsequent continual rain left even Hampshire sodden, its ditches brimming, its land springs never known to be so full, its roads in many places impassible from mud.

It was a shock to Becky Pither, then, that her mistress suddenly announced mid-morning on a cold damp day that she was walking to Abbotsbridge House to discuss her petit point with Miss Katharine Manningford. Becky protested: it would be folly to venture out, for while the rain had ceased at dawn, the clouds were once more sagging ominously overhead. Holding herself oddly rigid, Susannah insisted; she had neglected Miss Katharine too long, she would go. Becky was left with nothing to do but to sigh meaningfully and to coax her to wear pattens to save her shoes.

Susannah picked her way along the lane between its ivy-covered banks till she came to the top of the slope that led down into Abbotsbridge. There she stopped and looked cautiously about herself. Great mountainous piles of cloud were moving over the wintry sky, erratically rimed with silver by an invisible sun. Suddenly a broad beam of light descended from between two clouds to illuminate various parts of the village below, the houses, the River Test, the church, lighting them with a fierce pale glow that moved stealthily over the land and then as suddenly disappeared again. The landscape darkened and the cold intensified. She felt irrationally as if she would never see that scene again. She breathed deeply and the earth held a dank metallic scent.

The ruts in the road of which Sedley so often complained were deeper than ever, and running with water, the lane only wide enough for one vehicle to pass. It was definitely hazardous to the foot-traveller. She held up her head and listened. A rumbling sound came to her: it was an approaching carriage, but the noise in the cold lonely air seemed to strike her heart with fear, so that she clasped her arms about her swollen body as if to still its palpitating pain. There was something she was impelled to do though it took her to the verge of danger. As the horses came into sight she stepped forward; her foot slipped in the mud, she flung out her hands before her and, echoing strangely dramatically back from the banks on each side of her, came the sound of her voice yelling.

When Martha Pither bustled into a sickroom she brought with her an atmosphere of the homely and the everyday, an atmosphere that was comforting as a breath of spring air to men and women fighting pain and disease in airless over-crowded conditions. When she came into the vicarage Susannah gasped with relief.

Of all people's carriage to have fallen before, fate had selected the Blands' for her, and while Mr Bland had stopped his horses with a swiftness that had prevented a still nastier accident, they had been with her and fussing ever since. Sedley had returned from a discussion with Mr Waterton to find his wife complaining of tormenting pain from an ankle sprained for the third time in nine months and had ridden rapidly off to find Dr Huskett, and, on Becky's low-voiced advice, Martha. 'Just in case,' said Becky.

As Martha entered she summed up the situation in one comprehensive glance that took in the agonised look of appeal in the eyes of the curate's wife, and the flustered state of the Blands, plus the fact of her daughter giving a herbal tea to her mistress, the scent of which she knew well.

'Amazing, 'ent it?' said Martha, in an admiring voice, when Mrs Bland had poured it all out to her, 'how 'tis the Blands as comes to the rescue. What the villages 'ud do without 'em, the Lord only knows. But wi' Rector not so good as he should be, I reckon you should both return 'ome, Mrs Bland. Why, finding Mrs Stacey fallen that nastily must 'ave bin a shock, mustn't it?' And in less than five minutes she had the Blands off in their carriage and Susannah up on her bed, examining her with practised eye and hands.

'The fall seems to have started something up,' Susannah muttered through gritted teeth.

Martha nodded.

A knock on the door interrupted them and Susannah had just time to hiss: 'Say nothing yet!' before Sedley came in to report that Dr Huskett was in grave trouble with his gout, and reluctant to move from his fireside unless it was a matter of life or death. 'And besides,' Sedley added more prosaically, 'it is raining again, heavily. The doctor says there's nothing to be done save to avoid cold compresses and bind the ankle well.'

'That has been done,' Susannah said. She sighed. 'I seem to have a weakness in that particular ankle. Unfortunately I went over on a rut quite violently.'

'That road's a disgrace,' Sedley said angrily. 'I've mentioned it many times at Brambourne parish meetings. Had it been mended last autumn in the way I suggested we should not have this trouble now. Oh, and the doctor asked if you have any pains elsewhere.'

'My back's aching somewhat,' she admitted. 'I cannot tell . . . perhaps I've sprained that too. But it is nothing much.'

When Sedley left to change from his wet clothes into dry, Becky sidled into the room and the two women looked at Susannah.

'No doctor!' Susannah insisted. 'If my babe has truly started up so early, then you two will do better in my confinement than any old man.'

Martha chortled. 'We'll not call 'im 'less we're forced! All's as it should be with ye, far as I can tell. Now you drink that raspberry leaf tea and lie quiet and 'twill be over main quick, I'll guarantee.'

Susannah obeyed, turning on her side and closing her eyes. Dear God, she was grateful to have Martha there and not Prudence Paine. Not long ago Prudence had called in with her sharp eyes and her pious voice, wishful to discuss Mrs Stacey's delivery, whether Doctor Huskett would be in attendance, how many days Mrs Stacey would wish her to help after the event . . . Susannah had been forced to cut her short. It was extraordinarily kind of Prudence to offer, she said, but there would be no requirement for her services. Prudence had bridled: she recalled the dismissal of her cousin, Mrs Dismore, the employment of that Rebecca Pither from Abbotsbridge as maidservant: 'Brambourne folk not good enough for you, seemingly, Mrs Stacey?' Susannah had shaken her head and smiled reproachfully, telling her: 'Not so, indeed!' but asking in return how could she not have Martha Pither, being herself one of the first babies Martha ever delivered, and with her daughter working here, well, she was sure Prudence could see it would be an insult.

A pain slid low across her back, gripped her till she caught her breath, and retreated. Susannah gasped with relief and tried to compose herself. It had been a bad day when Prudence came, one of the worst of her marriage, the day after Sedley had struck her, and her cheek still red from his blows. Three weeks ago, was it now? It seemed like yesterday. She had lain awake till the small hours that night. It had been clear that Sedley's resentment was swelling with her body; the child had scarcely been mentioned between them for weeks, months even. She had shifted uneasily between the clammily cold sheets. She could wait no longer for him to break the silence, her time was drawing near – and that time would be an additional blow for him. How could she soften it? At last the thoughts had become clearer in her mind, crystallising into plans. Yes, she had thought as she finally drifted into sleep, that's how I shall deal with it, that's how I shall reassure him.

Rain streamed down the windows, darkening the room with a watery curtain, but Becky had kindled a fire before returning to the kitchen and its glow outlined the reassuring figure of Martha crouched over some sewing. The pains sneaked up on

Susannah, swiftly intensifying, clutching her with cruel strength until she gasped from them. 'Never 'old yer breath,' Martha told her without looking up from her patching. ''Twill make the cramps worse. Think o' summat else.'

Distraction ... She must keep her mind occupied while the baby made its slow entrance into the world. As Prudence had gone flouncing out that day so Susannah's mother and Jack had arrived with the latest news, that the petition had been ordered to be heard on Second Reading. Jack had handed Susannah a copy to read, which she found fascinating. The petition had been presented to Parliament in the names of Thomas Trotter, Yeoman; Joseph Stent, Yeoman; Mrs Sarah Pern, widow; Samuel Truckle, Small-holder, and others, who, it stated, were *a majority in number of the Freeholders and Customary or Copyhold Tenants having a Right of Common upon Abbotsbridge Common, whose estates and interests, should the Bill pass into a Law, will be greatly injured, and several of them totally ruined thereby; and, further, certain of the Petitioners, by Threats and Menaces, were prevailed upon to sign the Petition for the said Bill, but upon Consideration of the impending Ruin they should be subjected to by Inclosure, now beg Leave to have Liberty to retract from their seeming Acquiescence in the said Petition.'*

Jack had remarked that it was the Committee stage, not the Second Reading that would be of importance: had they friends in the House of Commons they might have some chance, but the local Members of Parliament had never responded to their attorney's letters. Susannah said indignantly that the petition had put their points forcibly and well – surely some notice must be taken of it? Jack retorted that the clerk could have transcribed the words of the nursery rhyme 'Little Boy Blue' on the contrary petition for all the effect it would have. They lacked status. He put his head in his hands. Susannah had hated to see him so disheartened and bitter: it had never been in his character to despair.

A beast had its talons in her body and was tearing at it. It was James Manningford's fault, all, all his fault. Jack and her parents' pain, the villagers' suffering, the agony that was wrenching her. If James Manningford were with her now she would curse him with every curse she knew. Damn him, oh, damn him! She thumped the pillows with her fist.

Martha was standing beside her; leather stays creaked as the vast body bent; warm knowing hands touched her. 'Not long now,' came her voice.

Her mind fastened eagerly on the words. But then, in a rush, came fear. She lifted her head. 'Does my husband know what is happening?'

'He knows,' Martha returned. 'Becky told 'im when she served 'is dinner. She gave 'im his favourite raspberry puffs an' said he'd be a father by the time he'd digested 'em. Fair put out about it coming early, he was, Becky said.'

'I can imagine he would be,' Susannah murmured, wincing.

'Ah. But you'll be glad to know he's being kept busy. Some'un delivered two tubs o' Moonshine under cover of the dirty night and him an' Becky's bottling it up.' She lowered her voice. 'Best Geneva, seemingly. That'll be summat to toast the child in!'

So Sedley was being distracted. Distraction ... think of the baby, Piers if it was a boy, Harriet if it was a girl. Sedley had hardly spoken to her that next day after he had hit her. But she had made much of him, anticipating his needs, warming his shoes at the fire, preparing his favourite foods. It had seemed unfortunate that he had come in from the church while her mother and Jack were there once more and discussing the bill, but no one could be more prodigiously tactful than her mother, who, barely pausing for breath, had changed the conversation to Sedley's sermons at Abbotsbridge, for which, she said, she had a deep admiration. 'So profound, yet so comprehensible. I am guilty of shocking sins of pride where my son-in-law is concerned!' Her words had dissolved Sedley's stiffness and when Susannah later suggested that they should be considering names for their baby, he dismissed the subject brusquely, but for once, not unpleasantly. She persisted, insinuating that names could be used as subtle compliments to persons of significance to Sedley's future. He grasped the point immediately. Piers had been Sedley's father's name. If his mother could be persuaded to come to the christening and to view her grandchild as a reincarnation of her dear late husband, she might consider augmenting her son's puny income. The more he thought of it, the more Sedley was sure she would. And a boy's second name could be James, after its godfather and as a compliment to all the Manningfords, and for a girl, the compliment would be to the Watertons, in Harriet, Mrs Waterton's name. Warming to the subject, Sedley then added Dorothy, for his mother, and Frances, should Fanny agree to be a girl's godmother. Susannah said softly: 'Piers James Sedley, for a boy, please!' and Sedley had actually patted her arm as he agreed.

Piers James Sedley Stacey arrived at eight o'clock in the evening, greeted the world with a lusty yell of shock, then fell to staring silently while he was washed, well-wrapped and placed in his mother's arms.

'Quick and easy,' said Martha. 'Like I told you. Here he is.'

Susannah had seen him briefly when he was born, held up naked and yelling in Martha's arms, his maleness somehow inordinately obvious on the tiny body. Now he lay in her arms and breathed quietly and made sucking movements with his mouth. A stranger: that was the disconcerting part. For months she had pictured him and vaguely expected to recognise him, but here was a miniature person whose features she had never seen before. Or had she? She stared into the depths of the round dark eyes, touched with a finger the soft brown wisps of hair, smiled at the minutely perfect ears. 'Hello, Piers,' she whispered. Yes, there was recognition here.

Martha's voice broke into her reverie. 'I'll go and tell Mr Stacey he can come and see the bouncing healthy boy you've given 'im.'

'Oh, Martha, no!' Susannah said urgently, giving her a conspiratorial look. 'Pray don't tell my husband 'tis a fine boy, else he'll forget it's been born – well, early – and he'll go boasting to his friends, and every eyebrow in the village will vanish into the wigs above!'

Martha's chest heaved and the kerchief over her bosoms shook and billowed like a rick-cover in a gale as she guffawed. 'Eh,' she wheezed, 'I've heard some funny ones, but I've never before 'eard a mother want the father to b'lieve he's got a puny lad!' She smoothed her kerchief down with a firm hand. 'But 'tis none o' my business, nor no one else's neither.' Her heavy tread shook the stairs as she went to break the happy news to Sedley.

Susannah lay contemplating her baby. In the fire a log settled, sending sparks flying up the chimney; rain rattled at the window.

Sedley shoved the oak door shut, stood staring by the side of the bed. It was clear he had been sampling the liquor he had been bottling.

'A son,' she said softly, inclining the bundle in her arms a little towards him, as if proffering it.

'Yes,' he said, a finger rasping his chin. 'It is small, very small.'

'But Martha says he will prosper.'

'Let us hope so,' he said heavily. His forehead was puckered, his breathing heavy. He added unexpectedly: 'He has my hair.'

'Yes,' she said. 'It is the same colour.'

'Well,' he said. 'Well. A son.'

'Piers James Sedley Stacey.'

A momentary flicker of amusement. 'A lot of names for a very little fellow.'

She smiled too. 'He will grow to them. Sedley, why don't you stay with us for a while?'

He seated himself on the chair where Martha had sat, eyeing his wife and the child. Upright and a little flushed, he spoke abruptly.

'He should never have been born,' he said.

She stiffened. He must not reject the boy, not now, not ever. 'No!' she flung back at him. 'No, he should not! But I hope you will never let him hear such words. Never ever!'

Their eyes met in challenge: his were the first to fall.

He turned his head, hawking morosely in his throat; he spat in the fire and the fire hissed back at him.

'What the deuce are we to tell people? What are we to say?'

'Naturally we say that the child was born very early because of my accident. Oh, I know everyone will be aware that it could not be that early – not at this date. But no one had much doubt as to the true situation when we married so unexpected and fast. If remarks are made it will be vulgar in those who make them. You know well how to discourage such persons, Sedley, I

have seen you do it. A lift of the eyebrows, a shrug of disgust –
you can shrivel them in a moment. As I shall do.'

'In my position ...' he began.

'In your position,' she interrupted shrewdly, 'folk are more
likely to be embarrassed to press the matter. And we shall face
it out as if all were normal. Some other gossip will soon arise to
take the attention of the petty-minded, and memories are
surprisingly short.'

'They had better be,' he said angrily.

'And our baby should be kept quietly here for some weeks,
away from all staring prattlers, till he is grown bigger and
stronger.'

James Manningford regarded breakfast as an important meal,
preferably to be taken alone, certainly without speech. To have
his female cousins indulge in gossip at such a time was the
outside of enough. He had been wakened to the noise of
torrential rain, pulled the covers over his head in disgust, and
thus slept too long to avoid meeting them over his ham and
fried beef. He followed his Cousin Ambrose into the room,
Ambrose with a book tucked beneath his arm, James armed
with a newspaper. Both men's faces lengthened at the sounds of
chatter and tittering coming from Julia and Jessica, who were
sitting at the table opposite Katharine and young Silvia,
scrunching toast and drinking cups of chocolate with a live-
liness fit to be repressed at this hour of the day.

'Good morning, Papa, good morning, Cousin James,' they
chorused, with the alert, challenging look of those brimful with
news.

The downwards seams on Ambrose's gaunt-cheeked, clean-
shaven face deepened as he jerked out: 'Good morning!' and
opened his book. James merely nodded, seating himself and
opening his paper with a flourish sufficiently brisk to warn any
female of sensitivity that he wished to eat in silence.

That Julia and Jessica were bereft of sensitivity became
evident within a minute of the two gentlemen pushing the first
forkfuls of food into their mouths. The chattering broke out
once more in lowered tones, accompanied by meaningful
looks, nudges, and remarks such as: 'Can you conceive of such
a tale?' 'How prodigious embarrassing for them!'

Ambrose marked his place in the book with a thin forefinger. 'Would you kindly refrain from servants' hall gossip!' he requested in austere tones.

Silvia's mouth ceased to masticate toast as she blurted: 'Not servants' hall gossip, Papa! Parsonage!'

Ambrose stiffened. 'Empty your mouth before you speak, Silvia! Only vulgars both gobble and gabble together.'

James's paper descended with a sudden rustle. 'Parsonage gossip? Which parsonage?'

Before any of them could answer, Beatrice hobbled through the door, took in the scene with a sweep of sardonic eyes and remarked with a grin: 'I see that the early birds turned into worms at the sound of the rain.'

'Far too wet to ride,' her father said. 'I trust you were not so foolish?'

'Oh no. Even I have to confess to worming my way back down my bed. Is that fried beef? Good. Then I shall have some.'

James flung his paper on the floor. 'What parsonage gossip? Could I please have an answer to my question!'

Jessica leaned forward, her eyelids lowered in a mixture of mock reproach and malice. 'Mrs Stacey had a baby last night. Imagine, barely six months after she was married. They say she had a bad fall ...'

'A fall!' James rapped out. 'What fall? Is she all right?'

Jessica shrugged. 'How should I know? I know only what my maid said. She fell, and it made the baby come.'

'If she had been badly injured I feel certain we should have had all the gruesome details by now,' Ambrose remarked cynically.

'She slipped in the mud on the rise to Brambourne,' Julia interpolated eagerly, 'right in front of the Blands' carriage. They had to pick her up, all wet and dirty, and convey her back to the vicarage. Imagine!'

'And do the rumours relate what sex the child is?' Beatrice enquired.

'It was a boy,' Silvia said happily. 'A dear little baby boy.'

A flood of emotion sent the blood to James's cheeks. He hid his face in his coffee cup, only to become conscious that his hands were shaking. He sipped slowly to steady himself, and counted in his head. By his reckoning the baby was, if anything, overdue.

'I remember now the injury she had,' Jessica said suddenly. 'A badly sprained ankle. It was twisting it on that dreadful bit of road that caused her to go over!'

James choked over his coffee, losing his breath entirely. By the time Beatrice had thumped him on the back and a servant had poured him a glass of water, his face was crimson; his eyes streaming. It would have been impossible to tell whether their moisture was due to emotion or choking or laughter – or indeed all three.

Six days passed. James had to possess his soul in patience. Godfather-to-be or not, he could not go rushing in to see the child before the danger period for puerperal infection was over, and Susannah out of her bedchamber. He flung himself into work, driving to Winchester to see the attorney, Mr Fewtrell, making innumerable notes and indexing them, and riding round the fields, swearing under his breath at the wet state of the land, the ruin of the winter wheat and the rotting of the turnips. Yet all the time his mind was on Susannah and the baby: he could not remember being so impatient to see anything since the gift of his first horse, the first to be his very own, not a pony passed down from his sister Charlotte.

At breakfast the following Monday, Rosalind announced her intention of walking to Brambourne vicarage with a basket of fruit for Cousin Susannah. 'I suppose somehow I shall manage to fit it in to the course of the morning,' she added, 'though I scarce can tell how with so much to be done about the house, not to mention the week's menus to be gone through with cook.'

'I will take it for you,' Beatrice and James said in chorus.

'I am riding to Brambourne to hunt toads in the manor pond with William Waterton later.' James said. 'The vicarage will be on my way.'

'I was intending to visit Cousin Susannah to admire her baby – we can ride together.' A mischievous look came over Beatrice's face. 'I can only hope that Mr Stacey has recovered his temper. He seemed vastly put out yesterday!'

James cast her a guarded sidelong look aslant his nose. 'Do you know of any reason why?'

'Yes, of course, and so do you ... But no, I forgot, you were not at church yesterday, were you? Father and I nearly disgraced ourselves. It was as funny as any farce at the Winchester theatre. You will remember we received certain tubs of moonshine a week ago? So did Mr Bland and Mr Stacey. Mr Stacey, like Papa, had sensibly bottled his off and disposed of the evidence. The Blands, in their usual muddle, had not. When they were warned, only just in time, that certain persons were a-snoop, Mr Bland told Dick and another lad to hide them. So they dropped one into a newly dug grave and back-filled the hole: the other they put in the pulpit. No one warned Mr Stacey, who, of course, is still taking the morning services!'

'How the devil did he contrive to preach his sermon?'

'First he stood back behind the tub, his face distant and disgusted, then he tried to kneel upon it but found it at the wrong height, finally, when he reached the high point of his peroration he leaned over it and almost over-balanced! And can you guess what was the text of his sermon? "Wine is a mocker, strong drink is raging" – directed at Barney Bidewell and his like! Papa and I were in agony.'

It was a typical March day: a high wind shifting curds and whey clouds sideways across a clean-washed blue sky; rooks cawing around the tops of the lime trees; blackbirds with their beaks full of nesting material flying in and out of the tangled hedges; snowdrops gleaming on the ivied banks below. James and Beatrice rode silently and briskly to Brambourne, he controlling his impatience with difficulty.

At the vicarage a beaming Becky flung open the door into the sitting-parlour to announce them. Afterwards, James could remember little of those first minutes. He was aware of Susannah, looking remarkably pretty and well, lying on a sofa with a rug over her legs and a small bundle in her arms. He was conscious of deep relief that neither Sedley nor any neighbours were in the room, only Susannah's mother, hiding her mingled pleasure and embarrassment beneath a dignified front. There were greetings and congratulations and the passing of a basket of fruit and a bunch of snowdrops, and Susannah holding the tiny flowers momentarily against her face, their delicacy touching her soft skin, and all the time her eyes watching him. There was laughter and a touch of shyness and constraint. He felt himself to be over-large and awkward and ridiculously tongue-tied. He could think of nothing sensible to say to her. Beatrice peeped at the baby and made all the expected remarks and then Susannah turned to him, her eyes challenging. 'Come and see him, Cousin James!'

Beatrice moved away and he bent to look. Susannah pulled a shawl aside and he saw a minute face, composed, apparently asleep, with wisps of brown hair above. Then as he gazed the child stirred and opened its eyes. James's heart began to beat with suffocating strength. The irises were of a richly dark blue: they were eyes he had seen thousands of times in dozens of looking-glasses and they gazed back with a serious intent look as if memorizing his face. A tiny fist broke free of the enveloping shawl and waved in the air; James touched it with a finger and at once the fist opened and closed, to hold his finger in a determined clutch. And then his heart felt strange, warmed and exhilarated as never before.

Susannah spoke softly: 'His name is to be Piers James Sedley – for his grandfather, his godfather and his father.'

James swallowed. 'Piers James ... How very handsome!'

From behind him Beatrice said: 'Goodness, is James to be his godfather? Handsome indeed! And does Mr Stacey know that his son's godfather-to-be did not listen to his sermon yesterday?'

'I promise to attend this Sunday,' James said with mock-solemnity.

Piers closed his eyes and yawned, as though making his own comment. James watched this extraordinarily adult grimace with enchantment, until suddenly his emotions threatened to become overwhelming. Then he knew he must leave before he betrayed himself. Somehow he managed to say the right things and to get himself out of the house, aware of the smile lurking in Susannah's eyes and of Beatrice's surprise at his abruptness. Beatrice would not go yet, she said, she intended to sit awhile by the fire and sample Susannah's refreshments; she would have a far more pleasant and civilised morning than James would, chasing toads in the Watertons' cold pond!

Once he was out in the cool air and on his horse, James decided he would not ride straight to Brambourne manor but would head for the open downland. He wanted solitude. The atmosphere at the Watertons' would stifle him.

He rode along the lane, turned into a wood where the narrow track made him duck his head from time to time to avoid low branches. It was a beech wood, its floor tawny with beechmast, sprinkled here and there with pale wood anemones that turned their heads from the currents of air. Far above him the tops of the trees moved vigorously in the strong breeze and birds sang in an endless outpouring of feeling, piercing and clear, that seemed to echo what was in his heart.

Out of the woods and up a green track, and man and horse emerged onto the downs. The lower slopes were dappled with sheep, each accompanied by a tiny lamb. The wind was pushing the last rags of clouds high above the land and their shadows raced across the slopes as if they, like the birds, were exhilarated by the coming of spring. James pressed on upwards till he could look down over the valley and see the silver ribbon of the Test and the far blue hills beyond it.

Then he urged his horse to a mad gallop across the short-cropped turf, stabbing with one hand at the air, shouting: 'My son, my son!' And the unhearing hills echoed back faintly, distantly, 'My son, my son!' And again James yelled: 'Piers James, my son!' and rode on laughing wildly as his words came back at him.

17

Spring came slowly, cold winds flayed hands and faces, the rain and mists returned, March went out on a flurry of snow.

But at last the weather had to relent. On a morning in late-April that was full of sunshine, Susannah carried her son out through the orchard to where the meadows began. Hedges and trees were breaking into shrill green leaf, and drifts of daffodils were bending before a soft breeze. In the orchard a robin was cascading the notes of his spring song and over the fields the larks were trilling, endlessly, effortlessly, far above the delicate blades of the young wheat, out of sight in a shimmering blue sky. Susannah settled her son in the crook of her arm, turning him to look at his new world, jigging him gently, laughing. 'Look!' she commanded him. 'Look at the sky and the trees and the flowers! It's spring, Piers, your first spring. Look at it, smell it, listen to it! Isn't it wonderful?'

She must not stay long outside: Sedley's mother had finally come to visit them. But for a few minutes she could be alone with her child, alone and happy. A brimstone butterfly appeared over the hedge, frolicking in the sunlight, and along the edge of the field were pheasants, their feathers glowing copper in the distance. The baby stared placidly ahead and blinked. Susannah hugged him closer. 'You'll see,' she said. 'You'll see!' Back through the orchard, where the apple trees at last had buds, and they paid a visit to the pigs, sunning themselves outside their sty. Gamma had gone the way of all pig flesh, but Alpha and Beta had been kept for productive purposes and were visibly about to fulfil that duty, their great bellies spread across their straw. Susannah picked up a stout stick with her left hand and leaned over the wall to scratch along Beta's spine while the sow encouraged her with short pleased grunts. 'Pigs, Piers,' Susannah said, and her son screwed up his face and sneezed.

In the walled garden the weeding man was working with the deceptively slow plod of the countryman. He was one of Prudence Paine's Dismore cousins, taken on by Sedley to appease Brambourne feelings, but unlike old Mrs Dismore, the one-time housekeeper, he appeared to enjoy his work, bent and gnarled though he was, and he was clearing out the weeds at a steady speed and for only a shilling a day. Susannah had plans for the garden: she had a vision of lavender and lilies and roses, of colour and scent. Already she had pots full of cuttings begged from her mother and the Blands sheltering beneath the south wall. She called a greeting to the weeding man, checked her pots for moisture and returned to the house. She would rather have had Pier's cradle carried out to the garden and started on the planting, but Sedley's mother would not like to be neglected.

Not that Mrs Stacey could be deemed demanding. Had Susannah suggested leaving her for an hour the huge sunken eyes would have regarded her with concern, the sweet voice have begged her not to have regard to her mother-in-law, of course she must continue with her normal life: Mrs Stacey was used to being alone, it had been her lot for many years. By chance Sedley had been out when she first arrived, called to the bedside of a dying old man; she was deeply hurt that after all she had endured he could not be there to greet her. But so sympathetic had Susannah been to the rigours of the long and arduous journey by chaise, so apologetic for the disappointment of her son's absence on her arrival and so full of the regret it would cause Sedley, that the querulous note had receded from Mrs Stacey's voice and the two ladies found themselves quite in accord. 'So very kind ...' Sedley's mother had sighed, making her feeble way up the vicarage path on Susannah's arms. Ensconced with her feet up on the sofa by Susannah and having consumed a bowl of strengthening broth brought by Becky, Mrs Stacey had revived sufficiently to comment on the furnishings of the sitting-parlour: 'Most charming, most elegant ... Indeed, the vicarage is far more to be recommended than Sedley led me to believe. I should not care for such rural seclusion myself … my health, you know, I am a sad invalid and I must have attendants of a level that only a city can afford … but such a place as this is not to be despised!' Piers James Sedley she had found a dear little man, with a remarkable resemblance to her adored late husband, whose demise, she had been sure Mrs Stacey would understand, she still lamented every day of her unfortunate life. If Piers grew up to be like his grandpapa he would be a saintly man.

In some ways she was an unexpectedly easy guest. She did not wish Sedley to take her gadding about, to visit places like Winchester or Stockbridge, she was content to lie languid upon a sofa. To talk was her greatest interest, to have sympathetic listeners her delight; she absorbed sympathy as a cut flower absorbs water.

As Susannah reached the house Becky emerged to tell her that Miss Beatrice Manningford had come calling and she'd put her in the sitting-parlour. Susannah relinquished the baby into Becky's arms and went inside to find the two ladies regarding each other with the same amazement they might have bestowed on a Chinaman.

'We have introduced ourselves,' Beatrice said briskly, rising to kiss Susannah on the cheek.

'I have had a most interesting conversation with your lame friend,' Mrs Stacey said in die-away tones, leaning back among her cushions. Clearly she had found contact with Beatrice's vigorous and astringent personality exhausting, even for a matter of minutes.

'I shall not stay,' Beatrice announced. 'No, no refreshments, thank you, Cousin Susannah. I came merely to ask for your help in a certain matter. More of your help, I should say.'

'Of course. What is it?'

'How finally to prise Katharine from her seclusion. She walks in the park unveiled now, and she will dine uncovered with kindly old friends such as the Blands, the Goddards or the Knights. But there it ends. She is too nervous of the Waterton ladies to dine with them – and she refuses to walk in the village.' Beatrice turned to Mrs Stacey. 'I should explain that my sister's face has been marred by smallpox, and despite Cousin Susannah's clever design of a cap and a special way to wear her hair to conceal the worst marks, she is still afraid to appear in public.'

'How sad for her,' Mrs Stacey said. 'But perhaps she is right to hide herself. The sensibilities of others must be considered also. I remember in Bath once meeting a lady similarly afflicted over the dinner table and she quite put me off the delicious food. My friends agreed that it was selfish to upset others thus.'

Beatrice drew in a sharp breath, but on catching Susannah's eyes she exhaled it again and contented herself with saying tartly: 'My sister is not an object to disgust. Nor does her family see itself in the light of jailors to imprison her for no fault of her own.'

'She is someone for whom I have a high regard,' Susannah said. 'And she must not continue as she is, my cousin is quite right.'

'I do have a plan,' Beatrice said. 'I thought that if several of us rode with her in a party she would attract less attention. To start with we would stay off the roads, but as she grew more confident we might one day find ourselves riding through Abbotsbridge, with Katharine hardly aware of how she got there.'

'An excellent scheme.'

'And one you must join, Cousin. I know there is the problem of your having no horse, but here you can oblige us twice over. We have a sick groom who can't ride, so that if you exercised my second horse or one of James's hacks you would be helping us as well as Katharine. Pray say yes!'

Susannah said: 'I should look churlish if I didn't. Yes, gladly.'

'Then that is settled and I must leave.'

As Beatrice rose to her feet and drew on her riding gloves the door opened and Sedley came in. Through the door with him came the sounds of the baby's vigorous protests.

In reply to Sedley's greetings Beatrice said with amusement: 'I can hardly hear you for your son's noise. A healthy pair of lungs!'

'I expect he's cross at being put in his cradle,' Susannah said. 'He prefers to be nursed by his grandmama.'

'I'm not surprised,' Beatrice said. 'Males like attention.

Goodbye, Mrs Stacey. You must be proud to have such a fine lusty grandson.'

There was a pause. Mrs Stacey's head moved in negative fashion on her cushions. Then her voice spoke with acidity: 'Perhaps proud is not quite the word one should use, eh, Sedley? Surprised, one should rather say, so early in the marriage as he arrived.'

'He came prematurely,' Sedley said with equal acerbity.

Mrs Stacey's eyebrows arched upwards. 'My dear Sedley!' she sighed.

The moment had come that Susannah had desperately hoped to avoid - and in front of Beatrice, too. She had anticipated some attack, but not like this. Yet perhaps this way was more clever, for Mrs Stacey evaded any open discussion, the unpleasantness that one like she would so much deplore.

Sedley crimsoned and Susannah saw that she must move swiftly to neutralise the poison. 'Oh, Sedley,' she said as if his mother had never spoken, 'would you be so kind as to see to Cousin Beatrice's mare for her? Becky put her in the stable. We'll meet you by the little picket gate to the lane, it's the shortest route for my cousin.' And as Sedley strode angrily off, she walked slowly with Beatrice through the front garden, between clumps of narcissus and daffodils, talking gaily of the new flower borders she planned here, but relieved when an unknown young man trotting briskly past the house on a dappled grey caught their attention by raising his hat and calling a greeting.

'Good morning, Miss Beatrice. Good morning ma'am!'

'But who ...? No, I have it,' Susannah said. 'The new physician. And in a hurry! I never saw old Doctor Huskett in a hurry. He clearly knows you – I trust you've not had to consult him?'

'Goodness no,' said Beatrice. 'No, I met him at the Blands yesterday. He is staying with them, didn't you know?'

'No! Yet I only spoke to them a couple of days ago.'

'He had taken a room at The Bull, but Mrs Bland naturally considered that unsatisfactory and whisked him off to the rectory - somewhat overwhelming for a stranger, but one does see advantages to the arrangement. He'll have sensible advice on which house to take locally, while they will have a tame physician on the spot to advise on Mr Bland's condition.'

Susannah was laughing. 'How reassuring for them all.'

'Mrs Bland is already convinced he is exactly what is called for in the village – someone intelligent, energetic, full of modern ideas, someone who will cure all our ailments!'

'In short, a miracle worker.'

'He seemed to me a sensible fellow,' Beatrice said. Her eyes gazed along the empty lane. 'And he rides a handsome horse.'

Sedley appearing then with her skewbald, he assisted her into the saddle and she rode off smiling. Sedley gave Susannah a long hard stare, appeared to be about to say something, but, changing his mind, swung round on his heel and walked off. Susannah looked after him, sighed and lowered her head, then, noticing with disgust several pieces of ground elder appearing beneath the hedge, she began to tug them viciously from the soil.

Late that afternoon Sedley went to the church with the intention of deciding various matters, including the re-siting of the font. Long rays of sunshine shone through the old stained-glass windows and spilled soft colours on to the sloping walls; a big brown moth, disturbed from its rest, fluttered up the nave; he did not notice. He stood contemplating the hewn stone of the Saxon font, his eyes unfocussed, his mind elsewhere. Sedley had never been a man given to introspection or self-doubts; he had always easily transmitted his natural self-confidence to others, and in turn their belief in him had confirmed his large assurance of his capabilities. Susannah was the first person to have made him stop and consider. That he had fallen a victim to her sensual wiles had shaken his confidence in his ability to resist temptation, and it had not been a passing and forgotten misdemeanour moreover, its results were with him daily in the person of his wife and now the child, and in his relative penury. He had made something of a comeback in that, as a married couple, he and his wife were widely welcomed at the dinner tables of the gentry, but it had been borne in on him recently that Susannah was more warmly received than he; while he recognised that a mischievous desire on the part of certain members of the Manningford family to tease Miss Waterton

212

and the Fulbroads might partially account for this, the fact that he had been courting Miss Waterton removed any salve to his injured self-esteem.

Now there was the matter of the child. Its early arrival had caused him the most acute embarrassment. It had been inevitable that he would have to account for its too swift appearance, but while six or seven weeks was easily accountable for in terms of a premature child, a good three months was not. He writhed beneath the mixture of ill-concealed glee and disapproval evident among his parishioners as they spoke of his joy at becoming a father. And his mother would not augment his income.

He turned from the font and began to pace up the nave. Joy! If he could with a wave of a wand have removed the child and its mother from his life he would have done so. He supposed Susannah was well enough. She ran the vicarage competently and with praiseworthy thrift; she entertained his occasional guests to a pleasing standard; when they dined out her youth and beauty did him credit – except when men such as William Waterton made their lewd interest all too clear; she discussed Church matters with him with a knowledge and perceptiveness that were laudable when they did not exceed his; she was an acquiescent partner in the marital bed. Had she come from a different class of person, had she brought with her to marriage a respectable portion, had it not been for the child, he could well have been highly satisfied with his wife. But these were stumbling blocks that could not be ignored: particularly the child.

It was peaceful in the church. No sounds here of his mother's plaintive voice, of the baby's crying – yet the noise of them were ringing in his head. 'My dear Sedley!' his mother had said. Scornfully, 'My dear Sedley!' What had she meant by it? She could have been implying merely that the weeks were too many to be credibly covered by the excuse of prematurity – or she could have meant that Piers was a full-term child. He could not ask her. He could ask no one.

He recalled Piers' face at birth: minute, it had seemed, a crumpled visage with features like dabs of putty, the hair a scanty fluff. He had no way of telling if that was how a full-term child looked, he had seen none so young. The brown

213

moth was fluttering just in front of him; he struck at it with his hand, sending it down to the floor where it flew in faltering spasms along the tiles. He ignored it and strode up to the altar, to stand there glowering at the showy cloth Miss Waterton had embroidered as a gift to the church, his mind recollecting, brooding. Mrs Bland had scolded Susannah for working too hard some weeks before the birth, as had Mrs Trotter; she had fallen from that weak ankle on a lane that he had many times censured as dangerous; surely she had been a virgin when he had first taken her: there had been the evidence of the blood on the sheet. And yet ... she had been strangely certain so soon that she was pregnant ... vehemently persistent in her demands that he must marry her. No, she would not have dared, no woman would dare, foist another man's child on him. The thoughts that had been fluttering in his mind were sick thoughts that he must obliterate. He turned to walk back down the aisle and encountered the brown moth again, now jerking in circles. He brought his heel down sharply on the little furry body, endings its life. The sudden violent act had a cathartic effect on him. He rubbed sweating palms along the seams of his breeches and breathed deeply, feeling the tension leaving him. Women could be the devil with their jealousies and their rivalries: his mother, Miss Waterton, they were both the same, craving to injure Susannah because he had made her his wife. In reaction he felt almost warm towards her. He would ask her for her views on the siting of the font: Piers would be the next child to be baptised in it.

In mid-May the villagers of Abbotsbridge heard that, the bill for enclosure having passed the Commons and the Lords, the Royal Assent had been given on the twelfth, and the commissioners appointed, led by Richard Haynes of Salisbury, to carry out the provisions of the act. Jack privately told Susannah that Counsel for those petitioning against enclosure had been allowed little time to put their case, the hearing lasting a matter of minutes only. The Committee found that the necessary majority of three-fourths in value had given their consent to the bill, and it was reported that the Standing Orders had been complied with. That was all the Committee cared for.

The commissioners were to come to Abbotsbridge at a bad

time. They would not have been welcomed by the majority of villagers in any circumstances, but this was a time of dearth and distress, of disease and rising prices. Prudence Paine had seen her three times three deaths and more; she and Martha Pither had no need to compete for work, the level of sickness was frightening; typhoid and measles were working their ravages in the poor house and silently extending their talons into the labourers' families; chest infections were rife and Sedley complained of the difficulty in making his sermons heard above the coughing and spluttering.

The price of food had risen beyond the reach of the purse of the poor and the dole of bread, meat and fuel organised by Mr James Manningford and Mrs Stacey continued on into the spring. In Basingstoke Corn Exchange at the beginning of March wheat had reached the great price of fifty-two shillings per quarter; by the end of March it had risen by almost twelve per cent to fifty-eight shillings and it continued to rise, shooting to an unbelievable peak of ninety shillings a quarter.

The distress was felt through all England, yet the actions taken to remedy it were piecemeal, local and fitful. There were civic and parish collections for the deserving poor; the army gave up the use of hairpowder and a royal proclamation trumpeted its discouragement of the use of flour for that purpose; the Middlesex magistrates ceased their normal consumption of pies and puddings; Parliament offered bounties on imported wheat.

Poverty and near-starvation inevitably led to sullen turbulence and to food riots. Hardly a county in England was free from disturbances. The mobs, often largely consisting of housewives and led by them, behaved with extraordinary restraint, confining themselves mainly to seizing food and then organising its distribution at what they decided were fair prices. When these mobs marched there was little plundering of shops, though several mills and their millers were attacked. The ringleaders of either sex were seized and punished. With the example of France immediately across the Channel the authorities were made nervous; the misery surrounding the rich in the countryside could not be ignored and those existing at starvation levels were becoming desperate. Mr Fulbroad fulminated across the Watertons' dinner table that it was as he

215

had forewarned, the Jacobins were on the march, and, with an angry glance towards Susannah, added his conviction that all of that persuasion should be arrested forthwith.

There were turbid undercurrents of feeling in Abbotsbridge, and with the commissioners arriving shortly to start examining all claims to land and common rights, and the surveyor and his men measuring and mapping every inch of the village, James knew that immense care and tact would be needed to forestall an outburst of anger. Twice since the news came of the passing of the Bill he had been stoned. He had spoken of it lightly when warning Beatrice not to ride alone: 'Only a handful of earth and gravel from behind a hedge – I was more in danger from my frightened horse than from the fellows attacking me – but *you* should not take risks.' Yet he was conscious of a deep unease: the men surveying the land would be highly vulnerable to stones and pitchforks.

On a showery May morning he sat in the library pondering the best course of action to take. Josh Pither, as constable, must be ready to act should trouble erupt. Josh at the forge and John Hayter at The Bull were well placed to hear any rumours of malice flying around, but while Josh was neutral, Hayter, with common rights to be extinguished, would balk at anything smacking of spying for the Manningfords. Then who could be the intermediary? The answer, when it came to him, was obvious – Jack Trotter. For both men it would be safer and more natural to discuss any approaching trouble with Jack. And the need to communicate with him would give James an excuse to visit Susannah and the baby: it was extraordinary, the irresistible urge he had to see them both. He was thankful that Stacey's sighing watchful mother had at last left.

A ray of sunlight struck his desk, causing him to blink. He glanced from the window and saw that the sun was shining on the trees and the park, and the rippling water of the River Test beyond was glinting with light. He looked down at the papers awaiting his attention. There was four or five hours of work there: he must compel his mind to concentrate on the estate accounts that he had now taken over from Ambrose; he must make notes of the points Ambrose and he wished to raise with Mr Fewtrell at a meeting in Winchester next day, and there were a dozen letters awaiting his attention . . . yet all the time the fitful sunshine was tempting him outside. It was mayfly time on the river, the trout would be rising strongly and for days now he had been imprisoned indoors by work and by rain: the temptation was almost too much. He glared at the laden desk; he would do all he could this morning, but he would fish this afternoon come what might. And at dusk he would ride to see Jack Trotter. That settled, he bent his head to his work.

As James walked down to the river he found his mind dwelling again on Susannah and the baby and when he would see them next. They intruded more and more upon his thoughts and he could not understand it: women had always played a part in his life, but not a major part; they were amusing to flirt with, delightful in more intimate relationships, but he had never cared deeply for any one of the females who had entered into his life, never worried about her health or her welfare, or whether his actions won her approval. And babies were entirely a matter for the other sex to endure: if he had thought of them at all it was as squalling creatures better avoided; yet here he was, ludicrously enslaved by a baby's toothless grin.

A heron rose at his approach and flew off up river, its long legs dark against the bright sky. He watched it absently. It really was incredible that a nursemaid turned curate's wife to whom he had behaved so badly should have rooted herself this deeply in his life. Originally it had been his guilt that had led him to strive in certain ways to help and befriend her, now it was for her own sake. He struggled to identify what it was in her that appealed to him. She was lovely, there was no denying that, but he had known many women in London quite as beautiful and far more worldly and sophisticated. But it was not just her looks: he liked her sense of humour, her directness, the courage with which, wrong-headed or right, she fought for what she wanted and attained it. He admired the way she guided her tiresome prosy husband without his realising it; James's instincts where she was concerned told him that the marriage was not proving a success, yet never by word or look did she betray this. Above all he liked her intelligence, the mettlesome intelligence that challenged his. It was as exciting to have an argument with her as it had been to fight a tough case at the Bar; there was no man among the local gentry who made the demands upon his mind that she did. And she had awakened him to new facets of country living, a new understanding of people. He had thought he knew about the country because he had hunted and shot with his friends, because he had read books on agriculture: now he saw the narrow bounds of his knowledge. He saw that he had lumped the poorer folk of the village together at one level, hardly bothering to separate them in his mind from the criminal poor of London, unaware of their sturdy pride and their endless fight to preserve an independent life. And though it seemed odd to him at times, he did not resent Susannah for her scoldings, rather they added to his respect for her. He had never cared for toadies, not of either sex.

He reached his favourite spot on the river bank and saw that the river was flowing full and fast, swelled by the recent rain, and above it hundreds of mayflies were dancing, sparks of pale gold in the light. He stood very still, studying the scene. For a moment he saw nothing, then a splash and a dimple by the opposite bank showed where a fish had snatched a fly, and then the sunlight glistened on the side of a trout as it leapt in greed.

He set down his tackle and began to ready himself, a smile on his lips. A small party of riders was to accompany Katharine along the meadows on the morning after next and James had been coerced into joining them; it would be tiresome slow work, for Katharine was no horsewoman, but Susannah would be there: he would be able to talk to her about the changes in the village; the spice would not be lacking. He fixed his fly and gave his line a preliminary swing. It was a dull day on which Susannah was not present ... His mind jumped with shock and his arms dropped: an old memory had come to him, a memory of a friend at the Bar, announcing to him with embarrassed pleasure his engagement to be married. James had demanded to know what the devil he meant by tieing himself up at so young an age, to which his friend had replied with simplicity: 'When a day without the lady is a dull day, then one knows what love is.' James jerked his drifting line from the water. What nonsense: his mind was playing tricks on him. He had an affection for Susannah, that was all; she was stimulating and amusing. And he felt a responsibility towards her ... and towards Piers ... and he did passionately wish he could do more for them than merely ensuring the Staceys a place in local society and acting as Piers' godfather. But that was not love, the rubbishy talk of the sentimentalists. Surely not. Widening circles on the water showed where more and more trout were rising to the lure of the dancing, dipping mayflies. Damn it, he would concentrate on his fishing, leave this nonsensical stuff to the poets and the philosophers. He took his rod in a firm grip.

It was an afternoon of excellent sport and he was mopping his forehead after a tussle with his second trout, when he became aware of someone walking down the river path from the house. He swore beneath his breath. Let no one come and disturb his fish with their thundering footsteps or inane remarks. At that moment he saw a trout that looked a monster lying in the sunny ripples at the tail of a weed clump: though he knew that the refraction of light could lend enchantment, he was certain it was truly big. This one he must have. The sun disappeared behind a cloud, the trout became invisible, but he had its lie to an inch.

It was a woman walking along the path, he could see her from the corner of his eye as he prepared, with heart-thumping anticipation, to make his cast. Silently he urged her to stand still. Now, have at you, trout! He cast and cast again. The fly barely touched the surface. There was a splash and a flurry of water and his line tightened; the fish rushed downstream. James stumbled hurriedly along the bank, his eyes glued to the water.

The woman had stopped and was standing motionless this side of a weeping willow tree some twenty yards away. It must be Katharine, no one else would be so quiet. The fish had stopped; he tightened his line steadily and the fish started up, tugging and turning and twisting and tugging again. Pray God his hook held! It seemed an eternity of fighting and manoeuvring before it was landed, but at last he had it, secure at his feet. He straightened his back and gazed at it in triumph: not a monster, but a damned good trout, the best he'd had yet.

'Bravo!' a laughing voice said. 'What a handsome catch.'

Not Katharine, Susannah. He turned in shock. Susannah, coming close to the water's edge, admiring his trout lying in the grass. Abruptly, he thanked her for standing so quietly.

She smiled. 'My brother Jack fishes when he has the chance. I have been carefully raised.'

'Clearly.'

She did not detract from his peace, standing beside him, watching the river, rather she added to it. A pair of coots was pottering upstream; from somewhere came the musical note of a moorhen. She said softly: 'I rarely walk this way; it takes more time. But it makes a pleasant change from the lane. I have come from a meeting of the musical club, you know.'

'Oh!' he said, giving her a comically guilty look. 'Oh, good Lord! And I should have been there to play some Haydn piano sonatas. I totally forgot. Am I in everybody's black books?'

Amusement lurked in her voice. 'Not quite everybody's. I must admit Miss Waterton was put out at first, but Beatrice assured her you were shocking busy, and she did understand that there were many business matters which clamoured for a gentleman's time. And I understand that fishing for trout in mayfly time is important business! Besides, they were all distracted by a plot to persuade Katharine to play her flute.'

James picked up his rod, running the line absently through his fingers. 'If they rush her too fast, she will dig in her toes.'

'You are right. And Timothy Goddard and I both said so. It was agreed in the end that she should be invited to come and listen until she is at ease, then, perhaps, she will consent to play just to a few of us.'

James bent his head to deal with a fly. 'I thought, once, that she was merely foolish. It takes those who do not know her some time to grasp the extent of her fear of people. I know now the courage it has taken for her to go out as much as she does.'

'I was the same,' Susannah said. 'Few people realise.'

'I did not know you would be at the musical club,' he said.

'I was asked to sing. A test of my voice.'

'And the verdict?'

'I sing true, Miss Waterton says, but it is a very small voice.'

'How unkind.'

'No, that was just. She put me exactly in my place.'

He said quietly: 'I should have liked to hear you sing.'

'And I should have liked to hear you play!'

'Touché! I shall be there next time.'

'It is to be at the Blands'.'

'It is agreed. We shall judge each other.'

He was ready to start fishing again. The air was cooling in the absence of the sun, but the clouds of mayflies seemed to be thickening and splashes in the water showed that the trout were feeding greedily. On a sudden impulse he turned to Susannah, the rod in his hands.

'Have you ever fished?'

'Goodness, no. Never.'

He proffered the rod. 'Would you like to try?'

She looked from it to him, laughing. 'Do you think I should?'

'If you would like to.'

She contemplated the proffered rod. 'Show me how to hold it, please. What do I do?'

He demonstrated the action a couple of times, laying a short length of line on the water and picking it up swiftly again. Then he handed her the rod, placing her hands in position. 'You hold it so, firmly.'

To show her he had to be close: his hands were on hers, their bodies touching, shoulder to shoulder. A remembered scent of youth and wild roses was in his nostrils; a wisp of her hair blew against his chin. He was at once intensely aware of every movement of her limbs, of every lock of her hair, of every breath she took. Nothing in his life had prepared him for feelings like this. He stepped back from her as if to step away from the emotion.

She lifted the rod. 'Yes,' he said huskily. 'Now swing it.'

Obediently, a little awkwardly, she did as she had been shown. Her young body moved and swayed with her efforts; her hair was ruffled by the increasing breeze, strands flying out and up in the air, the slim length of her legs was revealed as the skirt of her muslin gown pressed against them. James watched from a little behind her, taking deep slow breaths of the cooling air.

'Try by the far bank,' he told her. 'Trout will likely be lying in the slack there.'

She jerked the rod. 'Oh,' she said crossly. 'I am so clumsy, Cousin James. I cannot lay the line where I want it.'

Was it his imagination, or had a drop of rain fallen on his cheek? 'It takes time to learn the trick of it,' he said, smiling at her indignation.

He looked up. An odd dark cloud had advanced upon them unseen. It seemed that they might be in for a shower. As if to confirm his suspicions a spatter of drops fell on his face.

Susannah flicked her line smartly up from the water, peering at the rings appearing and spreading on its surface. 'Dear Lord! 'Tis raining. Oh, how annoying!'

The rain increased. 'It is one rascal cloud,' James said. 'Just one. But you must take shelter.' He looked around himself. 'Quickly, under the willow!'

The fronds of the weeping willow reached to the river in front of it and to the tall grass behind it. He seized her hand and ran with her, pulling her into a dusky green cave beneath its boughs. They stood just inside, breathing quickly. For a moment he looked without speaking into her flushed face, into eyes opened wide like dark flowers. The scent of water was very strong. The rain rattled on the leaves. A water-vole splashed into the river.

The dark eyes left his to flicker round and round; he saw her breasts rise and fall, the muslin of her gown, damp in places, clinging to her flesh. He knew suddenly that she was as emotionally aware of him as he of her. She attempted to move further beneath the tree's shelter, tripped on a root and caught at his shoulders to save herself. In a second they had reeled together in a passion of kissing. Once he caught at himself and paused but her hands held him close: 'Don't stop,' she breathed. Together they sank on to the cushioned softness of the mossy, leaf-strewn bank. Overhead the rain pattered gently, rhythmically. 'Dearest,' he said. 'My dearest ...'

Later, much later, she raised herself on an elbow to lean over him, her eyes caressing his face in the half-light. 'That was a revelation,' she said with reverence.

The sun broke through the wet willow fronds in streaks of gold and green. 'Yes,' he said slowly. 'Yes, a revelation.'

18

The baby was crying as Sedley left the vicarage two mornings later, crying in short angry gasps that were intolerably piercing and demanding. It was nothing to do with him, he could do nothing to placate it, yet somehow the cries seemed to rebuke him for his indifference. It was a relief to be out in the cool morning air, away from the fussing women, riding to discuss with Mr Bland the possible ways in which the repairs to the two churches could be funded, back to a world of men and men's problems.

Piers had cried in a similarly demanding fashion when Susannah was attending the musical club at the Manning-fords', but she had not appeared concerned when he had spoken to her about the nuisance of the noise and his consequent inability to concentrate on his work. In fact, he recollected as he turned the mare into the lane, she had been quite strange when she returned, staring at him with distant eyes as if she were seeing him through the wrong end of a spy-glass, and when the baby had started up again, seizing it from its cradle and disappearing upstairs to feed it as though he, Sedley, had not been there at all. He had been forced to follow her and stand at the window with his eyes averted from the full white breasts and the sucking child in order to finish what he had to say. He wanted to know why she had been so late in returning: quite apart from the problems with the child, Mrs Waterton had called to speak to her and he had found it impossible to explain his wife's absence since Mrs Waterton said her daughter had already returned from Abbotsbridge House. 'There was a shower as I walked back and I had to shelter under a tree,'

Susannah had said dreamily. 'Oh, and Cousin James and I were talking.' 'Hm,' he had said stiffly, 'I trust you were not rude to him.' 'No,' she had said, her voice so soft he could hardly hear her. 'No, I was not rude.'

And when Mrs Waterton had called again next day, Susannah had still that remote look. Mrs Waterton had been full of her usual trenchant comments upon village personalities, and complaints of the unreasonably poor spring weather and of how unfavourable the lambing season had proved from the great scarcity of green food, so that more milkless ewes had deserted their lambs than the shepherds ever remembered before – conversation that normally would have held Susannah fascinated, yet she had barely managed to say yes and no in the right places. Mrs Waterton had also asked whether Mrs Stacey now felt herself able to recommence her work with Brambourne's needy folk and expressed herself relieved when she said she did, for she quite despaired herself at the fecklessness of certain families and Mrs Stacey was so clever at setting their feet on the right road. And Susannah had seemed unaware of the great honour Mrs Waterton was doing her by praising her efforts and by calling at the vicarage instead of summoning Susannah to Brambourne Manor. It was a relief to perceive that such unconcern had done her no disfavour in Mrs Waterton's beedy eyes.

His mind was diverted from his wife's odd behaviour by a greeting from over a hedge. 'Good marnin', surr.' Prudence Paine, adjusting her shawl about herself. 'An' 'tis a good marnin' too, ent it, after all the unkid weather we've bin having!'

'Very good,' Sedley agreed, noticing for the first time that the sun was shining from a sky almost free from clouds.

'The Lord has made 'Is face to shine 'pon us at last. Praise him! An' how's that babe of yours that we've seen so little of?'

'He is growing as he should, thank you,' Sedley replied.

'Ah. Come early, so folks says? Weak an' pickèd, was 'e?' She licked dry and scaly lips. 'Must ha' bin, if 'e come that early. Very early, too, hey?'

Sedley looked at her.

'Ah, well,' Prudence said hastily, 'Mrs Bland did say Mrs Stacey done too much an' brought it on 'erself. A shame, after all her good works. An' all for Abbotsbridge folks, too. I 'ope as how they was grateful. I seen the new doctor riding past two days agone – met 'im, have you?'

'Not yet.'

'He looks healthy 'imself, I must say. But young. Now we'll 'ave a young man for the cure of our bodies as well as a young 'un for the cure of our souls. Young men,' Prudence observed with gloom, 'ever wants to change things, things as've bin so since afore time remembered. Time and times I've seen it. An' now there's you, Parson, 'as 'ave moved the lectern crost the church an put gaudy cloths on the altar, and now we hear ye wants to shift the font. Our font, as has bin where it is seven hundred year, so I'm told? Folks feels badly about that.'

'Do they indeed?' Sedley stared down his nose at her. 'Then perhaps you could reassure them that such changes are not made without great discussion. There were nine or ten men in the church to assist me to find the best place for the lecturn, and as for the font, many women have complained what a shocking draughty place it is set in. All those months of poor weather the families of the newborn shivered their way through the christenings, worrying lest their babes or they themselves would end up with nasty chills – or worse. That is no way to make the professions to God in the baptism, as I'm sure you'd be the first to agree.'

Prudence moistened her lips again and readjusted her shawl. Two hens and a cock had appeared round the corner of her cottage, scratching at the earth as they came. Now the cock threw back his head and crowed loudly, derisively. 'There'll be trouble, I shouldn't wonder,' she said with venom. 'Folks don't care for change. Nor they didn't care for us 'aving to walk to Abbotsbridge for our church services times when you an' Mr Bland puts Abbotsbridge services first when 'e was ill. But I've no time to stand here arguing 'bout such matters, I've work to do.' And she hunched her shoulders and disappeared into her cottage.

Sedley rode on, his lips compressed. The Methodists in his congregation were a thorn in his side. Not that they were not fervent members, the trouble was that they were altogether too enthusiastic after salvation, and enthusiasm, in Sedley's book, was bad form. He disliked anything excessive. His beliefs co-

225

incided with those of most of his fellow clergy in the Church of England, consisting as they did of a judicious morality founded on rationality rather than revelation, and an approach of sober common sense. Methodists he considered impudent and encroaching; in particular he disliked the way in which their conviction of their own personal salvation led them to ignore all differences of rank and education and criticise their rightfully ordained pastors. Sedley dug his heels into the mare's sides, fuming. It was for him to direct their feet in the path they should go, not for them to presume to question his ordinances. He had already had to speak to Prudence's husband, Samuel, about his tendency to break into vocal prayers and ejaculations of 'Glory to the Lord!' and other such unnecessary noises during the Sunday services. And instead of showing contrition the man had actually informed him that such overflowings of a passionate heart would always be welcome to his Lord, and asked him why he did not himself pray extempore instead of invariably reading the printed prayer. To let emotions flow unchecked was what Sedley most deplored. Extempore prayers led to emotional outbursts, and from an excess of the emotions came fanaticism and all the evils that implied. Sedley had been sternly repressive with Samuel Paine, a foolish uneducated fellow who could not be expected to understand the matters he was meddling with. Paine, indeed! There was the name of a troublemaker, Thomas Paine, author of *The Rights of Man*: it was from the excess of reforming zeal of men like him that the horrors of the Terror in revolutionary France had sprung. He was a low fellow, too, a stay-maker or some such thing.

There were times when Sedley was tempted to envy those parishes where the followers of Wesley had built a meeting house and taken themselves and their disruptive fervour out of the church, but he struggled to suppress such thoughts. The bosom of the Church of England was broad and could tolerate some variation in men's approach to God; besides, the breaking away of ever more groups of dissenters sapped its strength.

The mare negotiated the ruts down the slope to Abbots-bridge with an awkward gait that set him swaying in the saddle to compensate. Here was another matter that regularly raised his ire. Despite all his representations as to its dangers, despite his wife's fall, nothing had been done by Brambourne parish to repair and improve the lane between the two villages; in his view Mr Waterton was neglecting his duty as the local Justice of the Peace by failing to insist upon action. Sedley knew just how the work should be done. He had read an article in a journal on the work of a blind surveyor called John Metcalfe, who had supervised the building of many miles of turnpike roads in the north. He understood the need for good foundations and proper drainage runnels. In fact, he would relish managing the work himself. He had found the practical task of clearing his own two meadows surprisingly enjoyable, a relaxing contrast to the more cerebral demands of the church. As Coquette trotted into the rectory carriage-sweep Sedley decided he would offer to Squire Waterton to undertake the task, in the autumn, after the harvest, when there would be men available for the work, and provided that he was given all the necessary materials and no skimping. There was no reason why he should not; Mr Bland would not object, being annoyed himself by the state of the lane, and since Sedley constantly moved between the two villages he could keep a daily check on the work. Far better he should gain local fame as a road builder than as the progenitor of an embarrassingly untimely babe.

Half-an-hour later Susannah followed him, riding the young bay horse Beatrice had lent her on another unforgettable occasion. A groom had brought him over to save her the walk to Abbotsbridge before the first ride with Katharine, but at whose command she did not know and had not dared ask. She sat the horse with a straight back, her chin high, self-conscious in a newly-made riding habit with the very latest in buttons and trimmings, and telling herself she did not care whether James noticed, he was too much a man to bother with female fripperies. Yet she had dressed with great care, dabbing scent on the nape of her neck and scorching one ear with the hair-tongs as she wrestled with a new mode for her curls.

She rode with the sun warm upon her back, between banks all white and green and scented with elderflower and hawthorn blossom and Queen Anne's lace. For two days she had been absurdly happy, hugging the thoughts of James to herself, remembering the touch of his hands, the words he had spoken, what they had done. Now she knew why women would endure

227

those unimaginable vissicitudes to fly to the arms of their lovers: it was for the ecstacies of a passion that was shared in tenderness and in laughter, for glorious heights of sensation she had never dreamed of before, for she had had no introduction to their existence. And all that had been hers, given to her by James, without stint, caring for her pleasure before his own.

As she turned the horse into the lime avenue she could see the church and the rectory just beyond and she thought with pity of Fanny, who was repelled by men, afraid of childbirth, frightened of the implications of love: to her, none of this would be given. She would have none of the heightened awareness that fulfilled loving gives of the sheer happiness of living, of the joy of sharing a look or a touch, of the special charm that babies possess, of the beauty of the countryside that had such a limpid freshness today. And it seemed as if a cloud dimmed her contentment. Fanny might be in the schoolroom now with her brothers and sister, or she might be in the drawing room playing her harp, but in either there would be frustration, for while Fanny saw music as her road to fulfilment, that road was never clear of obstacles.

The young horse protested, straining and tossing his head against the apparent intention of his rider to return him so soon to his stable. Susannah urged him on absently. Poor Fanny. For nearly four months the plans for the concert had been held in abeyance: Mrs Bland had been fully occupied with caring for Mr Bland, who had made a slow recovery from his seizure, constantly complaining of headaches and lassitude; Fanny had been forced to spend so many hours with her brothers and her sister that she had barely had time for her weekly lesson with the master who rode over from Winchester, let alone the planning and rehearsals needed for a concert. Now its date was set for early-July, but Fanny was not happy with her performers, 'No one would call them musicians!', nor with the programme Miss Waterton was arranging. 'Paltry stuff – and have you heard the glees and the hearty sea-shanties she proposes for the finale?' Susannah had responded lightly that these would appeal to the less musical members of the audience dragged there by their spouses: 'They will forget how they yawned through the first part and say what a capital evening they've enjoyed!' But Fanny had not been impressed. 'Oh, what we do will be better than nothing in our dull society, but the gulf between our concert and that of true musicians will be as great as that between our family charades in the rectory barn and the plays performed by professional actors at the Winchester theatre.'

As she turned the horse from the lime avenue towards the gatehouse arch, Susannah could hear the clop of restless hooves and the sounds of voices ... James calling instructions to a groom, Beatrice exclaiming over some matter, Miss Waterton's well-bred voice in reply. A cold hand seemed suddenly to grip Susannah beneath the ribs; the sun went in. Who was she among these people of wealth and birth to cause James Manningford to care for her especially, even to notice her? A nobody – worse, a thrusting argumentive nobody, striving to stand upon the shoulders of a cuckolded country curate to reach into their world. How could she look into James's face after the way she had behaved, falling into his arms beneath the willow tree, allowing, even encouraging, him to make love to her? She had an almost irresistible urge to drop the reins and let her horse gallop away back down the avenue as clearly he longed to do. Somehow she got through the arch into the courtyard. They were all there, all talking at once, their horses' rears towards her, one of them evacuating its bowels as if in comment. Not for the first time Susannah asked herself why James had not called to see her yesterday and received no satisfactory answer: if there had been an important meeting surely Sedley would have known; hay-making had not yet started. Her lips tightened. She would meet James Manningford with cool dignity, behaving as if nothing had happened between them, her eyes lowered.

Beatrice turned first, waved a gloved hand, called a greeting; Timothy Goddard smiled and nodded; Rosalind murmured in abstracted fashion; Miss Waterton's horse swung her round till she could no longer ignore Susannah's arrival. 'Oh, Mrs Stacey. I was not aware you were to ride with us.' Susannah could have said the same of her, but refrained.

James ended his instructions to the groom and turned abruptly. 'Cousin Susannah, good morning!'

Her eyes refused to remain down. His eyes were on hers,

229

widening in private greeting, there was a little secret smile about his mouth. The courtyard blurred in a dizzying haze of golden light. The sun shone out. She said: 'Good morning!' demurely, and turned her head lest her face betrayed her.

And then she saw Katharine, her face white, every tendon in her neck rigid, as she sat waiting on a grey pony in a corner by the stables, and Susannah cursed herself and all of those present for thoughtlessness and inattention to the object of their morning's excursion. She urged her restless bay over beside Katharine and touched her hand.

'You look well, Cousin Katharine,' she said softly, 'most elegant. And you have a pretty pony. Is he yours?'

'Julia's!' Katharine gulped. 'He's ... quiet.'

'I wish mine were,' Susannah said ruefully as her mount gave a couple of bucks, then skittered round irritably.

'I warned you Handon needed more exercise!' Beatrice called. 'I am glad you could help with him.'

'I relish the opportunity to be of use,' Susannah said breathlessly. 'But I hope we move off shortly.'

'Unfortunately, Mrs Stacey, we have not yet agreed our route,' Miss Waterton said, evidently re-opening an acrimonious discussion. 'My own suggestion included glimpses of some delightful wild orchids, the bee orchid and the early purple in Bonnard's Copse ...'

Susannah was aware of negative movements from Katharine, closely beside her, of a hand trembling on the reins; the discussion and the anticipation were tautening her nerves intolerably. She said: 'But too many glimpses of crowded cottages in Bonnard's Close ...'

Miss Waterton said: 'Mrs Stacey, your views were not requested.'

Handon twitched his rear-quarters round to lash out at Miss Waterton's horse, missing a fore-leg by a hair's breadth. Miss Waterton's horse jerked sideways, nearly unseating her. To her surprise Susannah heard a gasping giggle from beside her: Katharine, with a hand to her mouth, momentarily distracted and gleeful. Miss Waterton opened her mouth to blister Susannah, but was forestalled by James's decisive accents.

'Let us for Heaven's sakes go, and by the route as first planned. There will be other days to go other ways. And

Samson will be playing pranks like Handon if he does not get the fidgets out of his feet soon.'

He clattered out of the stable yard so that the others followed him perforce, Susannah and Katharine in the rear, leading them behind the house, southwards down to the river and thence to a long grassy ride, inviting for a gallop. And all the time Susannah chatted to Katharine, carefully casual talk designed not to demand mental effort in response, but to halt the terrible darting of the eyes that glared from Katharine's frightened face, searching, always searching, for the people she seemed convinced would be waiting along their ride to stare and to jeer. But not a soul was to be seen in the quiet country-side, only the occasional pheasant or partridge, whirring away at their approach. Gradually Katharine's eyes became less anxious, her tremblings ceased, and when Timothy came to station himself on her other side, she was even able to volunteer some rational remarks about the ball to be held next month for Julia's come-out and tell them how much happier Jessica was now that she went about so much with the Fulbroads: 'Even to visit the silk manufactory in Winchester – and Mr Fulbroad presented her with three lengths of the finest silk, no less. Imagine!'

At the start of the long ride the party paused and James called back to Susannah that she should gallop Handon now. 'I have seen what an uncomfortable ride he is giving you, so over-excited as he is. And my lad here too – we must give them their heads.'

'They are amazingly alike,' Timothy commented. 'Both handsome bays, both keen to go.'

'Not surprising,' James replied. 'They are half-brothers, same stallion, different mares. They take after their father in temperament as well as in looks. But Handon is older by a year, normally less erratic.'

'He has been better schooled,' Beatrice interposed, grinning. 'We must match them against each other one day, James.'

'Race them? Why not now? Are you game, Cousin Susannah?'

'To race?' Susannah allowed the tugging Handon to carry her to the front of the party. 'I have not raced since I was a child teased by my brother. 'Twould hardly be a fair contest.' Her

231

hands adjusted the reins, her teeth showed: 'But yes, yes, I am game. To the old elm tree and back! Are you ready? THEN GO!'

At her shout Handon sprang forward, pulling fiercely at her arms. They shot ahead of James and Samson, Susannah laughing breathlessly at James' yell, struggling to curb Handon's impetuosity as he surged along the track. From behind them, dwindling but still clear, came Miss Waterton's mellifluous contralto, informing the rest of the party that she was surprised at Mrs Stacey. 'Such hoydenish behaviour in a married lady is not what one cares to see!'

James was just behind her and to the right; she could hear and sense him, rather than see him. The wind was whistling through her hair; the eagerness of the horse beneath her was exhilarating; her trick at the start had given Handon the edge. She settled to ride and to win, on Beatrice's behalf as well as her own. For some way the distance between the two horses was consistent, then, slowly, she began to gain ground, ground she needed to circle the tree. The elm stood where the grass ride divided at a fork, its branches were low and wide – she must not ride too close. Circling as near as she dared she caught a glimpse of James' face, stern and determined, barely a length behind her and now gaining on the inside. Suddenly he was level. With hands and feet she urged Handon back down the track; for a while Samson stayed grimly in place, then gradually he seemed to drift backward. The waiting party was near, the race was won, she had only to keep Handon going. Then, from nowhere, James was level with her again and grinning fiendishly, then he was half a length ahead and the shouting, laughing faces flashed past and he had won.

The horses slowed; she had no breath left; James wheeled his horse round and rode back towards her. 'That was . . . an unfair . . . stratagem!' she accused him, at once indignant and amused, struggling with her blown hair.

He was laughing in triumph. 'A perfectly fair stratagem,' he retorted. 'Far more fair than yours at the start! Had you not cheated then I might have let you win!'

She gasped. 'Let me win! Of all the arrogant and condescending men I ever met, James Manningford, you are the worst! Had it not been for that ruse of yours I should have won – I had the edge on you and you know it.'

232

'I will admit it was near thing. And that you rode superbly! It was a splendid race.' He gave his horse's steaming neck an appreciative slap. 'An antidote to the tiresome grind of yesterday.'

'Yesterday?' she asked quickly, too quickly. 'What were you doing yesterday?'

'Ah, so you had thoughts for me, too!' She turned her head to expostulate at so vain an assumption to find him smiling at her in a most disconcerting manner. 'I should have called upon you yesterday were I not caught in a meeting in Winchester, a meeting I could not miss. So do not be cross, not for that or the race. Cry truce, eh? Give me your hand.'

He leaned over, holding out his hand to her. She held hers out, right to his left, shaking her head at him but unable not to smile back. They clasped and a piece of folded paper slid between her fingers. Her heart beat in staccato quivers of feeling. She had barely time to slide the note into the palm of a glove before the others trotted briskly up.

'Close, very close,' Beatrice called. 'Less than half a length in it.'

'It was nothing,' James said. 'The horses are well-matched. We must race them again.'

'We shall,' Beatrice said with enthusiasm. 'And then I shall prove that Handon can win.'

'And you must tell me when, so that I can watch,' Katharine's voice came. 'I would not miss such fun for anything. Could it be next week?'

They looked round, startled. Katharine looked fleetingly embarrassed by their enquiring faces, but no more; her eyes were sparkling, and everything about her, the tilt of her head, the straightness of her back as she sat on the pony, showed her enjoyment of the occasion. 'It was the most exciting thing I ever saw,' she added softly, and scattered joyful looks around the party.

They turned to ride back and as they did so saw a middle-aged man and a youth about to pass them. The pair were trudging along showing no interest in the party, but nevertheless Susannah was aware of a shrinking movement from Katharine. It was Sam Truckle and his second son, driving a cow on a long rope. Katharine pushed her pony on, determined to get away from them, riding to the head of the string of horses. Her movement must have caught the men's attention, for they stopped and stared, exactly what Susannah had been praying they would not do.

Truckle nudged his son, remarking in his loud rough voice: 'Hey, look there, Ned, 'tis the poor pock-marked lass. Don't normally see 'er about, do we?' And then he added something else that only those at the back of the group could hear.

Smiling delightedly, Susannah caught up with Katharine. 'Did you hear what Sam Truckle said? You must have heard it!'

Katharine rounded on her bitterly. 'I knew how it would be. I knew how it would be. How can you smile? How can you be so insensitive? *The poor pock-marked lass* – that's what he said, and that's what they'll always say. I knew nothing had changed. Oh, why did I let myself be persuaded to come out?'

'But you did not stay to hear the rest of it!' Susannah reproached her. '*Whyever do she keep so hid? Why, she's a'most pretty!* That's what Truckle said. That's what they'll always say – pretty, Cousin Katharine! If you had only stayed instead of running away, you'd have heard. Pretty!'

'I do not believe you,' Katharine said, but she looked startled.

'I assure you it is so,' Susannah said.

'It is so,' Timothy said, riding up level with them. 'I heard it myself.'

'Well, there you are,' Beatrice concluded. 'And I tell you, I never heard so good of myself. Best I ever heard was, *That lame girl rides good.* I should burst with pride if someone called me pretty.'

'*Almost* pretty,' Katharine protested, but her lips were twitching. She spoke the words again, as if she were tasting them. 'Almost pretty ...' Happiness irradiated her face. 'Almost pretty! Me!'

The note was discreet and short to the point of terseness; it suggested a day, a time and a place. And yet it had its own charm. It began, "Dearest" and it ended with an outline sketch of a weeping willow that after a moment's study Susannah could see incorporated his initials, J.L.M., James Laurence Manningford; the J and the L forming part of the trunk and the

234

M sprawling above as the canopy. She memorised the contents and was about to burn it when she changed her mind; this she would keep all her life. She turned to her writing slope, in which she kept her writing paper and any letters from Mrs Waterton and others of importance in the parish. There was a secret drawer in one side, held in place by a pin and a spring, a secret Sedley had no knowledge of. She slid the note inside and fastened the drawer shut with the pin. He would never find it there.

It had been agreed with Beatrice at James's suggestion that Handon should be temporarily stabled at the parsonage; as James pointed out, it would be easier for exercising him, more convenient for Susannah. It was convenient in other ways, too.

She met James three miles away, in a quiet spot where two drovers' tracks met and mingled. It was a deliciously warm morning, the air thick with the scents of early summer, of honeysuckle and hawthorn blossom. Spring and its flowers had been late, with frosts persisting even to the end of May, but now spring and summer were colliding in a joyous burst of colour.

James was waiting behind a group of yews all tangled over with wild clematis. 'At last,' he said. 'I was beginning to think you had decided against coming.'

She leaned forward on the horse, her eyes amused. 'You are not accustomed to babies,' she said. 'They set their own routine, which to break is to court trouble. You forgot to consult Piers when you set a time for our meeting!' She made a light gesture of mockery. 'Just for once you have felt ... the drawbacks of parenthood.'

'A salutary experience, to wait upon the will of my small son.'

Her hand flashed upwards to silence him. 'Never say it!' she said, her voice low and urgent. 'Never say that word, there are ears everywhere. He is your godson, no more.'

They rode together to the base of a chalk hill known as Flintpen Ring and tethered the horses to a pair of beech saplings. The climb up was a breathless one, each slanting glances at the other and looking away again, anticipation trembling in their minds as warm and exhilarating as the summer breeze that fanned their faces. A golden and white haze

235

lay over the grass of the hillside where buttercups and cowslips and daisies bloomed, and when they reached the lip of the first of the great encircling banks that gave the hill its name they turned and looked back together, catching their breaths and laughing, looking at Hampshire spread below them like a map, hazed with blue and mauve in the far distance. Susannah was captivated by the view. Before her she could see cornfields and commons all soft greens, and between them, here and there, the chalky white of lanes and the River Test glinting in the light, winding past flint churches and the village thatches. She recognised the church of St Swithun at Abbotsbridge, but the tower of Brambourne's church was invisible.

'It is tucked behind that hummock, there,' James said, pointing. 'And there is Grateley, and look, you can just see Stockbridge. Have you never come up here before?'

'Yes, once, with Mrs Bland and the children, on an exploring party. But I was too busy watching the boys to have time to examine the view.'

When she had gazed her fill they turned to the deep grassy ditch that lay between them and the next rampart.

'The children must have enjoyed themselves here. I should have.'

'Goodness, yes. It was a windy day and they were like seagulls, screaming and tumbling everywhere. They rolled down the slopes. You can see how enticing they are.'

'Exceedingly,' James agreed.

He raised his arms and flung himself full-length on the turf, rolling with abandon down the slope, reaching the bottom with a bump. He lay on his back and looked up at her, laughing helplessly.

'You great child,' she called. 'Now I know you are just a schoolboy at heart!'

'Of course,' he responded. 'Men play their parts – silent, strong, authoritarian – yet inside there is always the boy longing to escape and play. Come down and join me!'

A little devil caught at her; decorum and her new riding habit forgotten, 'I shall. I shall indeed!' she said. And in turn she flung her arms in the air and rolled down, rapidly losing control of her progress, landing heavily on top of James and knocking half the air from his lungs.

236

'Oof,' he gasped. 'Dear God, Susannah ... what a weight you are. You have done for me! Ugh, I shall count myself ... lucky ... if my ribs are unbroken.'

She twisted round to kneel on the turf and look at him with concern. 'Oh dear! I did not intend ... I have not truly broken anything, have I? I did not know I should come down so fast. Forgive me!'

His arms came round her, powerful and demanding, pulling her down hard against his chest: nothing broken there. 'How could I not forgive you, when I love you so ridiculously!'

'You are teasing me again! You had me all in fright, believing I had damaged you,' she scolded. A pause, then: 'What was that you said?'

A hand smoothed back her hair. 'I said I forgave you.'

'No!' she protested. 'No, after that.'

'I remember nothing more,' he said with a wide-eyed look.

'You said ... Tell me what you said!'

'Ah. I remember now! I did mention another matter ...' He leaned over to whisper in her ear.

She looked at him with eyes transfixed in wonderment. 'That's what I thought I heard.' The warmth of him was in such contrast to the coolly formal indifference with which Sedley treated her that she could hardly believe in its reality. She was caught in a daze of happiness, lying in the sunshine on a bed of wild flowers. 'Cousin James ... and now what do you think you are doing?'

Delicately and slowly he was undoing the bodice of her riding-habit. 'Dearest. I am going to demonstrate to you the truth of what I have told you, in the manner most fitting.'

'But that is not the whole truth of love,' she said, teasing him in his turn. 'Though men may speak as if it is. It is also another word of four letters that begins with an "l". How do I tell the difference?' And for an unwelcome second the memory of Sedley's cold lust passed through her mind.

His hands were immediately still. 'You know because I tell you and because it is a part of the whole. What do you wish me to say or do?'

And at once she realised that he had misunderstood her and she cursed herself as a clumsy fool for having aroused an unwanted remembrance in him, too. Swiftly she said: 'Of

237

course. My dear one. And I know because I feel the same.' She took his head between her hands and kissed him, and sensed the momentary hurt vanishing. Then she lay back and helped him with what he called the comical complications of the fastenings of her clothes.

'Your breasts are beautiful,' he murmured, when that part of her was laid bare. He touched them lightly with his fingers: 'Your nipples are like raspberries.' He picked two cowslips and tickled her with them so that she wriggled and laughed and caught his wrists, to hold him away. Then he dropped the cowslips onto her skin, saying: 'Fruit and flowers!' and picked daisies and buttercups and piled them into the nest between her breasts. She told him: 'You are mad, quite mad!' and he looked at her, serious and tender, and said: 'I know, mad for you!' And then he took hold of her strongly.

19

One day they were not there, the next day they were, the
surveyor's men with their chains and their rods, outlined and
menacing up on the skyline. Then they were everywhere, crawling across the valley like beetles, measuring, always measuring,
reducing the villagers' grandiose and rounded claims of acres
to exact figures down to the last square rods, poles and perches.
And the commissioners were there also, demanding that all
claimants to land must send in those claims in writing in their
hands or the hands of their agents, distinguishing the tenure of
the lands concerned and giving all particulars needed to establish their claims exactly. They also demanded sight of title
deeds, bills of sale, copies of the manor rolls, documents that
had been written decades, even centuries ago and tucked away
in dark forgotten corners. The villagers grumbled and cursed
and men like Page and Pettifer trembled. How were unlettered
folk such as they to prepare their documents, or to have their
statements of claim properly drawn up? 'We can't afford no
lawyer,' Dick Pettifer stated in The Bull, 'but folks says if
there's aught put wrong in my claim they'll turn it down flat. It
didn't ought to be allowed.' And there was a growl of agreement from all those present. 'Aye,' Page said. 'My wife's that
worried she 'aven't slept fer a week. An' nag? Dear God! But
what can us do?' 'Ask Jack Trotter to help,' John Hayter said in
a sour voice as he poured Pettifer yet another pint. 'Reckoned
he could stop it, didn' 'e? So he ought by rights to help us now
we're stuck with it.'

Discontent rumbled through the village, affecting everyone.
Many were still short of food and their hunger fuelled their

anger against those who were fat and looked to grow fatter at their expense. Men turned away when the Manningfords or the Fulbroads approached and the surveyor's men reported threatening gestures and muttered curses as they went about their work. Sensibly, the commissioners had decided to stay at the White Hart in Brambourne; it was near, but on neutral ground, so to speak, and they were well looked after. And the surveyor's men also took themselves out of the village when dusk fell. So by mid-June there had been no violence, but the threat and the fear of it were always there, hanging like a sour smell on the air.

And then came the night of the Skimmington. It had been a hot day, one of the few hot days of the summer, and it was a hot night. The men were thirsty after a long day in the fields and they crowded into The Bull and spilled out again into the open space round the inn and the smithy to talk. And the subject of their talk was the state of Charity Bidewell.

Few of the men were averse to giving a woman the occasional clout if she spoke out of turn, but Charity's bruises had long been a cause of deep disapproval, not only to them but to their wives, who spoke forcibly on the subject. A black eye or a swollen jaw was bad enough, said the women, but now she'd lost a tooth and they knew of other bruises out of sight (with knowing shakes of their heads), and she well in the family way again. Barney was bringing bad fame on the village.

The men sucked down their pints and the more they talked about it the more strongly they felt that Barney should suffer for this. No one remembered afterwards who first broached the idea of a Skimmington, though several claimed it, but no sooner had the word passed round than the preparations were under way. Bidewell was said to be skulking in that cottage of his; if they moved sharpish they could shame him properly. John Hayter provided sacks and straw to make the effigy of his old enemy and some of the men ran home to fetch discarded garments to dress it, and to collect the component instruments for the rough music that would accompany its parading round Barney's hovel. Then the effigy was tied on to the most peaceable of Hayter's carriage horses, facing the tail; a battered hat was jammed on its head by a savagely jubilant old man Jurd; the men lined up with the music-makers at the back, and they were off, with many adjurings, one to another, of silence.

Along the road and over the common they went, to find Bidewell's cottage quiet in the light summer darkness, just one rushlight burning behind the half opened shutters. Sam Truckle crept forward to spy and indicated with a raised thumb that their target was indeed there.

'One, two, three, play!' yelled Berry Truckle and Nat Pither in unison and bedlam broke out.

Pots and pans were beaten, cow-bells were rung and posting-horns sounded; one man had a large drum, a member of the church players had brought his trumpet and Dick Pettifer fired off a musket. Round and round they paraded the effigy, shouting and jeering, with Black Betsey's shrieked obscenities clearly discernable above the loudest rough music, they afterwards claimed, that ever had been heard in Hampshire.

The light went out in the cottage; no other sign came of either of the Bidewells. When they had had enough of the music the men turned their attention to burning Barney's image. It burned briskly, sending a fountain of sparks into the dark, and the men and women danced wildly round it, breaking off at intervals to refresh themselves from the barrel some enterprising fellow had dragged there in a handcart. When the fire began to die down they raided the Bidewell kindling and the log pile and dragged out the staves Barney was using to fence off his land. The fire on the common burned until dawn.

But another fire was lit that night. And there was trouble and fighting elsewhere. Martha Pither always swore afterwards that it was from all the enquiries and the questionings and cross-questionings and accusations and counter-accusations that her Josh suddenly developed his shining bald patch. But that could no more be proved than anyone could prove who were the instigators of the fire that burned Mr Fulbroad's barn or the near riot in Brambourne. As Josh said, he couldn't be in three places at once, and all he knew was that a Skimmington was a traditional and allowable way of demonstrating village disapproval, and that he'd heard someone – and in the dark no one could tell who, mind – shout that they'd showed Barney Bidewell their views of him and now they should show Mr Fulbroad. And someone else had shouted that they should tell the commissioners in Brambourne where to go, too. 'Arrh, to the hot place,' growled the crowd. And then the crowd had started to move away, and dear Lord knowed who went where, that was all he could say.

The fire on the common could be seen throughout Abbotsbridge village; the fire that burned Fulbroad's thatched barn was seen for miles. Fulbroad wanted culprits, he wanted hangings and floggings at the cart's tail, he demanded to know who. The village faces were blank: if anyone knew, no one was telling. Normally Bidewell would have been the prime suspect, but Bidewell, to the equal regret of the villagers and Fulbroad, had his alibi. The colour in Fulbroad's face deepened from plum to mulberry; he shouted and cursed, even offered a reward, but the evidence never came.

There was evidence about the Brambourne business and it came largely from Luke Carter. Luke was now courting Becky Pither. He had been sad at losing his first love, Susannah Trotter, to Parson Stacey, but not surprised; he had always known she was too good for him. Becky had brought news of Susannah; sympathetic understanding had ripened into friendship and now to something more. To win Becky, he needed the approval of Josh and Martha, but while Luke was a common labourer, Josh was a man of some importance in the village. With drunken men vowing to cause trouble at the White Hart, thoughts of Becky and Mrs Stacey and Josh swelled in Luke's mind: he set off at a trot for Brambourne.

His intentions were of the best, it was their carrying out that went wrong. A warning to the landlord of The White Hart was all he had in mind, but as he reached the inn he found several men just leaving and a small crowd from the alehouse trooping along the lane, going to view the great fires they had glimpsed. All had been slaking a large thirst, most were scarcely less drunk than the Abbotsbridge men. When they heard Luke's panted warning and his muddled account of a Skimmington, their minds grasped two points: Abbotsbridge men were coming to attack them and it had something to do with Barney Bidewell. Brambourne village had scores to settle on both counts: Barney had insulted their women, Abbotsbridge folk needed to be taught a lesson.

''Twere a good fight,' Luke confided to Becky later. 'A dommed good fight, best I ever saw! Some was wrestlin' an' some was punchin' an' some was clashing with staves, bold as can be. An' Peter Page was blowing 'is hunting 'orn like the Devil was blowin' 'is last trump. Near as much noise as the Skimmington, 'twas, you!'

'Go on,' Becky breathed, enthralled.

'Aye, an' that there bull-terrier of Elias Dismore's, 'e gets his teeth into Dick Pettifer's leg an' he won't let go, not till Sam runs into the inn an' gets the pepper pot an' chucks it all at 'is nose. Then 'alf of them's sneezing so bad they can't see what they're doing and that there righteous gallibagger Paine, 'e got two black eyes, don't look so righteous now!' He paused to chuckle.

'But what set 'em off like that?' Becky demanded. 'You do tell a tale arsuppards, Luke Carter!'

'Oh, that. 'Twas Clerk Kimber, standin' in the lane like a dummle, telling our folks they couldn't go no further, when all they wanted was to talk to them commissioners. Couldn't take that, could they? Some'un floored 'im wi' a clunk, didn' see 'oo,' craftily, 'not in the dark, like. Then everyone joins in.'

Noses had been bloodied, a couple of men knocked temporarily silly, but no mortal wounds had been given and no one would say who had hit whom. Honours were about even. The authorities in both villages let well alone.

The blood-letting had relieved the fever, overnight the temperature in Abbotsbridge cooled. The threats to the surveyor's men stopped, and those who had turned away when the Manningfords approached now called a greeting. It seemed they were wishful to make amends. Josh told James via Jack Trotter that sensible folk felt that burning barns was going too far, moreover, that no one in the village had been caught and punished for their misdeeds had been a relief. For days folk had eyed each other and the reward notice Mr Fulbroad had posted and feared the worst. 'Summat like them nasty letters those Frenchies denounce each other with,' said Josh. But nothing had happened and the village was grateful for small mercies. 'Only,' muttered Josh, 'what'll happen when the land's redivided?'

Midsummer morning, and Arthur climbed over the flint and brick wall that encircled Abbotsbridge Park and slid into the narrow band of beechwood on the other side. He crouched against an old tree for cover, looking and listening, but the wood was quiet. Despite its apparent emptiness Arthur stayed where he was for some minutes, only his eyes moving. The Manningford gamekeeper was a young Jurd, energetic and determined and peculiarly ferocious against vermin, in which category he included Arthur. Arthur had a wild creature's terror of being caught and locked up; he disliked reconnoitring the woods and spinneys by daylight but at times it was necessary: Squire Waterton had been true to his threat and there were mantraps in the Brambourne Manor coverts; now the Abbotsbridge lands must be searched. Satisfied that no immediate threat loomed, Arthur moved off, his passage among the trees as silent as a shadow.

When he came to a patch of ferns he moved particularly carefully, his eyes searching. There was a passage through it narrowed almost to nothing by overhanging fronds, it was the only path, for on either side were brambles; this was a likely place for traps for man or fox. Towards the far end he stopped: his sharp eyes had seen what other eyes would not, a noose set a handspan above the ground and fastened to a peg hidden among dead ferns to his right. It was intended for a fox, but if it caught him then the crash of his fall would bring the keeper quickly enough. Arthur stepped round it. He knew now of its presence and to touch it would be to warn Jurd of his interests in the area. The snare reminded him of the snares he had set for Susannah Stacey at Brambourne parsonage. She'd been proper good to him, had Mrs Stacey, giving him that coat and all, and she'd been good to his old aunt Oram, too, taking soup to her as she lay a-dying. There weren't many about as kind as her. And you could talk to her. He'd shown her the faint marks in the ground that betrayed where the rabbits entered her garden, always landing in the same places in the long and short hops of their run, making marks known as squats; it was from these marks that Arthur knew exactly where to set his snares. She'd been fascinated, said she knew nothing of such matters. He'd told her that he'd teach her babe how to find his meat when he was old enough and she'd been properly appreciative: she knew there were few folks he'd make that offer to. Arthur continued his prowl beneath the trees. He'd teach young Piers how to get hares on the open down, luring the animal through its taste for blackthorn, planting a strong stick with twigs on it in the turf and concealing the trap nearby with grass and moss. And he'd teach him to carve and use a throwing stick weighted with lead to knock down a roosting pheasant.

The sun lanced down through the trees in stripes of gold. Insects danced in the light, while above him the wood-pigeons cooed. He leaned against a tree to scratch his back on its bark, then was sharply alert as he heard an unexpected sound, a sound of singing. His legs folded beneath him and he slid down the trunk on to the dead leaves and beechmast beneath, where sapling and ferns gave him cover. He listened. It was strange singing, muted and soft, as though the singers, like him, were in fear of discovery. His first instinct was to get away, but he controlled himself and lingered, curious. The singing continued, a man and a woman's voice blending together in a wordless tripping *dah de dah de dum dum*. His belly to the ground, Arthur wriggled forward till he could see and not be seen.

In a grassy clearing Mr James Manningford and Mrs Stacey were dancing, hand on lifted hand. Forwards, backwards, sideways, they stepped, and always to the rhythm of their strange humming, looking at one another and smiling, almost laughing, as they went through the precise little movements. Once Mrs Stacey missed her step and then she did laugh, soundlessly and breathlessly, holding on to Mr James' arm, and Arthur's sharp ears could hear her saying softly: 'I never do remember that bit aright, do I? Oh, how exasperating!' and his reply: 'Do it once more and you will have it, sweetheart.' And once more they danced their minuet and Arthur watched, entranced. This in no way resembled the country dances that village couples performed with boisterous enthusiasm on the common on feast days. He had seen nothing so clever or dainty before. When they had finished he saw Mrs Stacey give Mr James a look of triumph, her head tilted towards him, and Mr James nodding with mock solemnity and then pulling her into his arms. He seemed to be trying to persuade her to something, while she was demurring, glancing at the sun overhead as if to say, It is too late. But it seemed she must have capitulated for Mr James took her hand and ran with her across the grass and into the edge of the wood to Arthur's left.

245

He knew then where they were going: to the old abandoned summerhouse that had once looked over the meadow and up to the Big House, but now was hidden behind saplings and bushes that had crept out from the woods to surround it. Arthur had used it as a hiding place on several occasions. He thought of it as it would look today: an octagonal wooden house, silent and stuffily warm, cobwebs in the corners flecked with transparent insect remains; a couple of dry creamy moths lying on the floor, a heap of old cushions, a dusty quiet. Outside, the bright air pulsating with summer life.

Arthur shrugged his shoulders and scratched an armpit. He knew why they were going there, just as he knew why village men accompanied his mother back from the alehouse at nights. He made no moral judgments for it was neither in his up-bringing nor his character to do so. He turned and wriggled backwards; it would not be safe to stay now. But as he made his way round the edge of the wood to the wall his mind kept straying back to the grace of the dance, and its charm, and to the warmth and laughter that had been in their eyes. He knew he had seen something quite out of his experience today, something special that he would not quickly forget.

One of Beatrice Manningford's greatest delights was to watch dancing; as with riding, the aspiring dancer triumphs when his or her rhythms are under perfect control and perfectly attuned to another's: Beatrice, an excellent rider, knew in her veins that she would have made an equally good dancer; little beside it appealed so deeply to her physical senses and her sense of beauty. She had lied when she told Susannah at Jessica's ball that she had nothing to lament in not dancing, but there was no sense in repining, and to suffer the syrupy flow of her neighbours' sympathy would be a bore. So she watched with enjoyment the style and harmonies of the performers and developed a lively eye for pretension, hypocrisies and incipient scandals among their social group as they met and re-met at balls and parties. The dance in particular was a stage for the revelation of personalities and pride; a set for the country dance a microcosm of society with all its advances and retreatings, its bowings and its curtseyings, its movements up or down the set. Beatrice watched and noted and laughed to herself without malice at the sentimental and the cynical alike.

On the night of Julia's ball she was determined that her enjoyment should not be spoiled by pain as it had been in her exhaustion at Jessica's ball. When Rosalind fussed and demanded Beatrice's help she was firmly told to ask Jessica instead. 'Jessica seems set on marriage, let her practise the skills of that desirable state in readiness for her responsibilities and learn that life is not all fun and new silk gowns.' It was the second ball Rosalind had run, she should know the problems and the pitfalls now, she should not need so much help.

At the end of the second two dances Beatrice found her hand solicited for the next two by the new doctor, Edmund Breakspear.

She opened her eyes at him. 'Me, Doctor? Are you not aware that I cannot dance, that I am lame?'

'Lame, Miss Beatrice? No, I had no idea. Is this a temporary affliction, or something more permanent?'

'Very permanent. I am a cripple of many years.'

'Then I beg your pardon. But ... now I think of it, I do not remember ever having seen you walk. Apart from at the Blands' dinner table I have only seen you riding, and that to my admiration. May I instead sit with you?'

'You may. But, Doctor, if you are looking to dance, should you not be seeking a partner? I can introduce you to a number of attractive ladies who would be delighted to oblige.'

'But it was your company I sought,' he said, sitting down beside her, 'and it is yours I shall have, dancing or no.'

Beatrice contemplated him, her eyes narrowed now with interest. He was not a striking-looking man, being of only medium height and build, and with slightly rounded shoulders, but he had a pleasant face and an intent manner that was challenging.

'Tell me about your lameness,' he said. 'We will leave that unpleasant word "cripple" out of it, for I see no signs of the cripple about you. Were you born lame or was it caused by an accident?'

'Oh, an accident,' she said. 'A riding accident, and one that was entirely my own fault. Pride goeth before destruction and

247

an haughty spirit before a fall, Proverbs tells us, and that was how it was.'

'Tell me,' he said.

'It is a sad and sorry story, but if you must have it, here it is.' And she told him of how, at the age of twelve, she had taken her pony out, a relatively untried young animal, and put him at a wall too high for his capability. He had fallen and she with him, but worse, he had broken a leg and in his agony he had rolled on her, breaking her left leg in two places. 'Pegasus – the very name I gave him shows my arrogance then – Pegasus had to be shot, and I deserved to be shot with him. Instead my punishment was to lie abed for months while my leg mended. Only it didn't mend. Doctor Huskett was not a clever man with broken bones and it mended crooked and then the bone did not grow as I did, so my leg is short and I walk in a most unclever fashion.'

He said: 'It is a sad story and you have my sympathy.'

She made a vigorous gesture of rebuttal. 'Sympathy? I'd as lief have none. My leg is an old wound, and but a trifling annoyance nowadays. If you wish to show me understanding, treat me as a normal person. Many men speak to me as though I were an idiot.'

' 'Tis they must be mad,' he said. 'Your sanity and common-sense particularly struck me when we met at the Blands . . .' He stopped short. 'Not that I mean to imply that the Blands are anything but . . .'

Beatrice chuckled, rescuing him. 'Say no more, I understand you exactly.'

'Thank you, ma'am. That is most gratifying.' Their eyes met in a flash of shared amusement and then he turned to the dance floor. 'You could gratify me further by identifying some of the people on the floor tonight. Mrs Bland has told me several stories of local personalities and I should like to fit the names to the faces, particularly since many will become my patients. Tell me – which is Mr Hector Fulbroad?'

Beatrice indicated. 'Over there, holding court with several ladies at the upper end of the room, the heavy fellow with the powdered hair, the one with the ginger eyebrows and eyelashes.'

'He is prodigious fine – and just as I imagined him.'

'Ah yes! And there is a son, Elliot, equally as fine, and three red-headed daughters. Only one is here tonight, the youngest is not yet out, the oldest I gather is indisposed – you will have met her, no doubt?'

'Yes, briefly.'

Beatrice liked him the better for his silence on Miss Fulbroad's illness. Old Dr Huskett had been gossipy, not to say indiscreet, on the subject of his patients' maladies; she preferred her body should not form a topic for conversation. The dancing began again, and it was a minuet. A sober dance, its charm lay in its precision and its elegance, in the genteel bearing of the dancers, in the whitest of white gloves on the hands. Beatrice began to identify some of the couples nearest to them: Fanny, whom he knew, dancing with Timothy Goddard: 'There is particularity. Young Timothy is exceedingly ardent.'

Edmund Breakspear wanted to know if anything was likely to come of it: 'Mrs Bland is very hopeful, and I have never seen Fanny so animated.'

Beatrice doubted it. Fanny was at her best at a ball; she danced well, enjoying the music and the movement; indeed, it was probably the only form of exercise she did enjoy. And she was in a relaxed mood tonight: the last rehearsal for her concert had gone well, the performance was at the end of the next week, she was busy with all she enjoyed most. 'She encourages Timothy because it pleases her parents, but I should be amazed to see her marry him.' Was that fair of Fanny? he wanted to know. And, to her own surprise, whereas ordinarily she would have thrown out a flippant remark about young hearts mending easily enough, now she found herself choosing her words with care. 'I do not believe Timothy truly knows his own mind, nor that he understands hers in any way. Put at its most simple, Fanny is beautiful and he is in love with love. I pray I am right.'

Edmund nodded and accepted this, asking next whether the young man dancing with Jessica was Mr Fulbroad's son, for he thought he recognised the colouring. Beatrice told him laconically that it was, adding, 'But don't expect me to say anything more, else you'll say I have the tongue of a shrew.'

'Then I shall confine myself to enquiring who is the young lady dancing with your cousin James. Could that be "my cousin Susannah"?'

'Why, yes. Why do you ask it like that?'

'It's a name that constantly falls from your cousin's lips. Clearly, he thinks a great deal of her.' He turned to look questioningly at her.

'I think we all do,' Beatrice said. 'Certainly my sister Katharine and I have a high regard for her. She is talented, lively and stimulating in conversation. There are no dull moments with Cousin Susannah.'

'She and your cousin dance well together.'

A footman passed with glasses of wine on a tray. Edmund stopped him to take two glasses, handing one to Beatrice, whose hand closed on it automatically, her eyes fixed on the couple in front of them.

There was something unusual in the quality of James and Susannah's dancing. Forward and backward they moved in unison, a half-smile of something resembling triumph on their lips. Beatrice had never seen a minuet danced to such perfection; it was breath-taking in its faultlessness.

'They make a perfect couple, do they not?' Edmund remarked. 'Tell me, Miss Beatrice, would I be speaking out of turn if I asked when the announcement is to be made?'

Beatrice dragged her eyes from the scene to blink at him. 'I'm sorry. You said ... an announcement?'

He indicated with one hand. 'Your cousins. Surely I can't be wrong? The degree of affection and closeness between them is unmistakable.'

She smiled unbelievingly. 'You mean – marriage? But surely you must know, Doctor – staying as you have done with the Blands - my cousin is married already.'

'Married!' He looked stunned. 'No! Then I beg your pardon. I have made a most foolish mistake ...'

'She is married to Mr Stacey, the curate. More than that, they have a child, a baby boy.'

His face showed his embarrassment. 'I must have been very stupid. But you must believe me when I say I had no idea that Mr James' cousin Susannah and Mrs Stacey were one and the same person. 'Tis true Mrs Bland was for ever speaking of Mrs Stacey and how she had once been her children's governess – but it never occurred to me to connect the two names. I have spoken to Mr Stacey many times but I've never met Mrs Stacey. Forgive me.'

She touched his hand. 'It was an understandable mistake, given the circumstances. And a comic one, too. James and Susannah argue as often as they agree. Let us drink this wine you have so neatly procured and forget the matter.'

The little orchestra formed from the local churches' players was playing with unusual verve, perhaps inspired by the excellence of the dancers: she could see rather than hear that James and Susannah were gently humming the music, a pretty piece, the work of Mozart. Dah de dah de dum dum ... Their lips moved slightly; smiling, they glanced at each other, and as quickly glanced away. Then James bent to murmur something in her ear. Susannah shook her head, but seemed to be struggling to suppress laughter. And then James looked down at her, a long look, a look for which there was only one interpretation, and at that look heat flooded Beatrice's body and the light of the candles was suddenly dazzling in her eyes.

'Oh, dear God,' she breathed, and felt herself shaking violently, and knew that Edmund Breakspear had seen that look, for she sensed him stir in the chair beside her. And she scanned the room, for she felt certain that everybody present must have seen it too, and known what she had known, and yet the dancing had continued, and now it was finishing, and no one appeared to have noticed at all.

The doctor put his hand gently but firmly on her arm and held it for a moment. 'Sip your wine,' he said, so quietly that she could hardly hear him. 'Come, sip your wine, you have had a shock.'

She looked at him and saw that there was no use in dissembling. 'I cannot believe it,' she said. 'That I should have been such a fool, such a blind fool. And you come among us, who hardly know us, and recognise it at once.'

'I had nothing to blind me,' he said.

She sipped her wine obediently and knew what he said was true. The doctor was talking steadily and softly, and she did not know what he was talking about until he stood and drew her to her feet. He was telling her that the room had become too hot and close, that they must leave it, go out through the long windows and stand on the terrace in the night breeze, and then

251

he was steering her in that direction and she was limping beside him, hanging on to his arm as she had never hung on anyone's arm in her life. They walked to the edge of the terrace and leaned on the balustrading and the summer night breathed at her a scent compounded of grass and roses and lavender flowers. At the far end of the terrace she could see the outline of two silhouettes entwined against the low moon and knew it was William Waterton making passionate advances to some woman, and a wave of near-hysterical laughter welled up inside her that she could barely repress. That she should be out on the terrace with a man, she, lame Beatrice Manningford: dear Lord, what interpretation would the chaperons put upon this if they saw them? She leaned over the balustrade and picked a rose, putting it to her nose. Inhaling that familiar scent was calming; she breathed it deeply.

'Miss Beatrice,' Edmund was saying. 'You ride every day, do you not?'

'Yes, I do.'

'And I have several times seen you ride alone.'

'I expect you have.'

'Is that wise? You might fall and lie for some hours before anyone found you.'

'I am not a green girl to fall off, Dr Breakspear, nor do I put my horses at jumps beyond their capabilities, not nowadays.'

'You should never ride alone. There has been bad feeling in the village, I understand.'

'I do not believe any of the villagers would touch me.'

'Nevertheless, there could be unpleasantness.'

'Are you suggesting I should have a chaperon?'

She sensed rather than saw that he smiled in the darkness. 'Just someone to ride with. And in that capacity I should like to suggest myself. Will you ride with me?'

'In the capacity of chaperon, Dr Breakspear,' she said mockingly, 'I will ride with you.'

'That was not quite the capacity I had in mind, Miss Beatrice, but it will serve for the moment. Shall we say tomorrow, at three o'clock?'

'At the bottom of the lime avenue,' she said slowly. 'Agreed.'

He leaned, as she had done, over the balustrade to pick a rose, a half-blown flower. Then he took the rose that she was twisting between her fingers to place them both in the sash that circled her high-waisted gown beneath her breasts. On a quiet breath he said: 'One thing I think I should say to you before we return inside ... I am not a gossip.'

'I did not think it, Doctor.'

20

Six days passed, the night of Fanny's concert at last arrived and Sedley was going to be late. At first he was annoyed, but as time went on he became resigned. If one were forced to be late, one might as well be dramatically so. As he prepared to ride back through Brambourne he started planning how he would tell the tale. He had been called to the bedside of a worthy parishioner, the wife of a well-to-do farmer living a mile to the east of the village. Sedley had ridden off promptly, to find Prudence Paine tending a moaning and lamenting female, not, as he had been told by one of her sons, about to be taken through St Peter's portals by violent heart attacks, but suffering the results of a surfeit of food and drink, taken in celebration of her husband's half-century of life. But the woman would not let Sedley go. The pain had made her certain her demise was imminent and she needed to discuss the future world with her spiritual adviser. So far as Sedley could ascertain through her sobs, she saw the gate to Heaven as resembling the gate to Winchester on a busy market day, and could not perceive how she would meet her dear late parents in all the angel throng within. Manipulating his handkerchief against the gusts of mingled port and brandy, he reassured her that God would always find a way: He was all-seeing, all understanding.

At last he was free of her clutches and going to untether Coquette, only to have Prudence's sturdy form inserting itself between him and the mare.

'Wine,' Prudence observed heavily, 'is a mocker.'

Of course, she and her husband were abstainers. The farmer and his wife were bound to have suffered lectures on the wickedness of their ways from Prudence. For once, Sedley had some sympathy with the Paines' viewpoint. 'Any excess is to be deplored,' he agreed.

'You should preach one o' your sermons 'bout it here,' Prudence told him.

'I preached on the very text you mentioned not long ago ...' Sedley began and then broke off as he remembered the circumstances.

'Aye,' said Prudence in ominous tones, 'I remember, an' a fair sermon 'twas, taking all in all. But that was at Abbotsbridge and folks do say as there was a tub of the devil's spirits in the church at the time. Dear knows how it come to be there and dear knows who it belonged to, and I won't be accusing you, Parson, but 'twasn't fitting. I do say as you was right to be preaching the sober life to them people because they needed it, but there's plenty here as didn't fancy traipsing to Abbotsbridge of a Sunday, not even to the House of God, and so they missed it. And they need the Word here, the dear Lord knows.'

Softened by the praise of his sermon, Sedley remarked that he might indeed preach on the same text in Brambourne and tried to edge round Prudence to his mare, but Prudence was unbudging: she was determined to unburden herself in full; if Brambourne was a pit of drunkenness, Abbotsbridge was the same and more besides, a veritable Sodom and Gomorrah.

'From the bottom to the top,' said Prudence. 'From the bottom to the top. And them as should know better is giving an example to them beneath them of lax livin' an' lewd behaviour. Young men meetin' young ladies as is not their wives all unbeknown and riding with them goodness knows where. I've seen 'em with my own eyes, Mr Stacey, a-laughing and a-joking an' a-kissing of hands and heaven only knows what else when no one is looking.'

Stiffening, Sedley took his eyes from Coquette to fix them on Prudence, attempting to learn more from her looks, but her face was raised to the heavens. 'I am surprised to hear this,' he said.

'Ah, there's plenty you don't know about, Parson, nor others round here. But then they do say, don't they, that fathers and husbands is the last to know. They never see what they don't like to see – want to think their womenfolks is perfect. But I know, and you should know, Parson, that they're not.' She pulled her shawl more tightly round her shoulders. 'Well, I must be getting back sharpish. 'Tis going to rain, I reckon, and I've no fancy for getting wet.' She turned on her heel and trudged off, her tight back registering her disapproval.

But of whom? Sedley rode after her and soon passed her, his mind mulling over her words. Had Prudence been talking in general terms of lewd behaviour, or in specific? To be exact, of his wife? It was true Susannah had been behaving oddly for weeks, often absent-minded, at other times elated and laughing at nothing. And she had been evasive about the most important of her marital duties recently, complaining of headaches or tiredness; there had been many disappointing nights. Fathers and husbands were the last to know, Prudence had said. Did she mean Thomas Trotter, Squire Waterton, himself?

It was beginning to rain as he reached Brambourne Manor, a cold spitting of water in his face, and he was thankful that Miss Waterton had won the battle with Rosalind Manningford over which of the two big houses should have the honour of holding Fanny's concert; he would not have cared to ride further. He arrived between two items and managed to present his apologies and even make the Watertons laugh with his tale of the drunken farmer's wife before he slid into a chair next to Mrs Goddard.

Fanny's great moment had come. She plucked the strings of the harp and the company fell silent. Even in his distraction Sedley was not unaware of the picture she made, her slender arms lifted to the strings, the light from the candles shining on the fair ringlets and silhouetting the lovely pensive profile. She played a short piece by Petrini first and then Krumpholtz's fifth sonata. The rippling and vibrant sounds caught at her audience and held them still, but the beauty of Krumpholtz's adagio opening was lost on Sedley; he was looking from guest to guest for clues to the riddle of Prudence Paine's remarks. William Waterton, large, flushed, and dishevelled of lace at throat and cuffs, was asleep; clearly he had supped well. Sedley pursed his lips. Susannah was sitting at the front with the Blands and Timothy Goddard, nowhere near William, though that, Sedley thought, proved nothing. Beatrice Manningford was sitting next to that new doctor fellow, who was leaning forward, chin in hand, listening intently; he had not been in the area long enough to have set up an affair with anyone, surely. Beyond them came Jessica Manningford, brilliant in the finest silk, sitting between Elliot and Mr Fulbroad. Sedley noticed Elliot touch Jessica's arm and murmur a remark, to which she replied with a tap of a fan and the glint of an eye. Both Elliot and Timothy Goddard were too preoccupied elsewhere to have an eye to Susannah – or were they? The duplicity of men was endless. He remembered how he had been courting Miss Waterton yet sleeping with Susannah, and groaned inwardly. His eyes moved on. Only James Manningford, behind her and next to Mrs Waterton, was looking at Susannah and his appeared a gaze of mere abstraction.

The audience applauded with vigour; Sedley joined in, pushing his hands weakly and almost soundlessly together. William awoke with a loud grunt. There were calls of 'Superb!', 'Most moving!', 'I never heard a better performance!', 'Give us more!' Fanny looked pleased and excited, her face for once free from sadness. She rose and curtseyed, then seated herself again to play an encore, a short piece by Handel.

The evening continued. Fanny was praised in what Sedley considered over-extravagant terms; he had heard her playing at the rectory too often to be impressed now. His wife sang a duet with James Manningford, 'Hark! Hark! the lark at heaven's gate sings'. Their voices rose and fell, blending: 'My lady sweet, arise, arise, arise ...' Arise from whose bed ... whose bed ... whose bed?

'Most creditable,' approved the guests. Most discreditable, moaned Sedley's heart. The sea-shanties and glees that ended the concert passed him by. His neighbours joined in the choruses, singing heartily. Sedley sat in silence, brooding.

The brief flowering of summer was over, the weather became unsettled and wet more often than not. Moulds and fungi flourished, but little else. The hay crop was poor and late; it was possible to count the ribs of most of the cattle on the common, and the sheep flocks were depleted by disease. Again James Manningford and William Waterton were in agreement that the year's harvest would be disappointing, if not disastrous.

On a still morning in early-August Susannah surveyed her

257

garden and decided with her usual optimism that the damp weather had been kindly to her new plants and they were bound to be a fine sight next year. The rose cuttings had taken, and the lilacs and lavenders too. But dead-heading was needed, and the fallen mulberries from the big old tree were white with mildew. She was going riding with Katharine and Beatrice later in the morning, but first she would tend her garden with her baby son for company.

She laid Piers on cushions under an apple tree and he cooed at the leaves above him and tried to catch them with waving plump fists. He was a contented greedy baby, more alert and awake with every day that passed, and growing fast. He was large for his age, and forward too, something which alternately pleased and alarmed his mother.

She crouched to snip at the fading heads of pinks and pansies and then stood to shear the lavender. She would dry the seed heads and sew them into sachets to put among her linen. Ladyship appeared from a bed of thyme to inspect the work, then curled up nearby to sleep. She was about to produce her first litter, her body seething with kittens, and she spent most of the day resting. Susannah saw that Piers, too, was dozing; she smiled and worked on, enjoying herself. She had just begun to rake up the mulberries when she heard Sedley's voice, loud and peevish.

'Oh, there you are! I have been looking for you for ever. Why did you not let me know where you were?' He was striding aggressively down the gravel path towards her, the hem of his cassock flapping behind him.

'You were busy writing. I was afraid of disturbing you. Besides, Becky knew where I was.'

'It is not good enough. I've told you before, Susannah, I need to know at all times. People may call, people of importance who wish to speak to you and it is ridiculous for me to be caught on the hop, with no idea of my own wife's whereabouts.'

'Very well, Sedley. At half-past eleven I am going riding.'

'Oh! Going riding yet again,' he pounced. 'And with whom?'

Susannah told him, adding: 'We're to ride over the downs, a ride Cousin Beatrice has chosen; it's further and more open than we have ridden with Katharine before. She is become ever more brave and sure of herself; we're all proud of the progress she has made.'

'I shall ride with you,' he announced.

'But you can't,' she protested, startled. 'You haven't been invited.'

'Because of my devotion to my duties, which is widely known. I'm sure the Manningford ladies will be delighted to have my company this once.'

He was watching her with the same intent suspicious look that he had worn now for a couple of weeks, since about the time of the concert. She hated to think what had provoked this, yet she was sure he could have no real knowledge of the truth, or confrontation would have been immediate and violent. She pushed with her rake against a heap of mouldy mulberries and an idea came to her.

'But you cannot come,' she repeated. 'You told me at break-fast you must christen a sickly child.'

'That I am to do in a few minutes, then I shall be free to ride with you and the Manningford ladies.'

'But you should not, Sedley. It would be encroaching in you.'

'Encroaching! Encroaching! How dare you!' His voice cracked on a shout. 'What a disgraceful thing to say of your husband. I cannot believe you should have such gall.' At the sound of the angry voice Piers woke and began to wail. Sedley ignored him. His hot eyes glaring at Susannah, he said: 'You are trying to stop me from riding with you for some other reason. Could it be that you are meeting someone other than the Manningford ladies? Could it? I can imagine no other reason for such disgusting impudence.'

Susannah deepened her voice to great hurt: 'These are ter-rible charges you are laying against me. It's impossible to conceive that you should mean them. I can only ignore them.'

She turned to rake mulberries with long strong strokes, disturbing two wasps which flew angrily up at her. She ducked and they swerved to head for Sedley. He batted at them with his hands, stepping backwards almost on to Ladyship, who fled in shock, spitting. Sedley cursed the wasps, the cat and his wife, impartially and noisily. The baby cried vehemently. Susannah picked him up, snuggling him into her shoulder and patting him comfortingly.

259

' 'Tis all right, sweetheart,' she told him. 'Papa was angry, but 'twas all over nothing. I am sure he is sorry now.'

Sedley struggled for control, his chest heaving. It would be undignified to continue the argument over the yells of the child, and he was due in the church immediately. He flung back his head, a Roman senator rebuking the unruly populace. 'I am going to the christening now. We shall ride off when I return. Do you understand?' And he stalked off with what dignity he could muster.

They rode in silence to Abbotsbridge House, Susannah's mind full of churning, anxious thoughts. Were Sedley's suspicions instinctive or had some person seen her with James and dropped hints? Her mind returned to the concert; she was certain they had in no way betrayed themselves there, yet Sedley's mood seemed to date from that time; he had returned with narrowed eyes and a taut cruel look about his mouth. And since then had come the questioning. At times his mistrust seemed focussed on William Waterton, but in other moods he appeared to doubt all men and women, blindly seeking information that would discredit anyone among the local gentry. She could only wait for his suspicions to subside, and double her own watchfulness. Her moments alone with James were brief, dependent upon blurring the times of her meetings with others, yet she longed for them more than ever, as an antidote to Sedley. Sexual contact with him was now more a punishment that any act of marital felicity; he used her with only half-suppressed cruelty, grasping and tugging at her limbs with hard fingers that bruised where they touched.

As they rode up to the gatehouse she sensed him watching her. She was certain he thought Beatrice and Katharine would not be there, that he would catch her in a foolish pretence of having mistaken the day. But the sounds of clopping and clattering hooves were unmistakable and when they rode through the arch they found James and Katharine and Timothy Goddard already mounted, with Beatrice testing a girth.

Their reaction to Sedley's presence was exactly as Susannah had anticipated: a well-bred surprise coupled with a faint hauteur. 'I thought – with your permission, of course – to accompany my wife on one of these famous rides . . .' Sedley managed. A high flush was on his cheeks.

'You will find it dull work, Mr Stacey,' Beatrice remarked as a groom assisted her into the saddle. 'A gentle ramble through the countryside for my sister's sake.'

They rode off immediately, skirting Brambourne to the south, and it was there, at an outlying cottage, that they met Dr Breakspear, unhitching his horse from a gatepost. It was James who invited him to join them: 'If you have an hour to spare.' To Sedley's annoyance, the ladies seemed pleased at the doctor's acceptance, rather than put out, and he gathered that the man had ridden with them on a previous occasion.

They cantered along a track above the river, then, when it narrowed, the horses dropped to a walk and the party split naturally into three couples, each talking busily, leaving Sedley to bring up the rear. It was not the place he considered proper for himself. He rode alongside Beatrice and the doctor, wondering what Mr Manningford would think of his daughter riding with someone who made a profit from loathsome diseases.

He found them discussing her lameness. Dr Breakspear wanted to know if Beatrice had ever worn a shoe built up to reduce the disparity in length between her left and right legs.

'Oh, faith, yes! Foul torment it was, on top of the other torments Dr Huskett had devised for me.'

'How was that?'

She ducked her head under an arch of hazels. 'It hung upon my foot like a lead weight and my leg throbbed all night from the pain it caused.'

'It had a thick heel?'

'It did. Do not remind me. And why all these questions?'

'I am concerned at the severity of your limp. A properly designed shoe, gradually raised in height, could help it greatly. It might also ease the pain Miss Katharine tells me you sometimes feel in your back.'

She said sweetly: 'You are taking a deal of interest in my case, Doctor. Do you always go to such trouble?'

'You are a special case,' Edmund Breakspear returned calmly. 'I never met one quite like it before.'

She broke into a low laugh. 'You have all the answers.'

The fellow knew on which side his bread was buttered, Sedley thought sourly, fussing over Miss Beatrice like that, worming his way into Mr Manningford's favour through the good graces of his favourite daughter. And their stupid conversation was most rudely excluding him. He pushed Coquette forward to join Timothy and Katharine, to find Timothy lauding Fanny's playing at the concert to the skies and demanding of Katharine why she had not been there. 'There was no one to whom you could have had the least objection, all kindly people, intent only on the music. Your friends. You should have joined us.'

'That is what my sisters say. Perhaps next time.'

'Next time you will be playing your flute,' Timothy said.

Katharine shook her head in agitation. 'I couldn't!' she said. 'That I never could do. Oh no! People staring . . . a nightmare!'

'Not if they were staring in admiration. No, listen! At the concert Susannah suggested that the candles should be put at Fanny's right shoulder. They illuminated her music but put her and her harp in silhouette. It was most effective. Why should not you and Fanny play together like that? – the flute and harp blend delightfully – and you would both show your lovely profiles and no one would see your skin.'

Katharine was silent, her eyes on the swallows skimming the river below between the plumes of reeds. 'I . . . I do not think . . . I would have to consider it. It is something of which I never dreamed . . .'

'I will not press you,' said Timothy, his boyish face grave and intent. 'But I do believe you have the courage, if you choose it.'

Their conversation, Sedley thought, was even more dull than that of Beatrice and the doctor, and beyond a polite smile as he drew alongside they too had ignored him. Such lack of manners was really the outside of enough. But what of Susannah and James Manningford? They were talking quietly and quickly, their heads turning, their bodies inclined one to the other, as if deeply held by some subject. Ah, but what? His inner compulsion drove him close behind them, as near as Coquette would allow.

At first he could hear snatches of sentences only. 'Along the valley . . . near the river.' '. . . Somewhere well sheltered . . .' He felt himself go cold. The idea slithered snakelike through his mind that they were planning an illicit rendezvous. He began to shake, repugnance nauseated him, but he must hear. He leaned forward in the saddle. 'I think it is an excellent idea,' Susannah was saying softly but eagerly. Coquette tossed her head and jibbed. She was too near the hindquarters of Samson for her liking. He urged her on. 'Down near the river,' James was saying, 'the soil is stronger and deeper, better suited to wheat. The round of wheat, turnips, barley, clover is common, but Mr Coke favours a six-course rotation using wheat, barley, turnips, barley again, then clover, ryegrass ... broken up about midsummer and so to wheat again.' Sedley could not believe his ears. Had they become aware of his nearness and so changed the conversation? 'If I did have such a farm I could try one against the other to discover which answers best on our soul.' 'And as you said,' Susannah added, 'demonstrate the results to your tenants and the other farmers; then they'd have no personal expense in such trials.'

Samson lashed out with a hind leg at Coquette and jerked suddenly to the right so that both James and Susannah looked round to discover what had upset him. Coquette dashed into the gap created and Sedley had to rein her hard back. There was a moment's surprised silence while he stared at them in shock, and then Susannah broke into unintelligible speech. Recovering, he discovered that she was telling him of some experimental farm that James Manningford was hoping to create on Manningford land once the enclosure award was published. 'And he would try all different crops and breed special sheep for wool – for after all, sheep are vital to our village economy, and – oh, it does sound tremendously exciting!'

Sedley struggled to produce suitable comments, comments that would not reveal his incomprehension of James's wish to be involved in such matters. To hunt and to shoot, that was exciting to Sedley's mind, those were the prime reason for living in the country. But to dwell upon turnips and mangel-wurzels and bleating brainless sheep was no occupation for a gentleman: the Manningfords should leave that to a Scottish bailiff who could be trusted to be efficient and thrifty. His mutterings died away.

Susannah said: 'My brother Jack would relish the opportunity to do something similar, but he has neither the money nor the land available.'

'I have told you,' James replied, 'he must buy land on

mortgage. Already there are small parcels available. Oh yes, I know the argument on principle of not making a profit from the changes, but at this stage it is a foolish one. Let me tell you, Cousin Susannah, rising land values . . .'

They were off again, caught in the sort of argument that Sedley had so often instructed Susannah to avoid. Thank heavens, they were arguing without animosity. From the trees came a woodpecker's raucous laugh and he saw suddenly that he was being absurd, conducting himself like a half-wit. No one could ever imagine those two caught up in an affair; they could not meet without some dispute arising. These morning rides were the most innocent, the most tedious event imaginable. Susannah had told him that William never rode with them; he could believe her now; he would not stand it for five minutes. As the party at last turned up towards the downs Sedley heartily wished he had stayed away himself.

Over the summer weeks the villagers judged the new doctor. They were slow to accept outsiders, but when they discovered that Dr Breakspear, despite having lived most of his life in London, was Hampshire born and bred, they were more ready to drop their guard. The doctor peered at his patients with deep-set brown eyes, large and gentle as a deer's and as long-lashed. That his close contemplation was made necessary by myopia was unknown to them; they were touched by it. 'He do truly care,' they told one another. Like some of them, he was dark-haired and darkish of skin. 'One of the black Hampshire men,' said Mrs Bland. 'Jutish,' the rector said absently, lifting his head from a volume of Fordyce's sermons. In late-August an unprecedented event gave the doctor fame. It was a difficult birth and the anxious father actually had the temerity to call in both Martha and Prudence, and both, to their chagrin, had to admit defeat. Dr Breakspear, using iron forceps, succeeded where they had failed and saved both mother and child. To have Martha and Prudence in agreement over his high skill was a triumph in itself. The villagers judged the new doctor acceptable.

But there was one person who did not find Dr Breakspear acceptable. 'My father!' said Beatrice. Had she been capable of it she would have been pacing the vicarage floor, instead she could only vent her fury by beating the arms of her chair with her fists and swearing in a most unladylike fashion – and that in a low tone because Piers was asleep in his cradle beside Susannah, and Ladyship in her basket with her four kittens was watching Beatrice with suspicion. 'Some damned interfering person informed Papa that I have been riding with the doctor without a groom in attendance. Secret assignations – that was what he said. Intolerable!'

'How did you reply?' Susannah asked.

'With the truth. Edmund rides with me because he thinks it safer at present.' She hit the chair arm again. 'And Papa knows we are a groom short still.'

'The truth, but not the whole truth!' Susannah remarked, smiling. 'You cannot pretend that Dr Breakspear has not shown interest in you.'

'Oh that!' Beatrice said caustically. 'For my position, for my money – not vast fortune, but any money would be of interest to a mere sawbones.'

'Mr Manningford did not say that, surely!'

'He did not use the words fortune-hunter, or toad-eater, or encroaching tradesmen, no. But he might as well have done – the implications were all there.'

'If that is so,' Susannah said carefully, 'then it was insulting.'

'It was damnably insulting. Edmund is not wealthy, but I understand he has sufficient to live on, did he choose so. And he comes of an old-established family. His grandfather has an estate in the Meon Valley, but Edmund is the younger son of a younger son and must largely make his own way. He became a doctor after he left Cambridge because medicine fascinates him, and,' defiantly, 'I admire him for it.' She scowled out of the window, then burst out: 'And devilish insulting to me, too!'

'Yes, I see that,' Susannah said, 'but it must be your father's concern for you. He cannot truly believe it.'

'That I should never attract a man's real interest? Oh, easily! For I believed it myself for many years and thought I had come to terms with it. But then ... when a man whom one finds congenial shows a definite wish for one's company, when he talks to one at length ... and with certain looks ...'

'When he even kisses you?' Susannah murmured.

There was something of exceptional interest beyond the

window. 'He has kissed my hand, my cheek, my hair, and once, just once, my lips,' Beatrice said, so low that Susannah could scarcely hear her.

'And you thought yourself in Heaven, and now this – this tattle-monger – has forced you down to earth.'

'With my father's words ringing in my ears, all that was natural and free and delightful between us will now seem false.'

'Only if you choose so,' Susannah said firmly. 'For myself, I never saw so hopeful an inclination. If you care for him, if you love him, you'll not hold back.'

'Love, what is that?' Beatrice asked with a return of spirit. 'People say it is when one is blind to a man's faults, but I have never found myself so.'

'No . . .' Susannah said slowly. 'Nor I. Perhaps it is . . . when even the man's faults have a certain wayward attractiveness . . . Dear Lord, it is impossible to define.'

The sounds of trotting hooves and male voices in the lane caught their attention. 'Here is your husband and Cousin James, too,' Beatrice said. 'Has he business with Sedley?'

Susannah rose. 'He comes to see his godson and sometimes he leaves a message for my brother. I expect he met Sedley on his way.'

Piers woke at the stir as the men entered and began to wail for attention. 'Give him to me,' Beatrice said to Susannah. 'You will need your hands free for dealing with refreshments.' Piers seemed pleased at this and dabbed his fingers at her hair, her chin, the brooch at her neck.

It was drizzling rain outside and James and Sedley both complained of the wet, James that the harvest would soon be worthless, Sedley that riding in damp breeches chafed him and made the carrying out of his duties deuced unpleasant. Becky appeared with a tray and they drank coffee and ate fresh biscuits and spoke of how many French emigrés there were in Winchester and of how many Catholic priests had deserted their flocks to come over, which shocked Sedley. Then James wondered how William Waterton was enjoying the three weeks he was spending in London, and whether he would have fresh news of events in France and elsewhere. 'He'll be back any day now,' he said. 'He'll not want to be away for the harvest.'

The drizzle had ceased. 'I think we should leave,' Beatrice

266

suggested, 'or we'll be caught by the next shower. Cousin Susannah, would you take your baby, please? He's slobbering down my riding habit.'

'I'll take him,' James said. He leaned over and plucked the baby from her lap to dandle him on his own knees. Piers stamped and braced sturdy legs, gurgling, clearly enjoying a game he had played before. 'Good Lord, young man, what strong legs you have!'

Beatrice stared at them. 'I never saw a man hold a baby so young before,' she said.

Susannah removed the child from James's arms, summoning Becky to take him. Then James recollected the purpose of his visit, giving Susannah a note which he said was for her brother, on a matter of land prices.

Clouds were moving heavily across the sky as Beatrice and James rode off. They went swiftly and it was not until they slowed for the turning to the avenue of lime trees that Beatrice spoke. 'I don't think, James, that you should fuss over the baby so much. It looks odd in a man.'

'Nonsense!' James urged Samson to a canter as the rain began to fall again. 'My own godson!'

'Godson?' Beatrice queried, kicking her own horse on. 'Oh, I don't think God came into it, do you?'

21

The old summerhouse was empty. A smell of warm dust and old wood came to Susannah's nostrils as she opened the door and slipped inside, and there was a silence made deeper by a distant wood pigeon cooing across the park. She left the door open and sat on a pile of faded silk cushions, watching the first yellowed leaves of autumn drift down through the cool air. She had never arrived before James till now and it made her feel uneasy, allowing fear and remorse at what she was doing to Sedley to surface. Intermittently, as when she caught Sedley watching her like a cat at a mousehole, guilt flamed through her and shock at her own behaviour. Adulteress, Jezebel, cried the remnants of her childhood teaching. But when James was with her all that was swept away by the happiness of knowing herself loved: she was drunk and uncaring with bliss.

Her heart jumped as the bushes rustled, but it was James in the doorway, his figure outlined suddenly against the brighter light outside. He flung himself down on the cushions beside her and she started to speak but what she wanted to say was stopped by his lips, fervently caressing hers. She held his head between her hands and at length pushed him gently away. He sat up and contemplated her face against the tattered cushion.

'What is it?'

'I . . . Nothing.'

'Something is wrong. I can tell it, my Susannah.'

'I cannot stay long, that is all. Sedley is about.'

'Sedley is always about, damn him.'

She sat up, and her shawl slipped back onto the cushions. 'He has become suspicious. He knows, James. Not about us, thank God. But he senses ... something, someone. He measures every minute I am out of the house – he questions me endlessly – 'tis dreadful. But he is determined the man must be William Waterton. William has always flirted with me.'

'William would!'

'I know. But Sedley believes I am naive enough to fall for it. He was almost normal when William was in London, but now William is back.'

'And Sedley has you frightened.' James loosened his cravat, his eyes closely upon her.

'Yes. No ...' She made an anguished gesture with both hands as if striving to sweep the problem of Sedley away. 'He is impossible.'

James caught her right hand and prisoned it in his. With his free hand he swept up the puffed half-sleeve on her arm. 'Bruises! I thought so! Bruises on your wrist and marks on your upper arm, marks made by fingers. What the devil is happening between you and that man, Susannah?'

'Nothing!' She pulled her arm away, tugging her shawl concealingly over herself. 'It is nothing. I mark easily. I bump into things ...'

'Nonsense!' James said quietly. 'I saw bruises on your thighs last week and you told me some cock and bull story about falling over a stool. No! He is being brutal to you! Tell me the truth.'

She fingered the fringe of the shawl, her head down. 'He is angry ... and ... and hurt! He does not realise ... what he is doing.'

James was silent; a baffling mixture of emotions worked in his face. He drew a great breath of the warm dusty air, expelling it out in disconnected hopeless phrases: 'What I could do to him! Your poor lovely arms ... your body. Oh God, what spite – what a brute!'

'He does have reason,' Susannah reminded him.

'I don't care how much ...'

'Sssh!' She stiffened. 'Somebody's outside!'

Silence. A head, then a body, appeared in the doorway, outlined half-crouching against the light.

James and Susannah were on their feet.

'Who ...?' snapped James.

'Arthur!' Susannah gasped.

The gaunt young face turned to hers. 'You mus' go. Hurry! The parson – he's a-comin' fast. Saw 'im I did, follerin'. But you moved too quick an' he don't know where exact.' He turned to go, added urgently, 'He's comin' from behind!' and was gone like a fox to earth.

'Who the devil was that?' James demanded.

'Arthur Tandy.'

'The poacher? Heaven preserve us!'

'I believe this time Heaven has!' Susannah whispered. She peered out. 'Best do as he says. Sedley told me he would be in the church with his clerk this morning – he must have lied. Pray God he doesn't see me – or you!' A flickering smile, a movement in the bushes and she was gone, as silent and fleet as Arthur.

James walked out, pulling the old door to behind him. A cold breeze blew a scattering of leaves from the trees, the sky was low with clouds and there was a damp smell on the air. As he looked back at the summerhouse it seemed to him that the summer, what there had been of it, was finally over. He straightened his shoulders and slowly walked away: he would not advertise his presence, but no one, no man on earth, would make him skulk.

It was more than a week before they could be alone together again, but at last Susannah had the opportunity to murmur a time and a place and the following day James waited for her under the weeping willow tree.

It was late-morning and he sat on an old cloak, waiting. The willow fronds in front of him swayed and twisted in the wind, showing green and yellow, but they were not the fresh bright colours of spring, they were bleached and blemished. The swifts and the swallows had gone; only a party of wild geese honked beside the river. September, he thought, and the harvest barely half in. Normally he loved autumn, the scent of bonfires, the brilliant golds and bronzes of the beech leaves, and the start of the shooting season, but this year autumn and winter threatened dearth, cold, famine and unrest; the beauty of the fading year would mock him. He stood restlessly and looked for Susannah through the leaves, worrying, and then he saw her coming, not too fast, not too slowly, but steadily as though on some worthy errand, a basket on her arm, her hair blowing.

He had missed her; he had missed her shockingly. As she ducked beneath the willow fronds, he seized her and kissed her long and demandingly. 'Dearest, dearest, I was afraid you would never be able to get away. I had a bad feeling – '

'Sedley is spending the day in Winchester; he is dining with one of the canons from the cathedral. I saw the letter myself.' She pressed her head against his shoulder, holding him with a curious force; he could not see her face.

On the old cloak he sensed desperation in the way she clung to him, an oddly silent urgency in the response of the body beneath his in love-making. Afterwards he sat looking at her, feeling surges of tenderness press in his heart, troubled by her tenseness, wanting still to caress her and murmur reassurances. But she drew away, huddling on her clothes as if she feared at any moment to see Stacey part the willow fronds and come crashing in on them. He put out a hand to draw her down beside him.

'If Sedley is in Winchester you can be at ease, my Susannah. I have not talked to you for days and days. Stay. Please.'

She sat, but it was more the crouched position of an animal ready to flee at danger. 'I daren't stay long, but there is something I have to say to you, James.'

She paused – and in that second's hesitation he knew. 'No!' he said violently. 'No!'

She shook her head, her eyes staring past him. 'We have to part. There is no other way. Oh God, James, if it were possible to go on, don't you think I'd risk anything, *anything*, to be with you?' She turned her head to him. 'But it isn't.'

He felt as if she had hit him beneath the ribs: he gulped in anguish for breath to speak. 'We could wait for a week or two – even a month – until Stacey's suspicions die down. We could be very careful ...'

'No,' she said, and her voice was adamant. 'Don't you see, I cannot do this to him? He married me, James. He married me and gave Piers his name, a child who is not his. And he is suffering in his own way. And there is more to consider – how could I live with myself if I had another child that was not his? How could you?'

271

The wind rustled in the reeds by the river, a dry and dusty sound.

'Stacey does not deserve you! He does not care for you. I care for you, damn you!' He felt his hurt and despair curdle into hostility. Her eyes were fasted on him, watchful and troubled and yet detached, and he had an impulse to lash out and hurt her, to break the taut calm with which she was regarding him.

'I know,' she said, so low he could hardly hear her. 'I know. And I care for you. But that does not affect it.'

And at the tone of her voice he saw that her calm was unreal, a screen for the pain that was in her, too. He remembered unexpectedly how she had lashed out at him time and time again when she was carrying Piers, wanting to hurt – and succeeding too – and the impulse died within him.

'Please,' he said. 'Please, think again. We cannot let this happen to us. We could go away, you and I and Piers, and build a life for ourselves somewhere where nobody would know us. Yes, why should we not?'

'Because the scandal would follow us everywhere, even abroad, even to Italy. We could not escape it.' Then tenderly, pityingly, she added: 'Nor could you bear to leave Abbotsbridge. You could never abandon your enclosure plans now, half-way to success, nor the village folk with difficult times coming.'

And when he was silent she said, 'You see, I know you better than you think.'

They were both standing now. He grasped her arms above the elbow. 'Wait.' He was lacerated with pain, pain that would be unbearable when she was gone. Knowing that he was being foolish and that the words were empty words, he still had to argue. 'Give me time to think. There must be some way we can still be together.'

'There is none!' she said, in a whisper that was almost savage. 'My mind has gone round and round the problem like a squirrel in a cage. James, if Sedley found out he could throw me out – but he'd keep Piers. You know the law, you know I would have no rights over my own baby. Oh James, there's no answer to this. None!'

'Dear God – ' he was held rigid by emotions he had never experienced before.

Still he would not let her go. She added: 'I believe there are people who do know already. Someone, I am sure, hinted to Sedley.'

He remembered Beatrice's words and was silent. She pressed a brief hard kiss on his lips. On a gasp she said: 'You know you can visit Piers any time you wish. Goodbye, dearest James ... at least we have had our lovely summer.' As she turned to go the smooth arms slipped from his hold. She ducked beneath the dying willow fronds and he did not stop her.

Her steps, half-running, faded in the distance. Beyond the tree the wild geese honked again, then flew away; he could hear the beat of their wings as they went. Then came a softer sound, the sound of rain on the willow branches, persistently pattering. It reminded him of that day in spring when they had first made love here; it was four months ago and it was yesterday. He remembered the great trout he had caught, and Susannah trying to fish and their laughter and the happiness, here, under the willow tree.

After a while the rain began to penetrate down into the green cave in which he stood, his head bowed. He picked up his cloak, shook it free of leaves and grass and walked out. The river was a grey streak of water wincing at the rain. Big drops coursed down his face and if there were already drops of moisture upon it, nobody could have told.

22

It seemed to James during the next weeks that nothing was going right in his world. He sat working at the mahogany desk Ambrose had put specially for him in the library, he forced himself to attend meetings, he drove in his curricle to Winchester, everywhere he was beset with difficulties and the news was bad.

The enclosure process was becoming bogged down with problems. Richard Haynes, the senior of the three commissioners, was a pedantic plump little man, thoroughly put out by uneducated villagers who did not produce their statements of claim in exact legal form. Under the terms of the act the commissioners' powers were virtually absolute: if Mr Haynes chose he could dismiss claims that were technically irregular, but he chose instead to worry Ambrose and James with them, assuring them every second minute both of his wish to be just, and of how he was compelled to be meticulously exact. Ambrose took to vanishing when Haynes's one-horse phaeton was seen driving up the lime avenue; James must cope on his own.

The politics of that autumn were taken to crude extremes: Charles James Fox, while capable of warm fellow feeling for rebellious radicals or the poor and ignorant, did not appear to James to be the man to understand the complex problems facing William Pitt's government – the enormous financial strain and burden of the war, the impossible task of fighting in many areas of the world at once with a navy that was over-stretched and an army ill-trained and ill-organised. Far from supporting Pitt at a time of national danger, Fox himself was withdrawing more and more from Westminster, while permitting his followers and their more radical friends to attack the government, inside and outside the House, in inflammatory speeches that compared its members with Roman tyrants and fermented discord and hatred. And Pitt appeared to be doing little to counteract this; he had made no effort to draw any members of the present opposition into the government, no move to unify the House. A dry and distant man, he was becoming ever more reserved and contemptuous of criticism.

Nor, in James's opinion, had the government been sufficiently resolute in its continuation of the war. The fiasco of the invasion of Brittany in the summer by a force of emigrés under the Comte de Puisaye jointly with a British force had made him despair, showing yet again, and bloodily, the ineffectiveness both of the army and of the coalition. At least no one in the local villages had been killed, though a young Kimber had lost a forefinger to a musket ball in fighting the forces of atheism. The full extent of the disaster was only now being realised. The army of invasion had been formed in Hampshire, under the Bourbon flag, but while arms for twenty thousand men had sailed with the advance guard from Southampton on June 17th, an urgent request for troops for the West Indies had left only five thousand available for Brittany. Rather than upset the French princes and risk the coalition with the Portland Whigs, the government decided to allow the depleted expedition to sail. When James had read the *Hampshire Chronicle*'s bleat in early July, 'It is yet impossible to say at what place the emigrant troops will effect their landing, as it must depend much upon contingent circumstances . . .' he had thrown the paper on the floor. In the Vendée the royalists had frequently behaved with as much bestiality as the republicans, massacring them as they had been massacred, according to the *Chronicle*. Now the disorganised risings in the Vendée and Brittany had been crushed by Hoche and the guillotines in those areas kept endlessly busy. It all went to confirm the Hampshire villagers in their contempt for Frenchmen and all things French.

There were more immediate worries at home. The harvest was even worse than James and William had feared: thunderstorms with heavy rain in late-August and early-September mashed whole acres of grain into the mud and the total finally garnered was a quarter down on the previous year.

At the midsummer quarter sessions held at Winchester Castle in July the magistrates had deliberated upon a report on the general condition of the poor. They had resolved, as their colleagues in Berkshire had resolved at a meeting in May at the Pelican Inn at Speenhamland, near Newbury, that while the prices of necessaries had increased more rapidly than the wages of labour, that it was not now expedient to make a general regulation of wages. The Hampshire magistrates recommended that the difference between the labourers' incomes and 'their lowest outgoing under the best management' should be made up in relief granted by parish officers. Each parish was to come to its own decision as to the level of relief paid, at a parish vestry.

These had seemed to James short-sighted ways of dealing with soaring food prices and the distress of the poor, and in those happier days before they had parted, Susannah had urged him with her usual vigour to fight for higher wages. But this week Abbotsbridge and Brambourne had both agreed to adopt the system decided at Speenhamland. This joined the level of relief to the price of a gallon loaf and the numbers in the claimant's family. James condemned it as a paltry remedy: 'With prices as high as they will be this winter, you will make hard-working men doing a full day's work into paupers asking for charity,' he told Mr Fulbroad. 'If you wanted deliberately to cause unrest you could not have found a better method.' But Fulbroad and Munday and others in favour of subsidising wages from the rates were unrepentant. 'Prices are unnatural high this year,' Fulbroad pointed out. 'They may well fall – but try to make wages fall back if we raise 'em now – pough! An impossibility! We shall wait and see how the events of the war move, and whether the next harvest is good – that is the sensible man's way to judge.' 'And in the meantime no person will starve,' Munday had added.

Sitting at his desk late on a bleak afternoon, James longed for the relief of pouring out his indignation to Susannah, but that was denied him. Her absence was a void he could not fill; the thought of her made him quite frantic with love and regret. The stillness of the dark and heavy library fell about him with smothering gloom. He felt cold and exhausted as though he was suffering some sickness of mind and body.

Of recent days he had felt himself more and more isolated: old friendships seemed of little importance; Ambrose was leaving him largely to his own devices. He had supervised the harvest this year for the first time, sharing his interest and his concern over its paucity with Susannah. Now she was gone, the harvest was over. The villagers had withdrawn behind closed doors and fastened shutters; the nights were cold. The fields of stubble, the woods, the lovely downs no longer drew him; he stayed in the house, alone and tired. Each day he struggled to plan for the next season; frequently he reminded himself of the great time to come when the commissioners would have departed, when there would be new and changed acres to supervise, when he might have his experimental farm, but with the slow death of the year planning was impossible. His mind revolted; unfinished piles of notes drifted about his desk as the leaves drifted beneath the elms in the park. His lack of progress intensified his detachment and his melancholy.

When Beatrice came in he was sitting in semi-darkness, his eyes gazing unseeingly as the last of the light faded from the park.

'My dear James!' she said, as the glow from her branched candlestick found him. 'Why ever are you sitting in the dark? Could you not have sent for candles?'

He stirred in his chair. 'No matter. In any case, I have a headache.'

'A headache? You? I cannot believe it!' She put the candlestick down on the edge of his desk and scrutinised him. Her voice was soft. 'Oh James, poor James. Perhaps it is this bleak day, affecting everyone. I have been visiting Brambourne vicarage and Cousin Susannah was low, like you, very low. She said she had a cold coming and certainly her eyes were red.' She put an arm round James's shoulders and hugged him.

James made an odd small sound like a groan and shook his head.

Beatrice straightened. 'I shall send for wine. And this fire must be made up.' She limped across the room and tugged the bell-pull. When the wine came she thrust a glass into his hand. 'No, it is not Canary! I know you consider that too sweet. You

277

will find this more palatable – it is a new discovery of Papa's, a hock. Try it.'

James sipped obediently. 'Perfectly pleasant,' he agreed.

Beatrice drew up a chair by the fire. 'You will never guess what I was doing this morning,' she said. 'Indeed, I quite surprise myself with the variety of my occupations, not to say preoccupations, these days.'

'What have you been doing?' James forced himself to ask.

'Helping to set a small boy's broken leg!' Beatrice said. 'A perfect monster of a small boy, and, indeed, he did not seem so small when it came to holding him down for the operation! He had been playing on a haystack and fell off – to disaster. His mother was hopeless; she could do nothing but lament and bewail the absence of his father, who had gone to market. So I found myself the doctor's assistant, and fascinating it was, too, as well as exhausting and ear-shattering.'

'How did you come to be doing this?'

'Purely by accident. I was riding behind Bonnard's cottages and saw Edmund Breakspear as he emerged to find some sensible person to help him with the child. He seemed to think me suitable and who was I to deny it? He said afterwards that he could not have managed without me.'

'And couldn't he?'

'By threatening the child with the horror of growing up to hobble like me if he did not allow the doctor to set the leg properly and splint it, I eventually persuaded him to let the job be done. Truth to tell, I would not have missed it for the worlds ... it was ... worthwhile. I wish Edmund had been our doctor when my leg broke: I might have been less crippled myself.' She drank her wine, smiling dreamily into the fire. 'There is something so totally unromantic in holding down a screeching writhing small boy that it quite restores my faith in Edmund, whatever Papa may say.'

On the following day Susannah made a resolution never to think about James. The fact that she had made the same resolution every day for three weeks did not deter her. She must not allow herself to brood over him – that way madness lay. Sometimes she thought her misery was driving her mad; she could not concentrate upon the most simple matters in her life:

she forgot to take the bread from the oven when it was cooked, and had to make a whole batch over again; she mislaid items all over the house and had Becky in a turmoil searching for them; she had even forgotten that Mrs Waterton was to call on her the previous morning and was out, so that Sedley had to apologise for her, and was so shocked he was almost past anger.

Today she and Sedley were to eat with her parents and Jack. At the farmhouse there was a new issue burning in her family's minds: the prospective purchase of land. Peter Page, one of the smallholders, had been made an offer for his acres by Mr Fulbroad and was thinking of selling up. Like Sam Truckle, he was already in debt, a debt he could have managed to pay off had times been good, but with the upheaval of enclosure and the lawyers' fees to pay and all the other costs, including the fencing of his new land at the end, it was just too much for him and his wife.

'Mr Fulbroad has offered him work if he'll sell to him, but Peter doesn't trust him – the first bad weather, the first word out of place, and he'd be turned off,' Jack said, passing a dish of vegetables to Susannah, 'so he came to see what price I'd offer for his acres – and his work.'

'How many acres?' Susannah asked.

'He has fourteen. He would retain three acres for his wife to have a cow, so eleven on offer.'

'Could you afford them?'

'With difficulty. I should leave myself a touch short.'

'Then why not take out a mortgage?'

'A mortgage?' Mrs Trotter flashed, looking furiously up from her roast duck. 'They are wicked things. A trap for fools like my father.'

'I suspect he used the money he raised to fund his gambling,' Jack said gently. 'To borrow money to buy land when the price of it is rising is a very different matter. I admit I have thoughts of it.'

'Such opportunities are rare, Mama,' Susannah said. 'Jack should seize it and any more that come his way. The price of corn will stay high while we are fighting the French. A mortgage could be easily repaid.'

'What do you know about it?' Sedley asked her sharply. 'Mortgages are no matter for a lady's concern.'

Susannah took a deep breath. 'Mr James spoke to me about it,' she said simply. 'You remember, Sedley, when you came on Cousin Katharine's first ride to the downs. He says that in the present state of affairs there is little risk.' There, she had spoken his name without colouring up or wanting to burst into tears; she must be getting stronger.

'The extra acres 'ud never come amiss to us,' Thomas said, pushing a vast forkful of meat into his mouth.

'I wish it were that simple,' Jack said. 'He laid down his knife and fork and looked at them all. 'How can I, who opposed enclosure so bitterly, now rush to make a profit from those who are suffering because I failed?'

Sedley remarked: 'It was a foolish endeavour, doomed from the start.'

Susannah jerked with irritation. She spoke to Jack across the table. 'You are talking nonsense. If you don't buy the land, then who will? Mr Fulbroad, or Mr Munday, or perhaps the Manningfords. But most likely Mr Fulbroad. He's greedy for fresh acres. Will he give a generous price? Never! Does he treat men aright? No! But he will hint at ills that might befall those who thwart him – indeed, we know he already has. Ricks are easily set alight and he has the score of his burned barn to pay off. Small men are vulnerable men. But if you offer to buy land at a fair price to save Peter Page and men like him from Mr Fulbroad, you'll be seen again to have their interests at heart.'

'Ye've a good point there, Sukey,' Thomas said.

Mrs Trotter shook her head. 'A dangerous business,' she muttered.

Jack pushed his chair back with a rasping sound. 'I do want to buy those acres,' he said with quiet passion. 'And others too. I dream of having the wheat and oats thick on our land at harvest time so we have sizable surpluses to help feed those who've gone hungry this year. I dream of increasing our pigs fivefold, even tenfold, buying in weaners and fattening them fast to sell to the navy – there's a clamouring market there. And when we do have separate enclosed pastures, then I'd dearly love to have made enough money to buy prize rams and strive to breed sheep for higher quality wool. Mr Robert Bakewell is one of the greatest improvers and I've read sufficient to follow

280

his stock-breeding principles. Peter Page's acres would be a small beginning – but from them many more could come.'

Emily Trotter looked taken aback. She rose and there was a stir as plates and dishes were removed, and a great apple pie with cream, and pears, nuts and raisins were brought in. There was an effort to change the conversation to less controversial matters, but insidiously the subject of Peter Pages's acres crept back. By the time Sedley and Susannah rode off it was decided that Jack should enquire at Winchester, purely in principle, of course, as to the costs of a mortgage on the land.

'That,' said Mrs Trotter, screwing up her eyes into mere slits of disapproval, 'will, I trust, settle the matter once and for all. The interest on a mortgage is pure usury. Never should one a borrower be.'

Susannah and Sedley rode home at a brisk trot, their heads bent against a light but penetrating rain, passing on the rise the first signs of digging on the rutted road, the first piles of materials glinting wetly.

Indoors hastily after stabling the horses, and they plucked off sodden cloaks and Becky brought them cloths to pat their faces and hair dry and steaming hot drinks. Ladyship emerged from her basket and came to rub round their ankles, and behind her tumbled her kittens, ears twitching and tails erect, three tabbies and a black.

'I should be happy to see your family increase their acres,' Sedley acknowledged. 'To see them improve their position would be pleasing.'

'Dear Lord, it would.' Susannah sat by the fire to sip her drink. 'Sedley,' she asked, 'will you be seeing Mr Bland tomorrow morning?'

'Yes. Yes, we are to discuss preaching similar sermons upon certain issues in both villages. The unrest is worrying.' He stared and the skin on his face seemed to tighten. 'But what's it to you when I see him?'

She forced her voice to the calm propitiation she had recently used so much. 'I told you that tomorrow I ride again with Cousin Katharine. If we set off together you could explain to me exactly how you plan to mend the road. I saw there were cartloads of stones and gravel ready.'

He was not propitiated. He slapped his cup and saucer down

on the hearth and leaned forward, his hands gripping his knees. 'I know why you ask! You have plans for the morning you would not wish me to discover, plans to meet a certain person secretly – isn't that it?'

'Oh, Sedley, why do you say such things?'

Two kittens chased each other up his right leg, their claws piercing through his stocking as they scrambled. Sedley yelped and shook his leg violently. 'Damn the creatures! Why d'ye keep the little beasts in here? Put them in the kitchen.'

The kittens dropped from his leg, turning neatly in the air to land on all fours. 'Careful!' Susannah gasped as his foot lashed out at them. She scooped the tiny animals up and put them back in their basket.

'Well?' Sedley demanded. 'You do not deny it, do you?'

The irritation that had been in her all evening erupted. 'Whatever I said you would not believe! For weeks now, months even, you've suspected and cross-questioned me. I know you think I'm having an affair with William Waterton. I am not, nor ever would do! A man who attempts to seduce every dairymaid for miles around? It's an insult!'

Her fierceness took him aback. He said: 'But you must admit your behaviour has been odd. Last month you were for ever out for walks and rides alone – or that you said were alone – even in the rain. And your absent-mindedness is shocking.'

'Perhaps my mind is preoccupied by hurt at my husband's suspicions.'

Sedley shook his head like a horse tormented by flies. 'It does not have to be William. It could be someone else.'

She said hotly, loudly: 'There is no one else. I am not having an affair with anyone.' It was the exact truth, dear God, and how she wished it could be otherwise. And at the thought of James and all she had renounced her eyes and throat began to smart. 'I will swear it on the bible if you wish,' she blurted, and burst into tears.

Sedley was shocked and fussed and clearly took her tears as an indication of her innocence. 'No, no,' he said. 'I will take your word as truth. We have no need to be so dramatic.'

'I shall do it,' she insisted, hiccoughing, wiping her eyes with the back of her hand. She flung out of the room, seized the great leatherbound bible from where it always lay on the desk in his study and returned to hold it up, her arm trembling with its weight. 'I swear before God that I am having an affair with no man.'

Sedley was deeply flustered. 'There was no need ... please put the bible down. The dear Lord knows ... now dry your tears, do. Becky may come in for the teacups and whatever would she think?'

The tears were a relief after all the strain; for a moment or two she indulged herself while he patted her shoulder awkwardly, and then she groped in her reticule for a handkerchief.

'Ah, that's better,' he said as she found the square of cambric and mopped. 'Now we will say no more about it, no more at all.'

They were both silent as they prepared for bed and for once he did not press his attentions on her. She caught his eyes turning pensively towards her once or twice and prayed that he would remain satisfied with the oath that she had sworn, that he would not think to seek for what it did not say. She could not swear to a lie. At bottom, she thought, he ached to be reassured: he might not care for her but he cared still less for scandal.

The rain had ceased when they rode off next morning and the sky was washed a pure blue. Where the road-markers were working they stopped for Sedley to give instructions and when they trotted on he explained to Susannah his ideas on foundations and camber and drainage, and said how difficult it was to stop the men from simply shovelling stones and gravel into the ruts as they had always done.

'In the village they tell me I'm mad to dig up the whole road,' Sedley said, 'but when it's done they'll see! My mendings won't be washed away in the first winter rains.'

'No more nasty accidents,' Susannah agreed, repressing unwanted memories.

By the lime avenue they parted. Thoughts of her uneasy life with Sedley occupied Susannah as she cantered up between the yellowing trees, but as Abbotsbridge House loomed the thought of seeing James pushed out all other thoughts; the anticipation was painful. She had seen him only twice since their parting. The first time she had been walking to Abbotsbridge to visit Fanny and her family and he had come suddenly into sight, riding up the rise with William Waterton, the pair of

283

them talking and William joking, and both had had their hair cut short in the newly fashionable Brutus crop, elegantly dishevelled. It was James and yet it was not James, he looked so different. And she remembered the big horses sidling and snorting above her, with William leaning down and chatting easily, on and on, and she absently responding where it seemed demanded, and William's loud laugh, and all the time James staring sombrely and silently at her till she could hardly bear herself. The second occasion had been at the next of Katharine's rides. At first he had tossed greetings and comments to everybody but her, behaving as if she were invisible, but then when she had dropped behind the others, her body strained and her head aching with the effort of behaving normally, then he had appeared beside her and spoken to her with a formality that seemed to deny everything that had been between them, asking after her husband and the baby as if they were people with whom he had only a distant acquaintance. And she had answered in a daze as if the meadows and the trees, the riders and he were all part of some unquiet dream, some nightmare that would not fade with the day.

The group in the courtyard was small today, Beatrice and Katharine, and Fanny, unusually, for she did not care for riding ... and James: James with his back to her, addressing the groom, Harry, in a sharp voice, and then swinging himself on to his horse and turning to ride beneath the gatehouse arch and lead the way down the avenue, barking out: 'Cousin Susannah!' as he passed her, his face set.

Katharine murmured apprehensively: 'But where are we going?'

James turned his head. 'For a short ride only, to that patch of open country beyond the Winchester road where we can gallop the horses, and back again.'

'But that means riding through the village!' she exclaimed.

'Yes,' James said, 'it does. We shall ride through at a trot and it will be over before you know it. It is time enough that you took this step.' And his tone and the set of his face brooked no argument.

'I can't, I can't!' Katharine said to Susannah and Fanny in an anguished undertone. 'I am not prepared for this ... not the village ... not yet!'

284

'Nonsense, the village stares are nothing,' Fanny said calmly, patting her pony's neck, 'they mean no harm, those people, but they have such dull lives, any change is an excitement. I expect they will be pleased for you, even startled, to see how normal you look, after all the old rumours.'

Katharine was silent, but the reins in her hands shuddered and the tendons on her neck stood out. Susannah looked into her face and an intense awareness came to her of the girl's real panic and dread.

'It will be all right,' she said reassuringly. 'There will be few folk around at this time of day, and none of the young and silly – they'll be at work. Remember what Sam Truckle said of you? A'most pretty? Now you must give the rest a chance to agree!'

Katharine swallowed drily.

'Stares cannot hurt, and we shall be beside you, I promise.'

The village street was far from empty: there was a clutch of women talking outside Duckett's shop and two young lads driving a pig, and all the old men were gossiping under the smithy chestnut tree in the autumn sunshine. With her awareness of Katharine's suffering still strong in Susannah she saw these people as a great blurred crowd, avidly watching the five riders as they trotted forward, waiting to comment and to gossip, and tension rose in her, knotting itself in her stomach. Katharine's hands were taut on the reins and her pony was dropping back, back behind the rest of them ... and then Susannah's mind cleared, and she saw the groups of people looking across with their placid country faces and she reined Handon back till she could lean over and give the pony a sharp clout on his flank. Then as Katharine perforce was taken forward Susannah called greetings: 'Good morning, Mrs Page, Mrs Truckle! How are you, Josh!' And the faces that had been staring in wonder broke into smiles and nods and greetings.

Old man Jurd tottered forward on his bow legs the better to see that his eyes were not deceiving him: 'Eh, miss, a good marnin' to ye!' he called, his voice hoarse with excitement.

They rode round the smithy and into the lane leading to the Winchester road and there were half a dozen cottages to pass and a woman shaking a mat and two small girls staring with their fingers in their mouths and it was over.

'There,' Beatrice said triumphantly, 'they were pleased to see you!'

Katharine moved her lips and then licked them with her tongue as though her whole mouth was dry. 'They smiled at me,' she said in a voice hoarse with wonderment.

'Naturally,' said Susannah. 'They like a pretty young woman.'

'But at me!' Katharine said. She sat very straight in the saddle and the colour flooded into her pale cheeks. 'I did it – and they smiled!'

'You see,' said Beatrice, 'it was easy. Wasn't it?'

'No,' came James's deep voice unexpectedly from behind them. 'It was ordeal by burning stares, but she came through magnificently.'

'I agree,' Fanny said. 'And Timothy Goddard will be disgusted to have missed being with you on such an occasion. He's been so admiring to see you coming out of your shell as you have done recently.'

'Oh!' Katharine gave a shy laugh. 'I know you are all quizzing me, but thank you for being so kind.'

'Kind? To put you through that ordeal?' said Susannah. 'Now you are quizzing us.'

James and Beatrice cantered briskly up the lane; the others followed more slowly. As Katharine rode in happy silent relief beside them, Susannah asked Fanny about the rector's health, and about her one-time charges. 'I know that your father is taking all the church services now and Sedley tells me he is busy about parish business, but is he able to teach William his Latin again?'

Fanny's lovely petulant face broke into a smile. 'Yes, I am thankful to say, and William is far better behaved now. William Waterton is not the best godfather in the world for the more serious aspects of his upbringing, but he did offer to teach his namesake to shoot – William was in seventh heaven. But Papa said he would permit it only if he was satisfied with the progress of his work.' Fanny giggled. 'My brother changed overnight.'

'A clever scheme. And it must have taken some pressure from you.'

Fanny shrugged. 'But there are other pressures on me,' she

said ruefully. 'Marriage! Timothy Goddard is praised to the skies - endlessly. In some ways it makes my life easier ... if I'm frantic to escape the schoolroom I tell Mama that I'm to walk with Timothy, or that I'm to visit the Goddards, and difficulties miraculously evaporate. But the more I escape through Timothy, the more encouraged he is ... and Mama and Papa.'

'Has he spoken to them?'

'They've said nothing, but I suspect so. And I swear he was determined to propose to me yesterday. Mama pushed us to take a walk in the garden and he was forever taking my hand, and deep breaths, and saying, "My dear Fanny, there is something I must say ..." and I was forever interrupting him to exclaim over the lovely late roses, or the dear little robin singing in the cherry tree, even the dear little snails' trails on the path! And then the gardener came out and I rushed to speak to him, and you know what a dreadful old curmudgeon he is and how Mama and I loathe him. So the moments passed and the worst was averted, but, oh dear, what do I do now?'

Susannah was laughing, but Katharine was shocked and reproachful.

'Poor, poor Timothy,' she said, 'he must have been dreadfully disappointed not to speak to you. Do you really not wish to marry him, Fanny?'

Beatrice and James came trotting back impatiently to rejoin them.

Fanny said: 'I don't wish to marry anybody.'

'How strange you are,' breathed Katharine. 'How can you not love someone who so clearly cares for you, and who is so thoughtful and kind?'

Fanny shook her head. 'Love does not come to order,' she said.

'How right you are, my dear Fanny,' James said, reining in beside her. 'Love neither comes nor goes to order, though there are those who behave as though it did.'

'Truly?' Susannah said coolly. 'Then I am glad my acquaintance is so small that it does not encompass such persons.'

They crossed the Winchester road and she kicked Handon to a canter and then to a gallop on the grassy ride opposite. Divots of turf and mud swirled upwards as Handon's hooves attacked the wide track. Behind her, James, galloping too, received a spatter of mud on the cheek. Swerving, he drew level with her and they rode together, grimly, swiftly, for nearly a mile. Then, as if moved by a common will they slowed to a trot, then to a walk.

'I wish,' he gasped furiously, wiping the mud from his face on his glove, 'that I could cut off love as you seem able – you must explain to me how it is done.'

Susannah glanced behind; the others were tiny figures in the distance, coming steadily. She looked stonily back at James.

'Devil take you!' he said. 'Will you answer me?'

Before them was a distant view of Hampshire hills, but the hills were vanishing into mist and the sun, too, was being swallowed by clouds lying like fingers across the sky. A thin breeze blew cold over them.

'You appear to know the answer already,' she said. 'A month nearly, and you have not visited Piers. We have waited for you, he and I.'

'When you have deliberately cut yourself off from me,' James said, 'do you expect me to come seeking further pain?'

'I cannot help the pain,' she said passionately, 'not for you, not for me. Events have inflicted it and perhaps one day it will ease. But Piers should not suffer. Sedley – I don't know why, perhaps because he has some deep unconscious knowledge that Piers is not his, perhaps because he is not a man to care for children – Sedley takes little interest in him. He does not talk to him, he does not play with him. But Piers has learned to love you. Are you going to let him be hurt, too?'

'No,' he said slowly. 'My son ... no, your command forbids me to say that word, my godson ...? No, never, not if I can help it.'

'Then visit him. Not alone. That would be ... would not be right. But you could come with Beatrice. Or with Katharine. Yes! Make Brambourne village her next ride.'

'Very well,' he said. 'I will try.'

'Then you can both admire his progress. James, he is so obstreperous and comical – he can roll from his back to his front now, but when he has been there two seconds he dislikes it and roars to be put back, only to do it again. I swear I have turned him over thirty times a day!'

288

'Losing him,' James said, 'has been a part of my pain in losing you.'

'Then do not inflict it upon yourself,' she pleaded.

23

Autumn became winter, the days were short and cub-hunting began. The mornings were cold and often misty, but when the mists lifted the air was bright and sharp in a way that braced the body and cleared the mind. Beatrice Manningford rode every day as had been her custom for many years, but of recent months she had ceased to ride alone. Much of the time a groom rode with her, a taciturn middle-aged man; when, as happened surprisingly frequently, Dr Breakspear happened to join them, the groom rode a discreet distance behind and kept his own counsel.

Beatrice loved all the seasons of the year but best of all she loved autumn and this autumn had been brilliant. As she had ridden with Edmund Breakspear along the valley in the short, unexpectedly warm October days there abounded with her a feeling of such exhilaration and happiness as she had never known before. She dismissed her father's mistrustful thoughts, she refused to think about the future, she rejoiced in the happiness of the present, most of all in the pleasure of his company and his gentle serious conversation about her life and her difficulties, and of his experiments comparing the results of the uses of different foods and certain ointments in cases of scurvy and the skin diseases. In helping Edmund with the boy with the broken leg she felt she had contributed something actual and real to his cure, now she sensed windows opening wide in her mind.

With the coming of winter nothing had changed but the coolness of the air, the widening brown bands of the winter ploughing in the stubble fields, the loss of the beech leaves. Each day was a time of suspended wonder.

She was cantering home through the woods in the slanting late afternoon sunshine one day, skirting Brambourne to the south, when she heard the doctor call her name and the sound of his horse's hooves behind her. She reined in slightly and turned her head to exchange greetings.

'No groom?' he said, looking round with a frown as he caught her up.

'As you see,' she said sweetly. Then she relented. 'I started off with him, poor man, but his horse began to limp and we discovered he'd lost a shoe, so I ordered John home. I saw no reason to shorten my own ride, however. The countryside is quiet.'

'I see that,' he returned. 'I also see that this path we are following is rough. Badgers' holes or fallen branches could be covered by leaves and prove treacherous. You might lie here injured and undiscovered for hours.'

'Oh, nonsense,' she protested. 'Handon is most sure-footed. Follow me and you'll see.'

She kicked the horse back to a canter and moved ahead of him along the track. Two minutes later she was laughing over her shoulder as they came to the end of the wood, 'You see?' she called, but almost on that instant Handon encountered a hidden tree root, stumbled and threw her.

Caught unawares she tumbled heavily, inelegantly, half-winding herself, and lay on the path in a fury, her eyes closed against the oblique rays of the sun that were not only blinding her, but illuminating her in all her folly.

Edmund, scared for her, drew his horse up almost on its haunches, flung himself from it, knelt beside her and pulled her head on to his lap.

'Beatrice! Beatrice, tell me you're not hurt! Tell me!'

Her dignity had been lost, her hair was muddied and full of leaves. Yet she felt his hands smoothing the tumbled locks, touching her gently, probing with concern. The sensation was amazing, delicious; she could not bear to speak, to break the spell.

'Dearest,' he said, his voice abruptly sharpening to fear, 'my sweet! Speak to me!' He turned his head to shout: 'Help! Over

291

here!' Then, despairingly: 'Oh God, there's never anybody about at this hour.'

Reluctantly she moved, easing her shoulders.

'Dear one.' His hands clutched her. 'Quick, tell me where it hurts.'

Beatrice opened her eyes. 'Nowhere!' she said and shut them again.

'Oh – and you gave me such a fright. I thought you concussed. Why are your eyes closed, you wicked girl?'

'The sun. And my embarrassment. Such folly – like the green girl I swear I'm not!'

He laughed at her, he quizzed and mock-scolded her. He had told her, he had forecasted this. What luck that he had been with her and that she had not been injured. He could not have borne for her to be hurt. His tenderness and his mockery pierced her, a feeling of almost unbearable happiness flooded her. She felt that they were suddenly very close and she looked up at him, trembling and yet confident and he leaned to take her face in his hands and kiss her, full and warm.

Then he lifted his head and said: 'You need someone to look after you all the time, every day. That's what I believe, my foolish, careless, lovely Beatrice. You need me. Will you marry me?'

She did not reply at once, her throat thick with happiness and love. She saw his face in the sunlight, tanned, the skin of his jaw dark and slightly rough, and she reached up with her hand to put it against his cheek. Everything she had not the words to express of her joy and wonder was a part of that movement of tenderness. 'Yes! Oh yes!' she said, and reflected what a very little word 'yes' was for so big an occasion.

Later, as they rode, she remarked with laughter that only she could have had so unromantic a proposal, covered in leaves and mud. And how the news was to be broken to her father she did not know. Edmund wanted to approach him at once, but Beatrice told him: 'Not yet.' His mind, she said, would have to be opened to the thought that one of his daughters was to marry, not an idea she believed he had ever seriously considered, and unless he was carefully prepared he would be set against it.

'Edmund did laugh,' she told Susannah later, 'and he did

agree to leave it to me. But I think he was a little hurt. And now, somehow, Papa has to be persuaded that it will prove a good match.'

'It will be a wonderful match,' Susannah told her fervently. 'And Cousin James could speak on the doctor's behalf, couldn't he? They seem good friends.'

'You're right. How sensible. Papa is more fond of James than anyone could have imagined possible who knew how once he resented his coming to Abbotsbridge. He will listen to James and weigh his words.'

But it was by chance a couple of days later, while Ambrose and James were riding along the track above the water meadows looking for the man known as the drowner, that they encountered Edmund Breakspear riding in the same direction to visit a patient with bad rheumatics. Polite greetings were exchanged and Ambrose explained whom they were seeking. Edmund knew the man they meant, but he had seen no one.

He added, with a regretful smile to Ambrose: 'You know, sir, I am a Hampshire man by birth, yet was forced to live much of my life in London. Now I've returned I find myself ignorant of what others take for granted. Can you explain to me, pray, the principles upon which the drowner works in the flooding of these meadows?'

'It is to give an early bite of grass in the hungry months of March and April. Briefly, the object is to cover the grass with a thin layer of running water from the chalk stream, before and after Christmas. This, you will understand, acts as a blanket against the frosts and also deposits silt around the roots. We have a skilled man in our drowner who controls the weirs and the hatches and keeps the channels clear – he's nearly as important as Josh Pither in the village. The great advantage of water meadows like that below us is in the feed for our sheep.'

'I understand,' Edmund said. 'But I am surprised the sheep don't get foot-rot.'

'Oh, no. This is quick-drying land and they're not left there long. Next they are folded on the land for barley, to give it their dung.' Ambrose pushed aside some overhanging willow branches as he rode. 'Well, by the time the young barley is showing the sheep can be pastured on the downland by day and folded on the fallow land by night.'

'And a watered meadow produces far more hay than unwatered ground,' James added, 'and,' with a triumphant smile, 'there is no need for manuring.'

'Fascinating,' said Edmund. 'An excellent scheme.'

He had several further questions to ask, including a searching one on how the system would be organised after the enclosure of the land, before the conversation moved to the desperate state of the labouring classes this winter, and the inadequacies of the justices' response, on which all three found themselves in agreement. James noticed Ambrose giving Edmund something approaching a look of approval.

Abruptly Ambrose said to Edmund: 'I understand from James that your grandfather is a Hampshire Justice, though I cannot recall ever having been introduced to a Breakspear, or indeed hearing such a name.'

'No, you wouldn't,' Edmund agreed, smiling. 'You have been misinformed: not my paternal, but my maternal grandfather, and his name is Bridges, Hugh Bridges.'

'Ah, I know him,' Ambrose said, his austere face lightening. 'He was used to give me advice when I was first on the Bench, excellent advice, too. But that means your mother – why, she must be ... Do not tell me your mother was Louisa Bridges?'

'Yes, the very same.'

'Well, well, Louisa Bridges' son! She was one of my first flirts, you know, back in the mad old days of my youth. We used to meet at Christmas balls and summer balls, and out hunting, too. So pretty and lively she was.' He looked round at Edmund, his face breaking into a smile, 'Well, you must come and dine with us, at all events, and tell me about your family and how your grandfather fares. I should be delighted to renew my acquaintance with him and Louisa. And I am told you have struck up a friendship with my daughter, Beatrice. Yes, you must definitely come to dine, and soon. Can you manage tomorrow?'

24

As winter went on there were gales on land and storms at sea. The long-awaited expedition to the West Indies to put down rebellions there was forced back to harbour, and in December again was dispersed by the fury of the storms. Mr Fulbroad, concerned for his interests in Barbados, was beside himself with anger at the delays. After the last gale in early December, Susannah surveyed the damage to her garden with lacklustre eyes. It was battered and covered with twigs and other debris, and the mulberry tree had suffered a mauling, but she had no zest for clearing the mess or staking her damaged shrubs. She had no energy for anything.

When Jack had arrived to tell her of his successful meeting with the banker, Mr Jocelyn Forbes, in Winchester, 'I reckon I impressed him with the careful calculations I put into my plans for expansion!' and of how he had purchased not only Peter Page's eleven acres but seven additional acres from old Cornelius Nutbeam with the help of a mortgage, she had smiled and congratulated him, but found it difficult to produce the enthusiasm Jack had expected from his normally exuberant sister. Fanny Bland, too, used to Susannah's understanding and sympathy in her running battles with her parents, found her friend's responses unusually muted when she poured out her tales of the explosions of wrath that had burst over her head when Timothy Goddard finally cornered her and she had refused him.

'Mama was sobbing and shouting at me that I would turn into a long-nosed old spinster like Miss Waterton – and Susannah, I'm not twenty yet. And Papa said he wondered if the

Goddards would ever speak to us again, I had behaved so shocking. One would imagine no female had ever turned down an offer before!'

Susannah said in a faraway voice: 'Fanny, I'm sorry, but the rumpus was inevitable. They see your life so differently from you.' Then she had removed her crawling, insatiably curious son from his explorations in the log basket to hug him closely and wipe his grubby little hands, and barely responded to Fanny's plaints with more than a 'Yes?' or an 'Oh dear!'

Now she walked back up the garden path, staring half-blindly at a holly showing its blood-red berries, the only note of colour in the desolate scene. From a high perch somewhere a thrush began to flute its song: so many thrushes had died in last winter's cold that it was unusual to hear one; the rich joyous notes seemed to mock her and all human anxieties and troubles.

She was pregnant. She had suspected so for many days and now she was sure. It was right she should give Sedley a child of his own, consciously she recognised that, but in her deeper instinctual self she resented the insidious growth within her womb of a child that was not James'; she felt tired and nauseated and miserable.

The wind had not entirely died, its icy breath was penetrating her clothes; she shivered and forced herself back indoors. The house was silent: Sedley was in the church, Becky was in the kitchen brewing beer, Piers was asleep upstairs. She went into the sitting parlour to crouch beside the fire there and through the window, distantly, came again the mocking beauty of the thrush's song, and all at once she began to shake with sobs, dry, tearless sobs that hurt her throat and made her head throb, and all the time the question was pounding through her mind: how should she tell James? And the grief was as much for him as for herself, for the loneliness and despair that he would feel, for she had Piers for her comfort and James had no one.

At first her thoughts were all of the telling: there was no means of disguising it or lessening the hurt, it must be quick and sharp, like a surgeon's knife. Tell him herself she must; he would be deeply hurt to hear of it from some gossiping neighbour.

*

296

On New Year's Day James walked into Abbotsbridge rectory with his face as cold and set as stone, hardly hearing what Mrs Bland was saying. The rector's man took his riding coat and his bicorne hat and he was unaware of his presence. A child! Susannah pregnant with that man Stacey's child, damn him to perdition! and she told him as coolly as if she were observing what o'clock it was. Mrs Bland was rambling on, her voice like a stream bubbling over stones; what was that she was saying?

'... I must wish all my friends a happy New Year ... though how anyone could find it so with wheat at as much as three guineas per coomb and wheat flour difficult to get at all, I can't conceive! And how an honest labouring man can be expected to manage I don't know, either. Do pray, go into the rector's bookroom, Mr James, the fire is lit, and he should be home at any minute. Indeed, he should have been back half an hour ago, he must have been delayed across the common – the Bidewells again, another sickly child that should be christened for its poor little soul's sake ... But you must make yourself at home and I shall order refreshments ...'

'No, no refreshments, thank you,' James said, his voice harsh.

Mrs Bland looked at him doubtfully. 'I would stay with you, you know, but I am a slave to my children's education, and this is Fanny's sacred hour, the time to play her harp without interruption. You know that we are to have another concert in the spring, so great was the demand from our neighbours? Well, if you are comfortable ...'

'Perfectly,' James replied.

He stood in the centre of the room clenching and unclenching his hands. Always there had been the hope at the back of his mind that Susannah might relent, that she would sicken of her life with that prosy and unpleasant parson and turn again to him for love and companionship. Now that hope was dead.

From the drawing-room came the sounds of Fanny's harp, playing some piece in a minor key. Mozart was it, or Haydn? The plucked and plaintive sounds touched his heart, entering into his mood. He let the music flow over him, his eyes half-closed.

When the harp was stilled he opened his eyes. The room seemed very empty, the cold January light reflecting dully back from worn leather-bound commentaries and books of sermons piled on the rector's desk. Nothing to divert his thoughts from Susannah's words. 'You must not think of me, James, not ever. I belong to the past and you must look to the future. Someday soon you must marry. You need someone to share your life . . .' If he could ever have hated her, he had hated her then. The pain tore through him again; somehow he must numb it. In the distance the harp music started again, elusive sounds filtering through the walls. James swung on his heels: he would not wait alone, he would sit with Fanny.

She stopped playing immediately the door opened, her hands still lifted to the strings, her eyebrows imperiously raised. Her sacred hour, Mrs Bland had said. James understood.

'Please do not stop. Take no notice of me, Fanny. I only wish to listen to your playing while I wait for your father.'

A moment's silence. Fanny's back was straight, her chin up. 'You will find it dull,' she warned. 'I'm not playing for an audience. I am practising.'

'I understand.'

She said no more, but simply nodded and turned her eyes back to her music stand. James crossed the room and sat down. Fanny began to play, her head tilted forward as if to hear every vibration of every string to the full, going through the piece phrase by phrase, repeating sections again and again as she searched for the very essence of the music, the composer's deepest intent. It was clear that within seconds she had forgotten James' presence in the room; her mind was totally engaged with the music. At intervals she stopped to consider, flexing her slim hands, then worked on, now bringing to it her own interpretation, heightening the contrasts of mood, enriching the tone.

James sat very still, watching her, warmed by the murmuring log fire, losing some of his tension in his interest. He was impressed; this was an aspect of Fanny that he had never met before. That she played well, indeed, more than well, he had long known, but that she brought to her music so high a level of intellectual dedication was unexpected. This was an entirely different Fanny from the young woman who shrugged her pretty shoulders in boredom at dinner parties, or spoke with annoyance of her subjurgation to the rectory schoolroom routines; this was someone he could admire, someone who gave herself whole-heartedly to the achievement of the highest standards. She was beautiful and her playing was exceptional. When Mrs Bland poked her head round the door to tell him that the rector had at last arrived he was regretful, jerked back from a different world.

Mrs Bland was shocked that Fanny had not moderated her playing to her company. 'I did not realise you had come in here, Mr James. That doleful piece – you should have persuaded her to play you something more lively. If I had but known ...'

'It was exactly the music for me this morning, Mrs Bland, I assure you. And to listen to Fanny practising was an education.'

Fanny was putting away her music, but she looked up at him now, a sudden smile lightening her face. 'You are one of the very few people who can listen without making doltish comments or paying foolish compliments. I should be happy to play for you at any time, if you should wish it.'

'I should appreciate that greatly,' he said, and felt complimented himself.

In the following weeks James fell into the habit of timing his visits to the rectory to Fanny's sacred hour, and slipping into the drawing-room to listen to her playing whenever he had the opportunity. He had a multiplicity of matters to discuss with Mr Bland so that his visits were not infrequent. He found Fanny restful, undemanding; she wanted nothing from him, she was content to let him listen as she continued to pursue her own vision. Her pensive distant face and the reflective charm of her playing accorded with his own sadness, seeming unconsciously both to echo and to soothe it. On the days when he forced himself to visit Susannah and Piers his hurts came rushing back, together with a feeling of dispossession that left him spiritless and empty as a husk: it was then that he found Fanny's company particularly soothing. And so abstracted did he seem, so remote from the ardent beau of Mrs Bland's imaginings that even her optimistic eye could discern nothing to rouse her maternal hopes. Besides, there was always some objective in his calls.

In a second winter of dearth and high prices, the rector and James worked together to deal with the needs of the poor. Men like Mr Fulbroad and Mr Munday were coerced once more into donating to the fund for food and fuel, despite their grumbles.

'I contribute enough to the rates already,' Hector Fulbroad stated, 'and God knows they've risen to a shocking level.'

'Helping these people will keep down the unrest,' James said, appealing to his pet prejudices, 'and relief outside costs a deal less than forcing them into the poorhouse. It has already kept Nat Jurd and his family, the Nutts and the Carters safe in their own homes.'

Fulbroad eyed him and produced two guineas which James cheerfully pocketed, saying that he would regard them as a contribution for this month and be back the next for more, leaving Fulbroad swelling with annoyance.

Mr Bland made a patient mediator in the arguments that raged throughout the winter over what the farmers considered the high-handed behaviour of the commissioners for enclosure. It had been laid down in the Act of Enclosure that the commissioners were to direct the management and order of the land with regard to cultivation, including the flocks, whatever the usage to the contrary, from the time of the Act to the final award. Inevitably, men like Truckle and Pettifer complained bitterly, stating that they had no intention of allowing any townsfolk to dictate what was to be grown nor where they were to pasture their beasts, nor aught else. When the commissioners attempted to adjust the time-honoured calendar of grazing and folding of the sheep flocks there were scenes in The Bull and outside the smithy that threatened riots.

'Are ye men or are ye beasts yerselves that ye let these furriners dictate to ye?' demanded old Seth Carter, the retired shepherd.

James bluntly told the senior commissioner, Mr Haynes, that if he did not rescind his orders then the inevitable trouble would be laid at his door, and the changes were quietly abandoned. James and Mr Bland spent many hours riding together to smoothe the farmers' ruffled susceptibilities and with the help of Jack Trotter, an uneasy truce was kept.

After what seemed interminable months of cold and disease and high prices, winter at last drew to its end; the scent of spring came to the air, wood-anemones and celandines poked up their starry flowers on the roadside banks, and as the days warmed and lengthened the musical club began to meet again to arrange its next concert. As a boy James had been a keen student of music, but as a man he had found other concerns supervening and while he had continued to play, he had not given it the time that once he had considered essential. Now he found his old interest reviving and growing; encouraged by Fanny he played Rosalind's Broadwood pianoforte most evenings. He accompanied Katharine on the flute, too, often with Timothy Goddard as an audience as well as Rosalind and Beatrice, Timothy seeming to find a similar solace for the hurts he had suffered at Fanny's hands from Katharine's playing as James did from Fanny's.

Fanny was determined that Katharine should play at her next concert and said so to James. 'She has some pretty pieces in her repertoire that are just the thing to appeal to our neighbours – genteel tripping stuff they can all understand.'

'You must use your persuasive powers on her,' said James.

'Not me – Timothy. He would be the very fellow for the job!' Fanny's eyes were lively with mischief. 'If I were the matchmaking sort, I should be busy there. An ideal couple, don't you think, despite her pock-marks? Both so shy and quiet and good and earnest. And if it were to come about then Mama would be wholly silenced on the topic of Timothy and me, something devoutly to be desired!'

'Is it still bad?'

Fanny shuddered. 'Shocking. Oh, Mama only tells me that I am breaking her heart once a day now, instead of ten times, but it is still horrid – and Mr Manningford's announcement of Beatrice and Edmund's wedding date caused a bad setback! No, all my hopes are on this coming concert, James. If it is a success perhaps my parents will understand my wish to go to London and study with a famous teacher. And it would be such Heaven, too. I would live with my Aunt Anne, my father's sister. She is musical, truly musical, a widow on her own, and she has said she would be delighted for me to companion her.'

'It sounds a sensible idea,' James said. 'I wonder at your parents being so opposed to it.'

'They have only one idea for me,' said Fanny.

The topic of Fanny and her parents came up again after the

first meeting of the musical club, held at Abbotsbridge House. It had been a successful meeting, with broad agreement among those present as to the tone and style of the next concert and several of the items to be included settled amicably. When their business was finished Rosalind Manningford and Timothy disappeared with Fanny to supervise the servants as they transported the precious harp back to the rector's carriage, but the others remained, collecting up their music and chatting. Normally James would have removed himself immediately, but today he stood turning over sheets of music on a side-table, half-listening to the conversation.

On her return Rosalind was unusually animated, praising Fanny's skill and saying how much she had enjoyed her playing of a particular piece by Handel.

'It was written originally for the harpsichord, and Fanny tells me she adapted it herself. An enchantment, I declare.'

'I agree,' Katharine murmured, 'it was wonderful.' It was the first time she had ventured to come to a musical club meeting and she had sat wide-eyed and silent throughout the proceedings, but since everyone present, including Miss Waterton, had allowed her to sit in her corner undisturbed she was now feeling comfortable enough to give her opinion.

Rosalind said in lowered tones: 'To my mind it is a great pity that she is not allowed to do as she wishes and go to London. Her parents rail at her that she will end up a spinster, but for myself I do not see that as so very dreadful. I am unmarried and I'm quite content.'

Miss Waterton ceased a series of chords on the pianoforte to give her a pitying look. 'You have made your life around your family, and with them and this big house to run you are never at a loss for occupation or companionship. For Fanny it would be a quite different situation. Imagine what it would be like for her to grow old and lose her looks and be poor and pitied. I cannot think that music could ever recompense one for that, and you know how highly in my scheme of things I rate music!'

'I do not see that in Fanny's case, Augusta,' Rosalind said obstinately. 'Someone like her will always have friends and be admired.'

'One would imagine so,' James said from the side-table.

Jessica, who had come into the room in search of her work-box and silk thread to mend a tear in the flounce of one of her new silk gowns, looked up from her comparison of colours and said: 'For my part, I think Fanny should look to marrying an older man with an establishment of well-trained servants, one who could free her from the drudgery of domestic arrangements to live her life as she pleased. And one who would not force her to produce a baby every year. Goodness knows, one can sympathise with anyone's reluctance to commit herself to that!'

'Jessica! Not to want babies – you cannot be serious?' Katharine protested.

'You must admit that a married lady's life is shockingly narrowed by child-bearing,' Jessica returned. 'Look at poor Mrs Stacey. She's not with you today. She'll not sing duets with Cousin James at your next concert. No sooner has she produced one child than she's burdened with the next. And so it will go on. It's enough to make one shudder.'

It made James shudder. The atmosphere in the handsome faded room had suddenly become intense, unbearable. Miss Waterton struck another series of chords, loud this time, and forceful. He was abruptly aware of currents of feeling that he had never noticed before, aware that Miss Waterton despised his cousin Rosalind for having so soon relinquished all hope of a husband, that Rosalind sensed and resented this, and in turn despised Augusta Waterton for her frantic dependence on marriage as the justification for her existence; he saw that Jessica would write her own rules for her life, assured and resilient despite the defects of her puckered cheek and damaged arm. He tried not to think of Susannah. Unprepossessing visions of the narrow lives that women lived assailed him – lives and ways that he had always accepted, never before queried. Behind him the conversation continued, the cool well-bred voices dissecting Fanny, whose genius should have put her above their pity and their resentment. It was almost with relief that he greeted a manservant's information that Mr Haynes's one-horse phaeton was driving up to the house. He pushed the music sheets away and walked from the room.

The commissioner, his spectacles on the end of his nose, had queries about the running of the cow common, or cow pasture, after enclosure when the arrangements were to be vested in the rector, the overseer and the churchwardens. He told James that he anticipated the enclosure award being published in the late-summer, which was sooner than the pessimistic Ambrose had originally anticipated, and that he wanted all arrangements that could possibly be controversial to be thoroughly thrashed out by then. James found himself more nearly in accord with the pedantic little man than he had ever done before: at least Mr Haynes's queries and quibbles were over matters of fact and sensible management, matters upon which clear-cut decisions could be reached without undercurrents of feeling and emotion.

Yet when the man had gone and James stood by the library window where it looked into the park, all bright and soft with the coming of spring, he did not see the first haze of green lightening the branches of the trees, or watch the rooks busy with their nests among the topmost twigs, nor was his mind occupied with clear-cut factual matters. The emotions he had wanted to avoid when he left the drawing-room now gripped him; he stood by the window for a long time, struggling with thoughts that were desolate and cold. At the mention of Susannah his mild pleasure in the morning's activities had vanished; the knowledge that another man was possessing her and fathering his children on her was intolerable, the torture of the damned. He had called to see her and Piers yesterday at the parsonage in the company of Beatrice and found himself hardly able to look at her, her body distorted with Stacey's child. Instead he had concentrated on Piers and damned what Beatrice might think. And Piers had demanded attention; he could stand now, and he had pulled himself up on James's riding boots to stand between his legs, crowing with triumph and thumping him with his plump little fists. James stared out over Manningford land. Neither he nor Susannah could move out of sight of each other, but somehow he had to eradicate his jealousy and his anguish.

There were other women in the world, not the sun and the moon, but gentle creatures with soft bodies and compliant natures. Perhaps as Susannah had said – and Ambrose and Beatrice also – perhaps he should fill his sight with such a woman, a woman for whom his advances would be a relief, an end, as someone had said this morning, to loneliness and pity.

Then there would be two lonely people the less in the world. He remembered Ambrose's words. ' 'Tis time you looked about you, James. You need a wife and Abbotsbridge needs an heir. Serious, I mean it. Pretty widows and other men's wives won't do, won't do at all.' James leaned his heavy head on the cool glass of the window; it was his lowest hour.

25

When the musical club held its concert in early-June Susannah pleaded an indisposition and stayed at home. With only a month of her pregnancy to go she felt misshapen and gross and hated appearing in public, especially with James there; she was horribly aware of his averted eyes. Instead, once Sedley had left, she checked Piers lying in his cot with his face flushed with sleep and his fists clenched in tiny male pugnacity, adjusted his covers, and then retreated to bed with Goldsmith's *The Vicar of Wakefield.* Its charm soon caught her up and it seemed all too short a time before she heard Sedley's voice calling to Becky to know where her mistress was and then heard his heavy footsteps on the stairs.

He looked hot and irritable. 'A dull evening,' he said. 'Shocking dull. You did well to miss it.' He tugged off his cravat.

Susannah laid her book down. 'Was the concert not good?'

'Fair enough, I suppose, but everybody praised it to a ridiculous degree, ranting over Fanny Bland's playing and what a genius she is, James Manningford in particular lauding her to the skies. I do not see it myself. I cannot like that rarefied stuff with no good tunes to it. Besides, she thinks too much of herself as 'tis.' He sat down heavily on the bed to pull off his buckled shoes. 'And there is no sense in all this music for someone in her position. If I were her father and had to put up with her pettish ways I'd soon take a cane to her.'

Susannah wondered whether Fanny had snubbed Sedley, or merely ignored him. He stood to remove his breeches and his eyes fell on her book. 'Reading again? A novel and lent to you by Fanny? I wish you will not waste your time with such trash. Novels do nothing but unsettle females and give them foolish ideas.'

'This book does not come from Fanny, Sedley, it's Mr Manningford's. He told me he liked to lend his books to those who could give them proper appreciation.' She showed him the leather spine. 'Look, *The Vicar of Wakefield*. Most suitable reading for your wife, wouldn't you think?'

'Hm.' He flung his breeches at a chair. 'If Mr Manningford lent it to you then one cannot doubt that it is proper reading and you should be grateful. But that does not change what I said, Susannah.'

'I understand.' She eased her cumbersome body a little in the bed, moving away from him and the smell of stale port that hung on his breath. 'Do tell me, did Cousin Katharine play her flute?'

He stood on one leg to remove a stocking. His voice half-muffled as he tugged, he said: 'Yes, she did. Two short pieces in company with the harp.'

'Oh, I'm glad,' Susannah said warmly. 'That was amazingly valiant of her – and against everyone's expectations, too. How did she seem? Did she play well?'

'As creditable a performance as any, I thought. The candles were put behind her shoulder to hide her pocks and one could see her silhouette jerking, but she stuck to it.' He gave a short laugh. 'William Waterton bet she'd never do it, shy as she is. He wagered his guineas with Timothy Goddard and James Manningford, and lost – a typical folly. The man has more money than sense.'

'I'm so pleased she overcame her fears. Now she must feel equal to anything!'

'I daresay. I made her my compliments afterwards and she appeared most gratified by my interest. She is pleasant enough, poor creature.' Sedley paused to scratch the thatch of his naked chest and then pulled on his night-shirt. As his head emerged his eyes focussed on her body beneath the covers, then moved to her hair, long and lustrous, tumbled on the pillow. He seized her brush from the chest of drawers. 'Sit up,' he said, 'and I shall brush your hair.'

As the bristles scratched across her ears he remarked that

James Manningford had sung a duet at the concert with Fanny. 'He has a fine voice, but 'twas a pity he could not sing with you, as he did last year. It is just the thing to bring you to folks' attention.'

'Mm,' she said, and the memory of singing with James, their voices intertwining joyously, rose up in sudden pain inside her; she had to grit her teeth not to shove Sedley violently away.

At last he stopped tugging at her locks but his brushings and fondling had aroused further designs on her; in the trembling summer candlelight his body loomed enormous. He tugged at the bedclothes.

'No, no,' she said, clutching the sheet. 'Not tonight.'

'You are not going to deny me?'

His evening out had bored and irritated him; now he would use her coldly to relieve his frustration. Her stomach churned. 'You know my condition. You know I have not felt well this evening. Please, Sedley.'

For a moment she thought he would hit her but then he turned angrily away and made for his own side of the bed. ' 'Tis little enough enjoyment I have from marriage. Always some excuse to deny me my rights. Many men would insist. But for the child you carry I should.'

He tugged on his nightcap and scrambled into bed, grumbling in spurts of rancour for several minutes. At last silence fell, only to be broken by a sudden exclamation; Sedley sat upright in bed. 'Now look what you have made me do!' he said. 'Your unwifely behaviour has made me neglect my duty to the Lord. I have not said my prayers!'

On the first day of July the second child of the Stacey's marriage was born. Sedley had spent the day in Winchester, first on various shopping commissions for himself and Susannah and then dining with his friend the Canon in the Cathedral Close. He arrived home to find Fanny Bland swooning on a sofa, his vicarage full of people, and the short angry cries of a very new baby ringing in his ears. It was some minutes before he could sort out the component parts of this scene. He was not helped by Mrs Bland who was torn between her excitement at having called, all unknowing, moments before the birth, 'I must tell you – you have a beautiful baby daughter, Sedley!' and her concern for her own daughter, 'Lie quite still, Fanny, do! Allow the blood to mount to your head – of course nobody is dying, Susannah merely cried out for a second!'

Someone thrust a glass into his hands – was it Mrs Bland or was it Dr Breakspear? The doctor was now administering some draught or other to Fanny; his mother-in-law, Mrs Trotter, was clutching his arm and saying something, he knew not what, and then Martha Pither appeared, all smiles, with a bundle in her arms and he was pushed forward to peer at a tiny protesting face. As he looked the child stopped crying, its crinkled face smoothed out and it seemed to blink interestedly at him.

'There!' said Mrs Trotter. 'She knows her papa!'

He studied her. Apart from some wisps of brown hair, he could see no resemblance to Piers; this was a quite different child, rosy, the contours of the face rounded, female. Nor were the circumstances of the birth in any way related: the embarrassment and constriction that had attended that previous occasion were missing; behind him the room reverberated with murmurs of delight and congratulations. 'A pretty babe and your very image!' a voice exclaimed. His already high colour deepened with pleasure.

'Have you a name for her?' Mrs Bland asked.

'She is to be Harriet Dorothy Frances!' And he explained the significance of the names.

'Of course!' Mrs Bland exclaimed. 'Your goddaughter, Fanny. How charming!'

When his unexpected visitors had left Sedley first went upstairs to see his wife, who was sleepy but relieved, then sat down to write to his mother. He hoped her delicate health was not causing her attendants too great concern, and trusted that the news of the birth of her granddaughter would liven her spirits. If she could but bring herself to leave Bath for the country, so health-giving in the late-summer, then they would celebrate the christening with a large party in her honour. It was his dearest wish that she should be with them at this happy time. Susannah and he were, of course, giving the child her name. Surely, he mused, quill in hand, with his family increased to two, she would now see her way to augmenting his income. Smiling, he went on to describe the baby. 'All who have seen her,' he concluded, 'feel that she is destin'd to be a great bewty.'

*

While she was still abed recovering from the birth, Susannah was a captive audience for Fanny's rantings: far from being persuaded by her concert success to allow her to depart for London, the Blands saw it as a clear indication that she was required in Hampshire. She had every opportunity here: all their neighbours loved the concerts, they were discerning folk capable of appreciating the most noble and uplifting sorts of music, why should she seek the dubious attractions of London? 'Such nonsense!' said Mrs Bland. 'Fanny's health would undoubtedly suffer from the dirt and the noise and I should not be there to stop her from playing her harp till all hours!'

There was little Susannah could do, except to provide a sympathetic ear and condole with her. 'Perhaps you could go when you are of age.'

'But that means waiting for aeons of time, and I could not bear it!' Fanny wailed. 'Besides, I should have no money: I cannot depend on my parents' goodwill for an allowance – clearly they have none towards me.'

'Time may still change their attitude.'

'Nothing will ever change their attitude! I tell you, Susannah, I am in despair. Sometimes I think I should kill myself – or perhaps I shall die of boredom or despair first!'

'No one ever died of boredom,' Susannah assured her, shifting her sleeping baby from one arm to the other.

'I could, easily,' Fanny retorted. 'My meaningless existence is stultifying everything that is in me as 'tis. Dear God, Susannah, if I cannot get away somehow I do not know what rash extremes I may be driven to – I warn you, it is unendurable!'

Fanny often made such declarations, so that Susannah did not attach any particular significance to it until ten days later, the day of Beatrice Manningford and Edmund Breakspear's wedding.

She was dressing for the occasion in the bedroom when Sedley arrived back from the Blands, where he had been consulting with the rector about a new treatment for the death watch beetle in the church timbers, and began to change also.

'My new white satin waistcoat,' he complained. 'Where has it been put?'

Susannah showed him.

'Ah!' He put it on and paused to admire the effect, smoothing it down over his chest. 'Well! Well, Susannah, I have some strange and unexpected news from the Blands that I imagine will surprise you as much as it did me. Most unexpected.' He looked around. 'And my black silk stockings?'

'Here, in this drawer. What news is this?'

'James Manningford and Fanny are to be married. They say that one marriage generates another, but what d'you think of that?'

Silence. She said from between numb lips: 'You must be mistaken.'

'That was my own first thought. But I assure you 'tis true: Mrs Bland is in seventh heaven. The formal announcement will not be made for a few days, so we must not spread the word, but Mrs Bland told me in confidence, as a trusted friend. She knew I would not blab it about.'

She collapsed on the bed. Her words came thickly, seeming to clog in her throat. 'Fanny... and Cousin James. He must be mad!'

'I would not disagree with you there: you know what my opinion of Fanny has always been. And while I would never be one to advocate marrying purely for money, a sensible man should make a prudent connection – Fanny will bring the Manningfords nothing worth consideration.' Sedley shrugged on his coat and adjusted its high stand-up collar. 'Still, not many women would care to share a house with five plain spinster cousins, and there it is! Hurry up, Susannah, you will want to check our little Harriet before you go and you are barely half-dressed. It will never do to be late; I dare swear half the county will be present at today's affair.'

She stood up, drew on her blue silk gown, and began mechanically to arrange her hair in front of the glass. Her body seemed to have drained itself of blood; her knees were trembling and her lips were pale. 'They will never suit,' she told her shocked image. 'They are too unalike. They will never be happy.'

Sedley's face appeared behind her as he dealt with his own hair. 'I daresay they will contrive to rub along well enough, much as the rest of us do,' he said with faint malice. 'Besides, why should you worry? It has nothing to do with you.'

Susannah made no reply. She dropped her hairbrush on the

chest of drawers, went to check the tiny sleeping Harriet and returned.

'I am ready. Shall we go?' she said.

The church was cool inside to the point of dankness: after the warm July day its chill gave her goose-flesh. When she arose from praying she stared blindly across to where the open south door framed a dazzling scene of tall grasses and tombstones and distant cornfields against the sky, her hands absently rubbing her cold arms. There was a flurry outside, country voices exclaiming and calling good wishes in the lane; feet scrunched on the gravel path. The musicians struck up raggedly but vigorously, three fiddles, two bass viols, a flute and Peter Page on his trumpet; the congregation rose.

Beatrice appeared on her father's arm, outlined against the bright sky, walking with a slow and steady dignity so that her limp, improved considerably now by Edmund's special shoe, was scarcely perceptible, a smile of such pride and happiness curving her lips as she drew level with Susannah that Susannah had difficulty in choking back tears of over-stretched emotion.

It was then, through a gap between the heads in front of her, that Susannah saw Fanny, looking peculiarly attractive in her own cool remote fashion. Her soft fair hair was swept gently back and up into an artless chignon, a few curls wisped on her forehead, and the whole was bound round with a band embroidered in silver, echoing the blue and silver embroidery of her white crepe dress. That high-waisted style particularly suited girls of Fanny's figure, selecting as it did the beautifully moulded breasts for special attention and flowing unimpeded down the long slim legs to flatter them to their utmost. And on the opposite side of the aisle was James, looking at her in a way that was unmistakable.

The service passed in a blur for Susannah. She sat, rose, murmured responses, did as the rest of the congregation did, and all the time her body was shaking and the face of James was blotting out all other things.

At Abbotsbridge House she wished the couple happy, kissed Beatrice and admired her handsome white satin gown and the heirloom lace veil that was gracing the fourth generation of Abbotsbridge brides, all in a blind dream. Turning away, she took a glass of champagne from a footman and drank it standing mute beside Sedley. Faces swam into focus and disappeared. Miss Fulbroad, splendidly mourning a recently dead aunt in black and purple crepe, with gold fringe, cord and tassels, told her how much she admired her blue damask silk dress, 'Quite an old favourite, I do declare!'; Mrs Waterton remarked that Susannah looked pale and insisted upon her taking another glass of champagne, 'Nothing to match it for reviving the spirits!'; Miss Waterton hinted at further nuptial celebrations to come, 'But mum's the word . . . a delicate matter . . . such secrets are safe with me!'

She became aware of someone watching her, and, turning her head, saw that it was James. He detached himself from an animated group of guests and began to come towards her. She could not possibly speak to him here, now: she looked wildly for an avenue of escape and then saw Katharine standing alone by a window, her eyes wide, her head turning from side to side, the tell-tale tendons on her neck stiff with panic. Susannah cursed herself for not having noticed her before and slipped between the chattering men and women to the rescue, but even as she arrived Timothy Goddard appeared from nowhere, took Katharine's hand, pressed it reassuringly in his and drew her to talk to his dull and placid mother. James loomed behind her and Susannah was trapped.

'Cousin Susannah!'

'Cousin James!'

They stared at each other, the sound of the wedding party coming in distant roars, like the sea.

'I must speak to you,' he said. 'Something I must tell you . . . but here is not suitable. Perhaps tomorrow, at the vicarage?'

They were on their own in the window embrasure, no one could hear what they said.

'If you mean that you are to marry Fanny, don't trouble yourself. The information has already reached me.'

'How could it? Who told you?' His voice was sharp and stiff.

'Why,' sardonically, 'Mrs Bland told Sedley, who informed me.'

'I should have known,' he said in disgust. 'Damn it, I did mean that it should be me.'

'Yes.'

A pause. 'Will you not wish us happy?'

'Oh, certainly, I'll wish you happy!' she said caustically. 'But I'd doubt you will be – either of you! How could you do such a senseless thing? Fanny, of all women!'

'Are you angry because she is your friend?'

'No, no. Because she is Fanny. She will be no good to you, Cousin James. It is a ridiculous idea.'

'What on earth can you mean?'

She said in a furious undertone: 'Fanny has never wanted marriage.'

'I know – because she loathed the thought of wasting her life in running a house and dealing with endless servant problems. She would never be that sort of wife. But with me she need not endure such dull tasks; Cousin Rosalind will continue to deal with them, and be glad to do so.'

Exasperation swept through Susannah that the man she loved should be so foolish and so blind. It was impossible to explain to him without breaking Fanny's confidence, without sounding indelicate, worse, without sounding like an angry and jealous rival; yet she must do it.

With a tight throat she said: 'I was not speaking of that side of marriage, though that is true. But Fanny is afraid of ... of all aspects of marriage. James, she is afraid of the marriage bed!'

'I do have some ... awareness of that. Do you not believe me capable of gentleness, of patience?' He was beginning to sound angry. 'I can understand if she looks upon it with trepidation. I am sure many women must.'

Susannah shook her head vigorously, muttering: 'Not trepidation – revulsion. Can you understand that? Revulsion! The very idea sickens her.'

'Revulsion? What the devil do you mean? Am I so repulsive then?'

'Not you. Not specifically. Any man.'

'Rubbish!' he snapped. 'Now you are exaggerating wildly – and with what reason I would rather not speculate. I think this conversation should cease.'

Trying to warn him was hopeless; she wished she had never begun. But how could she not? 'I'm sorry, Cousin James. I do wish you happy ... I always would. And Fanny is my friend ... dear God, this is so hard ... please believe me, I only want to help you.'

314

The guests were eddying about behind them, gentlemen looking for the ladies to take them in to the banquet, the great feast that Beatrice had told Susannah her father insisted upon to mark the occasion and his pleasure in it. The room was slowly emptying; they could not go on arguing without drawing attention.

'It was you yourself,' James said with a cutting edge to his voice, 'who told me I should marry.'

'I was honest then for your own good, not for mine – as I am now.'

'Then yours is a strange and hurtful kind of honesty.'

She looked up at him and the annoyance at his obtuseness went from her, leaving only a deep sadness that all was so strained and changed between them. 'Honesty . . . and truth . . . they often are hurtful. That does not make them less right,' she said, and turned and left him.

She reached the door in a taut and brittle mood, cursing the pressure of emotion that had made her blurt out unpalatable truths before she had recovered from the shock of his engagement and had time to think out a reasoned approach. Dear God, what a gabbling fool: she had probably done more harm than good.

The meal now would be a long meal, dish following rich dish and course following course; wine flowing and footmen scurrying. It would be too much to hope for an interval for quiet thought, and, oh, dear God, here was William Waterton advancing upon her.

'Mistress Susannah,' William said noisily, escorting her to her chair, 'what luck that we're put together. There's chance fair opportunity, hey? Well, you've been hiding yourself away of recent. A sad loss for us all! But I'm told you've been busy in family matters.'

'My husband is delighted with his new daughter,' Susannah told him.

'Aye, so I hear. And named her for my mama. What a fellow the man is for compliments. I trust he pays you all he should. Damme, but I'll say this, your looks have not dwindled from the occasion!' His gaze examined her figure with unabashed interest, lingering over her breasts, fuller and more rounded now than before.

'You appear to be in good form yourself, Mr Waterton,' Susannah said, helping herself from an elaborately decorated dish of fresh salmon.

'What, me? Ready for anything, any time,' he agreed meaningfully.

The footman proffering the dish at his elbow coughed reproachfully. 'Eh what?' said William. 'Hah, food! Excellent.'

The guests sat shoulder to shoulder, crowding the long table, silks and satins gleaming, jewels sparkling from fingers and necks, shoulders and hair, talking clamourously. At the top of the table Edmund Breakspear was bending his head to his flushed and elated bride in the big carved chair and chuckling at her remarks. Edmund's groomsman, a stooped and lanky cousin, seemed to have found a common interest with Miss Waterton, who was listening to him with strangely rapt and silent attention. In a momentary interval of relative quiet his voice boomed out abruptly: 'Mr Gilbert White held that house-swallows hibernate in the banks of rivers, but I cannot agree. I suspect they pursue the sun south in search of warmer . . .' The renewed hubbub blotted out the rest of his theory. And beyond them James and Fanny, she for once not looking bored but laughing and spreading her hands expressively as she spoke to him, he adjusting her silk shawl as it slipped from her shoulders and watching her with a curiously thoughtful and searching look.

Susannah picked up her wineglass to drink in tense gulps.

'. . . Devilish good, hey?' William's voice rumbled in her right ear. He lifted his own glass and rolled the liquor round his tongue with relish. 'We should sample more of it, what d'you think?'

In a rush of relief that he had interrupted her unpleasing thoughts, 'Yes,' she said. 'Maybe we should.' Wine might blur the pain in her aching brain, help her endure the interminable hours before she could be alone. And after several glasses, though the desolation was still there, it had receded, helped by the exchange of mischievous pleasantries with William, who, at least, was hampered in his usual desire of proceeding further than mere talk by being at table, where the superb quality of the food was occupying a fair part of his attention. He was concerned that she was not eating with sufficient enthusiasm and insisted she take more roasted green goose, more boiled rump of beef, more artichokes, more syllabub.

'I like females of big appetites!' he told her when she protested she could take no more. His large hand encroached on hers where it lay toying with her glass, his eyes again scrutinised the low neckline of her gown. 'You don't want to grow lean and scraggy like that sister of mine.'

Susannah shook her head at him. ' 'Tis a matter of build, of natural shape. We're different.'

William ran exploratory fingers along her arm, feeling the soft inner flesh. 'Very different,' he said appreciatively.

Composedly she removed the arm. 'Careful – or you will tempt my husband to call you out.'

'Husbands are shocking spoilsports,' he grumbled.

'But 'tis natural in men to wish to preserve their sports for their sole use,' Susannah observed. 'Why, you and your father use mantraps in your coverts.'

'Ho! A sharp piece! Mantraps in bedrooms, hey? Is that what Stacey would have? Rue the day!'

'Then 'tis clear you value your ladies lower than your pheasants.'

William broke into his great laugh and eyes turned. 'Excellent sharp wit! But I have no wife, ma'am, no females to put a value on.'

Among the eyes that had turned were Sedley's, protuberant and glaring, but the goad of James's engagement still worked on her and the wine she had drunk had made her reckless: she ignored their message. She pushed away the hand that was now trying the contours of her knees and said:

'You should have a wife, Mr Waterton.'

He accepted her rebuff with a noisy sigh. 'You are not kind to a man, Mrs Stacey,' he said. 'A wife? Ecod, I think not. My life is pleasing enough as things stand – a deal of hunting, shooting and fishing in season, good food, drink and women all the year round. Why spoil it by shackling myself to some female who'd want to clip my wings?'

'What a sad picture of marriage you paint.'

'A true one as I see it. Those peaches look good, pass me one to try, will you?' He bit largely into the fruit and added with juice running down his chin: 'And I'll tell you someone who's

317

going to be under the cat's foot shortly, too – James Manning-ford. Heard about him and Miss Fanny, have you?'

Susannah gave a brief nod.

William mopped juice with his napkin. 'Too *noli me tangere* for my liking. If you take my meaning. Miss Touch-me-not.'

'I understood.'

'Ah. Encompass Latin, do you, atop of the rest? Of course, you taught my young godson the stuff. Well, Fanny's easy on the eye, I'll say that, but, frankly, I'd as soon bed with a cold poultice. Nor I couldn't endure her tantrums and takings. Can't imagine what James thinks he's doing. Told him so, too, but there's no moving him once he's made up his mind to a thing. My opinion is, it'll be a disaster.'

26

William was not the only person to express dismay to Susannah at James' engagement to Fanny: Beatrice said she was horrified.

On the first morning after her return from honeymoon she lost no time in riding to see Susannah, only to find her with Becky in attendance, putting little Harriet in her cradle preparatory to riding out to meet her family to view their new farmlands.

'Dear Lord,' Beatrice said. 'How maddening. Well, it will be no use my trying to delay you, for I imagine you and your family are as full of excitement over the enclosure award as mine. But let's at least trot down the street together, for I have such a multitude of things to say to you and ask you and discuss with you I cannot bear myself if I don't air them!'

'Have you?' Susannah returned calmly. She found her hat and tugged on her riding gloves. 'But first, tell me, was your time in Bath pleasant?'

Bath? Oh heavens, Beatrice told her as they mounted their horses at the stable mounting block, she and Edmund had enjoyed such a hilarious honeymoon, laughing together at all the delicate maidens and mewing tabbies and old toughs taking the waters, and the earnest medical men with their theories on the healing powers and medicinal properties of the hot springs. There had been concerts and a visit to the theatre to see a vastly amusing play by Mr Sheridan and truly, they had not been dull for a moment. But to turn to matters of importance at home – what was to be done about James' idiotic engagement?

'There is nothing to be done,' Susannah replied. 'Nothing

except pray that the marriage will turn out better than we pessimists expect.'

'It seems to me,' Beatrice said epigrammatically, 'that a pretty face may do much to a man's senses, but nothing for his sense! I never thought to hear myself say such a thing, but even Augusta Waterton would suit better in certain aspects. A man like James? James! Oh, I am so cross with him.'

Susannah shook her head. 'And I with Fanny. I cannot believe there is love there.' They were silent for a moment, both contemplating the folly of two people they cared for. 'And Fanny is my friend,' Susannah said softly, as if confessing some form of guilt at having criticised her by implication, at judging her less than worthy of James.

'Mine, too,' said Beatrice ruefully. 'And you are right, now it has been formally announced there is nothing we can do. A breach of promise suit? God forbid.' She snorted with reluctant amusement. 'It is not a disaster in everyone's eyes, you know.'

'Not Mrs Bland's!'

'No! Nor my sister Rosalind's. Rosalind tells me she had always dreaded James getting married, for it would have meant another woman taking over the running of Abbotsbridge House, someone else having all her responsibilities and interests. At a stroke she would have been reduced to a mere cipher, another spinster relation having to live, ghostlike, in the shadows. But Fanny has already said that she will be delighted to leave Rosalind in charge. Besides, Rosalind has always had a great admiration for Fanny – no, more than that, I have to say it, she doats upon her. To be able to minister to Fanny's beauty and genius, to have the glory of being able to listen to her playing the harp every day, that, to my sister, is a wonder, a prize to be valued above anything.'

'And Fanny is relieved not to be required to settle menus or control housemaids,' Susannah said drily. She had tried to remind Fanny that freedom to play the harp all day was not the only change that marriage would produce in her life, but Fanny was ignoring all words that smacked of criticism or might cause unwelcome thoughts. She was euphoric with relief at escaping the rectory schoolroom, immersed now in her bridal clothes and her trousseau, tossing her head at any friend who showed a sober face to her triumph. She had always liked James; he could speak of matters that interested her, books, clothes, the theatre, above all, of music. They would stay regularly with his father in London and go to great concerts; she would be able to buy all the music and books she wished without anyone preaching thrift; the dull chores of her parents' household would vanish: the narrow horizons of Fanny's life had widened to glorious vistas.

'One does see why she is doing it,' Beatrice said with a grimace.

Halfway along the village street the common came into view beyond the cottages at the western end. Beatrice reined to a halt. 'Cousin! Look! Those stakes marching across the common – what do they signify?'

Susannah stopped Coquette. 'Those? The lines of the new roads. The far one will join the road to Stockbridge, replacing the muddy bottom lane, the other will serve the new farmlands there. The old Winchester lane is to be widened to forty feet and straightened to come out further east.'

'It all sounds eminently sensible,' Beatrice commented. 'But I am surprised the stakes are still standing, considering village anger!'

'Ah, yes! Well, half of them were pulled up on the first night and tossed across the common, but within a day an information was laid as to the culprits.'

'Really? And who was it?'

'Sam Truckle and Dick Pettifer! Who else? Your father heard the case yesterday morning and fined them. The talebearer was old man Jurd, who is openly gleeful over the half-guinea reward Mr Fulbroad gave him. Since then the stakes have stayed in place.'

'The lull before the storm,' Beatrice said. 'Dear Lord knows what will happen when the harvest is over and the real work of change begins.'

'Or when Barney Bidewell is ousted from his hovel.'

'It is going to be a difficult winter.'

'Yes, it is,' Susannah said soberly. Coquette was becoming restless, but she tightened the reins and held her steady. 'We should look our fill on this scene, Cousin Beatrice, to remember it how it is, for within a few short weeks it will be changed utterly, and there will be no going back.'

Beatrice glanced at her and looked away into the distance.

Beyond the cottages the common and the great open fields stretched, the rough grazing of the common where it abutted on the village showing the mingled greens, browns and greys of worn turf and trodden bare earth, of weeds, molehills and coarse clumps of rushes. Beside it the north field was a pale sea of barley, the west field a wide and faded gold expanse of wheat; not a hedge, not a tree to divide or mark the land there, the paths and baulks hidden now by the corn; empty, save for the human ants to one side, working together to gather in the harvest.

But soon the farmers would make their marks on the land, compartmentalising their fields with hedges and trees into a neat patchwork landscape, building perhaps new farmhouses on their new lands, away from the cosy heart of the village. Susannah blinked as the wide expanse before her quivered in the unusual warmth of the August day. Would it be as James had said, that the land would become more green, more lush, more purposefully turned to the production of food? Her eyes focussed back on the village street: the sun shone golden on the lichen of ancient tiled and thatched roofs, beneath the forge chestnut tree the old men were silently contemplative; a clip-clopping horse, pulling a loaded wagon, plodded past them, the driver swaying somnolently on his seat. Would it be also as Jack sadly prophesied, that the self-contained, self-helping community of the village would slowly be destroyed, winnowing out the weak?

The horses began to move on of their own accord. Susannah shook herself free from doleful thoughts. 'Well, so great a change cannot but be exciting,' she said, 'whatever one's reservations. I wonder how Cousin James feels, now he knows exactly how the manor lands lie.'

'I've no idea,' Beatrice said, 'for I've caught no glimpse of him. I'm told he and my father have been riding out, hour upon hour, debating their potential, or they've been closeted in the library, deciding where James's experimental Home Farm shall be or mapping out the tenant farms.'

'One wonders,' said Susannah, her eyes on her mare's ears, 'how he will find the time to get married, with all that must be done.'

322

'Yes, Rosalind did say the one had been playing havoc with the other. But the wedding date is now set for the third week of October and the honeymoon will be in London.'

'Oh.'

They had arrived at the house Edmund had moved into shortly after his arrival in Abbotsbridge, Maynards, which he and Beatrice had been having renovated. It was a tall, narrow building that reared itself above its neighbours, more a slender mansion than a house, Beatrice said, with its elaborate cornices and ceilings and marble fireplaces. She was about to leave Susannah when she abruptly tapped the side of her head with her hand.

'Cousin Susannah – a thought has come to me about James and Fanny, a most tantalising wicked thought. I quite shock myself . . . yet it might solve things.' A deep breath, eyes alert. 'I must consider . . .'

'But what is it?'

'No. No, I must not tell you. It is but the genesis of an idea. We have been concentrating upon the wrong person, Susannah.'

'I have not the faintest notion of what you are speaking.'

'No. No more you should have. But tell me, have you never thought of playing the devil's advocate?'

'Devil's advocate? Sometimes, I'll admit. When the demon of mischief gets me.'

'He has hold of me now.' She laughed suddenly. 'I shall say no more. Cousin, you will be late with your family if I keep you any longer, but just one thing I must tell you on a totally different topic. Edmund and I went to visit Sedley's mama as he requested.'

'How was she?'

'Not well. Pale and drawn and with a sad tale of sickness and spasms and palpitations. She says her apothecary is in despair over her.'

'She has complained of similar miseries over some years,' Susannah observed delicately.

Beatrice nodded. 'I understand what you mean, but to my eyes she had gone downhill considerably in the past year. I was shocked. And Edmund said that from what she told him of her symptoms he would indeed be worried, were he her medical man.'

Sedley must be told, and he must discuss his mother's illness with Edmund, Susannah reflected as she rode on. Sedley had been annoyed and hurt by a letter from his mother saying that her state of health would not let her travel to Brambourne for her granddaughter's christening, nor could her apothecary predict when he might permit such a journey, she was so shockingly poorly. Of his finances she had written nothing. He had not replied. Now, Susannah thought, he must be persuaded to write in sympathy and understanding; he should also consider visiting her in Bath: it was not so far away that he could not be back within a week, not to miss the Sunday services. It was a pity, she thought wistfully, that Harriet was so small or the children and she could travel with Sedley; she would love to visit Bath.

At the farmhouse her mother suggested that Jack should saddle his Welsh cob and ride on with Susannah while she and Thomas followed on foot. There was a spot, she explained, a husky quiver in her voice betraying the excitement she considered undignified, whence it was possible to see almost all the acres that were to be theirs. The land lay to the north of the river, so the slopes faced south. Really, it was not to be despised.

'Which means,' Jack remarked as he and Susannah rode off, 'that she is delighted with what we've been allotted.'

'Is she still nervous of all you have taken on?'

'Less since again I sold my cattle for a remarkably good price. Mother may grumble and worry, but I suspect the truth is she is choked with pride over us both and the steady rise she sees us making in this world.'

Hissing geese scattered as they rode out through the little orchard. They turned right to ride over land that swelled gently towards the downs.

'Where, then?' Susannah demanded. 'Where? Where do your acres lie?'

He shook his head, laughing at her eagerness. 'We are on our land,' he said, and refused to tell her more till they reached a natural bank that lay above a slight fold in the land, dotted with clumps of hazels and brambles and late honeysuckle. He kicked his pony up to it, stopped and turned. 'Here is about the far boundary. Look!'

The shallow valley and its river were vividly clear in the summer light, the line of the river clotted with willows and alders, the village roofs visible here and there beyond. The dusty warm scent drifting from the cut barley in the west field mingled with the fragrance of honeysuckle.

'This is ours!' Jack said. 'That commissioner, Mr Haynes, he made no bones over running my allotment alongside Father's.'

With an outflung arm, as if he would embrace all the chalky acres before him, he showed Susannah how the river beyond the mill formed the south-western boundary, giving them some acres of water meadow, and how the ground widened in a wedge shape to the top end, taking in part of the north field and a slice of the sprawling common. 'To those thorn bushes way over there. The commissioners have been fair to us, at least. The soil is generally good, though 'tis thin up here. It is all workable – and, Sukey, taking what we had with what I've bought and adding in the land awarded in lieu of our common rights, we own not far short of a hundred acres! Think of that!'

'I am marvelling,' she said promptly, and her eyes crinkled in amused affection at his enthusiasm. She swung an assessing look back over the gentle incline of land running down to the Test, land that he and her father would have to fence and ditch and clear and plough in the coming winter: 'I am marvelling, too, at the months of work that lie ahead.'

'Not only farmwork,' her mother's voice came as she and Thomas arrived to join them. 'There are men who are certain Jack has nothing better to do than to act as an unpaid notary in their arguments with the commissioners and the Manningfords.'

'Pettifers and Smallwoods an' such like that,' Thomas added.

'Mr Manningford has refused to grant the Smallwoods a new lease,' Jack said to Susannah.

'Poor farmers,' Mrs Trotter muttered. 'I've no sympathy for their whinings.'

'The Pettifers, and most of the others who have only a few acres are angry about their allotments of land,' Jack went on. 'Some are at a shocking distance from their cottages and some awkward of access – and then, to add insult to injury, they get almost nothing in lieu of common rights. They have fair grounds for their anger, and I shall do what I can for them – could be they could get better land through exchanges, that's permitted.'

'Trouble is, folks've naught to fall back on nowadays,' Thomas said, pushing his battered hat to the back of his head. 'No merchants paying their wives and children to spin yarn, like when we were young. Anyways, look – Manningford land runs to the north and east of us, there, with the new road the boundary part way. They 'ull be fair neighbours. Sam Truckle has 'is acres down on goodish land by the river to the west of us, but then comes the Fulbroads, God 'elp us, flanking us all the way up here!'

'Never trouble trouble till trouble troubles you,' Emily Trotter said sententiously. 'If you keep our hedges and fences strong, I doubt we'll hear ought from Mr Fulbroad.'

'With Robert Page working for us now and a couple of good lads to help, we'll soon have the boundary fences up, at least,' Jack said.

'Good lads?' his mother commented. 'I never heard Arthur Pettifer called a good lad before!'

Jack laughed. 'Black Betsey ran out of neighbours sympathetic to her so-called borrowings of food, so she sent Arthur to Mother for a loaf ...'

'An' not for the first time,' Thomas interposed. 'I reckon if Betsey was dead she'd come in her skellington to borrow a shroud!'

'And if she does return the bread as she says, it'll go in the pigswill,' Emily Trotter muttered. 'Who'd fancy aught from her hands?'

'Arthur's not so bad as his mother,' Jack said, smiling patiently. 'Anyway, while at the door he said I'd need help and offered himself. He vouchsafed that my sister was some'un special and he calc'lated I'd not do 'im down! I thought him worth a try.'

'I believe you're right,' Susannah said.

The family turned to go back down to the farmhouse and saw a big man stalking swiftly up towards them, his head lowered.

'See there? I'll wager yon's another shorn lamb wanting Jack to temper the wind to 'im!' Thomas remarked.

The man lifted his head to reveal the dark face of Barney Bidewell.

'Surely,' said Mrs Trotter. 'But you'd best look out the shorn lamb doesn't turn into a ravening wolf that'll bite the hand held out to him. He'll demand you save it, but 'tis Fulbroad land his cottage now lies on.'

The sun had moved perceptibly across the sky. Susannah told her family that she must leave and rode off down the narrow track, having assured them, though in an undertone, in view of the advancing Barney, that she thought their new farmland as good as could have been expected, if not better. She was pleased and relieved for them. Her parents' commands to give their dear grandchildren kisses from them both followed her.

She urged Coquette to a trot. She must not be late for Harriet's next feed or Sedley would be angry. He took a very different view of this child from Piers. Piers' arrival had been resented; he had been a baby to be kept out of view and rarely commented on, for his birth had disgraced Sedley. But Harriet was the apple of his eye, no other babe could compare. He called on all visitors to wonder at her pretty face and the perfection of her little hands, while yesterday he had been quite comically elated when she produced her first smile – and for him! It was a deep relief to Susannah that he felt so warmly towards her. It helped to ease her feeling of guilt that Harriet had not twined her way into her own heart quite as Piers had from the beginning, while the topic of her progress gave her a precious source of conversation with which to beguile Sedley when his mood turned sour, as too often it did.

William Waterton's attentions at the Breakspears' wedding feast had awoken Sedley's demon of jealousy. Though he had said little after his first snapped rebuke to her for flirting and jesting with William in what he dubbed a most unseemly manner, there was a sullen watchfulness about him at times that made her skin prickle and creep.

27

The Blands gave an enormous engagement party for Fanny and James, cramming their house to its uttermost confines. 'Just a few close friends,' had confided Mrs Bland to Sedley on inviting him and Susannah to the occasion, rattling away like the prattlebox she was, he thought in some annoyance, about the difficulties of making the arrangements when so many of James' family lived in London, and how complicated it would be to fit more than a few into their little rectory – and it twice the size of his own vicarage. Now, hardly able to find the space to raise his drink to his lips, and already conscious of stains on his white satin waistcoat from some fool's inconsiderately flourished glass, Sedley set his lips tight and vowed to move out of the throng to somewhere more safe, somewhere, moreover, where he could have conversation of point with somebody of note, rather than exchanging shrieked expressions of delight on the occasion with persons like the Blands' daughter, Lucy, over-excited at the prospect of being a bridesmaid. Details of the lace and satin Fanny and Lucy would wear did not enthrall him.

At all events, he concluded morosely, edging round the room in the direction of Sir Francis Heanley, a neighbouring landowner with excellent shooting and livings in the Church to bestow, Fanny and James seemed to have a sufficiency of tastes in common that the marriage might stand some chance of happiness. And what tastes! He and Susannah had been invited to join them and the Breakspears in an expedition to a concert in Winchester, two weeks previously. He could not ever remember having been more bored, his jawbone nearly fractured from yawning, but the others had expressed themselves as delighted, Fanny as animated as he had ever seen her, her eyes sparkling at James as they discussed the brilliance of Mr Mozart. 'One marvels at his melodic invention,' he heard her say, and then, 'This seems to be an entirely new conception of the role of the solo instrument!,' to which James had responded warmly: 'A dialogue, a grand discussion between opposing forces which brings one to the edge of one's seat!' It was only a collection of fiddles and bass viols and what not playing, after all, and heavy stuff at that: Sedley thought the pair of them affected and pretentious, and was relieved that his wife stood quietly by, not allowing herself to be drawn in. Still, it had been clear that Fanny and James were at one on this subject; Fanny had even hugged his arm, unusual in so cool a female. But she had been swiftly brought down to earth by the new Mrs Breakspear saying that she hoped their future offspring would be as musically inclined as their parents. She envisaged a round dozen for them, they could form their own orchestra. Sedley smiled grimly to himself: that thought had sobered Miss Fanny in her silly posturings: such a face she had pulled. She would soon learn she could not escape the condition the Lord rightly imposed upon all women.

Across the room Susannah had been introduced to James' father, Peter Manningford, a big man of imposing presence and bristling white eyebrows, and now to his sister, Lady Wardener, too. She was tall, long-necked and decidedly elegant, with heavy-lidded eyes that examined Susannah with one long sweep. Sedley thought it too bad that his mother's refusal to help him with money had forced his wife to wear her wedding dress yet again to an occasion. Three days of dancing attendance in Bath while his mother lavished money upon doctors, attendants, servants, medicines and hot-house fruits had been productive only of whining complaints to her poor son, with never a penny for him or his family. Susannah had altered her gown again, of course, trimming it with pale bronze ribbons and sash in an attempt to pass it off as new, but it was wrong that his wife should be put to such contrivances.

The Manningford family was talking now, his wife was talking, a hint of a smile on her lips. He hoped she was not putting herself forward – ah, but she must have said something witty for there was a sudden burst of laughter and they were all responding to her together, their voices rising above the many others in the room, and now there was more laughter. James said something to his father, evidently in praise of Susannah, for the old gentleman dropped his hand on her shoulder, and James gave her a look of kindness, yes, almost of fondness, Sedley thought, relieved.

A second later he saw William Waterton shoulder himself a way through the guests and arrive at Susannah's side to add his boisterous part to the gaiety, then as James introduced yet another guest to his father, claim Susannah's attention. Sedley went stiff. His wife had her eyes on the bridegroom to be, shrugging and smiling in brittle fashion at William's sallies. When James drew Fanny aside to murmur in her ear, Susannah looked away, spoke to William, apparently excusing herself, then wove her way through the guests to the door.

Hmm. Sedley turned again towards Sir Francis only to find himself caught by Miss Waterton, flushed and excited, shrilly recounting a preposterous folderol about some correspondence she was having with Dr Breakspear's cousin and groomsman on wild orchids. What the devil were they to do with anything? 'Fascinating, yes, fascinating,' he assured her. Was that William Waterton following Susannah? His head swivelled; yes, William had ambled purposefully from the room. Sedley mumbled an excuse to Miss Waterton and headed for the door.

In the hall he could see only servants dashing about, but there were voices in the bookroom. Pretending to be deep in thought, his hand clasping his chin, Sedley crossed the hall to loiter by the half-open door.

'... You must sit beside me at the meal, m'dear. There'll be a need for leaven to lighten this doughy occasion, don't you think?'

'We must sit where we're placed, Mr Waterton, you know we must – 'tis not our choice.'

'Nor 'ud Fanny be my choice to sit beside, were I James, still less to lie beside in time to come! Told you so before, haven't I? I'll warrant that you and I 'ud have more fun of it than ever James will with Fanny as his bride!'

'Dear's my soul, Mr Waterton, you go too far!'

'God's my life, Mrs Stacey, you don't go far enough! Not even a paltry kiss to reward me for all my devotion to your charms? 'Tis really too bad!'

The rector's manservant, Dick, came along the hall, his face, his stiffly tied back hair, his brass buttons, all gleaming for the occasion, two tray-carrying maids scuttling in his wake. Sedley straightened himself and sauntered nonchalantly in the direction of the Jericho, glancing over his shoulder. His wife emerged from the bookroom to walk swiftly away, one hand to her forehead. William came out to pounce upon Dick and whisper a request in his ear; the rector's man grinned and nodded, stood aside for the maids to whisk by, then disappeared down the cellar.

Sedley decided to make use of the facilities he found himself beside; as he relieved himself in the odorous little room he pondered his overhearings. His wife had properly rebuked Waterton, without going so far as to offend him. Just as he had instructed her to do with the lecherous fellow. Not even a paltry kiss, Waterton had said. Sedley buttoned his breeches and patted his clothes back into position. He sighed; perhaps he had been wrong in his suspicions of Susannah. But not of Waterton, no, not of him. The man was the worst sort of lecher, making lustful advances to a clergyman's wife.

Sedley was back in the throng, at last on the point of button-holing Sir Francis Heanley, when a sinister thought struck him. An icy hand clutched the back of his neck, his hair seemed to stand on end, his flesh shivered and crept. Could his wife and Waterton have known he was outside the bookroom door? Expected him to be there? The conversation had been all too pat. His heart beat with an angry thump. Why had she gone to the bookroom? It was a shabby room, dark and dull, and she had no reason to leave the party – except for an assignation. She had known of her unfortunate husband's suspicions. She had glanced across at him, Sedley, with those seemingly innocent great grey eyes of hers, and murmured something to that man ... plotting to deceive him? He had not heard her rebuking William. She had not smacked his face. She had not behaved as any truly good woman would do. Indeed, the more he thought of it ... he could have sworn he had heard suppressed laughter in their voices as they spoke together. Very clever, very subtle – but he was not deceived. He knew now, knew the depths to which she could descend. But he was the more clever. He had only to watch and wait and he would catch her: he knew he would. And then he would punish her. He licked his lips and clenched his fists and a wave of sweat broke over him. Yes, how he would punish her!

After the engagement party Susannah was more distraught than she had been since she parted from James beneath the weeping willow tree. Hateful images invaded her mind, images of James and Fanny enjoying themselves at concerts, at the theatre, laughing together, of him caressing her, of him teaching her to make love. She devoted herself to her children, rocking Harriet in her arms and teaching Piers new words and phrases, but Piers looked at her with James' eyes and smiled at her with James' smile, and Harriet was Sedley's child. Even her visitors, instead of diverting her as she hoped, tormented her instead: Beatrice was intrigued by James' new farming plans and talked incessantly of his brilliant schemes, Katharine spoke wistfully of the bride's great beauty and how it was no wonder that everybody should admire her, and then Mrs Bland sat with Susannah for nearly an hour worrying whether she would ever have sufficient warm clothing ready in time for the honeymoon and whether Fanny's new maid would watch over her with sufficient care: 'So chilly as those great London houses are that they are to visit, my dear, and Fanny quite hopeless in these matters, especially where her undergarments are concerned!' Susannah's inflamed imagination at once produced disturbing visions of James' hands travelling about Fanny's body to remove such undergarments and she hustled Mrs Bland out of the house in a way that quite hurt her affectionate one-time employer and enraged Sedley when he heard about it at the garden gate.

He stormed into the parlour. 'Mrs Bland was concerned that you seemed too pressed with work to have time to talk to her. What is this nonsense? How dare you dismiss my rector's wife in so cavalier a fashion!'

'Nothing cavalier, Sedley,' she returned, her eyes avoiding his, 'but there is table beer to be brewed today and Harriet must be bathed and fed shortly or she will grizzle.'

'Becky brews the beer. You are planning to run about the villages again.'

'No, indeed not.'

A kind of fretful agitation had on occasion driven her from the house to seek diversion visiting Beatrice or Katharine, her parents or the Blands, but wherever she went, there Sedley appeared also, looming on his mare from behind trees or knocking at doors and expressing amazement at the chance that had sent him calling where his wife was already to be found. 'Dear me! Our minds so in tune – but a single thought between us!'

That suspicions were racking Sedley was beyond doubt. In the privacy of their bedchamber at nights he would rage at her for imaginary faults before he fell to handling her hair with a ferocity that aroused a thousand pinpricks of pain. She cringed when he approached her. His presence – the look in the bulging eyes, the thick wet sensuous lips, the stocky hairy body – was loathsome to her in its malignity. Their nightly couplings were achieved with an animal ferocity that left her bruised and aching. Twice she protested and asked him why he used her with such unkindness; twice he hit her. Now she waited helplessly for the mood to subside in him as it had before.

She could not understand it. This . . . this rage seemed to have sprung from the engagement party. True, she had left the drawing-room because the shrill chatter was making her head ache and William had followed her in hopes of a kiss and a pinch or a fondle, but she had evaded him quickly enough; if Sedley had been listening at the bookroom door he would have heard nothing objectionable, or not on her part. Then why? She had spent the rest of those agonising hours talking to Katharine or Beatrice, or at table, and always within Sedley's sight. Once Beatrice had murmured in her ear that she presumed it inevitable that her sister Jessica and Elliot would marry, but how could anyone bear a father-in-law who pawed her as Hector Fulbroad did Jessica? Susannah turned her eyes to see Mr Fulbroad's hand slip from its avuncular position on Jessica's shoulder to slide caressingly over her neat little bottom before he moved away. She had whispered back that if she were Jessica, somehow she might just slip and he find the heel of her shoes grinding his instep. Momentary glee had curved both their lips and she remembered seeing Sedley staring and scowling: perhaps he had thought their mirth was at his expense – but that could not account for his behaviour, surely?

Contemplating her life with him as she picked up Piers' toys from the parlour carpet, she thought: I do have Piers – and Harriet. She pushed a fallen bloom back into a vase of late roses, plumped up a cushion on a chair, and mentally added to her blessings, those of a comfortable house and a garden in which she loved to work or sit with her babies. She moved in a level of society that had once been beyond her wildest dreams, and which included intelligent and well-read friends with whom she could ride and walk and talk. Then, at the thought of all this inevitably including year upon year of Sedley's distrust and ill-treatment, misery rose up in her again. She walked through to the kitchen to tell Becky to prepare hot water for Harriet's bath, marvelling how it was that reflecting upon one's blessings gave so little comfort.

But life did not consist solely of melancholy: as Mr Manningford said of Shakespeare's plays, when tragedy lay like a cloud upon the scene, some comic happening was bound to arouse one's sense of humour despite oneself. She found Becky furiously kneading dough and complaining to Ladyship, who was quietly washing her ears in her basket beside the range, her kittens long since gone. ' 'Tis so unfair, puss. Not a body cares 'bout my feelings, not the least mite. Uh!' She pummelled the dough.

'Who is without concern for your feelings, Becky? Not us, I hope.'

Becky jumped at finding her mistress so near. 'Oh no, ma'am. Dear, oh dear! Not you. 'Tis my father and mother. Luke Carter 'ave asked me to marry 'im, but Father says he'll not say yea till Luke's got good furniture ready in a good cottage, and - wait till you hears this, ma'am – a pig in a sty! 'Tis true, as I'm a Christian, puts a pig afore my happiness, Father does!'

In pacifying Becky, holding down her own bubbling mirth until she had persuaded Becky to share it, in laughing together with her at the mental image Josh's stipulation produced of a pig standing shoulder to shoulder with Luke to shield big Becky from the cold winds of life, Susannah regained some equilibrium, melancholy was set at bay.

Fanny had an invitation to go to London to stay with her Aunt Anne to order some part of her bridal clothes and her trousseau there. At first Mrs Bland was doubtful, but the thought of London fashions for Fanny's gowns and pelisses was alluring, and so, barely a month before the wedding day, Fanny went to spend ten days with her aunt, accompanied by a maid.

'All that journeying for so short a time and at so great an expense,' Mrs Bland fretted to Susannah, 'but really, when I think of the dearth of choice here, and then I picture the rich and lovely fabrics that she will find and I consider the new position she has to fill, well, I tell Mr Bland, nothing is too good for our beautiful daughter, so well as she is to marry.'

So Fanny, nothing loath, departed for London and clothes and the concerts she was certain her aunt would arrange for her to attend.

'There is no sense in my remaining here,' she told Susannah. 'Mama is in a constant flurry over the wedding arrangements, and James thinks and breathes and talks his new farm all day and every day. Crop rotations and the Tullian system? Sainfoin and ryegrass? The boredom is excruciating. Beatrice tells me I should ride out with him in the mornings and learn more about the new ways. Can you imagine it, Susannah? I should never have time for my music. Beatrice is reading treatises upon medicine and discussing them with Edmund. So disgusting. It quite curdles my stomach. If my marriage were to be like that I do not think I should care for the state at all.'

On the day after Fanny left for London Susannah consigned her babies to Becky's care and walked through the cool September sunlight to visit her mother and discover how the fencing and the ploughing of the land was progressing.

The farmhouse and its outbuildings, like many in the village, had been built in a large paddock, or close, as it was known, Godsgrace Close, for a long dead owner. The house was half-timbered and mellow, the date above the front door 1627.

She found her mother hard at work in the kitchen, for the pig-killer had come on the previous day, and she had the hams and sides of bacon to salt and the chitterlings to clean, as well as lard and hogs' puddings to make. But, Mrs Trotter told her daughter as she rinsed and dried her hands, she would welcome a short break, and she had something to show her from the orchard. They walked across the yard, skirting the muck-heap, and went behind the sheds to the rickyard, where she handed a pewter tankard of ale to the old thatcher perched high on the first straw rick. It was a measure of the Trotter family's increased prosperity and busy state that they had hired him this year, rather than making do with their own amateur efforts, Susannah thought, watching the gnarled fingers working with speed and certainty.

They passed through the side-gate to the orchard and at the far end Emily Trotter told Susannah to sit on the stile there, while she climbed on to the first step. With a triumphant flourish of her arm she pointed.

'Look! You can see a fair part of our land from here. That's your father ploughing over there, and Jack beyond him to the right, working with Peter Page and Arthur on the fencing.'

'I see them. You can actually watch them progressing.'

The autumn had been mild and the ploughing was well advanced, brown earth replacing the pale stubble, clouds of birds following the nodding plough horses. Susannah watched, enjoying the faint scent in her nostrils of damp grass and freshly turned clods and smoke from someone's distant field fire.

'The boundary fencing is coming along fast – that to the west is Mr Fulbroad's – and when it's done and the ploughing's completed, then the land'll be truly ours. 'Tisn't the same till every part has felt its men's feet and their mark has been laid upon it.' Mrs Trotter nodded her satisfaction as she said: 'And that'll be soon, please God, the weather holding.' Her face turning serious, she added that the fencing was a sore expense, and how folk like the Pettifers and the Truckles would manage it atop of their share in all those legal costs, she failed to guess. Jack had calculated the total at one pound and eight shilling an acre, but she'd not suppose folk like them cleared as much as twenty pound in a full year, not in actual cash.

As they returned to the house she spoke of Jack's plans to make a trial in an eight-acre field of Mr Jethro Tull's seed drill and his horsedrawn hoes, along with Farmer Stent. 'To plant seed in rows seems downright unnatural – going agin the Lord's ways, Sam Paine says – but to be able to hoe swiftly between the rows would be excellent. Saving time is saving money, Jack says, so these machines will pay for themselves, especially if he can hire them out.' She smiled, half proud, half rueful. 'There'll be more changes coming, I know it. Your brother's mind is restless the way the wind is restless; you see nothing, yet things move.'

No sooner was Susannah back through the parsonage picket gate than Sedley erupted from the house, furious at her absence, for Miss Manningford had called with messages from Miss Katharine and two books Mr Manningford thought she might enjoy. He grasped her arm with bruising fingers to hustle her inside. Miss Manningford had gone on to pay a courtesy call on Miss Waterton at the manor, but she would be back at any minute, and where the devil had Susannah been and why was she wearing that dowdy old gown? When she began with forced calmness to remind him that he had known for two days that she was to visit her mother today, he cut her short. She must not waste time, she must change immediately; his wife must always do him credit. He shoved her. Susannah was starting up the stairs when there was a crash and a yell from the kitchen doorway: in toddling to greet her Piers had fallen and bruised his forehead.

She ran across the hall, snatching him up. 'Ow,' he told her, sobbing. 'Ow!'

'Poor sweetheart! I shall have to bathe this with tincture of arnica,' she said to Sedley.

'But you have not the time!' he protested.

'That can't be helped. A bruised temple must never be neglected.'

'Then I shall fetch down your Norwich silk shawl; that always gives an elegant appearance. Where is it kept?'

'In the top drawer of the tallboy.'

She dealt with the graze on Piers' forehead and carried him to the sitting-parlour, putting him on the sofa. 'There, my handsome, stay quietly with Mama and you will soon be a better boy.'

There was an exclamation and a crash upstairs. Was it Sedley who had bruised himself now?

'You stupid, careless, clumsy girl!' he was shouting at Becky. 'Look at the damage you have done!'

From her place by the fire Ladyship jumped and looked round in alarm. Sedley must have bumped into Becky. What had she dropped? No time to worry now. Swiftly Susannah tidied herself in the mirror, smoothing back straying wisps of hair. When she heard Sedley thundering downstairs she turned to take the shawl from him, but it was not the shawl he was carrying.

His face was suffused with the red blood of anger. Beneath one arm he clutched her writing slope, the little secret drawer on its spring hanging drunkenly out, in his other hand he flourished a scrap of paper.

He was shouting, but from the drumming in her ears she could not hear the words. She knew at once what he had – dear God, that cherished note James had written her so long ago, arranging their meeting at the foot of Flintpen Ring.

He slammed the door and advanced on her. 'You evil woman! You lying, adulterous evil woman. Becky dropped your slope, and when I looked to see the damage, this ... this filth was on the floor.' He hit her with the note, clumsily, brutally, on the face.

She retreated out of his reach, gasping for breath. 'Sedley, it is not as you believe ...'

'William Waterton! I knew it, I knew it ... you swore on the bible to me ... and all the time you were lying. And lying to God! He will punish you!' He came after her and tripped over the cat, which scuttled, spitting, to the protection of its mistress.

'It was not William Waterton ...' But she could never say who it was, never admit to anything. Her brain searched frantically for the impossible, a reasonable explanation for something so damning, her grey eyes moving from side to side like the tail of the agitated cat. 'That note is old, nothing, a childish infatuation, someone I knew before you.'

'Liar!' He mouthed the word with relish. 'I always knew you lied.'

Another blow to the face. She stumbled backwards and fell

on the sofa beside Piers, who let out a wailing cry of fright. Again a slap and Piers' cry turned to a scream. Susannah pushed herself to her feet, stumbling sideways to evade Sedley. Then she turned to defend herself. For her children's sake he must be made to believe her: her inward guilt must not stop her from fighting back.

Somehow she managed to keep her voice low, conscious of Becky somewhere nearby. 'I have never, never, so much as kissed Mr Waterton. What I swore to was the truth, and I will swear to it again and again. You've built up a great tissue of lies in your mind because you've always hated him. You've always been jealous of him, Sedley. He has the splendid horses you've always coveted, he stands to inherit his father's estate, he jeered when you courted his long-nosed sister. Your jealous mind has longed to see evil when none existed. None existed, ever.' She struck with words like rapiers but they were blunted by the armour of his anger. She flung at him: 'You don't believe me when I say I've permitted him nothing. Ask him then, he'll admit he's never succeeded!'

His chin came up and he stared at her along that arched nose of his. In his gaze there was something cold and hard, the evil of which he had accused her. The suave look of the Roman senator had vanished, replaced by the cruelty of the Roman soldier. And of a sudden she recognised the depths of her dislike of him; her mind flicked back over the past and she knew that she had always disliked him, however hard she had struggled to bury that feeling and create a real marriage with him. In shock she saw for the first time that she could never have married him without disliking him, could never have foisted another man's child on any man for whom she had any true care or respect.

'I shall!' he said. 'I shall thrash the truth out of him if necessary. And then I shall return and thrash you. You shall both admit the dreadful depths to which you have fallen.'

Where would Waterton be now? Sedley did not know, but he would discover him. He shrugged on his coat and grabbed his whip and ran from the house. His anger was barely under control; it surged in hot waves as he thought of William's treachery and Susannah's betrayal. He strode to the stable to saddle Coquette, but he was half-drunk with emotion and his eyes were blurred: he fumbled and cursed, his fingers refusing to obey his will. At last he mounted her and kicked her hard; speed and action only would help. As he turned into the lane the low winter sun found him and set his head throbbing with a scorching painful light. Sickness rose in his throat and a strange kind of grief threatened to overwhelm him. Susannah! After all he had done for her – betrayal! One could scarcely credit it. Waterton must be found and made to suffer for this: both of them must suffer. The mare was galloping now. His mind pondered with sick relish the various forms such suffering might take.

At the manor house the startled servant who responded to his thunderous knocking said he could not say where Mr William was. He believed he had gone shooting with Mr James Manningford and some other friends on Abbotsbridge land, but where exactly they were to be found was beyond him. Would Mr Stacey care to leave a message? No message, Sedley snarled, he'd find him, never fear.

Mounted once more on Coquette, he turned her head towards Abbotsbridge, lashing her hard. He was coming to the portion of road he'd had built, alongside the great beech hanger, when he heard men's voices from the other side of the old flint wall that bordered Abbotsbridge park, somewhere beyond the bottom of the hanger. Dragging at Coquette's mouth, he pulled her up so fiercely that she slid on her haunches, then he stood in the stirrups, riding beside the wall until he could see them, William and James and a couple of other men, just visible walking along the park boundary away from him towards a coppice of mixed ash and beech and elm. A pair of jays flew out from the bottom of the hanger, screeching, making him start. For a short way here there were no trees on the far side of the wall. Sedley jerked Coquette back, to put her at it. She rose, just clearing it, and it was then he saw another wall, lower, set at right angles to it, between him and his quarry. He turned Coquette sharply, too sharply he realised a second later, but William was less than fifty yards away.

Yelling to him, mouthing abuse that emerged as no more than a jumble of wild sounds, he hit Coquette hard with his whip. The mare quickened, but there was no room to gather herself before the wall loomed. She took off too late, catching the top brick course on her forelegs and somersaulting herself over somehow in a flurry of tossing hooves. For a brief moment Sedley glimpsed heads turning, eyes staring, then he was catapulted from the saddle, the ground rose up to hit him, and all sight was gone.

28

His body was brought back to the vicarage on a farm cart, Coquette, unhurt, trotting behind.

Susannah received his corpse, as she had received the news of his death from Edmund Breakspear and James, dry-eyed and shocked and full of horror. Her actions had driven Sedley to his death. She could hear her angry voice repudiating his accusations, accusing him in turn of jealousy and evil thoughts, challenging him to seek the truth from William Waterton. The shameless prevarications she had used racked her with guilt.

She did not know exactly where or how he had died. Thrown from his mare on jumping a wall, James said briefly, giving her to understand that he and William Waterton had witnessed the death. A violent concussion, Edmund said, making her drink some nauseating concoction which he told her would ease her shock. She did not wish to be stupefied, she said, pushing the cup away; she was perfectly calm. Nevertheless, he returned, you shall drink. And between the two men and Rosalind Manningford she was coaxed to swallow it. She needed desperately to be alone with James to discover whether Sedley had hurled his accusations at William before the accident, or whether, please God, the words had been smothered before they had been uttered. But there was no opportunity, for Rosalind Manningford was always there, twittering, agonised with embarrassment, struggling helplessly to be of help, and James would not meet her eyes.

There were always people there. If Susannah had thought of death, it was as a time of peace, with the silent departed lying in a darkened room where a single candle burned, and the drooping widow left quietly to mourn. It was not so. In the dreamlike state which Edmund's draught had imparted, she received caller after caller with condolences: Mrs Bland, enveloping her in plump and tearful embraces, smothering her in affectionate misunderstanding; Mrs Waterton, her beady sardonic eyes hooded, sparing with sympathy but generous with offers of practical help; Clerk Kimber from the church; her parents and Jack, her mother, calm and sensible, assessing the situation at a glance, sending her menfolk back to their ploughing after their shocked and loving hugs, staying herself to nurse Harriet when she woke up fretful, and keep Piers occupied in the nursery.

They gave her no time for grievous thoughts, all these people. She responded to them automatically, and when she did not cry as they expected, they said: 'She's stunned!', speaking in front of her as if she was witless. Beyond the sound of their voices she became aware of other things, of the sound of the passing bell tolling from the church tower, of the pigs squealing because Becky was too busy producing refreshments to feed them, of Martha Pither and Prudence Paine arguing at the kitchen door over who should have the honour of laying out the curate's body.

Later in the day, when Martha had finished the laying-out ritual and the wide accusing eyes of the dead man were held shut by two pennies on the lids, Mr Bland came to pray with Susannah by the body. The murmured prayers flowed through the room, steady familiar cadences, interspersed with readings from the bible, the same readings, she came to realise, that Sedley had made to Mrs Bland at the time of Daniel's death; it seemed fitting and right that the spirit of the dead man should be lulled with the words he had himself chosen. The gentle intonations continued, soft and tranquillising as a stream's babbling. She looked at the face on the bed, pale and bleak and remote, and the nerves that had been intolerably tautened gradually loosened. He was gone: that face would never awaken again. She hid her face in her hands and permitted relief to come.

Through the nightmare days to the funeral there were three people whose calm strength was there for her to draw upon when she needed it. James organised the funeral together with Mr Bland, consulting her only upon essentials. He found

Seddley's will, a simple one made shortly after their marriage, and told her she inherited all that was Sedley's at the time of his death. He brought Harry the groom with him to exercise and groom Coquette. He wrote to Sedley's mother on Susannah's behalf. Beatrice came each day and kept at bay the frightening and accusatory silences that at night, alone in the curtained great bed, pressed in upon Susannah. She helped her to pack up Sedley's clothing and shoes for Mrs Waterton to distribute to Brambourne's needy folk, knowing, without discussion, her need to banish the ghostly presence that his riding boots and his caped coat and all the other evidence of him gave to the vicarage, and she conspired with Becky to make her mistress eat and drink when such matters seemed unnecessary, even repellent. And in the evenings Jack came to keep Susannah company. Her mother came too, at intervals, but, though strong in practical help, Mrs Trotter was not perceptive of others' thoughts and emotions. She had been pleased by Susannah's good marriage and genuinely admiring of her son-in-law's devotion to his work; an undemonstrative woman herself, it had never occurred to her that Sedley's cool approach to his wife and son had been anything other than evidence of good breeding: she was saddened by his death and her sympathy was of the kind that hurt Susannah the most.

On the night after the funeral Susannah tossed and turned miserably, every inch of her skin prickling with tension. When she did sleep, nightmares tormented her. A letter addressed to Sedley had arrived from Bath yesterday to tell of Mrs Stacey's death; she had died the day after her son. Through Susannah's half-conscious mind visions of plunging horses and staring dead eyes floated in endless succession. In the morning the haunting sense of another world persisted, and her ears seemed to echo with screams. She stumbled to the window for light to find a thick October mist pressing against the panes, and starlings fighting on the stable roof. She felt crushed and overpowered with dread; she must get out of the house, out where she could breathe and think clearly again.

She fed Harriet, saw to Piers' needs, refused Becky's urges to take something herself, saddled Coquette and rode off. The mist was a cloud blanketing the village. Squire Waterton's horsemen, out early to their ploughing, glimmered through the whiteness, their hair mist-sprinkled with tiny droplets; they nodded and grunted to her, embarrassed by her fresh widowhood.

She rode down the lane to where Edmund had finally told her Sedley died, straining as he had done to look over the wall. A stoat undulated through the grass in front of the mare, who blew uneasily down her nostrils. When Susannah reached it, the only sign of the place where Sedley had fallen was the grass trampled from men's feet, and the muddy churnings of the cart. She sat looking. It was very still; the mingled odours of grass and mud and wet leaves was not unpleasant. Through the mist came the sounds of rooks cawing softly amongst themselves. A rabbit hopped slowly alongside the beeches, paused, looked, and vanished with a flash of its pale scut. Susannah let out a long breath; there was no evil here, nor any trace of her husband, he was gone, completely gone.

She nudged Coquette on absently, letting her choose her own path, surrendering her body to the motions of the mare, her mind now free from horror.

James woke and rose early, hoping to shake off the miasmas of the night, the unproductive thoughts that dogged him even in his sleep. He walked into the closet next to the bedroom and sloshed water from the ewer to the basin. It was icy, but he preferred it so; it was stimulating and invigorating to mind and body.

He splashed the water over his face. Oof! That was better. But not even the cold shocks could wash away his dissatisfaction with himself. Engaged to Fanny, who, it had become more and more clear, liked him well but loved him not, and not, most certainly, in the way any normal man would want. It was difficult to remember how he had arrived at this situation. Sheer folly, as he now saw it – but at the time? Fanny had always welcomed him at the rectory, she had become his friend – yes, and she had flirted, too, albeit holding him at a distance. He had wooed her with talk of fashionable clothes to enhance her beauty, with books, with visits to the theatre, above all with music. And it had worked; she had been as light-hearted and gleeful as he had ever seen her, flushed with the excitement of it all, flirtatiously grateful to him, taking his hand, kissing his cheek – like a delighted child. With Mrs Bland always about he'd had little chance of delving into Fanny's deepest feelings, opportunities just to kiss her were rare. When he had his kisses had been awkwardly accepted, never returned, but he had put that down to her unawakened state, to sheer inexperience. Then had come the announcement of their engagement, the shocked outburst from Susannah, the warnings from Beatrice.

He soaped himself impatiently. He had tried, then, to get closer to Fanny. But even when Mrs Bland was absent, always there was someone present, a brother, a sister, a maid. Then one day had come his chance, Fanny and he alone in an empty drawing-room. He had managed to take her in his arms, and then he heard her suck in her breath on a stifled scream and saw her pointing, and there it was, a spider, a fat, long-legged, hairy spider, quite the largest James had ever seen. It was on the sofa beside him, squatting in all its hideousness, seeming to watch them.

He had dealt with it swiftly, clapping his hands over it and running to fling it from the window. 'A nasty brute,' he said, 'but it's gone now.'

'It could come back,' she said, pale and shuddering.

'I'll shut the window,' he said, and did so.

'I loathe them,' Fanny said.

He had put his arms back round her, ready to give comfort and reassurance, but she had wanted none of him. She shrank from the embracing arms: almost, he thought, images passing across his mind in the half-light, almost as if his arms were the giant spider's hairy limbs. The same tremors of aversion had racked her. And on other occasions before she left for London he had felt the same reaction, the spider of her repugnance crawling between them.

James towelled himself with vigour. He remembered how as a growing boy he had taken pride in the development of his manhood. Nature had been munificent in her endowments: he had the hardest sinews, the broadest chest, the most swiftly deepening voice of all his friends. Now there were times when he saw himself through another's eyes, insensitive and gross in his maleness, something to disgust, not to attract. Could Fanny be coaxed from her shrinking? Would marriage change her? He could not tell. One thing he did know, the wedding must go ahead. For him to cry off would cause a scandal of proportions that no gentleman could contemplate.

He dressed and ran down the stairs. He would ride out. In the stableyard the grooms came running but he said brusquely: 'No, leave it!' He wanted to be alone, he would saddle the horse himself. As he rode away from the gatehouse arch he was glad of the obscuring mist, the mysterious half-colours in the lime avenue; no hearty person could hail him with foolish gossip, and he did not want to talk, he had too many bitter thoughts to contend with.

Towards the bottom of the avenue the mist was less thick, the lane beyond just visible. Stark against the whiteness, a woman in a black cloak was riding by, a woman with a look of Susannah. His memory produced her in her red cloak, flushed and lovely against the snow. This could not be her, he was conjuring visions from his thoughts. Yet he leaned forward – yes, it was. Mourning black, inevitable. He called; she stopped and smiled.

'You are about early, Cousin Susannah.'

'To be alone with my thoughts. And you?'

'I too.'

'Then we should part!'

'My thoughts were unprofitable.'

'And mine. Dear me! Then shall we ride together?'

'If you will – I should like it.' Here was a woman who had not found him repellent; the memory was balm to his hurts.

'Cousin James, yesterday I heard that old Mrs Stacey died just days ago in Bath. I don't know the terms of her will, but I thought you might know the law when two people die within so short a time of one another.'

The horses walked on, tossing their heads in a jingle of disgust at the slow pace.

James asked: 'Who died first, Stacey or his mother?'

'He did.'

'Then I am sorry to break the news that you will undoubtedly prove unlucky. Had she died first, her money would have gone in theory to Sedley, and would have been that of which he died possessed, if only by a day, even hours. As it is, unless you have been specifically mentioned . . .'

'Little likelihood of that.'

'Then your children will be wealthier than you. When they reach the age of majority, that is.'

'I rather thought it would be so.'

'Have you planned what you will do now?'

'Those were my unprofitable thoughts as I rode. I shall go to my parents. They have already offered to take me and the children.'

Momentarily shocked, he did not speak, but the way she looked across at him, her grey eyes sad and resigned, suddenly dispersed the tension of his bitterness, the edginess of his self-reproach, filling him instead with concern and regret.

'A poor solution. I know you cannot stay on in the parsonage, but surely you could afford a house of your own?'

The farmhouse was well enough, above average for its type, but caught up in the Trotters' striving struggling farming life her vivacity would be quenched, her beauty dimmed. Over the past two years she had developed a charm and a personality that had carried her into a different social world, a world that had learned to respect her, and where she had demonstrated her worth to the two villages. It was unthinkable that all this should be lost.

As they rode along the village street he tried to dissuade her, but she shook her head. Hers was the right plan. The costs of running her own home would reduce the small income that would be hers to penny-pinching levels, but at Godsgrace Farm the expenses would be shared, there would be the fascination of their enlarging acres and all that was happening on them, and she would be with those who cared for her. Besides, she added wryly, a flicker of amusement curving her lips, alone she would be prey to all the prowling William Watertons of this world.

'In that case,' he said in the same rueful vein, smiling himself, 'I support your decision!'

They had reached the farmhouse. He said: 'When you are ready to move, call upon me for carts and men to load them.'

She thanked him, and attempted to thank him also for the care and kindness he had shown her over these last dreadful days. 'I don't know how I should have managed without you.'

'Competently, excellently, as you always would do,' he said.

'No, don't cut me off with meaningless compliments, Cousin James. I leaned on you, and you know it.'

'That was no meaningless compliment,' he said. 'I d think you understand how highly I regard you. I would alway want to help you' And the thought of his total helplessness regarding her future life hit him with a blast of intolerable mockery. Savagely he burst out: 'How ironical that Sedley should die now!'

Her eyes flashed to his, abruptly arrested, and then suddenly, noisily, raising his fists above his head and shaking them in gestures of mingled fury and impotence, Barney Bidewell strode at speed round the corner of the farmhouse and into the lane past them, swearing and stamping and spitting some deep and searing anger, his dark face suffused with the blood of his bitterness.

James had just time to jerk his horse sideways to avoid the blow that Barney aimed at its nose, and then the man was past, fragments of his fury reaching them in dislocated phrases as he pounded up the street. 'Bastards! Thievin' rich bastards! Schemin' and stealin' and ruinin' us ... My 'ouse. Ah'll show 'em ... make 'em curse the day ... Bury 'em ... burn 'em to hell!' His head turned momentarily: 'Ah, an' you, Mrs Stacey! I knows you, yer bitch, prissy an' two-faced like yer brother!'

James tugged furiously at his reins to wheel his horse, his riding crop raised ready to strike but Susannah stopped him sharply. 'Leave him! Let him vent his spleen, so long as 'tis no more than air. He has cause to swear – him and many others. Don't give him more to avenge.'

James sucked in his breath and stopped. It went against the grain, he was fretted by a recurrent sense of trouble, but he saw the wisdom in her words.

He had just said an uneasy goodbye to her and kicked his horse to a brisk trot when he became aware of hoof-beats approaching from behind. Someone in a hurry, surely nothing to do with him. He tugged the aggrieved Samson to one side without turning his head, but the rider drew alongside, addressing him in the brisk and resonant tones of his cousin Beatrice.

'Well met, James, well met. I was intending to ride over to see you later, but luckily as I was mounting Handon this devilish mist lifted a touch and I recognised you and Samson.'

'If you wish for gossipy chatter, Beatrice, let me tell you I am not in the mood.'

but a matter of vital importance, James.'

   breathless, animated, and full of some about to
ormation. Against the mist, with her lively eyes
face, in clothes that had colour, unlike the stiff
that covered Susannah, she seemed peculiarly
and vibrant, full of some barely suppressed emotion,
mischief even. He was in no mood for Beatrice's sense of
mischief; it was misplaced this morning.

'What do you want of me?' he enquired disagreeably.

'Dear me! I want nothing of you, James, I assure you. Only
to give you advice, advice you may relish. No, don't shake your
head at me. I gave you advice once before, you remember,
despite your protests, and in the end you gained the day. You
never thanked me for it, but I will pass that by. Now I come to
produce a transformation in your life, so listen, and listen
carefully.'

29

It was while Susannah was settling into her old home and her mother was admiring the effect of Susannah's handsome Turkey carpets and the best of her furniture in the farmhouse rooms that Barney and Charity Bidewell's habitation was pulled down and their few sticks of furniture flung out into the mud. The part of the common where he had built was now Fulbroad land; Fulbroad was putting it under the plough; Barney had been given fair time to move and he had not done so: force was unavoidable.

Violence was used on both sides, according to the stories told afterwards in the village. Men clutching cudgels arrived in an icy dawn, surrounded the meagre cottage, then shouted for the Bidewells to come out. Barney, swollen and black-faced with anger, cursed from a window, while his wife screamed abuse from behind him. When the men advanced the shutters slammed. Thirty seconds later the rickety door burst open and out charged Barney and Charity, pitchforks levelled, murder in their faces. It took two strong men to hold Charity while she kicked and screamed and spat. It took four finally to subdue Barney and march him off to the village lock-up. One man had a nasty jab to the knee, two had black eyes, and their foreman's hand had been torn by a bite from Charity: 'Worse'n any mad vixen 'ud give, you!' But the woman could show sickening bruising – 'That never arose out of nothen',' said her grandfather Jurd.

The episode left a foul taste in the mouth and divided village opinion. Both Fulbroad and Bidewell were feared and loathed, but to beat a woman and throw her and her child out into the winter's cold were shocking acts; sympathy tendered to Charity somehow extended itself towards Barney.

Two days later Becky, who had accompanied Susannah and the children to the farm, Luke not yet having acquired his sty and his pig, was doing a late night check of the kitchen fire, when she heard a scratching at the door. She told Susannah later that she had thought it was Ladyship, wearying of her nightly battles with the farmyard cats, but when she unbolted the top half of the door she glimpsed Arthur, barely visible in the shadows of the starlit yard. She fetched Jack, as he wanted, and Susannah joined them.

Arthur would not come in. He hung back, as nervous of the light as a nocturnal animal, his eyes restless. His mumbled half-sentences were hard to catch, but a dismaying story eventually emerged. Since Bidewell had been let out of the lock-up several hours earlier he had been drinking heavily. Tonight he had been accompanied to the ale-house by Smallwood and Pettifer. Grievances were aired, more pints sunk down gullets dry from furious tirades, till finally, emerging on the other side of drunkenness to a cold sodden malice, they decided their wrongs must be avenged. 'Barney, 'ee say 'tes Mester Fulbroad's ricks to be fired, but Mester Smallwood, 'ee say 'ee 'ave 'is men an' dogs a-watchen. So 'tis Squire Mannenford's barns they be goen' fur.'

Susannah's brain worked fast. 'Don't bother to catch your pony, Jack. Take Coquette, she's in the stable. Warned in time, they can maybe stop the fools on their way, so no harm's done on either side.'

Jack nodded. They turned to speak to Arthur but he was gone as if he'd never been.

'You'll not need a lantern,' Susannah whispered. ''Tis light enough – and safer without. Go, quick!'

Jack turned and sprinted across the yard. When he returned an hour later he said little. He had been just in time. Men had been sent to conceal themselves in the barns, so that when the three arrived their fuddled minds were startled at finding themselves surrounded by men apparently emerging from the ground. There were sullen arguments, and threats uttered on both sides, but eventually the trio had slunk away. 'And should think themselves lucky!' Jack said. 'Having done nothing, they'll not be charged.' He sighed. 'Mr Manningford wants to give me a reward, but that I'll give to Arthur.'

'Tell him to be careful where and how soon he spends it,' Susannah advised.

'Strange that he should have brought a warning,' said Jack.

'Oh no,' said Susannah. 'Arthur has his own simple notions of right and wrong. 'Tis mainly on poaching that they'd not run with ours!'

Fanny brought beautiful materials and shawls and shoes and trinkets back from London, together with the very latest in gowns and pelisses, but to Mrs Bland's annoyance, they were not the high spots of her stay. That was a memory, a very special memory.

'London was wonderful,' she told Susannah over refreshments the next morning at the farmhouse. 'My aunt was truly kind, and so understanding.'

'Spoilt her,' her mother observed tartly to Mrs Trotter.

Fanny ignored her. Aunt Anne had discovered that the famous harpist and singer Sophie Corri was to give a private recital at an evening party shortly before she left London. Her aunt had moved heaven and earth to find an acquaintance who might give Fanny and her an introduction to the hostess, a lady famous for such entertainments, even, Fanny said, laughing, to approaching persons whom she quite detested. And her efforts had paid off. When Fanny described the event her voice caught in her throat, rapt and stumbling as she attempted to convey what it had meant to her; to give her listeners even the least notion of the harpist's virtuosity. After a solo for harp by Herr Carl Bach, Madame Corri had played her husband Mr Dussek's harp sonata in C minor, a work written not long ago in Paris. Infinitely demanding, Fanny said, requiring the most perfect articulation of the fingers and playing of a crisply incisive nature: it had been a revelation of new heights to be scaled. The whole concert had been exceptional, while to sit listening in the gilded salon of a great house, surrounded by handsome and favoured people who discerned justly what was admirable both in the music and in the player's interpretation of it, had intensified the pleasure. Then afterwards, Fanny said, her voice deepening huskily in her effort to draw her audience into her own feelings of awe, she had been able to talk to Sophie Corri in an anteroom. At first the harpist had been off-hand, discouraging to the young lady from the country who was delaying her tired return home, but at the last moment some comment of Fanny's had made her realise that this admirer did possess true understanding, and she had unbent.

Susannah understood that they had spoken together for some time, that Sophie Corri had promised Fanny copies of the music she had played, and in fact had sent them round by a servant the very next day, and that Fanny had been permitted to play her harp. 'A most perfect instrument, decorated Vernis Martin,' she added, anxious that none of the splendours of this encounter with the famous should be missed by her little audience. Fanny had played the first movement of Krumpholz's fifth sonata and Madame Corri had discussed her playing, giving her praise and encouragement. She had spoken with the judgment one would have expected, Fanny told them with seriousness, her eyes intent on some far point beyond the parlour window, a tiny pulse beating beneath the skin of her throat. Momentarily she stopped speaking, her head tilted to one side; she might have been searching for the source of a distant elusive voice, barely heard, yet sharply real. Then she gave her head a little shake. 'Mr Dussek recently dedicated a duo for harp and piano to Madame Krumpholz,' she ended quietly. 'The servant delivered a copy along with the other music. Rosalind and I will be able to play it together, perhaps, of an evening.'

Her mother leaned forward. 'You could play it with James,' she pointed out.

'Yes,' Fanny murmured. 'Yes, of course, I could play it with James.'

When the two older ladies went to admire Piers and Harriet, Fanny rose and began to pace about the room; her face, pale and smooth above the delicate stalk of her neck, looked suddenly intent. The expression made her look older, somehow more mature.

By the long low latticed window she stopped. 'Susannah, I must spend part of each year in London. I must, I must! As a married woman there is no reason why I should not, is there? So many families go there for the Season, or to spend the winter.

James could come with me after the harvest – we could stay with his sister – or if he would rather not, I could stay with Aunt Anne. To have that to look forward to and to enjoy would transform my life, I cannot tell you by how much! Do you think James would agree? Oh, if he only would! Mama is quite doubtful, she says he has too much to keep him here, but I am determined.'

'You must ask him,' said Susannah.

Fanny's gaze was fixed on something out in the garden. 'I tried to broach the matter yesterday, but James was very busy and quite grumpy. We sat in the drawing-room with Rosalind and one would think one could have a sensible conversation there, but we were forever being interrupted by a message from the surveyor, or that commissioner, Mr Haynes, or a farm tenant with some query or other on land boundaries, and when he was not attending to them James was grunting of nothing but land management and mangel worzels. I gave up in despair.'

'Try again,' said Susannah. 'James is really such a kind man.'

To sit in the drawing-room at Abbotsbridge House each evening now that Beatrice was gone was swiftly becoming purgatory to James. The room was invariably over-hot and filled with females, all of whose eyes seemed to be fixed upon him either in reproach or sour resentment, God only knew why. Tonight he had his cousins Rosalind, Katharine, Jessica and Julia. Three weeks ago Jessica had received an offer of marriage from Elliot Fulbroad and, after several days of prevarication and evasion, had, to her family's deep relief, refused him. Bereft of the trips to the theatre and the evening parties and all the petting and spoiling that had been part of the Fulbroads' hopeful attentions to her, she was at a loose end and finding a vent for her resentful boredom in provoking her sister Julia. Even the kindly Katharine had been heard to remark that they were both unpardonably nasty these days, fighting and scratching like two cats confined to one basket. Tonight an argument had erupted over a borrowed silk shawl that Jessica had never returned and now considered hers, Julia having, she said, no call for such a luxurious item, and had ended with the pair of them scowling ferociously from opposite sides of the great fireplace while Katharine silently mended the rent to the fringe that their fight for possession had produced.

Thus when Rosalind lifted a hand to her temples and remarked in a tired voice that she had promised to take poor Mrs Stacey some books today, and now would be thought to have quite forgotten her, James immediately offered to go.

'I should myself have called at the farmhouse to thank Jack Trotter again for his warnings of last night, but so busy was my day that I never did. I should be delighted to act as your courier, Rosalind.'

It was a moonlit evening with a light frost. He enjoyed the ride, the cold air that bit pleasurably into his lungs and cooled his over-heated face, the evening peace of the village. He handed Susannah the five volumes of a novel Cousin Ambrose and Rosalind were sure she would enjoy, Miss Fanny Burney's *Camilla*. She and Mrs Trotter were shocked at his riding out so late, and in the cold, insisting that he stay to take a warming drink.

The big low-beamed farmhouse parlour was warm and sweet-smelling from a fire of apple-wood. James was made to seat himself on an oak settle and given mulled ale to drink, and the light of the flames flickered in the spicy hot liquid, and picked out the room's gleaming ornaments, the polished old spinet and the kindly silvery face of the grandfather clock. Thomas Trotter and Jack came within a few minutes to join in drinking the ale and soon they were deep in village affairs, Thomas speaking of the 'fair old wrastling-matches' he and the others concerned had fought over which villagers should be granted rights to use the new cow common, and of Nancy Carter's deep gratitude that she could put her Alderney there. 'An' gratitude,' opined Thomas, 'is rare as silver in a cesspit hereabouts!'; of how John Hayter at The Bull had been forced to rent pasture for his carriage horses from Mr Fulbroad at a truly shocking charge: 'Count the blades o' grass they ate if he could!'; and of how Barney Bidewell was rabid with fury over the blocking of his revenge and determined to hit back somehow. 'But,' concluded Thomas, 'folks reckon 'tis but the bellowings of a gelded bull.'

James listened and responded, appreciative of a different perspective on village affairs from that of Abbotsbridge House or the local landowners. Susannah's father had a pithy realism about him that was healthy and invigorating. Thomas might be ill-organised in his approach to farming and too easy-going ever to be successful in any worldly sense, but he was not stupid: he made a good churchwarden and he understood the village people and their ways; his comments upon their vanities and their follies had a wicked aptness that made James chuckle. Jack and his mother, of course, James had long considered as two of the most sterling characters Abbotsbridge possessed. He turned his head to look at Susannah, seated a little to one side of them, the firelight glowing on her reflective face; she was quiet this evening, as she had been since Sedley's death, but she looked well despite the disfiguring black, and her comments, when they came, were, as always, worth having.

When the chimes of the grandfather clock sounded eleven, James was surprised how late it was and rose hurriedly, knowing that the Trotters would normally be abed by this hour. He thanked them warmly for their hospitality and nodded acceptance of Jack's offer to bring a lantern out to the stables.

When Becky opened the door he knew in a moment something was wrong. Mist ... drifting yellow across his path ... He caught the smell of smoke, stepped out, and the smoke-stench thickened, catching him by the throat.

'Fire!' he said urgently. 'Fire!' and set off towards it.

Jack ran beside him across the yard and behind the sheds to the rickyard. The first straw-stack was on fire at its base, tongues of flame creeping like the ruddy tendrils of some noxious plant up and up the stack, widening and deepening even as he spotted them. Behind them Becky was screaming with all the power her heavy body could produce: 'Fire! Fire!' and he heard her running and then the clank and splash of her vigorous jerking of the pump handle. Mrs Trotter arrived to chase the squealing pigs into the paddock; Thomas shouted that he'd move Mr Manningford's horse and Coquette to safety, Susannah clutched a bucket in each hand as she came. James and Jack ran to grab pitchforks and rakes to drag the burning rick apart. As he panted back through the thickening smoke James glimpsed figures moving behind it. Neighbours, surprisingly soon on the scene, coming to their aid.

'Hurry!' he gasped. 'Get sacks from the barn! Start beating!'

But the figures seemed to swirl and vanish with the smoke. James rubbed his smarting eyes. 'Come on!' he shouted again. 'Over here!'

And then, over the ever-increasing roar of the flames, he heard a man laugh, low and triumphant. A great flame shot up from the rick and he saw two figures vanishing into the shadowy paddock. Cursing, with fury hot and sickening in his stomach, he joined Jack in fighting the fire, working till his eyes and his throat were raw from the smoke and steam, his hands and arms flecked with burns, and his body and his legs drenched with the icy water that the family and their neighbours were hurling. Stopping for a second to clear his vision he saw wisps of burning straw floating above the thatched barn. 'Look to the barn!' he shouted. This first rick was doomed; throwing water on it was of no more use than spitting on a furnace: it was the other ricks and the barn and the house that were in danger now.

It was half-way through the night before the chain of bucket-bearers could ease their aching shoulders and pray the place was safe. They would have to watch for some hours yet, but the raging ferocity of fire that threw out its burning brands to the constant danger of all around was beaten now. As he descended the ladder on which he had been perched for the last two hours James could see people congratulating one another that no worse harm had been done – and then he saw Susannah, plodding wearily from the rickyard with an empty bucket, outlined against the red glow of the still incandescent embers of the rick. She stood for a moment and he saw the glow of her skirt increase at one side to become a flame and the flame shoot upwards at fantastic speed. He leapt from the ladder and hurled himself across the yard to grab her and thrown her down in the mud and the black ashes, smothering the flames with his own body, beating frantically at the last vicious spurts of fire that would not surrender.

She sat up slowly, rubbing bemusedly at the back of her head where it had hit a cobble. 'Whatever happened . . .? Ouch! Why did you knock me down?'

'Dearest girl!' he said, rising to his feet and holding out his hand to help her up. 'You were afire. Look at your skirt – it was the only way to save you!' And then he realised the words he'd used, realised too that if the staring exhausted villagers did not remark them now, they would remember them later. Calmly, slowly, his voice light, he spoke to redress the matter. 'Cousin Susannah! Dear Cousin, I do apologise for my roughness, but it was in the best of causes. Can you imagine how my family would have berated me had I let your burn!'

By the merest flicker of an eyelash he saw her comprehension. She looked down at her filthy skirt and back at him. 'Cousin James. My goodness, I had no idea! But I believe you may have saved my life ... I cannot thank you enough for knocking me down!'

He heard the men begin to exclaim and chuckle behind him, and then Mrs Trotter was beside Susannah, shaking her head at the ruined skirt and thanking him again and again. Somebody passed him the coat that he had slung off God knew when, and several voices remarked that Mr James had worked like a Trojan tonight, that he had, and finally he could sluice his face and hands free from filth at the pump, and find his trembling horse in a neighbour's shed, and ride back home under the light of a dying moon.

Several things arose from that night.

Barney Bidewell was sent to Winchester prison to await trial at the next Quarter Sessions. Ambrose Manningford thought it best not to deal with Barney himself, so Squire Waterton heard the matter and Barney was gone within thirty-six hours. He swore on his baby's head he'd had nought to do with any rick-firing, but James knew it was him he had heard and seen. Nobody came forward to give the accomplice a name, though most villagers reckoned they could hazard guesses. In The Bull and the smithy men spoke of Barney's bitterness that Jack Trotter had never saved his cottage like he could if he'd wanted, and his suspicions that it had been Jack whose warning had saved the Manningfords' barns: 'A reg'lar boiling up of hate, 'twas, you,' the men agreed disapprovingly.

Overnight James found himself popular. Hats that had never shifted at his presence now were flourished, wary weatherbeaten faces broke into smiles. Men had observed and deduced from the evidence of their own eyes. Their conclusions filtered through their womenfolk and Duckett's shop to become Abbotsbridge lore: Mr James was game to the backbone.

Mrs Bland scolded him. Popular in the village James might be, but not with his future mother-in-law. A man in his situation should not hazard his life in such a careless way. There were other people more suitable to deal with such emergencies. Fanny, she told him, standing four-square in the lane where she had caught him riding past, Fanny had been most shocked and concerned, quite trembling with anxiety for him when she heard.

'I think,' she concluded with sternness, 'that although it is Fanny's sacred hour, and a time I should not normally think of interrupting, that you should speak to her now and apologise and reassure her. I see some small burns upon your face and hands. I trust that if you are more burned elsewhere you will keep it from her.'

James tried to look suitably meek and contrite and went obediently to talk to Fanny. He found her practising in the diffused wintry light of the drawing room. She did not at first look up when he entered, her serious meditative face turned to her music stand, her entire concentration focussed on the rippling notes of her playing. He had to speak twice before she broke off to stare at him almost blindly.

'Who...? What...? Oh, James. I'm sorry, I was immersed in my work.' She took her hands from the strings and flexed them, pushing them finger tip to finger tip. 'What is it?'

'Your mother spoke of your concern at my adventure with the fire last night in the Trotters' rickyard. I came to apologise for any dismay I may have caused you. Having done so, I feel I should leave you to continue your playing and I shall withdraw.'

'No,' she said quickly, putting out a long thin hand. 'No, no, pray stay a minute. There is something I wish to discuss with you, something important pertaining to our life together.'

'Really? What can that be?'

She looked at him with a long look that was half doubtful, half something resembling defiance. Her eyes seemed to have grown darker, the pupils of them very large and black; she paused as if marshalling her words, her lips held delicately rigid.

Then she spoke and he saw that what she was saying was desperately important to her. She was not pleading, Fanny would never plead, but she was putting a case with all the arguments she could array.

'I should like it very much, James, and I hope it would be possible, for us to spend a part of each year in London. Oh, not a large part, I know your interests in the estate and the village would not permit that, but perhaps two or three months in the winter, in the more slack time of year?'

He said nothing, simply looked at her, his eyebrows raised.

She went on, smiling faintly, her voice level: 'I cannot believe that someone of your intellectual attainments, someone with your interest in literature, the theatre, and especially in music, could forever be satisfied by country life alone. Why should not we, like so many others who live generally on their estates, enjoy a revivifying time in London, a holiday from cares to be looked forward to for the rest of the year?'

'We have no house in London,' James replied.

'We have your sister Charlotte and her establishment, which is roomy and lively. We have your father's house to go to. We could even stay with my Aunt Anne. They all would be delighted to see us.'

'No doubt. But whether I would care to stay with them for so long is one matter, while whether I *should* is a moot point. I am needed here.'

'You could journey there with me and stay for a short while, I could stay a few weeks more.' Her voice was still level, but her eyes were wide and urgent. 'It would be so delightful for me there, so stimulating.'

James face was impassive. 'I have never believed in husband and wife living apart from one another. They should be together in all things, side by side.'

Her eyes slid from his face, the thin hands were clasped together now and held against her breasts, the knuckles standing out, thin shiny white bone emphasising her delicacy and tension.

'Two or three weeks would be nothing that anyone could cavil at, James, and the journey from here is no great thing.'

He felt a brute now, but he had to make his point, had to paint a picture plain for her to see: to give in to fantasies about

London life could destroy the real future he desperately desired for himself. He braced himself and heard himself say with a curious brutality:

'Fanny, this is nothing but playing with ideas. As my wife you will have to face a reality that in your maiden state has perhaps not occurred to you. Children, my dear, babies. I imagine the first will arrive nine or ten months after our marriage, and soon there will be others. Where in this imaginary life of yours will you fit them? My children will not be tossed aside to nursery maids while you go gadding elsewhere, nor will they be lugged in coaches with us like so much inanimate baggage. There may be those who behave like that, but I do not intend for it to happen in my family.'

He shook his head in a gesture of finality, turned away and began to walk to the door. Behind him Fanny stirred, her hand plucking the strings of her harp with a plangent sound.

Very quietly she asked: 'Will you not even consider it, James?'

'No,' he said, and left.

30

Five days later a shock like no shock before struck Abbotsbridge and radiated out to Brambourne and the farmhouses
beyond. Never had Duckett's shop been so full of matrons and
maidens alike anxious to buy goods there, while the bench
round the forge chestnut tree was so packed that old man Jurd
had to threaten to break bald pates with his stick before he
could place his backside on its normal resting place.

Jilted! Mr James jilted! A Manningford disdained. The story
was repeated a hundred, a thousand times, and never palled in
the telling. Miss Fanny Bland had run away. Quite how she had
run differed according to the teller: some said she had ridden
off at dead of night with but two bandboxes fastened to her
horse; others maintained that a secret lover had called for her in
his curricle at dawn; the story that eventually gained most
currency, but was sadly lacking in drama and romance, ran
that she had bribed the rector's man, Dick, to hire a carriage
and pair from John Hayter at The Bull and had calmly been
driven off mid-morning, while the rest of the family was out
visiting, to meet the stage-coach on the Winchester road, and
thus had gone to London, not to join her unknown lover, but
to the house of an aunt.

Opinions on who was to blame for this scandal differed,
sympathy for one or other of the two people concerned fluctu-
ating wildly between them. Many opined that Mr James had
spoken harshly to pretty Fanny Bland, forcing her to flee. The
world knew that he was a hard man, only look at the troubles
and misery he had brought on the village. Serve him right to be
abandoned almost at the church door, made to look a fool.

Others maintained the opposite: the rector's daughter was lovely, they granted, but she was a cold piece with no care for anyone but herself and that harp of hers. Mr James was well rid of her.

His family was as divided in its opinions as the village was; Katharine went to pour her heart out to Susannah.

'Poor, poor James!' she said, tears standing in her eyes. 'He must be devastated by such a blow. He has taken it on the chin, Papa says, as a gentleman should do, and he shows nothing, but oh! the hurt to his feelings, and with only days to go to the wedding. I do feel for him so much. And so does Rosalind – she was almost in hysterics when the news came at luncheon – and Jessica and Julia were quite horrid. Can you believe it, they actually said "Good!" in front of her? Rosalind is so particularly fond of Fanny, she feels it as a personal blow for herself also. She is prostrated now on her bed, truly prostrated.' Her chest swelled; she went on with a fierceness that was oddly at variance with her normally placid and kindly nature: 'They say that in the letter she left for her parents she said she was going to companion her widowed aunt, who is musical and will allow her to study the harp as she wants. It seems that is the only thing she cares about. How wicked! Not just to cause James to suffer, but the poor Blands also. And so many blows as they have had, the rector's illness and losing Daniel ... and now they must feel they have lost Fanny, too. My heart bleeds for them. And the embarrassment. How could one show one's face in public after such a let-down?'

She took a gulp of the cordial Mrs Trotter had brought to sustain them all after such a shock and continued: 'I cannot conceive of anyone being so cold and calculating. Well, I would not say it to everybody, but I agree with Jessica and Julia that James is well rid of her. And Timothy Goddard, so kind as he is. He will be shocked that one he admired could behave in such a callous fashion. I think perhaps I should call on him on my way home.'

After Katharine had gone, Susannah tugged a shawl round her shoulders and went out into the cool of the orchard. Here and there a last shrivelled apple lay among the leaves in the grass, and she kicked at them without knowing she did so. She was tormented by the idea of James being jilted, the subject of pity or village jokes, yet at the same time a guilty excitement and relief flared in her at the knowledge that he was free, and somehow both these thoughts lurched round and round inside her head without prompting a single further idea.

When Beatrice's voice called and she saw her limping towards her beneath the gnarled and naked branches, she startled violently.

'Well, Cousin Susannah,' Beatrice said, smiling and wholly composed, 'the events of today have proved us both right. Fanny and James were in no way suited and now Fanny has done the right thing – though, being her, in a totally wrong fashion – and we can rejoice.'

Susannah opened her mouth as if to speak, but refrained.

'Let's not put up a pretence between ourselves. The relief is extreme. What luck that Fanny took fright at the thought of all that marriage with James would entail and fled. It would have appeared better had she spoken to him with honesty and given him back his ring, but given her excessive desire to live in London and do nothing but play the harp, and the horror with which her parents would have regarded any thought of her calling off the engagement, this at least solves the matter at one stroke. Taking all with all, I think it has been excellently managed.'

'Excellently managed? Pity poor Cousin James' embarrassment!'

'He was an ass,' Beatrice returned, 'and has been made to look one. In the achievement of the right end that couldn't be helped.'

Incredible thoughts were crowding into Susannah's head. 'Beatrice! I have a terrible suspicion ... I can't believe ... But I heard you speak of acting as devil's advocate. Cousin, what have you done?'

'Only speeded the inevitable course of events,' Beatrice responded airily.

'... Speeded events?'

'James and Fanny were each bound to conclude that they had made a mistake – eventually. I ... attempted – in all kindness – to ensure that they each realised it before the fatal knot was tied. To persuade Fanny was not over difficult, I have to admit. I placed the humdrum realities of married life before her eyes, I painted James as a would-be patriarch, even something of a bully. I showed her how the demands of the domestic life frequently wear down my sister Rosalind, I pointed out how much work the chatelaine of Abbotsbridge House would be expected to do with the sick and the poor ...'

'And Fanny detests any form of sickness!' Susannah interpolated, a smile beginning to spread.

'Precisely. One way and another, over the days, I saw her grow pale and wilt. And I felt a very brute, I do assure you. But the invitation from her Aunt Anne was the sheerest luck, none of my devising. The contrast of the two lives was absolute. After that I had only to stiffen James's sinews. And today the deed was done – and with a drama only Fanny could have devised!'

Susannah blinked, caught her breath, then let out a gust of laughter that was followed by another and then another, shaking her body so that she had to hang on to the trunk of an apple tree for support. 'Oh,' she gasped, 'how shocking of you, how amazing, how clever!'

It was some seconds before their laughter allowed either of them to speak.

Then Beatrice said devoutly: 'Thank God, now James is free to marry a woman he truly cares for.'

Susannah's life at Godsgrace farm that winter was very different from her life at Brambourne vicarage. To be dressed in black made her detest each day afresh the loathsome necessity of clothing herself in its hypocrisy; mourning, too, kept her days quiet, her social life minimal. But against this she balanced the freedom from the endless pretence and show of her life with Sedley, the mental and physical relief of being free from his uncertain temper, his suspicions, his unpleasant demands on her body.

Her life was not the only one to be undergoing a transformation; it made her chuckle to perceive how her mother's was changing because of her move to the farmhouse. Mrs Trotter now had a white-painted picket gate and fence to her tidy little front garden, and new paint and shutters to the farmhouse. The rough clothes she wore for early-morning chores in the yards were changed by mid-morning to something suitable to receive

Mrs Breakspear or Miss Katharine or Mr James, or others of the gentry who called, even, once, Mr Manningford himself: the great smothering apron she wore was soon swiftly torn off and cast from sight. William Waterton came, and with a regularity which Emily Trotter was inclined to greet with satisfaction until Susannah explained, with what Mrs Trotter thought unnecessarily vulgar clarity, the strictly dishonourable nature of his intentions. Henceforth she remained present while he consumed the refreshments it was only good manners to offer, and confessed that she found him shockingly engaging and amusing despite his moral culpabilities. 'And he owns to four children in Brambourne and one in Abbotsbridge? Well, even if he were to offer for you, that is really too much for any wife to overlook!'

James was discreet in how often he called. By a miracle of his mischievous cousin Beatrice's contriving he was free, but six months was the very least period he must wait before making any approach to Susannah. He did not want to stir up the gossip that too easily would attach itself to a young and attractive widow.

As a counterpoint to the hard and down-to-earth toil that took a large proportion of his hours, was the dulcet examination of his feelings for Susannah. He had never before paused to analyse them with quite such thoughtfulness. Why, he did not know – except that he had flung himself into their affair with a passion quite outside all his previous experience and had retreated badly hurt from the outcome which he now admitted had been inevitable. Coherent thought then had seemed impossible. But why, he asked himself now, why Susannah? Some singular blend of the physical and mental attributes that called to him in a way no other could ever do: a beauty of looks, of movement; a combination of tastes, of feelings, of perceptions. This woman and no other. Marriage: when her period of mourning was over, marriage was what he wanted. Once, and it seemed singular now, once he would have thought marriage to one of her background and upbringing impossible. When she had announced her pregnancy with Piers the thought had not even crossed his mind, but now he did not give a toss what the world thought. He only prayed she would have him. There were unpleasant moments when he had to wonder. Even if she did still care for him, what might be her reaction to the responsibilities of becoming the mistress of Abbotsbridge House, to being forced to live with five spinster cousins and Ambrose too, never mind Rosalind's inevitable jealousy? It was a great deal to ask any woman to contemplate. And did she still care for him? James was far from certain. Since they had parted more than two years ago, she had shown him no more than conventional friendliness.

Beatrice remarked to him that she felt Cousin Susannah to be lonely. 'She has her mourning to consider, but if she were to be invited to join small parties to go to the concert or to dine quietly with old friends, who could wonder at her acceptance? The seemliness of such mild entertainment would be beyond question.' Her eloquent eyes met his making their own observations.

'How very thoughtful you are, my dear Beatrice. Such seemly kindnesses from one's friends could never be other than acceptable.'

Seemliness. James savoured the word. He would be thirty next year and he was aware of certain changes in his outlook that had developed during his Abbotsbridge years, and especially since his abortive engagement to Fanny. The word was appropriate to the situation and to his feelings. It would be important to Susannah, too. Her situation at her marriage to Stacey had been invidious, the too-early arrival of Piers an embarrassment. This time all must develop in proper fashion. Seemliness. He would appraise his actions by its measures. Pictures came to his mind of rides and drives through the Hampshire countryside, (he would enjoy teaching Susannah to drive his curricle), of sitting beside her at the concert, (the scent and the nearness of her), or at dinner at the Breakspears; of playing with Piers at Godsgrace Farm. They were appealing pictures.

At Christmas Mr Manningford announced with pleasure the engagement of his daughter Katharine to Timothy Goddard. Beatrice had not had to nudge Ambrose to ask the shy Timothy his intentions, as she had jokingly announced she feared; Timothy opened the matter formally and correctly in the old library, while Katharine sobbed her ecstatic incredulity to her sisters and Susannah, James, and Edmund Breakspear, gathered in the drawing-room. 'Me! Me! He wants to marry me! Oh, how can I bear being so happy?' Her older sisters and Susannah were almost touched to tears themselves, and even Jessica and Julia for once did not look down their noses. If Katharine with her damaged face could secure herself such a husband, the outlook for them must surely be good. Ambrose Manningford was genuinely pleased; Timothy he declared to be just the right sort of man to care for his innocent and retiring daughter, while the Goddards had been his friends for ever. Unusually, it occurred to Susannah as she emerged from Duckett's shop one morning, she had not heard a single dissentient voice among those who heaped good wishes on the young couple.

The old year faded, the cold early months of the new year passed slowly. Then in late-March there was one of those days of extraordinary warmth and beauty that come rarely but memorably. The first buds were stirring on the bushes, the first daffodils were flourishing their trumpets, and all the birds were singing with a throaty sweetness. Emily Trotter, busy in her vegetable patch breaking the soil into a fine tilth ready for sowing, straightened her back and looked round with pleasure at a particularly brilliant serenade from a blackbird in a fan-trained apple tree on the east wall. His mate she discovered preening herself in an apricot similarly trained on the south wall. It was, she thought with unusual sentimentality, a day for lovers. Bent once more to her task, savouring the sun on her back, she recollected with pleasure her Thomas's rough and ready but genuine courtship of so many years ago. She wished that Susannah might marry again; but while Susannah was often invited to houses where there were unmarried men of the party, there were no signs of courtship in the air, nothing that one could sensibly rely on. Two young children, she must admit, would be something of a bar. A pity, but there, Susannah was still lovely and still young, there was time yet for some man to appreciate her qualities. Not only lovely, but good: so hard she had worked this last winter with Mr Bland and Mr Manningford to ease the state of the poor. Mr James now, he was undoubtedly fond of her, they were often together in society, and recently he had even taken her and Piers out driving with him, but try as she might, Emily could see no more than cousinly friendship. And dreaming of a marriage there would be beyond the bounds of all possible likelihood, into regions of romancing. She shook her head, tugging a last dock from the ground and throwing it on her weedpile. Jack, too, he should marry. She raked slowly, to and fro, turning over in her mind the young ladies in the village as to which might be suitable, but concluding, not for the first time, that none were good enough, not for a young man who dined nowadays with the Manningfords and the Breakspears and the Goddards. When in the distance the church clock struck eleven she went indoors to brew tea, for she felt dry. She was surprised that Susannah had not thought to bring her a drink, for normally she was thoughtful in these matters.

She unlaced and removed caked old boots at the door and plodded in on stockinged feet. Her hand was out to lift the kettle on to the hob when she heard voices from the parlour. A visitor? Her lips tightened in self-reproach – and here was she in an elderly gardening smock and shoeless. Or was it Jack, come in from the fields for some reason to talk to Susannah? She listened. A deep male voice spoke, gentle, yet somehow holding emotion. She concentrated, her head bent.

'... The day being so beautiful and the thought of you also being beautiful, dearest one, it occurred to me that we might decide upon a date together, a date for our marriage. I could not hold back any longer.'

Susannah's voice: 'Did I hear you aright? A date for our marriage? Just like that, Cousin James?' A short pause, a bass murmur of words Emily Trotter could not catch. Then: '... taking me wholly for granted! Such vanity – such shocking ...'

'I know, I know! No need to repeat it!' An odd note in his voice she could not place, a distinct tremor. 'How many times in the past have I not had my shocking character thrown at me – arrogant, vain and – what was it – condescending?'

Susannah had spoken in that terrible way to Mr James? The flagged floor shifted and spun. Emily sat heavily down on her wheelback chair, her hand at her throat with shock. Surely she could not be going to refuse him?

What was he saying now?

'I wonder you ever could speak to me at all, let alone care for me! No, no, I apologise. Every woman's right ... and your right especially. Wait ... Mrs Stacey. Cousin Susannah. My dearest Susannah. You know how long I have loved and admired you, would you do me the honour of marrying me? The pleasure and happiness it would give me would be greater than life itself, and could not prove less than everlasting.'

'Oh James, dear James. That was a most handsome proposal – yes, and yes again!'

Was Emily hearing aright? From horror to happiness in seconds: emotions arose in a warm and transporting torrent that became too strong for her; Emily leaned back in her chair and let a flood of happy tears stream down her cheeks.